Praise for the Novels of Anna Jeffrey

Sweet Water

"Jeffrey mixes just the right amounts of soft, sweet, and funny, making Agua Dulce hard to resist."
—*Detroit Free Press*

"*Sweet Water* . . . is filled with wonderfully complex characters whose personalities are gradually revealed. There are no easy answers for any of them, but the ones they find are mostly happy and satisfyingly realistic. A pleasurable read!"
—*Romantic Times*

"A warm contemporary romance starring amiable lead protagonists and a town of eccentrics who meddle, matchmake, and mother the stars. . . . Fans will enjoy this slice of life in West Texas." —The Best Reviews

"Refreshing, appealing, and authentically romantic . . . moving and sensual, *Sweet Water* is not soon forgotten."
—Michelle Buonfiglio, wnbc.com's Romance: B(u)y the Book

"*Sweet Water* is her best yet! Sexy, tender, romantic don't begin to describe how wonderful this story is."
—RomanceJunkies.com

The Love of a Lawman

"Real characters come to life in this heart-wrenching tale littered with imperfect characters readers come to love and root for." —*Rendezvous*

"Engaging . . . the story line is loaded with action and the cast is a strong ensemble . . . a warm romantic tale."
—The Best Reviews

"If you like well-written, character-driven romances . . . with engaging characters and lots of internal conflict, I highly recommend *The Love of a Lawman*."
—Romance Reviews Today

continued . . .

Salvation, Texas

Anna Jeffrey

A SIGNET ECLIPSE BOOK

SIGNET ECLIPSE
Published by New American Library, a division of
Penguin Group (USA) Inc., 375 Hudson Street,
New York, New York 10014, U.S.A.
Penguin Group (Canada), 90 Eglinton Avenue East, Suite 700, Toronto,
Ontario M4P 2Y3, Canada (a division of Pearson Penguin Canada Inc.)
Penguin Books Ltd., 80 Strand, London WC2R 0RL, England
Penguin Ireland, 25 St. Stephen's Green, Dublin 2,
Ireland (a division of Penguin Books Ltd.)
Penguin Group (Australia), 250 Camberwell Road, Camberwell, Victoria 3124,
Australia (a division of Pearson Australia Group Pty. Ltd.)
Penguin Books India Pvt. Ltd., 11 Community Centre, Panchsheel Park,
New Delhi - 110 017, India
Penguin Group (NZ), cnr Airborne and Rosedale Roads, Albany,
Auckland 1310, New Zealand (a division of Pearson New Zealand Ltd.)
Penguin Books (South Africa) (Pty.) Ltd., 24 Sturdee Avenue,
Rosebank, Johannesburg 2196, South Africa

Penguin Books Ltd., Registered Offices:
80 Strand, London WC2R 0RL, England

First published by Signet Eclipse, an imprint of New American Library,
a division of Penguin Group (USA) Inc.

First Printing, January 2007
10 9 8 7 6 5 4 3 2 1

For my mother
1922–2006

ACKNOWLEDGMENTS

In writing this story, I relied on my friend Wanda Hines and her husband, Alan. She's a former sheriff's department employee, and he's had a lifelong career in law enforcement. They were generous with their time and patient in answering my questions. I came away from visits with them grateful that a man of Alan's caliber is looking out for the citizens of the small town where I live. I might have stretched reality slightly for the sake of the story, so if procedural errors have been made, they are all mine.

I also want to thank Heather Poole, a dedicated reader and supporter. Heather read for me, tossed around ideas with me and advised me on legal procedure. Plus, she stocks all of my books in her bookstore and constantly promotes me.

Author of historical adventure, Laura Renken, was my critique partner on this book. As an outstanding storyteller and plotter, she helped me immensely.

Last, but not least, I appreciate my editor, Laura Cifelli. Her frank commentary and wise story advice have benefited me again.

As always, I thank my cheerleaders, my husband, George, and my daughter, Adrienne.

"The rich are different from you and me."
—F. Scott Fitzgerald

"Yes, they have more money."
—Ernest Hemingway

Chapter 1

The warble of the phone sluiced through Elena Ryder's semiconsciousness. Without opening her eyes, she fumbled the receiver to her ear and mumbled a hello.

"Elena? Está eso usted?"

"Yes, it's me."

"Es Paula. La ambulancia ha ido a la casa de su hermana."

The words came in a string of Spanish so frantic that Elena's half-asleep brain translated only three of them: "Paula," "ambulance" and "sister." "Paula, slow down. Speak English."

"Ambulancia. She go to Carla."

Carla? Elena's eyes popped wide open to a hazy gray room. She switched the receiver to her opposite ear as she glanced at the red numbers displayed on her digital clock. 7:20 A.M. After working a long shift at Sanderson County Hospital, she had been asleep only three hours, but this news from Paula Flores, a nurse's aide, had snapped her wide awake.

"What happened?" she asked, now on her feet and making her way to the bathroom.

"I don' know. He hus' call. *Ella cayó en la arena.*"

Fell in the arena? It was barely daylight. Carla being in the arena made no sense. "Okay, thanks."

Elena disconnected. No sense wasting valuable time trying to pull useful information out of Paula.

Her heartbeat thumped steadily in her ears as she brushed her teeth. She ran a brush through her long hair and gathered it off her face into a scrunchie, then shucked her pajamas, threw on jeans and a flannel shirt and pulled on boots. Quickstepping through the kitchen and utility room to the garage, she keyed her sister's number into her cell phone. No answer. She climbed into her SUV and headed for Carla's house.

Sheriff Rusty Joplin cruised through Salvation, Texas, uncomfortable in his starched white shirt. He was so sunburned his skin felt sore and stiff. He had spent Labor Day weekend, the first long weekend he had taken off since being sworn in as sheriff, water-skiing with friends in Fort Worth.

He dreaded what awaited him in his office. A draft of next year's budget, the first official request for money he would be making when the county commissioners met next Tuesday night. He had tinkered with it for weeks, wanting to get it right.

His cell phone vibrated at his belt. He unhooked the device and glanced at the tiny screen. The time showed it was seven thirty and the caller was Cheryl Hopkins, his assistant and a Sanderson County deputy. Cheryl was one of the few people who had his private cell phone number.

"This is Rusty," he said into the phone. "I hope this is important, 'cause I'm headed to Mansell's for breakfast. I'm hungrier than a wolf. I came home to an empty refrigerator."

"Hey. How was your long weekend?"

"Good. How about yours?"

"Same old thing. Clean house, take the kids somewhere. Do laundry, take the kids somewhere."

Rusty chuckled. Cheryl might complain good-naturedly, but she was a devoted parent. "Anything good happen while I was gone?"

"No, it's been boring. But that might change. I just monitored a dispatch for the ambulance to go out to Carla Ryder's place."

Carla Ryder's *last* name had been Blanchard for ten years, but the Salvation citizens still called her Carla Ryder. "You mean to Blanchard's or to the old man's? What's up?"

"Sorry. I mean Blanchard's. I don't know what's going on. No nine-one-one call came in here. I contacted the hospital to see if I could find out, but the only person I could get on the phone was Paula Flores. You know how that went. I couldn't understand her. But it sounds like it wouldn't hurt if someone went out there. Since it's the Ryder clan, I thought you might want to handle it personally."

Cheryl Hopkins was Rusty's go-to girl. He had hired her when he took office this past January. Besides having years of experience in a neighboring county's sheriff's office, she had a deeply ingrained sense of right and wrong and had been thrilled when Rusty defeated the corrupt former sheriff, Jack Balderson, in last fall's election. She was more loyal than a wife and was almost psychic when it came to recognizing trouble. If she thought he should go to Blanchard's house, he probably should.

"Guess breakfast will have to wait. I'm on my way." He disconnected and accelerated, rolling west on the Eunice highway.

Rusty had never been to the Blanchard horse ranch, but he knew it was ten miles west of town. He had passed its entrance many times. He arrived in twelve minutes at the turn-in identified by an oversize mailbox. A sign in the corner of the fenced pasture read: LITTLE RED LENA STANDING AT STUD. In the distance, a cluster of buildings dotted the horizon.

He rumbled across the cattle guard entrance and

plowed up the long caliche driveway, slowing when
he reached a Y in the road. The left fork turned
off toward a sprawling ranch house, its red-tiled
roof a sharp contrast to its white walls. The straight
leg went to a cluster of outbuildings and corrals
where he saw activity. He headed in that direction.

Nearing an arena close to a huge beige barn,
he saw one of Sanderson County's two ambulances
backed up to the gate and a Lexus SUV parked at
a crooked angle beside it. He recognized the silver
Lexus as belonging to Elena Ryder, Carla's
younger sister. He couldn't imagine why she was
here at her sister's house so early in the morning.
The sun had been up less than an hour.

A blanket-covered mound lay on a gurney just
outside the ambulance's double doors. A sinking
feeling filled Rusty's chest. One of Blanchard's kids
was his first thought, but the blanket's profile
looked too large for a child. Pulling the sheriff's
department's Crown Victoria to a stop beside the
ambulance, he swung out of the driver's seat and
rounded the front end.

Jimmy Don Estes, one of the volunteer EMTs
who most frequently rode in the ambulance, stood
beside the gurney awaiting Rusty's approach. His
mouth was set in a grim line and he was running
a loop of rope through his fingers. He spoke before
Rusty asked. "Carla Ryder," he said.

A burst of adrenaline shot through Rusty's system and his heartbeat kicked up. He had known
Carla since he was ten years old. They were the
same age, had been in the same grade all through
school.

He glanced toward the shed attached to the
arena, where a female EMT was cradling a wailing
Elena Ryder in her arms. "What happened?" he
asked Jimmy Don.

The EMT tilted his head toward a sleek, midnight black horse standing regally on the far side of the arena. "That sumbitch right there."

Rusty stared at the horse. A young stallion. Rope halter, no saddle. A dozen scenarios ran through Rusty's head, tugging his brow into a frown. "He throw her off or what?"

"Nobody knows," Jimmy Don answered. "Mr. Blanchard found him standing over her. One thing's for sure, he drug her. She had this rope around her neck." He handed over the lead rope.

Rusty took the rope and fingered it, studied its surface. Typical lead rope: heavy-duty nylon, half-inch, stained and covered with barn dirt. Nothing unusual for a horse handler. For a few seconds he speculated on what Carla might have been doing with the rope and the horse. "Where's Blanchard now?"

"He was here 'til a few minutes ago. He went to stay with his kids. The maid's husband came out and said she was having trouble with them, so Mr. Blanchard went back to the house."

"Did he see what happened?"

"Said he didn't."

Rusty turned that information over in his mind for a few seconds, wondering about a man whose wife lay dead on a gurney leaving her. "Where'd he find her?"

The EMT pointed toward the center of the arena. "Right there."

Rusty looked toward the area the EMT had indicated. "Where was she when *you* got here?"

"Right there. He said he didn't move her. He just took the rope from around her neck."

"Fuck." Rusty disliked the unfolding story more with every second.

"We tried to resuscitate, Rusty," the EMT said in a tone that bordered on being apologetic, "but hell, she was gone before we ever got here."

Jimmy Don Estes had been a corpsman in the navy, had just returned from deployment with a Marine platoon in Iraq. If anyone could have saved Carla's life in an emergency, he could have.

"What's Elena got to do with this?"

"Nothing. She just got here. Somebody called her."

Rusty walked out into the corral, to the area where Jimmy Don had pointed, where the black barn dirt had been stirred and churned. He squatted and studied the ground. No rain had fallen in weeks, making the soil dry and loose even in the early morning. There had already been too much activity by too many feet for him to detect any telling information. A low-grade anger began to simmer within him. He stood up and walked back to the gurney and Jimmy Don, at the same time noticing that the barn's double doors stood open.

"Why wasn't the sheriff's office called?"

"I didn't know it wasn't," the EMT said.

Rusty stared at the rope in his hand, then at the horse again, still trying to picture exactly what had happened that had resulted in a fatality. Finally, he looked down at the blanket-covered form on the gurney, working to overcome his dread of doing what he knew he had to. "Let me see her," he said.

The EMT lifted the blanket edge, exposing the victim's face. It was covered with dirt, but Rusty could still see the waxy, translucent skin and pale lips, signs of death. He stalled at the eyes. They were open and bugged, the whites red with hemorrhage.

Rusty had worked as a Fort Worth street cop for several years, then as a rookie homicide investigator in one of the city's most brutal crime areas. He had witnessed his share of corpses. Out of necessity, he had developed an ability to objectify the sight. But seeing the results of fatal trauma applied to this woman hit him like a fist to the chest. They had competed in high school rodeo together. He shared a hundred memories of his youth with her and her two sisters.

He swallowed the lump in his throat and moved the blanket edge farther down. Several scrapes showed through the layer of grime on her hands. He saw several broken fingernails. She had on a gray sweatshirt covered with dirt. He lifted the blanket higher and saw she was wearing gray sweatpants and one rubber shower thong. The other thong lay on her abdomen. "Where's her boots?" he asked.

"Wasn't wearing any," Jimmy Don answered. "This is just like we found her."

Rusty shot a sharp look at Jimmy Don, who lifted his shoulders in a shrug. The EMT was a horse owner. Like Rusty, he knew that many catastrophes could befall bare feet in a barnyard. Or an arena. No one who knew anything about horses would approach even the gentlest one without wearing protective footwear. "So run it down for me."

"See the halter on that horse?" The EMT tilted his head toward the black stallion. "Mr. Blanchard said that rope was hooked to the lead ring under the chin. He said it looked like it somehow got twisted into a loop that was tight around her neck. He said he didn't know how she got herself tangled up like that."

Rusty tried to form a mental picture of how such an accident could occur, but it failed to come to him, especially with an experienced horsewoman like he knew Carla to be. Hell, he had seen her ride a bucking bronc.

Rusty blew out a breath, an effort to hide his irritation at the mishandling of a fatal accident scene. He plucked his cell phone from his belt and called his office. "Cheryl, I'm at Blanchard's. We need a JP out here."

He didn't have to explain why to Cheryl. She knew that in rural Texas towns where no one held the office of coroner the law required a justice of the peace to witness and pronounce an unattended death. "Oh, my God," she said. "Who is it?"

"Carla Ryder."

"Oh, my God, Rusty. . . . Listen, I'll take care of it. I saw Helen Grayson's car over at the courthouse earlier."

"Who's on today?"

"Lowell and Art Rodriguez. Matt, too."

"Is Alan around?"

"He's not due back 'til Monday."

Alan Muncy, the sheriff's department's only investigator, had taken off a week for a family reunion in Lubbock. "Send Matt out here pronto, but tell him not to come running hot. I'm not ready for everybody in Salvation to know about this. Tell Lowell to go to my house and get my truck and horse trailer and bring it out here. Tell him not to drag his feet. . . . And Cheryl? Y'all keep this quiet."

Cheryl had questions, but Rusty stanched them.

He walked over to Elena. She turned to him with grief-stricken eyes. Recalling her devotion to her family, he felt a new pain begin at his deepest center.

"Oh, Rusty. Did you see?" She came to him, breaking into a spate of sobbing. He could do nothing else but open his arms to her. She fell against his chest, her voice hitching. "Did you see . . . what he did to her? . . . Oh, Rusty . . . her kids. . . . What'll we do?"

"Shh-shh. Try to calm down, darlin'." He stroked her hair and held her close, murmuring to her in soft words. There had been a time when he had felt like his arms belonged around Elena Ryder forever. As kids, they'd had a thing, but since his return to Salvation three years ago, he had seen her only in passing. "I know it's hard."

He held her and petted her, mumbling reassurances until he saw a car slow at the driveway entrance and turn in. As the vehicle came nearer, he recognized it as the JP's car. It parked beside the ambulance and he put the weeping Elena into the care of the female EMT.

He walked out of the arena and met Helen Grayson, one of Sanderson County's two JPs, at her car door. The middle-aged woman looked like somebody's grandma, more at home in the kitchen baking cookies than traveling Sanderson County observing corpses.

"What've we got?" she asked as they made their way to the gurney.

"Strangulation, it looks like. Carla Ryder. I don't know what happened yet. Everything was all screwed up when I got here. Some things don't look right, Helen. I'm thinking we better get an autopsy."

They reached the gurney and Jimmy Don. He lifted the blanket, exposing Carla's face.

"Dear God," the JP mumbled. "Poor girl."

Jimmy Don pointed a finger at one eye. "I'm not an expert, but there's a couple of indications of asphyxia."

Rusty wasn't an expert, either, but he had seen the signs before. He had been the first arrival at suicides by hanging. He had assisted in investigating murders by strangulation. He had heard the crime scene techs talk and had witnessed autopsies. Those experiences and the victim's appearance told him she had suffered a torturous death, fighting to breathe.

Jimmy Don gingerly moved Carla's dirt-covered

red hair away from her injured neck. He moved her head from side to side. "She might have a broken neck, too."

At the movement of her neck, Rusty glanced at his watch and noted the time as 8:33. The fact that her neck still moved easily told him she hadn't been dead long enough for the onset of rigor mortis. "We can hope it was a broken neck that did her in," he mumbled, perhaps to console himself.

For Helen, he ran through the list of what he believed was wrong with the accident scene. Only she could authorize an autopsy.

The JP shook her head. "Such a shame. I think you're right about the autopsy, Rusty. I'll go ahead—"

"Nooo!" The outcry came from behind them. "You can't. I won't let you—"

Rusty wheeled and saw Elena coming toward her sister's body. He had no idea how long she had been behind them. He grabbed her shoulders and stopped her. "Elena, we have to. It's important to know how she died."

Elena broke into sobs again and he crushed her against his chest, pinning her. Over her head he nodded to Jimmy Don and Helen to go ahead. He wanted to hold her and comfort her in her grief, but he had to do his job. He turned her away from the gurney and guided her toward the silver Lexus, speaking to her softly. "Elena, you're a nurse. You know this has to be done. When you think about it, you, too, want to know what happened to your sister."

After a few minutes of weeping and protesting, she calmed and allowed him to seat her in the passenger seat of her SUV. His chief deputy, Matt Mercer, was standing behind him, waiting. Rusty hadn't even noticed when he arrived. "Take her home, Matt," Rusty told him, "or wherever she wants to go."

The deputy nodded. "You coming in soon?"

"Not for a while. Get Cheryl to bring you back out here to get the county car."

Rusty stuck his head back into Elena's rig. "You're still living at your dad's house, right?"

She was visibly trembling, but she nodded.

"Matt's gonna take you home, okay? Is your dad at home?"

She shook her head, her eyes set in a vacant stare.

"If you want me to, I'll ask Matt to stay with you a little while."

She looked down at her hands, clenched together in a knot. She shook her head again. "It isn't necessary. I'm all right."

Rusty knew nothing else to say, but he was concerned about her being alone. When they were kids, she hadn't had an abundance of friends and he suspected that hadn't changed. Like him, she had always been a loner among a host of family.

"What about Blanca? Do you—"

"She's out of town."

"Look, I'll come by and see you a little later, okay? When I finish up here."

She nodded, but didn't speak.

He closed the SUV's door and Matt drove it away.

Chapter 2

By the time Rusty returned his attention to the gurney, it was already being loaded into the ambulance and Helen was readying to leave. With Sanderson County having no medical examiner, standard procedure was to take a body for autopsy to the Ector County ME in the small city of Odessa thirty miles away. He knew he could rely on Helen to start the process, do the paperwork and do it right.

After the ambulance and the JP drove away, Rusty found himself alone at the arena gate. He was sweating profusely, though the early-morning temperature was cool. Except for a few birdcalls, an eerie quiet descended around him. The incident that had cost Carla her life smelled like something more than an accident. He couldn't keep from wondering if eyes were watching him from some hidden place. He drew a deep breath, seeking to calm the shaking in his gut.

His thoughts began to organize, taking him to times in his life when he had seen upheavals between men or women and wild and crazy horses. Any twelve-hundred-pound horse was a powerful animal, but an upset stallion was a freight train rolling down a track at a hundred miles an hour. As a prey animal, his instincts for self-preservation were formidable. A melee between him and a human that was violent enough to be deadly should have made enough noise to get the attention of somebody in the house, especially in the quiet of an early morning.

Planting his hands on his hips, Rusty looked toward the house for long seconds, judged it to be less than the length of a football field from the arena. Close enough to hear something.

The view from where he stood was of the back elevation. A long covered patio ran the length of the house. He could see what he believed was a hot tub on one end of the concrete. He assumed the patio door it sat near opened into the master bedroom. Had Carla's husband, Gary, been in the bedroom while his wife was engaged in a life-or-death battle with a horse?

Or had the man known of the commotion from a much closer place? The rich weren't often the victims of murder and if one of them was, the bad guy was usually someone close, like a husband. The fact that the man hadn't even returned to the arena to ask where his wife's corpse was being taken still bothered Rusty.

The stallion had kept his distance by remaining on the other side of the arena all through the earlier activity. Now, from the corner of his eye, Rusty saw the animal moving toward him. He turned and cautiously waited. The horse sauntered across the arena in a leisurely gait. Calm, not wired or upset.

Horses had been a part of Rusty's life for as long as he could remember. He had a sixth sense about them. As the stallion neared, Rusty opened the gate enough to edge through. He walked up to him, grasped the halter with his left hand and placed his right on the smooth black neck. The animal didn't back away or even flinch. "Whatcha doin', boy?" Rusty said softly, looking into the deep brown eyes and patting the muscled shoulder.

The horse whickered and sniffed at Rusty's shirt

pocket. So he was used to people and accustomed
to getting a treat. Rusty looked at the animal's left
side but saw no injury, no indication that anything
was amiss. He then walked around him and
checked his other side, then his face.

Just then he heard a clatter in the distance. He
looked away from the horse and saw his old Ford
truck wending up the driveway, pulling an equally
old two-horse trailer behind it. He noted the distance the noise carried in the quiet morning air.
The outfit came to a stop beside the Crown Vic.

Deputy Lowell Giles climbed out of the truck
and came over. "My God, Rusty. What happened?"

"It looks like this horse dragged Carla to death."

"You're shittin' me." Shock passed through the
deputy's eyes and his Adam's apple bobbed. He,
too, had known the Ryder daughters for years. He
gave the stallion a cursory look. "How'd he get the
best of her, Rusty? She's been fooling with horses
her whole life."

"Offhand, I don't know. Look, I want you to
haul him out of here. Take him to my dad's place
and don't say anything to anybody about it."

"Okay. Just let me get a rope."

Rusty held the horse's halter while Lowell went
to the truck bed and lifted out a lead rope, then
went to the rear of the horse trailer and opened
the gate. One of the traits Rusty appreciated about
Lowell Giles was his unwavering loyalty and faith
in Rusty Joplin. He rarely questioned a request or
the motive behind it.

When the deputy returned with the rope, Rusty
gently pushed against the horse's rump to turn him,
then handed the halter over to Lowell. The horse
stood still as a statue while the deputy hooked the
lead rope onto the halter ring beneath the animal's chin.

"He don't act like a wild horse," Lowell said. "Your dad be expecting me?"

"I'll call him."

The lead rope proved to be unnecessary. As the deputy turned and started out of the arena, the horse simply followed him.

Rusty continued to watch him. He was beautiful, with the look of a well-conditioned athlete in excellent shape. His black coat shone like obsidian in the early-morning sun. He appeared to be three or four years old, obviously strong and intelligent. A lot of people didn't like stallions. Too high-strung, too unpredictable. Rusty felt different. With a little patience on the part of a trainer, stallions could be turned into reliable horses, their strength used to advantage. Something about this one was certain— if Carla and Gary owned him, he was most likely a trained cutting horse and he was one valuable sonofabitch.

At the trailer gate, the horse walked up the loading ramp and into the interior without balking or causing a fuss.

Lowell slammed the gate shut and secured it. "He's awful tame to be a stud. Hard to believe he'd kill somebody."

"Yeah," Rusty muttered.

After the horse was driven away, Rusty unhooked his cell phone and keyed in his parents' phone number. His mother answered.

"Dad around?"

"Well, good morning to you, too. He went into town to the vet's office."

"Morning, Mom. Sorry, but I had something on my mind."

"How was your trip to Fort Worth?"

"Fine. Listen, Lowell's—"

"Did you see, um . . . what's her name again, Amber?"

His mother was referring to a woman in Fort Worth Rusty had dated off and on, one he had even brought to Salvation once. "It wasn't that kind of weekend. I just stayed at the lake at Mark and Kristy's house. Listen, Mom, Lowell's bringing a horse out to your place. Tell Dad I need for him to pen him up close to the house so y'all can keep an eye on him. I don't want anybody to go near him and I don't want anybody to know he's there."

"Is it your horse? Is it sick?"

"He's okay. I picked him up from some people. I just need somewhere private for him to stay for a few days."

"Sure, sweetie. I'll tell your dad when he comes back."

Rusty thanked her and disconnected.

He returned to the center of the corral and continued his examination of the accident scene but found nothing he could label as telling or even helpful. Still, for the sake of caution, he took the Polaroid camera from his car and made shots of the area from several angles. In a perfect world, a CSI team would have been present before the scene was destroyed. But in Sanderson County, population under ten thousand, the world wasn't perfect and no CSI team existed.

He kept a small spiral notebook in his shirt pocket. He pulled it out, along with his pen, and jotted some notes, including his own unofficial estimate of the time of death at roughly six a.m. In parentheses he wrote, "Pitch-dark."

Jimmy Don's remark—*Hell, she was gone before we ever got here*—stayed in his mind.

Though the ambulance was dispatched from the hospital, 911 calls came to the sheriff's office. Somebody must have called the hospital directly. Somebody like Gary Blanchard, who must have known his wife was dead when he made the call.

The question that had been needling Rusty since his arrival came back to him. *Why the hell didn't he call 911?*

Had Blanchard not followed the common practice because he had been too rattled to think clearly? Had he hoped to keep law enforcement away from the scene? Or had he bypassed the sheriff's office out of rancor? Rusty had defeated the candidate openly endorsed and vigorously supported by the Ryder family, which included Gary Blanchard. During the bitter campaign, bad feelings had run deep.

Rusty decided to give Blanchard the benefit of the doubt. He had often seen people behave in inexplicable ways when confronted with the sudden death of loved ones, especially violent death.

He turned his attention to the big beige barn a hundred feet away and the gaping maw made by the open double doors. He started toward it, unsnapping the safety strap on the .45 he wore on his belt. He was cautious by nature and he had learned to be even more so early on. Once, when he had been a part of a warrant service team, a fellow officer had been ambushed and killed with a shot to the head by the hidden suspect. From that moment, Rusty never forgot that the bad actors were usually able to see him, but he might not see them. And he was growing surer by the minute that somehow, somewhere, a bad actor had played a part in Carla Ryder's demise. This morning, he dared not be casual about what he might encounter in the barn.

He drew the pistol and stepped through the two-story building's dark doorway. Familiar barn smells filled his nostrils—animal droppings, hay and oats and barn dust. He waited a few seconds, listening, but heard nothing except horse sounds. As his eyes adjusted to the gray light, he scanned the high ceiling and saw several fluorescent light fixtures pro-

tected by metal guards. They ran the length of the
building. On a wall to his left, beside a closed door,
he saw a bank of light switches. He walked over
and tried them and the overhead lights flooded the
area with brilliance.

The door beside the light switches had no lock.
Rusty slowly pushed it open with his left hand, the
.45 heavy in his right. Scanning the room, he saw
typical riding accoutrements—saddles, blankets,
miscellaneous ropes and bridles—and a few small
tools and veterinary supplies.

He closed the door and returned his attention to
the barn's interior. With the huge space now
brightly lit, what he saw left him in awe. Finished
in rough-hewn cedar, extremely well kept and organized, the Blanchards' barn was built of better ma-
terials than many of the homes of Salvation's
citizens.

From where he stood, there appeared to be three
rows of spacious dual stalls with sliding partitions
that would convert each dual into a single. The
rows were separated by two wide aisles. He moved
up the center of the first aisle, placing his steps
carefully, watching and listening. He saw nothing
and heard nothing out of the ordinary for a barn
housing horses. He counted five horses, all alert
and waiting to be fed.

He passed a concrete slab with a drain in the
center and a faucet mounted on the wall. A rubber
hose hung looped on a cast-iron peg. A horse
shower area. The rich Ryders had nothing but the
best, even for their animals.

He found another set of closed double doors at
the far end of the barn. He pushed against them
with one hand and found them locked from the
outside.

Against the wall to the left of the doors, a
wooden stairway ascended to a mezzanine. At the

top of the stairs, he saw a long walkway, almost like a catwalk, with a wooden rail on one side. A closed door and a wide glass window were at the end of it. The window was covered on the inside. An office?

He climbed the stairs, tried the door and found it locked. Tightly drawn slats of a venetian blind hid the view of the inside and he could see nothing. He swore. He could pick the lock, but didn't dare enter without Blanchard's permission or a search warrant. He gave up the idea for the moment.

Standing at the railing in the echoing silence gave him an unobstructed view of the lower floor, including the second aisle. No horses were penned in the stalls accessible from the second aisle, but there was room for a dozen.

A new question rose in his mind. This was a big setup, with some number of cutting horses constantly in training, an operation that would require a lot of daily work and time on somebody's part. Surely the Blanchards had a caretaker of some kind. Perhaps the closed room was not an office after all. Maybe it was some kind of sleeping quarters or even an apartment for a caretaker. But where was he? Or she?

He switched off the lights and walked outside, no less interested in what lay behind the locked door on the upper level. He rounded the barn's front corner so he could see the side of the tall structure. At the far end, another set of stairs rose to a small wooden landing and a door to the area that was closed off on the mezzanine inside. A back door.

No longer worried that somebody was hiding in the barn, Rusty holstered his firearm and returned to the county car, determined to ask Gary Blanchard for permission to enter the locked room. He grabbed a roll of crime scene tape and covered the outside door with a big X of tape. Then he walked back inside the barn, climbed the stairs again and posted the interior door and the window in the same way.

As he left the barn, he considered posting the big double doors, but decided it would be useless. The horses would have to be taken in and out of their stalls and, this being Sanderson County, crime scene tape would likely be ignored.

Chapter 3

Rusty drove from the barn to the house and parked in front on the red-paved circular driveway. The house was a one-story hacienda-style structure made of off-white stucco. Spanish contemporary was how he had heard people in town describe it.

The Blanchard ranch had become an urban legend, a little more exaggerated each year. The state-of-the-art horse facility and the house with its manicured grounds were an ostentatious layout. Both had been custom-built by a contractor out of Midland in the middle of several hundred acres. All of it had been a wedding present from Randall Ryder after his daughter had up and married Gary Blanchard in California. The wedding had taken place ten years ago, but the locals still talked about the wedding present.

A long veranda stretched across the front of the house, behind wide archways. Rusty walked through one of them to the dark brown double front doors and rang the doorbell. The door was opened by a Hispanic woman. He lifted off his hat and asked for Mr. Blanchard.

She gestured to her left and stood back for him to enter, never raising her eyes from the floor. Rusty wondered if she was an illegal alien from Mexico. It was no secret that the whole Ryder family was partial to Mexican help and turned a blind eye to the immigration status of their employees.

And Rusty had made it no secret that he personally was opposed to the out-of-control immigration
that was going on in Texas and the practice by
some citizens who hired the illegal immigrants without regard to proper documents. In the wake of
9/11, he considered the flood of unknown bodies
sneaking into the country a threat to security and
a type of arrogance, a slap in the face of the many
legal immigrants who tried to play by the rules.

Beyond that fundamental hypocrisy, the hordes
that continued to come were a huge burden and
source of frustration to hardworking law enforcement officials who had to deal with the problem
but could basically do nothing about it. Immigration came under the federal umbrella. Rusty
couldn't think of a time when an employer of illegal
immigrants had even been cited, much less fined or
prosecuted by the Feds. A small-time county sheriff
could do almost nothing about federal policy.
Therefore, Rusty didn't ask his deputies to spend
a lot of time and energy hunting down illegals because they were illegal. But if they committed a
crime in Sanderson County, Rusty and his deputies
jailed them and charged them. Unfortunately, that
happened more and more often lately. More than
half the methamphetamine floating around Sanderson County came from Mexico via illegal aliens.

Following the Hispanic woman's direction, Rusty
found his way into a huge dining room with carved
bulky hutches filled with dishes hunkering against
two walls. A honey-colored oak table took up the
center of the room. Rusty counted ten chairs
around it. Above it, a massive light fixture hung
from the ceiling. It looked like an oval wagon
wheel at least six feet long. Black wrought-iron sil-
houettes of horses encircled its perimeter. No
doubt it had cost thousands.

From the dining room, he looked across a spacious kitchen to a breakfast àrea. The sun cast a long slice of pale golden light through the panes of a pair of French doors, the softness of the glow belying the sense of chaos Rusty felt all around him.

He hadn't often seen Gary Blanchard, but he had no trouble recognizing him sitting in a chair at the table, his arms wrapped around three kids. Blanchard was dressed in a gray T-shirt and faded jeans. Dark stubble shadowed his jaws. The kids, wearing pajamas, all had tearstained faces and clung to him. As Rusty skirted the dining chairs and the polished table and walked toward them, the stares of all four of them pierced him.

From red-rimmed eyes, Blanchard's glare came at him, hot and demanding. "What're you doing here, Joplin?"

"Gary," Rusty said quietly, hanging his hat on his fingers. "Looks like you've had a real bad morning."

Blanchard held Rusty's gaze a few seconds, then looked to his right. *"Jacinta! Venga tomar a niños!"*

Rusty had grown up hearing Spanish and had studied it in college. Even so, he wasn't conversant in the language and made no attempt to be. But he knew enough of it and his ear was attuned to it. He was able to decipher that Blanchard had called for someone to come and take the children. The same Hispanic woman who had answered the door appeared and lifted the boy from his arms.

"Tóme a niños en el cuarto de la familia y gire la TV," Blanchard told her.

Rusty thought he had told the woman to take the kids into the family room to watch TV. The small boy in his arms began to cry and cling, but the woman patiently pried him loose and carried him from the room, continually speaking to him in soft Spanish words. The two girls hung back with their father and the younger one began to cry, too.

"Maggie," Blanchard said to the taller child, "take Renata and go with Jacinta into the family room. Find the cartoons."

"No, Daddy. I'm scared."

"Don't be scared. I'm right here. Nothing's going to hurt you. Go on, now. Help Jacinta with Austin. I need to talk to this man."

The little girl looked up at Rusty with soulful brown eyes as she dutifully reached for her younger sister's hand and led her away.

The minute the kids were out of the room, Blanchard jerked to his feet, almost tipping his chair backward. He was a few inches taller than Rusty's six feet and probably outweighed him by twenty pounds. "Where'd you take my wife?"

"The medical examiner in Odessa for an autopsy."

"I didn't give permission for that and—"

"It's not up to you," Rusty said, intending to quell the debate before it started.

Blanchard seemed to consider that for a few seconds. A muscle in his jaw flexed. "I want that black sonofabitch shot. If you don't do it, I will."

Something like this was one of the things Rusty had feared. Glad he'd had the horse hauled away, he shook his head. "You don't want to do that, Gary. I know you're upset. I had Lowell haul him out of here so you don't have to look at him."

"It won't do any good to protect him." Blanchard stabbed the air with a finger. His eyes teared. "I don't care where you hide that fuckin' dog meat, I'll find him. And I intend to kill him."

Rusty leveled a firm look into Blanchard's eyes, hoping to calm him. "Gary. The horse is a dumb animal. Let's worry about him later." Rusty placed a hand on his shoulder and gestured toward a chair at the table. "Sit down with me and let's talk a minute. See if you can piece together for me what happened."

Blanchard jerked his shoulder away. "I don't want to sit down with you, Joplin."

Rusty ignored the vitriol. He was more interested in how Carla had managed to get herself strangled by her horse.

"Sit down, Gary," he said firmly, "and talk to me."

Blanchard dropped onto the chair to which Rusty had directed him. Rusty took an adjacent chair and laid his hat on the table. Blanchard sat on the edge of the seat, his palms braced on his knees. A muscle worked in his jaw. "I don't know what happened," he muttered. "I was in bed asleep. It's none of your damn business anyway."

"Well, Gary, you're wrong about that. When a citizen turns up dead unexpectedly and nobody seems to know how it happened, it becomes my business. Over at the arena they said you're the one who found her."

"That's right."

Rusty leaned forward, seeking eye-to-eye contact. "Well, how did you find her? I mean, it's pretty early in the morning. Were you in the barn? In the arena? What?"

The young boy could be heard from the next room. He had continued to cry since being taken from his father. Now he broke into breathless sobbing and gasping.

Blanchard's head jerked in the direction of the sound. "I got up to take a piss. I noticed her door was open. I walked down to her room, and she wasn't in her bed."

"You two weren't asleep in the same room?"

"That's none of—" Blanchard stopped, drew himself up and exhaled.

Rusty wondered if he had stopped talking because he had unintentionally revealed something about his relationship with his wife or because he had resigned himself to answer questions.

"She has . . . had her own bedroom."

The child's crying from the other room escalated into screams. "Shit," Blanchard whispered. He leaned forward, his elbows propped on his thighs, and rubbed his eyes with both hands.

Rusty, too, was distracted by the child's crying, but he didn't want to lose momentum. "Then what?"

Blanchard looked down at the floor. "I went out on the patio looking for her. I didn't find her, so I came back in and put coffee on. After it was made, I walked around outside. That's when I looked over at the arena and saw something on the ground. I couldn't tell what it was. I went closer and saw it was . . . Carla."

Blanchard's voice nearly broke before he said his wife's name. It was the first real waver Rusty had seen in him.

Rusty tried to imagine if anybody could have seen something lying on the ground in the arena from this house in the gray light of dawn. "What time was that?"

"How the hell would I know? Finding a clock wasn't on my mind."

Rusty nodded. "I understand. Was Carla . . . uh . . . still alive?"

The taller child, the one Blanchard had called Maggie, came to the doorway. "Daddy, Austin's screaming."

"I know. I'll be there in a minute."

"But, Daddy . . ."

Blanchard jerked to his feet, strode to the kitchen cabinet beside the refrigerator, pulled down a glass and yanked open the refrigerator door. He dragged out something that looked like apple juice in a clear bottle and poured some into the glass. He handed the glass to Maggie. "Here, give him some juice."

The girl trotted from the room carrying the glass and a pang of guilt pinched Rusty. He should be feeling sympathy for a man who had just lost his wife and was left with three small children. But under the circumstances, he couldn't afford such a soft emotion. Too much about the accident scene didn't add up. He pressed on. "Was she, uh, alive at that point?"

"I don't think so," Blanchard finally said, shaking his head and looking at the floor again. He didn't come back to the table.

Rusty stood up and walked into the kitchen, closing the distance between them. "Is that when you called the hospital for the ambulance?"

Blanchard looked Rusty in the eye, back in control just that quickly. He didn't answer.

Cool dude, Rusty thought. "Was there any particular reason you didn't call nine-one-one?"

"I just wanted someone out here soon as possible."

"I understand," Rusty said, bracing a palm on the countertop. "Before that, did you, uh, hear any noise coming from the arena?"

Blanchard glared. "I said I was asleep."

"Do you have any idea what Carla could have been doing to have gotten herself tangled up in the rope?"

"No." He closed his eyes and rubbed his forehead. "I don't know." He drew a breath and planted his hands on his hips. "She had this habit of . . ." He lifted a palm and shook his head, his eyes locked into a thousand-yard stare, as if he were seeing something inside his head. "Of looping a rope around her shoulder. I always told her not to . . . Maybe it got fucked up. I don't know."

Rusty ran that scenario through his thoughts, tagged it as something he would think about in more detail later. "Did you notice any vehicles in and out of here late last night or early this morning?"

The little boy's crying and screaming came from the outer room again. Blanchard stamped to the doorway and called out, *"Jacinta, lo trae de nuevo a mí."*

The Hispanic woman returned carrying the screaming child. Gary took him from her and cradled him on his arm. The little boy buried his reddened face against his father's neck and Gary began to rub his back and talk softly to him.

Rusty could see he was getting nowhere. Blanchard was vacillating between being calm and wired. Rusty returned to the breakfast table and picked up his hat. "Okay, Gary, we can take this up later. There is one more thing. I'd like to take a look inside that room upstairs in the barn."

"I suppose you've already snooped all over my barn. No damn way are you going to take it any further."

"Gary, I'd like to have your permission, but I don't need it. I can—"

"What, you're going to tell me you'll get a search warrant?" Blanchard's eyes bugged. Both he and the little boy in his arms stared at Rusty. "I got news for you, buddy. If you think ol' Porky Potter's going to let you tear into my barn, you'd better think again."

"Judge Potter's an officer of the court. He'll give a request for a search warrant its due consideration."

"Bullshit. He's a friend of mine. Better yet, he's a friend of Randall's."

Before Rusty could muster a comeback, Blanchard strode toward the phone mounted on the kitchen wall by a wide breakfast bar. "I've got to call Randall. I don't know how he's going to take this."

Rusty didn't envy him the call. That one of the most powerful men in West Texas adored his three daughters and his grandchildren was common knowledge. "Elena just left. Don't you reckon she'll tell him?"

Blanchard picked up the receiver and keyed in a number. "He's in Houston. On business. What was Elena doing out here?"

Rusty had the same question. If she was here so early in the morning, why wasn't the older sister, Blanca, here, too? "Are Blanca and Bailey at home?"

"They're in Europe."

Rusty's thoughts veered to Elena. In the back of his mind, he worried about her. Not only was her dad out of town, but with her older sister and brother-in-law out of the country, she was truly all alone. "I see," he said.

A part of him wanted to grant Blanchard privacy, but another part wanted to hear what he would tell his father-in-law.

Ever since the two girls had left the room, Rusty had been worried about them, too. Remaining within earshot of their father's phone conversation, he walked a few steps to the doorway and looked into the family room. The girls were huddled together with the maid and a Hispanic man Rusty took to be the maid's husband on a giant tan and white cowhide ottoman in front of the TV. A cartoon showed on the screen and music played at a low level.

Maggie stared up at him and Rusty saw in her dark brown eyes the resemblance to her mother.

The smaller girl was looking at him, too. She freed herself from the maid's grasp and came toward him. A cartoon character of some kind covered the front of her pink pajama top. She was a beautiful child, with Carla's deep red hair and huge dark brown eyes. Rusty guessed her to be five or six years old.

She stood in front of him and looked up, twisting the hem of the pajama top around her fingers. "Are you the sheriff?"

She had a soft little-girl voice that traveled straight from Rusty's ear to his heart. "Yes, I am," he said, keeping his tone gentle.

"Mommy's horse killed her. Are you gonna 'rest him?"

Chapter 4

Rusty left Blanchard's house in late morning. The sun had climbed high. Small, thin clouds scudded across the sky like veils. Another ninety-plus day lay ahead. Inside his car, he pulled his sunglasses from over the sun visor and shoved them on, dulling the brightness.

As he covered the distance between the house and the state highway, he thought of the irony of Cheryl's just happening to monitor the call to the hospital for an ambulance. If she had not, and if she had not followed up by calling him on his cell phone, perhaps Carla's body would have been hauled away and no one would have even wondered if she had died in something other than an accident. That loose approach to serious incidents was something Rusty hoped to correct as sheriff.

The haunted expression in the eyes of the Blanchard children stayed with him. He had seen that look more times than he wanted to remember. He had always had a soft spot for kids who became victims of tragedy.

His attempt to get information from Gary Blanchard had yielded little. He knew there was more the man could say. There always was. He hadn't heard Ryder's end of the phone conversation with his son-in-law, either, but he figured he knew how it went.

There's always tomorrow, he told himself. With

Randall Ryder's grandkids to take care of, Blanchard wasn't going anywhere.

He reached the highway and made a left turn toward town. His thoughts shifted to the arena and the black horse and he began to mull over his observations. A horse so out of control that it would drag its rider to death typically showed some signs of unruliness. The stallion hadn't even worked up a lather. Then there were the sweats and shower shoes. Too dumb even for a greenhorn.

Why hadn't the barn lights been on? It had been barely light enough to function in an outdoor environment when Cheryl called him and told him about the ambulance being dispatched. Was Carla in the arena working her horse in the dark, wearing what amounted to sleeping clothes? He believed these questions were adequate for a search warrant based on reasonable suspicion for at least the locked room in the barn, if not the house. He became even more eager to know what time of death the Odessa ME would establish.

He plucked his cell phone from his belt and called his office. "I'm headed to the Rocking R," he told Cheryl. "Call the hospital and find out who took the call on Carla Ryder this morning and what time it was. Ask exactly what was reported. If there was any paperwork, get us a copy of it."

"Okay," she replied. "You coming in soon?"

"Soon as I can." They disconnected. He was hungry, but his stomach was tied in such a tight knot he couldn't eat. He didn't have time anyway.

He took a shortcut over a caliche back road that passed through pastures of scrub brush, stunted mesquite trees and scattered pumpjacks rusting from poor maintenance. Crude oil was no longer the engine that made the West Texas economy second to none. Oil companies, particularly small ones, had less to spend on keeping their well sites neat and pretty.

Drawing closer to Randall Ryder's Rocking R Ranch brought his thoughts back to the tragedy at hand and the local talk. In Salvation, rumor and innuendo floated through the air as easily as dandelion tufts on the Texas wind. Nosing into the neighbors' activities was a way of life.

The Ryder family in particular, because of their wealth and influence, had always been the subjects of gossip. There were plenty of tales about Carla and Gary Blanchard. Among the many stories that circulated was that they had a stormy relationship. They had divorced once, which had resulted in a long, heated battle over custody of the two daughters. They had just remarried each other when Rusty returned to Salvation from Fort Worth three years back. Soon after the new marriage, Carla got pregnant with their third child.

More recently the gossip was about their liaisons outside their marriage. Rusty didn't know who Carla might be seeing on the side, but when he had worked as a deputy for former sheriff Jack Balderson, he had personally witnessed Gary's disregard for his marriage vows. Rolling on a trespass complaint late at night, Rusty had found Gary and a naked-from-the-waist-up Rosa Linda McDowell parked behind an oil storage tank on the Hanson ranch. Rosa Linda managed the Owl Club, a tavern in Precinct 4, the only wet-for-liquor precinct in Sanderson County. Precinct 4 was right up the road from the Blanchard ranch and Gary liked his liquor, the rumor mill said.

Rusty also recalled another fact from when he had worked as a deputy. A couple of times Sheriff Balderson had gone out to the Blanchard home on domestic abuse calls. Apparently Carla and Gary didn't just argue. They physically fought, with Carla being more violent and abusive than Gary. Even when the Ryder girls were kids, Carla had had an explosive temper and had handed rough treatment to both of her sisters.

Blanchard had attempted to have her arrested once. Rusty witnessed Sheriff Balderson refusing. The sheriff didn't want to jail the drunken daughter of one of his prime benefactors. Rusty remembered thinking at the time that if they had been in Fort Worth and he had been dispatched on a similar "domestic" complaint, he would have hauled in both Carla and her husband and charged them. Having money didn't set people above the law.

He hit a farm-to-market road and headed southeast toward the Rocking R's entrance. On the way he passed his own hundred sixty acres, which wasn't one half of one percent the size of the Rocking R. In the Fort Worth/Dallas Metroplex area he would have never been able to afford a quarter section of pastureland, but in Sanderson County's struggling economy these days, land was cheap.

Well before he reached the ranch's entrance, he began to see fat grazing cattle showing the Rocking R brand. The Rocking R went back generations, all the way to when, after the millions of buffalo that had once grazed these plains had been slaughtered, wealthy Easterners and Englishmen began to import cattle and put together empires.

Among the herd, active black pumpjacks worked, their seesaw action methodically sucking crude from the bowels of the earth. Being born. an heir to a cattle ranch had made Randall Ryder a cowboy, but inheriting oil wells had made him a filthy rich one. Since the bust of '85, many of the wells in Sanderson County had been plugged, but Ryder still had the contacts and the contracts to keep his own wells pumping. The increasing price of crude on the commodities market did him no harm, either.

A few miles later, Rusty passed over the cattle guard between the two massive red limestone stanchions that guarded the Rocking R's entrance. A couple of miles after that, he reached the ranch house.

He came to a stop behind Elena's silver Lexus. It was parked in the driveway in front of a four-car garage. The garage doors were closed and he saw no other vehicles. A Mexican man was buzzing a WeedEater around the edge of a flower bed where pathetically few flowers grew. As Rusty slid out of the county car, the Mexican turned his back. As he always did when he saw that behavior, Rusty wondered if the man was in the country illegally or guilty of some crime. Most of the native Mexican-Americans and the legal immigrants were friendly people who had no reason to turn away from the sheriff.

Approaching the antique front door, he was reminded how much he had always liked the Ryder ranch house. It was over a hundred years old, but so well preserved that a person had to make himself remember its age. The red limestone veneer was the only feature that dated it. That, and the architecture. The mansion had once been a "dog-run" house, the story went, a type of dwelling going back in Texas history all the way to the days before the Alamo. Only Comanches, Apaches and a few brave Mexicans had lived in West Texas that long ago, but some Ryder back in time had copied the old architecture.

A doorbell button was embedded in mortar beside the massive carved door. Rusty pushed it and heard a chime echo on the other side. Before the sound faded away, a Mexican woman, neatly dressed in a black skirt and a crisp white blouse, opened the door. Rusty removed his hat and asked for Elena. The woman answered in English and gave him entry.

Rusty stepped inside onto the dark red Mexican tile of the dim, cool entry. The tiles held a soft sheen and looked clean enough to eat off of. Through the quiet, he could hear the music of trickling water. Fifteen years had passed since he had last been in this house, yet he knew the sound came from the summer porch, where rivulets of water trickled down a rock wall into a narrow trough, then were recycled upward by a pump to fall down again. It was a type of air-conditioning system that was so effective in the dry West Texas air that sometimes the house was cold in the hottest part of summer.

The maid told him Elena was in the study, pointed to her right, then disappeared.

The house's layout began to come back to him. Gray-lit hallways led left and right off the entry. He recalled that the living and eating quarters were located on the left side of the house and the bedrooms on the right, with the two areas separated by the summer porch, which was the "dog-run" part of the house. Heading up the tiled hallway to his left, he saw the study's wide double doors where he remembered them to be.

Most of the cops he knew hated conversations with a victim's next of kin. He felt no different. Discussing a loved one's death was difficult even when calling on strangers. His history with Elena made today's visit even harder. He paused before knocking, steeling himself, then gently tapped on the door with his knuckle.

"Yes?" a voice said from inside. Elena's voice.

He eased the door open and saw her sitting on a long tan sofa. She looked at him across her shoulder. A table lamp cast an amber aura on the sofa's arm and on her face. Her eyes were red and swollen, her face blotchy. She had a tissue in her hand.

The smell of something clean and lemony surrounded him as he entered the room. "Hi," he said softly.

She didn't reply or ask him to sit down, but she didn't ask him to leave, either.

He eased the door closed and crossed the huge room to an overstuffed leather armchair, his footsteps silenced by thick carpeting. He sat down on the edge of the chair seat, bracing his forearms on his thighs, his hat hanging on his fingers between his knees. She was wearing a thin pink robe, he noticed. Her long dark hair draped over the collar and fell down her back to her waist. It looked damp. No doubt she had come home from her sister's house and showered. "You okay?"

Stupid thing to say, but what *could* be said at a time like this?

A photo album lay open on the coffee table in front of her. "Yes," she answered, appearing to be engrossed in the album.

Rusty let his eyes roam the room. The heavy draperies were open, but outside the window lay a wide covered porch that cast the room in shadow even on a day as sunny as today had turned out to be. Various hunting and fishing trophies hung on dark paneled walls, including a long and thick blue marlin Rusty remembered Randall catching years ago off the coast of Cabo San Lucas in Mexico. He saw no object out of place. A substantial wooden desk, obviously old and obviously the territory of the family patriarch, took up one end of the room.

As his police career had evolved over the years, Rusty had grown more fascinated by the silent stories told by people's homes. He was maybe twenty years old the last time he had been in this room and he hadn't paid attention, but now he looked at everything, including life, with a different eye. This room was a chieftain's lair, he thought now, and it looked much the same as how he remembered it from years back.

"You're out here all by yourself?"

"I just talked to Daddy," she said, her voice altered by a stuffy nose. She didn't divert her attention from the photo album. "He's on his way home. He'll be here soon." She turned a page.

"He's flying in? He still has his plane, then?"

Ryder had once owned a jet he kept at the airport in Midland. Salvation had an airport, but its one runway wasn't long enough for even a small jet to land.

"No. He sold it. He doesn't travel as much as he used to, so he uses a charter." She sighed and dabbed at her eyes with the tissue. "He's so torn up. I'm trying to pull myself together so he won't have me to deal with, too."

"Have you talked to Blanca?"

She nodded again. "She and Bailey can't get here before tomorrow. They're in Italy." She turned another page in the album.

Today was the first time he had been close to Elena in years and he couldn't keep from studying her. At eighteen, with her abundant dark hair, her clear green eyes, lips full and lush as a ripe peach, she had been a beautiful girl. Now, as a thirty-three-year-old woman, she looked like every man's fantasy. She still had a great body and he suspected that this morning the pink robe was all that covered it. For some damn reason he felt a tightening in his pants. Why now, of all times, he didn't know, because sex was the last thing on his mind. Especially sex with this woman.

"People have been saying for years a horse would kill Carla," she said. "But you know how she was. She never listened to anyone."

He recalled that about Carla's personality. "Willful" was the word that came to his mind.

She turned another page in the photo album. "Remember that one year when Daddy bought me that camera? I was just looking at the pictures I made."

Rusty couldn't hold back a smile. The summer before he left for college. Elena was sixteen and he was eighteen. She pestered her two sisters, him and all of his friends for the entire summer wanting to snap a picture of everything that happened. Her sisters were mad at her half the time. Carla was especially hateful. Once she even snatched the camera away from Elena and deliberately exposed the film to the sun. Rusty hadn't thought of the incident in years. "Yeah, I remember."

Elena looked closer at a picture. "There's some pictures of you in here."

Rusty supposed looking at pictures from the days when they were all in high school was some form of grieving process. "Elena," he said, "how did you happen to be out at Carla's this morning?"

"A friend called me from the hospital. Paula Flores. She told me the ambulance had been sent out. So I drove out there."

Rusty recalled his conversation earlier with Cheryl. "I didn't know Paula spoke English."

"She doesn't very well, but I don't have any trouble understanding her. I speak Spanish, remember?"

Elena's mother was Mexican-American, killed in a car accident when Elena was eight. That was the year Rusty had moved to Sanderson County. From then on, Elena and her sisters had lived in the care of various Mexican housekeepers. The result was that all three were fluent in Spanish and had a close affinity to the Mexican community. "I didn't forget.

I just didn't think of it. Uh, can I ask when was the last time you saw Carla?"

"Oh, not in months. Christmas, maybe. We weren't the best of friends, you know. I mean, I know we were sisters, but we didn't hang out or anything. The kids stay with me sometimes. I see more of them than of Carla and Gary."

This was September. Christmas was nine months back. So in the way Elena and her sisters got along, it appeared nothing much had changed from when they were kids. Carla and Blanca had never wanted Elena around.

"I suppose you knew Gary pretty well?"

She gave a sarcastic grunt. "No one knows Gary. He just suddenly appeared in everyone's lives. The handsome stranger. Daddy says Carla rescued him from the land of fruits and nuts."

Rusty had heard there was no love lost between Randall Ryder and his number two son-in-law, but he didn't know why. Perhaps the reason was as simple and as complicated as Blanchard's not being a man Randall had selected to be Carla's husband, as he had done with Blanca and her husband, Bailey Hardin.

"I'm assuming Carla knew him, though," Elena said. "At least well enough to get pregnant three times." A frown creased her brow. "Well, actually, she managed to get pregnant five times. She had two abortions."

A bitter laugh came from her throat. "Ironic, isn't it? Blanca and Bailey have spent thousands trying to conceive. When we were in high school, who would've thought Carla was the one who would turn out to be the fertility goddess?" She looked up at him again. "You didn't know about the abortions. Except for Daddy, you're probably the only one who didn't. You were in Stephenville. Or Fort Worth. Or wherever you were."

Rusty arched a brow at the uncharacteristic sharpness he heard in her last remark. "You're right. I never knew."

She bent forward and studied a picture. "Look, here's a good one of you and Carla. Come look at it. Y'all are sitting on the corral fence."

He rose and walked to the sofa. Laying his hat on the corner of the coffee table, he sat down beside her, his left thigh touching her right knee. The scent of something clean and pleasant met his nose.

The yellowed snapshot on the album page was of him and the red-haired Carla, all right, and they were sitting hip to hip on the corral fence. Carla's hand was lying possessively on his thigh, though at the time, he was sure, he had paid no attention to the implication of the gesture. He recognized the where, but he couldn't remember exactly when the picture had been snapped.

"I think this was that last summer that . . ." Elena paused, turned and looked up at him again, her green eyes made brighter by a shimmer of tears. "That everything went haywire."

Uh-oh. Rusty felt a little pinch in his gut. This meeting was going in the wrong direction. He had come here to offer comfort and hopefully discuss Carla and her husband's relationship while the atmosphere was still rife with shock. "Elena, I need—"

"The summer my sister couldn't be content with screwing all your friends. She had to screw you, too."

The temperature in the room suddenly dropped. "What?"

Her eyes drilled him and he couldn't look away. "Just be honest, Rusty. You don't have to deny it."

No statement was a bigger trap than *that* one. If a woman you were supposed to have been with accused you of screwing somebody else, you had damned well *better* deny it. He hadn't learned much about women in his thirty-five years, but he thought he had learned that. He stared at her, struggling to put together a reply.

"She told me," Elena said, swinging her gaze back to the album pages. "She even told me about the birthmark on your bottom."

The birthmark was a small strawberry on his right ass cheek. How Carla would have known about it he didn't know. "Elena, I never—"

"You want to know something?" She turned another page in the photo album. "I was so much in love with you that summer, Daddy could have never broken us up. Even if I was just a kid, I would have never agreed to be shipped out of town just because he wanted it. But after I heard what you and Carla did—"

"Elena, God as my witness, I never laid a hand on your sister."

She looked up at him again, her brow tented above troubled eyes. Her lower lip began to quiver. "It doesn't matter anymore, Rusty. It's been fifteen years. We've all moved on." She paused and new tears came to her eyes. "And now Carla isn't even here."

The sight of Carla Ryder's corpse lying on the gurney this morning now seemed a thousand years away. His thoughts were glued to this moment and the lie that might have changed the course of his life. "It matters to me, Elena. I never knew that's what you thought. I didn't know she told you that. I swear to you, it never happened."

Their faces were only inches apart and he could see a storm of confusion in her eyes. "Damn you, Rusty," she whispered. "Damn her. Damn everything. How did it all get so messed up?"

Suddenly she grabbed his open collar with both hands, pulled him to her and kissed him. Stunned and intending to back away, he gripped her wrists, but her tongue swept into his mouth and the stir in his shorts became a demanding monster. He didn't force himself away from her mouth like a sane man would have done. Instead, he took her tongue and they kept kissing like savages.

Her hands ran down his front to his belt and the next thing he knew his fly was undone and his erection was protruding like a spike. He felt embarrassed and awkward and confused. "Elena, listen. I can't—"

"Shh. Don't say anything. Don't spoil it." She rose on one knee and straddled his lap, at the same time untying her robe. Just as he had suspected, beneath it she was naked. Rational thought fled as her warmth surrounded him and her woman's scent reached him. His nostrils flared, his erection stood tall. He thrust, but his aim was poor and he missed the target. He was out of practice. Or maybe he had never been in practice for what was going on. She reached between them and guided him. In another frantic move, the tip of his rigid penis was inside her and he pushed home in one powerful stroke.

"Oh!" She gasped and sighed as her inner muscles squeezed down on his cock.

She began to move frantically and he took the cue. They humped each other brutally, both huffing and panting, her hanging on to his shoulders, him gripping her ass, helping her work up and down.

Her robe slipped from her shoulders. She cupped her breasts with both hands and guided one to his mouth. "Suck me. Hurry." He latched on to one nipple and sucked her hard. Her head fell back, her fingers dug into his biceps and her breath came in gasps. "That'sit, that'sit. Makemecome."

She was slick and hot and tight and his brain had turned to mush. All he could think of was the driving desire to mate, to couple, to explode inside her.

"Makemecome," she gasped again. "Please, Rusty."

He shoved his hand between them and fumbled to find her sweet spot. Then she cried out. Her deep muscles milked him. Tiny bright stars darted behind his eyes. He couldn't stop himself. He let go, a cry tearing from him as his seed spurted deeply into her.

"Aww, God," he groaned, still gripping her ass. He let his head fall against the sofa back. "Shit . . ."

She collapsed against his shoulder, huddling over him, her shoulders lifting and falling from her labored breathing. He could scarcely breathe himself. Even so, he could still smell the flowery fragrance of her hair and he could feel it soft and cool against his cheek. His thoughts raced. Among them was a hope that she was on the pill.

She straightened and looked down at him, her hair touching his face, the corners of her full lips tipped up into a smile. "You don't have to worry. I'm on the pill."

"I'm not worried," he lied, as a sense of guilt overtook him.

She braced her hands on his shoulders and lifted herself to her knees. He felt himself come out of her, felt the wet warmth of his semen draining from inside her and wetting the front of his pants.

"Yes, you are," she said. She leaned down and placed a soft kiss on his lips. "I know you, remember? You're a worrier."

"Look, Carla—"

He stopped. The horror of what he had said hit him only a second after it hit her.

Their eyes locked. Her expression was indescribable. Nothing moved. For a few seconds, he ceased to breathe.

Without a word, she crawled off his lap and stood up. He grabbed for her hand, but she pulled it back and stepped away from him, gathering her robe about her and tying it. "You know the way out," she said and quickstepped from the room. She didn't even slam the door.

He was shaking. His pulse pounded in his temples. *Good God.* What had he said? What had he done? Had he lost his mind? He had always been a little crazy where Elena was concerned, but how could he have let himself fall into what had just happened?

He sat forward and waited a few beats for his heartbeat to slow and his self-possession to return. Elena's remark about her sister and his high school friends battered him. It was true Carla had made the rounds. Even his best friend, Josh Logan, had had sex with her, but Rusty Joplin hadn't been and would never have been one of her conquests. All these years Elena had thought he screwed her sister?

At last he felt able to stand. When he got to his feet, his pants slid past his hips, dragged down by the weight of the .45 he wore on his belt. It was a damn wonder the pistol hadn't gone off and shot him or Elena or both of them. "Jesus Christ," he mumbled.

With shaking hands, he adjusted everything and zipped up. A wet stain had blossomed for the world to see on the front of his khaki pants. *Shit.* He picked up his hat and held it over his fly as he walked out.

Chapter 5

Chewing on her thumbnail, Elena watched from the summer porch. The white county car with its blue SHERIFF insignia slowly backed in an arc and drove away. Rusty's words echoed through her mind. *Elena, God as my witness, I never laid a hand on your sister.*

Though she had thought she had no tears left, one slid down her cheek.

As painful and persistent as a cactus thorn, guilt gnawed within her for the meanness she had felt toward her sister. For her entire adult life, her attitude toward Carla had been colored with the certain knowledge of her betrayal with Rusty Joplin.

I swear to you, it never happened.

She should have had more trust. She should have gotten in touch with Rusty. But she had been so devastated and so confused, she hadn't been able to.

Looking back, she could think of no time when Rusty had told her a lie. But, if she allowed herself, she could remember many times when both of her sisters had lied to her or when her father had manipulated her. Daddy had always been very good at orchestrating events to an outcome that suited him and enlisting her sisters to help him.

Of course, that didn't mean she didn't love all three of them or feel unwavering loyalty to them. Everyone had faults and as Daddy had always said, blood was thicker than water. Daddy was her only living parent and would deny her nothing. Her sisters were the only family with whom she was in touch.

After Carla's gloating confession so many years ago, Elena had never mentioned Rusty's name to her again. Just as Daddy had wanted, she went away to college in Lubbock and Carla went her own way in the horse world. In the years since, they had maintained a cautious, strained relationship for Daddy's sake. Perhaps they could have made up and been close if she, Elena, had only tried.

The early-morning hours slammed back into her memory. She had reached the arena too late. When she arrived, the EMTs had already given up. The sight of her sister's lifeless body would live with her forever. She squeezed her eyes shut, wanting to hide from shame of the hateful feelings she'd had for Carla all these years.

These days, now that they were older, thank God, she and her older sister, Blanca, finally had a better relationship. Blanca was now thirty-seven and trying desperately to get pregnant, hoping to compete with Carla for their father's time and affection by giving him grandchildren. Toward the same end, Blanca had married the man Daddy chose, educated and made a part of the Ryder businesses.

Her thoughts swung back to the scene with Rusty in Daddy's study, setting off another onslaught of conflicting emotions, not the least of which were regret and humiliation. She had practically forced him into sex with her. Being moral and honest, he might never speak to her again. And it was her own fault.

She didn't know what came over her, but she remembered reading in college something crazy about how life-threatening or traumatic events often drove couples to have sex afterward. It had nothing to do with lovemaking, but everything to do with fighting death with life.

Was that an explanation for what happened? Or was the encounter in the study an inevitability that found its time and opportunity? She had, after all, believed from the time she was fifteen that Rusty was her soul mate.

There had been other men in her life since those teenage years. Daddy had chosen one or two. She had met ambitious, well-educated men in the medical field. But she had become hard to please. No one lived up to the image that held a place deep in her heart of the handsome brown-haired Rusty Joplin and his sky blue eyes.

"Elena, you want the lunch?"

The voice startled her from her reverie and she turned toward the Mexican maid. "I don't think so, Benita. I'm going to my room to dress. Daddy'll be home soon."

She could spend no more time regretting what had been impossible from the beginning. In the coming hours, Daddy would need her to be strong and supportive. She returned to her room to prepare for the ordeal ahead.

She showered again, washing away the traces of the man she had practically assaulted. As she dried her hair, she concluded that the part of her that had always loved Rusty Joplin would continue to love him forever, but she had to lock those emotions away with her memories, where they had been for fifteen years.

A man shouldn't have to bury one of his children.

Aboard the sleek Learjet bulleting him from Houston to Midland, Randall Ryder sat in a buttery leather seat with his eyes closed. He felt as if he were functioning from outside his physical body. The message he had received from his son-in-law made no sense. Only after he called Elena and confirmed it did he believe it. How could his beautiful middle daughter be gone?

As his eyes burned anew with tears, he called back the last time he had seen her. She had been astride a prancing horse, her red hair tied back with a yellow ribbon. She was laughing and teasing him. *Climb on behind me, Pops, and I'll take you for a ride.* She had always teased him and called him "Pops."

What had he done to deserve this affliction again? Hadn't he already said good-bye to the mother of his daughters, someone he loved more than life itself? His beloved Magdalena's passing had nearly torn his heart from its roots. If not for their daughters, he might never have recovered. Since those terrible days, he had tried to be a good man, a fair man. He took care of his family, he went to church on Sunday when possible. He gave to those less fortunate than he.

His thoughts drifted to Carla's children. His grandchildren and his joy. Maggie, so much like her mother and named Magdalena for her grandmother. Renata, petite and charming. With her huge brown eyes—Carla's eyes—and small size, she reminded him of a pixie. And Austin, the two-year-old, the only one of the children who was blond and blue-eyed.

And he thought of his grandchildren's father. Where had that careless sonofabitch been while a wild animal was dragging his wife to death? Perhaps he hadn't even been at home. Perhaps he had been in another woman's bed. He had warned Carla that she had married a scofflaw and an adulterer.

Sensing the plane's descent, he opened his eyes

and glanced at his watch. He had been in the air an hour. It had taken only slightly less time to book the charter and get to the Houston airport than to fly from the Gulf Coast city to Midland. Air travel was one of man's most wonderful achievements.

In a landing soft as a kiss, the jet touched down and rolled to a stop. He lifted his briefcase off the floor. Inside, he found his cell phone and called his home. Elena answered. "I'm on the ground, sweetheart," he told her. "I'll soon be there."

She broke into tears. "I'm waiting for you, Daddy. I'm so glad you're back."

Ah, Elena. His gentle, sweet Elena. As beautiful inside as she was outside. "I'm on my way, sweetheart."

Deplaning, Randall saw his limo and driver waiting for him. "I heard about your loss, sir," the chauffeur said in a subdued voice. "I was sorry to hear it. I'll see to your bags."

"Thank you." Randall climbed into the backseat. He still had an hour of travel ahead of him before he would see home.

Soon the driver slid behind the steering wheel and started the engine. As the limo pulled onto the highway, he settled his thoughts on his children still living—Blanca, who constantly worked to please him; Elena, who looked and behaved so much like her mother.

And John Cruz, the son he shared with his former assistant at Ryder Oil. A lieutenant in the U.S. Army, John now served in Iraq. Randall hadn't done much for his bastard son. He had enjoyed John's mother, but he hadn't loved her like he had loved the mother of his daughters. Perhaps it wasn't possible to care about another woman as much as he had cared about Magdalena. Maybe life gave a man only one of those opportunities and if he lost it, perhaps that was his own private hell.

Because he hadn't loved Pilar Cruz the way he had loved Magdalena, he hadn't allowed her to give their son his last name. But he had looked after her and given the boy something more valuable than a mere name. He had given him an education at one of the finest institutions of higher learning in the state, Texas A&M.

Then, to Randall's dismay, thanks to the ROTC program at A&M, John had shown his gratitude by joining the damned army after graduation. Not that Randall Ryder could ever be labeled an unpatriotic man, but he had helped John to a degree in petroleum engineering. He had expected him to work for Ryder Oil.

In so hostile an environment as Baghdad, Randall wouldn't have been shocked to learn it was his son who had become a fatality. His daughters, on the other hand, were safe. The fact that Carla had died at her own home was terrible beyond belief.

Chapter 6

For the second time today, Rusty left his home, freshly showered and wearing clean clothes, headed to his office. He was back in control of his emotions, though he still felt wired from a double dose of adrenaline.

He wanted to dwell on what had occurred with Elena in Ryder's study. He wanted to figure it out and understand it, but he couldn't let himself be distracted from the more pressing catastrophe. In only a matter of hours, news of Carla's death would explode and rain unbridled speculation all over West Texas.

As he drove, he keyed in his dad's number. Marvin Joplin had his finger on more than the cattle market in Texas. Being a lover of horses, he also kept up with the horse world. Rusty caught him in the house just finishing lunch.

From him, Rusty learned the black stallion was a three-year-old with a pedigree two feet long. An article had appeared in a horse magazine about Gary and Carla buying him at the Futurity in Fort Worth back in July. Paid a small fortune for him.

No surprise there. The horse looked like a champion and cutting horses with premium bloodlines were selling for astonishing prices these days. Knowing that made Rusty wonder if Gary's threat to shoot the black stallion had been strictly for show. Even with a dead wife to avenge, would a man really kill a horse he had paid two or three hundred thousand dollars for? It was a question worth any cop's consideration.

He reached the sheriff's department in the courthouse annex after noon. The annex was a squatty fifty-year-old redbrick building across the street from the courthouse's back door. When Rusty was a teenager, it had been a medical clinic. At some point during his fifteen-year absence the county bought it, moved the sheriff's department into it and called it the law enforcement center. Little had been done to change the basic interior, so offices were not much larger than closets.

Over time, as other county government agencies needed space, the sheriff's department had been squeezed until its twenty-five employees now crowded into the front half of the building. The facility was no longer known as the law enforcement center, but as just the courthouse annex. The agencies that utilized the back half of the building reached their offices via poorly lit, narrow hallways. The county might give the building a lofty label like "courthouse annex," but everybody who worked in it called it the mouse maze.

As Rusty strode through the front doorway Cheryl scowled at him over her half-glasses and thrust a handful of pink messages at him. "Where you been? I've been calling you."

"Couldn't get here sooner," he said, shuffling through the messages to avoid looking her in the face.

One note was from the Odessa medical examiner. Suspicion snaked through Rusty's brain.

He walked on into his cramped office, with Cheryl following. She closed the door behind her. "Matt told me what happened," she said, almost breathless. She pushed her glasses to the top of her head. "I checked with the hospital. It was the nurse on duty in the ER that took the call and it was Gary himself who called."

"Who was the nurse?"

"Wendy Thayer. You know her. She's Bob Thayer's daughter."

"So what time was it?"

"Seven thirteen. All Gary said was that his wife was down and needed an ambulance."

Rusty laid his hat on top of one of half a dozen gray filing cabinets that lined the wall behind his old wooden desk. On top of the farthest file cabinet in the corner sat a fan that was rarely switched off. It created a low hum in the small room. He sank to his desk chair, running the time line of events as he knew them through his head. The time the ambulance had been summoned did not conflict with his own unofficial estimate of six o'clock as the time of Carla's death.

File folders and documents were stacked neatly on the corners and sides of the desktop, he noticed as he sat down. Assorted shapes and sizes of paperweights prevented papers that were loose from being blown off the desk by the moving air from the fan.

He could see Cheryl had been at work straightening things. In the middle of his desk blotter lay a file folder labeled BUDGET. His original intention on his return from the long weekend had been to spend the next two days working on next year's budget proposal for the sheriff's office. He set the budget file aside. "Were you up at seven?" he asked Cheryl.

She gave him a frown and a gasp. "Of course I was up. I come to work at seven."

"Do you remember if it was dark then?"

"Um, kind of gray. You could see a little bit when I left my house around six forty-five. I had to have headlights driving in."

Rusty mulled over the time, remembering that when he had first talked to Cheryl, at seven thirty, he had been driving, but he hadn't had to use his headlights. He tried to visualize again how clearly someone might have been able to see something lying on the ground in the arena from the Blanchard backyard at seven thirteen.

"I saw the crime scene tape on the barn door when I took Matt out to get his car." Cheryl's eyes widened. "Rusty, you really think it's a crime? You really think someone *killed* her?"

"I don't know. Look, Cheryl, I don't want everybody in the office talking about this."

"Oh, don't worry. I know when to keep my mouth shut."

A disputable fact, Rusty thought. Cheryl might be a loyal employee, but when it came to gossip, she wasn't much different from everybody else in Salvation. "That door where I put up the crime scene tape—do you know what that room is?"

"Good grief, no. I've never been to Blanchard's house, much less their barn. Though my bunch might be more at home in the barn than in the house. We ain't on their guest list."

"Not many in Salvation are. What'd the ME say?"

"Randall Ryder's lawyer's been on the phone with him. Apparently Mr. Ryder wants to halt the autopsy."

"That was quick," Rusty said. "He can't do that."

"He must not know that. He's filed an injunction. I don't know where things stand. I didn't even know there was going to be an autopsy."

Rusty lifted a different message from the stack. "Who's this guy?"

"A reporter from Channel Seven in Odessa."

Mental groan. The publicity madness was already

starting. A second TV station besides Channel 7 existed in Odessa and two in Midland. Soon all of them would be in town. With Ryder Oil's offices being in Midland, Rusty was surprised the Odessa channel had showed up first.

Cheryl leaned the heels of her hands on the outer edge of his desk. "Just tell me this. If this is supposed to be kept quiet, how would a TV reporter in Odessa already know about it? And why would he even care about a horse accident in Salvation?"

"She's—" He stopped as a picture of Carla's face flashed in his mind. A lump sprang to his throat, but he quickly swallowed it. "God only knows how Channel Seven found out. Carla's Randall Ryder's daughter. If she wasn't, no reporter would care."

At the truth of that statement, Cheryl straightened and frowned. "Asshole," she muttered. "He showed up a little while ago in one of those TV station vans. When I told him I didn't know when you'd be back, I think he might have gone out to Blanchard's house."

"Shit," Rusty grumbled. "They can't find any dead bodies in Odessa?"

Still, as distasteful as he found dealing with the press to be, he knew better than to alienate its members. He placed the message on a spike he kept on his desk for messages and phone numbers he didn't want to lose.

"How're those poor little kids?" Cheryl asked.

"They looked pretty shell-shocked this morning."

Cheryl shook her head, the frown not leaving her face. "I hope they'll be all right. Maggie's in my daughter's class."

Rusty looked up at her, curious now about the ages of Carla and Gary's children. "Fourth grade? That's what, nine years old? What about the other two kids? How old are they?"

"The youngest girl, her name's Renata, is six, I think. And the little boy, Austin, must be about two and a half or three."

Rusty shook his head, as a memory from that morning of the younger Blanchard daughter's pixie face and her huge brown eyes slid through his mind.

"Everybody thinks Gary's an ass, Rusty, but he does love those kids. He comes to every little program the school has, no matter how trivial or what time of day. He pays most of the expenses for every party. He even bought some playground equipment. Far as I'm concerned, he's a good dad."

Rusty couldn't afford to let himself get into any hand-wringing over the Blanchard children. Their father seemed to have their welfare under control. He reshuffled the phone messages, leaving the Odessa crime lab's number on top. "Okay. I'll call the ME and see what Ryder's up to."

"Now that you're back," Cheryl said, "I'm going to lunch. I've got to take some cupcakes to the school. I'll be back in forty-five." She started out the door.

Uh-oh, Rusty thought. He could think of no better place to fuel talk than the middle school. "Hey, Cheryl," he said behind her. She stopped and turned his way. He raised his hand to his lips and made a motion with his fingers like turning a key. "Remember what I said."

"Oh, I know. Mum's the word."

The medical examiner soon told Rusty about the injunction filed by Randall Ryder against an autopsy's being conducted on Carla Blanchard's body.

"Why?" Rusty asked him. Any family member could protest an autopsy, but few ever did and Rusty couldn't recall a time when one had prevailed in an attempt to halt it.

"Something about desecration of her body."

"He doesn't care what killed her?"

"I don't think it's that," the pathologist answered. "He's just arrogant, trying to throw his weight around. I notified your JP's office. They'll get it sorted out, then we'll do the cut."

"You got an opinion on the time of death?"

"Early. Around six o'clock."

"Before daylight."

"That's how it looks to me. Right now, it's just a guess."

Rusty said good-bye and dug in his desk drawer for an unused file folder. He made a note of the name of the ER nurse and the time she took the call from Blanchard, stuffed it inside the folder and anchored it with a paperweight. Then he found a blank crime scene report form in the bottom drawer of the file cabinet. He started on the report using the notes he had made at the Blanchard barn and house this morning, just in case the incident turned out to be a crime.

Just in case, hell. He *knew* a crime had occurred. And the facts he knew were more mysterious than the ones he didn't.

The paperwork was the part of police work Rusty disliked the most, but it was the most important. A cop's most effective tool was his pen. A crime scene report was a tedious document if done right. It covered dozens of details that might be pertinent later, from the background of the deceased to the precise description of the crime scene itself, details that might be forgotten if not noted on paper. Unfortunately, with no forensic investigation of the Blanchard arena, much of that information would never be known, so Rusty's written first conclusions became even more important.

When he had done the best job he could with what he had, he turned his attention to the search warrant he wanted. He went back to the file cabinet for a blank application form, then rolled his chair over to an old electric typewriter on a stand in the corner. Cheryl was back at her desk and fielding phone calls and Rusty was able to focus on the documents with few interruptions. When he finished, the nine-to-five workday was nearing an end, but he picked up the phone and punched in district judge Phil Potter's office number to request a signature on the search warrant application. Rusty's experience with Judge Potter was sketchy. The judge was part of the small good ol' boy network in Salvation, which included Blanchard and Ryder but did not include Rusty Joplin.

The call to the judge's office produced no results. He was out of town until tomorrow. Rusty missed the convenience of the city. In Fort Worth, there had been a dozen officials he could ask to sign a search warrant. Frustrated, he left a message.

As he hung up, a tap on the door took his attention. His sister Denise stuck her head through the doorway. "Can I come in?"

"Sure."

"So what happened, Rusty?" Denise asked, her gaze furtively roaming his desk.

"Close the door," he told her as he shoved the search warrant into the file folder holding the information from the hospital ER.

"I heard Carla Ryder got drug by her half-million-dollar horse. This morning, when Hayden was at the hospital delivering some meds, the nurses were talking about it."

"I can imagine." The hospital, as well as Denise and her husband Hayden Albretton's drugstore, were gossip mills. Rusty motioned for her to sit. "Give me the skinny on Carla and Gary. What do the rumor queens say when they come into the drugstore?"

She flopped into a chair and swung her long

brown hair behind her, too obviously eager to tell all. "I thought you didn't like gossip."

"I don't, but I want to know who those two are fooling around with these days."

"Well, let me see. Do you want the short list? Lately, Gary's been with"—Denise began to tick off on her fingers—"Bobbie Jo Branson and Patty Speck. Then there's Rosa Linda McDowell. He's been seeing her for a long time. She sort of comes and goes."

Rusty was casually acquainted with all three of the women. "Whoa. Two of those girls are married."

He felt foolish for the statement. If anyone should have known a marriage certificate was no guarantee of a wife's fidelity, he should have. He had married just out of college. The union had lasted just long enough for his wife to finish law school, go to work for a Fort Worth firm of defense lawyers and take up with one of the partners. Those memories seemed like a hazy bad dream now and he didn't dwell on them, but he hadn't forgotten them.

His sister lifted her shoulders and opened her palms. "So? This is Peyton Place. You act like you've been living under a rock."

"Yeah, yeah. What about Carla? Who was she seeing?"

"Don't know. She must be more discreet than Gary. Guess she worries what Daddy might say. What I heard was she doesn't—" Denise paused and looked away. She, too, was acquainted with Carla. She cleared her throat, swallowed and sniffed. "Um, she didn't do the locals. She goes . . . or went, out of town."

A lot of adjectives fit Carla, but "stupid" wasn't one of them. No doubt, if she really had had affairs outside her marriage, she would have been smart enough to do it out of town. If Rusty knew anything from personal experience, he knew a control freak like Randall Ryder wouldn't hesitate to take charge if his daughter was engaged in something he didn't like, even if she *was* thirty-five years old. "Does Randall know about these affairs?"

Denise's blue eyes came back to his. "How could he live in Salvation and not know it? That has to be part of why he doesn't like Gary." She arched her brow and cocked her head. "Of course, he probably thinks Carla was home baking cookies while Gary was out chasing women. You know how he's always been about his daughters. He would never believe one of those perfect angels could do anything so tacky as cheat on her husband."

"When we were in school, Carla was friends with Rachel Jones and Rita Massey—"

"Forget that. Take my word for it, Rusty. Carla and those women have nothing in common these days."

"She must have had a friend of some kind. She couldn't live in a vacuum."

He rethought that statement. In fact, the vast difference between the comfort level of the wealthy Ryders and the economic situation of most of Salvation's population had always left the whole family more or less in their own separate space.

Denise shook her head. "Honest, Rusty. Her wild and woolly ways put a high wall between her and most of the girls we all went to school with. Most of the people in this whole town, actually. Anyway, what's it all got to do with her getting killed by her horse?"

Rusty hesitated, gazing directly at his sister. Seeing her face was like seeing himself in a mirror. They looked so much alike many thought they were twins. They were tight and always had been, but to discuss his thoughts about Carla's death with her, or anyone, felt like a violation of a covenant. "I don't know, sis. I'm still thinking about it."

"Randall must be taking it pretty hard. Elena came into the drugstore and picked up a prescription for something for him to take."

At the mention of Elena's name, Rusty felt a tiny flutter in his heart.

"I heard Randall and Gary already had a big fight over where to bury her," Denise said. "Randall wants her in that family plot on his ranch, where all the Ryders are buried, but Gary says he might even take her to California where all of *his* family is. I can just imagine how the S-H-I-T hit the fan."

"That's bullshit, Denise. It's too soon for her husband or her father to begin to plan a burial."

But Rusty didn't doubt that it was a fight that would come in time and he suspected he knew who would win it. That Randall would want his daughter buried in the Ryder family cemetery on the Rocking R Ranch was to be expected.

It occurred to Rusty that the entrance to the Rocking R was on a state highway. Without a doubt, the turnout for the funeral of the daughter of a man as powerful as Randall Ryder would be larger than his small crew of deputies could manage. His department would have to work with the state cops to provide an escort.

"That Elena's a pretty thing all dressed up," Denise went on. "You know how she usually goes around town wearing those ugly blue scrubs and her hair in a braid? Today in the drugstore, she had her hair down and she was wearing one of those soft dresses like those actresses in *Desperate Housewives*. You know, the kind that sort of floats and sort of looks like a nightgown? It was tan.

Probably cost more than Hayden and I made last month."

"Hm," Rusty said, the morning's incident in Randall Ryder's study spinning inside his skull. Only a few hours had passed since he'd had his hands on Elena's naked body beneath a thin pink robe. He had no trouble imagining her in a floaty tan nightgown.

"I felt so sorry for her, Rusty. She looked like she was lost. Like she needed a good strong shoulder. It made me remember how she used to come to you when she was upset about something."

Rusty felt a muscle clench in his jaw. Instead of replying, he looked down at the phone messages and sorted them by priority.

"Do you ever think about her anymore, Rusty?"

"No."

"Liar. I know what Randall and Daddy did was tacky. I never did understand how you could just turn it off like you did. My God, y'all were hornier than rabbits. Every month Hayden and I used to bet on if Elena would turn up pregnant."

"Cut it out, Denise."

"Now that she's grown-up, you know who she looks like?"

"No."

"That movie star Angelina Jolie."

"Hm," Rusty said again. He knew few movie stars by name, but Elena was prettier than any one of them he could think of. Her looks didn't matter. To him, she was more dangerous than a black widow spider. A *female* black widow. He didn't fear much, but when it came to women, he feared being eaten alive.

"You know, if Hayden and I screwed like you and Elena used to, I'd have twelve kids."

"You need to get out of here and let me get to

work," he told his sister, getting to his feet and picking up his hat. With the autopsy and the search warrant stalled, Rosa Linda McDowell had come to the forefront of his thoughts.

"Okay, I can take a hint." She rose from the chair and started for the door. "You coming out to Mom and Dad's on Sunday? Hayden Junior's dying for you to see how good he's getting with his roping."

Hayden Albretton Jr., Rusty's thirteen-year-old nephew, made no attempt to conceal his hero worship. Because Rusty was the heeling half of his and his dad's winning roping team, Hayden Junior wanted to be a "heeler," too. The first Sunday of every month, the large Joplin family had their own family rodeo, which included a lot of roping and riding. Also good friends, good food and good music. With several family members out of town over Labor Day, the event had been postponed until the coming weekend.

"I'll see," he said, wondering how he could escape it. It wasn't that he didn't enjoy the gathering and all that went with it, but these days, his mother and his three sisters all ganged up on him about getting married again and starting a family. Even his elderly grandmother joined in. His youngest sister, Marilee, sometimes brought an extra woman along for him to meet. He hated being fixed up.

"You should do more than see. Samantha and her brood are going to be there. You know you want to see them. They won't be able to come back until Christmas. They'll be too busy bringing in their crop."

His sister Samantha and her husband farmed cotton up by Amarillo. She hadn't been to Salvation in months. It was true he didn't want to miss an opportunity to visit with her and her family.

"Besides," Denise added, "Mom and Dad put

everything off last weekend just so you could go water-skiing in Fort Worth."

He hadn't expected them to, but that's how his family was. They functioned as a unit and wanted him to be a part of it. "Hey, I wasn't the only one who went out of town."

As she left his office, he glanced at his watch and noted the time, four thirty. Rosa Linda would likely be at work at the Owl Club.

Chapter 7

Sanderson County was a tangible example of the inconsistency of the laws governing the sale and dispensation of alcoholic beverages in Texas. Of the four voting precincts in the county, one had been voted "wet" for the sale of alcohol by its citizens, while the other three remained "dry."

The liquor election had taken place before Rusty returned from Fort Worth. Winning the vote had to have been a Herculean effort on the part of a couple of special-interest groups because if Rusty knew his hometown, every church in town would have mounted a vigorous campaign against bringing booze into even a portion of the county.

The rationale for voting the precinct alcohol-legal had been that Sanderson citizens, who used to drive to New Mexico to buy liquor at the state line, could instead stop off before they got there and not take revenue out of Texas. Added to that was the fact that the county to the north was entirely dry, so now the population of that county didn't have to buy alcohol in New Mexico, either. Apparently the point that liquor could be bought in Odessa, thirty miles to the south, had been ignored.

The highway leading into New Mexico bisected the one wet precinct, now known as Precinct 4. It was the smallest precinct in the county. Buster Arnold, the ringleader of one of the special-interest groups, had activated his "special interest." He owned the Owl Club tavern and a liquor retail store called Buster's. He had recently moved a large building in from somewhere, shored it up where needed and opened a cowboy bar-café–dance hall called Boot Scooter's, open on Friday and Saturday nights.

The tavern and the dance hall provided social activity for many of Salvation's citizens as well as for revelers from the county to the north. The joke in the sheriff's department was that they all had to be out of jail on Sunday morning early enough to get to church.

Precinct 4 was also the area where much of the local crime occurred. The sheriff's department deputies patrolled it heavily. Small-scale drug activity took place in the Owl Club parking lot and even inside the tavern. Frequent complaint calls had to be answered, especially on weekends. There were fights, incidents of spousal abuse or disturbances of the peace in general—or sometimes all three at once.

Since Gary Blanchard had a reputation for partying hard, and Rosa Linda McDowell was an Owl Club employee, it was probably more than rumor that he spent some of his time in Precinct 4. If Rusty had learned anything about drunks and junkies, it was that they gossiped among themselves just like the citizens who were sober. That somebody somewhere in Precinct 4 had heard or said something pertinent to the accident at the Blanchards' was almost a given.

Half an hour later, Rusty parked in front of the Owl Club, his eyes focused on the door as he killed his engine and the air conditioner. The temperature was still in the nineties and the blast of hot, dry heat that engulfed him in the Crown Vic didn't make his sunburn feel any better.

He hadn't visited the Owl Club recently, but as

one of Jack Balderson's deputies he had been here many times for various reasons. The place was what he classified as a dive, pure and simple. The building was a gray doublewide mobile home from which most of the features that identified it as a "home" had been removed. Even so it looked like an old mobile home, right down to the rust trail from the rivets that secured the siding to the walls. Just as many in Salvation enjoyed the entertainment Precinct 4 offered, an equal number hoped for a tornado to swoop through and blow it away.

He stuffed his sunglasses behind the visor, slid out of the county car and headed for the plate-glass sliding patio door. One of its three-foot panels had been painted black and the other was filled in with unpainted plywood. Some months ago a drunk had thrown another drunk through the glass and evidently Buster Arnold hadn't seen the necessity or the practicality of replacing the panel with more glass. Probably sound judgment on his part.

Rusty paused just inside the doorway waiting for his night vision to kick in. The place was dark as a cave. Alan Jackson sang from a brightly lit juke-box in the far corner of the barroom.

Rosa Linda, the room's only occupant, was working behind the bar, spotlighted by an orange-colored aura coming from assorted beer signs hanging on the wall behind her. She had a dish towel in her hand.

Rusty made his way to a barstool across from where she stood and hitched a hip onto the wooden seat. Every time he saw her he wondered if she remembered he was the deputy who had caught her a couple of years back, late at night, in a half-disrobed state in the front seat of a truck with Gary Blanchard. If she did remember, she never gave a hint.

She folded her dish towel into a square, laid it

on the counter and crossed her arms under her breasts. "Come for a beer?" she asked, her tone dripping with sarcasm.

Rusty had a beer now and then on his private time, but for him to consume alcohol in public around Salvation, especially in a tavern in Precinct 4, defied good sense. He reacted to Rosa Linda's mockery of his office with a chuckle. "No, thanks. What's going on?"

She shrugged, her gaze boring into him. He read a host of emotions in her dark eyes—caution, resentment, extreme dislike. Rosa Linda had come from somewhere in Mexico. Though slightly overweight, she had an exotic appearance, with long, thick black hair, intense brown eyes and full lips fixed in what seemed to be an everlasting pout. She always wore bright red lipstick. Rusty had met her soon after his return from Fort Worth. Then, she had been married to Danny McDowell, an oil field hand, but the gossip said he kicked her out because of her affair with Blanchard.

Rusty had asked her about various individuals before, at which times she had been cooperative, even friendly. That attitude clearly didn't prevail in today's visit, so she must have known why he had come. "Gary Blanchard," he said, getting straight to the point. "When's the last time you saw him?"

Her shoulders lifted, her mouth turned downward into a horseshoe smirk.

"Look, everybody in town knows he spends a lot of time here."

She looked away, but didn't uncross her arms. "He has not been here in long time."

"How long's a long time? Yesterday? Last week?"

She lifted a shoulder again. "Don' know nothin', Sheriff. I busy. Him, too."

She had slipped from the nearly perfect English

Rusty knew she spoke when she wanted to. Rosa
Linda was an enigma. The moment Rusty had met
her he judged her to be smarter than average and
on top of things, which had made him wonder what
kind of education she had gotten in Mexico. Sanderson County was home to a .small number of
smarmy characters who routinely passed in and out
of the justice system and she seemed to be acquainted with most of them, yet she had never been
arrested. She had managed this tavern since its
opening, but so far as Rusty knew, she didn't drink.
She even went to mass on Sunday. And she had a
legitimate work permit.

Now, a spike of annoyance drove through him.
He was in no mood to be jacked around. "Let's
have an understanding, Rosa Linda. If I wanted to,
I could park a deputy in front of your door every
day all day. And every night all night."

Her defiance drained away, as he had known it
would. Buster Arnold would not be happy if one
of his employees did something to cause a deputy's
car to become a permanent parking lot fixture.
Rosa Linda knew that as well as Rusty did.

"Before the holiday," she said insolently.

"Was he alone?"

She smirked again and opened her palms, as if
her questioner was too stupid to be alive. "*Sí,
señor.*"

Rusty continued to give the sarcasm a pass. "He
came especially to see you?"

"He married, Sheriff."

"I know. So what was he doing here? Drinking? Partying?"

She didn't reply.

On a hunch, Rusty asked, "Does he usually come
to see you after he's been fighting with his wife?"

Her eyes sparked with anger and she let out a

cynical grunt. "He don' fight her. She black his eye, scratch his chest, but he does nothin'."

"How do you know about that?"

"I see." She pointed a finger with a long red nail to one eye. "With my eyes, I see."

"His wife came here with him?"

She gave him another insolent look. "No. Not her place."

Indeed. A woman who had been surrounded all of her life by the finery that immense wealth could buy would feel more at home in the Midland Country Club than in Precinct 4's Owl Club. "Okay. So Gary came without her. I'm asking you again. How long ago?"

She held up two fingers. "Two weeks."

"That's a long time to go without seeing your boyfriend."

"I tell you. He married."

"You've heard what happened to Mrs. Blanchard?"

"They should hang the flowers around that horse's neck. He is a good horse."

Rusty sat back on his stool, surprised by the unbridled display of venom. "Do you know Gary's hired help?"

"Luis Ramirez. He is a boy."

Rusty had figured Blanchard's hired help would be Mexican. He wasn't acquainted with Luis Ramirez. He suspected Luis might be the lone employee, but there could be a dozen helpers who were the Ramirez family's relatives or friends from Mexico, paid in cash, and no one, least of all the government, would know anything about them. "That's all? Just one boy?"

Before Rosa Linda could answer, two men Rusty didn't know came through the door. He could see the relief in her face. He didn't want to ask her

questions in the presence of somebody else, so he
left his card and phone number and told her to call
him if she thought of something she wanted to tell
him. He figured she would trash the card as soon
as he left her sight. It didn't matter. He would be
returning to the Owl Club.

The sky was still white with light and the temperature was still ninety-something when Rusty left
the tavern. He headed back to the Ryder mansion.
If Randall Ryder disliked his son-in-law as much
as gossip had it, he would be eager to talk about
it and concur with Rusty's suspicions. Rusty hadn't
learned much new or worthwhile information about
Gary and Carla's marital relationship from Rosa
Linda, but he had confirmed that Gary and the bar
manager were still well acquainted and were most
likely sleeping together.

The Ryder ranch was all the way across the
county from Precinct 4, but Rusty made the trip in
under half an hour. Nearing the house, he saw Elena's SUV parked where it had been earlier in the
day, but at a slightly different angle. It had been
moved. Rusty recalled that Denise had told him
about seeing her in town at the drugstore.

At the front door, the same Hispanic woman
from earlier answered the door chime. "I'd like to
see Mr. Ryder," Rusty said.

She invited him into the entry and told him to
wait. This morning when Ryder wasn't at home,
she had told him Elena was in the study and
pointed him in that direction. This evening, with
Ryder present, that kind of informality was probably not allowed.

Rusty stepped inside and immediately a chill
passed over him. The temperature in the entry hall
bordered on being cold and his shirt was damp in

places from perspiration. He removed his hat. While he waited, he perused an oil painting depicting a nineteenth-century Indian and U.S. Calvary battle. The painting was so large its images were almost life-size. Naturally it was an original. Rusty hadn't looked at it when he was here earlier. He knew a little Western history, and as he studied the artwork closer, Little Big Horn came to his mind. He strained to read the artist's name, but it was indecipherable.

The maid returned and led him into the study where he had met Elena this morning. A visual of the two of them in desperate fornication flashed in his memory, but he willed away the image and fixed his eyes on Ryder. The older man stood over six feet tall and usually carried himself as if he were far younger than his seventy-something years. Tonight, wearing a casual shirt, his body slumped in his chair behind the giant desk, he looked as if he had shrunk. His eyes were red and swollen and held a look of pain if Rusty had ever seen one.

"What is it?" Ryder asked.

Though he had been only too aware of Randall Ryder's influence during the election last year, Rusty hadn't often seen him and couldn't remember the last eye-to-eye conversation with him. Typically, the man's face appeared to be younger than his years, but now, with the length of his jaw emphasized by a dolorous expression, the face showed every hour of his age.

"I'm sorry about what happened to Carla, Mr. Ryder," Rusty said solemnly. "All of us who knew her feel her loss."

Ryder looked down at the desktop, elbows resting on his chair arms, hands folded across his stomach. "My daughter was a unique person." His head slowly shook.

Rusty wished he were anywhere but here. "I'm sorry to intrude on your grief, sir, but I've got some questions that need answers."

Ryder gave him a narrow-lidded look, contempt bleeding from his eyes. "Of me? You came here at a time like this to question *me*?"

"I'm gathering information, Mr. Ryder. If I can complete it while memories are fresh, so much the better."

"Isn't it enough you sent my daughter's body to be sliced up like a side of beef? We can't even lay her to rest until the weekend."

"This is an awful thing that's happened, Mr. Ryder. I know how upset you are, but if you'll just help me—"

"What is it you're after? What's so all-fired important that it can't wait?"

Of the many things Rusty intended to look into, one was Carla and Gary's finances. Rusty had heard that Carla had married a penniless fool and he doubted the couple maintained their lifestyle on what they earned from their horse business. Fundamental to any homicide investigation, as well as being common sense, was to look at everybody who benefited from a victim's death. "I'd like to talk about Carla and Gary's marriage, about their income."

"Why, that's none of your business."

Rusty pressed on, refusing to be intimidated into relinquishing control of the conversation. "I know you gave them the horse ranch as a gift. I'd like to know if Gary's name is on the deed."

Ryder didn't answer right away, sitting in his big leather chair as rigid as marble. He seemed to be thinking. "Yes," he said finally.

Yes, what? Yes, he had gifted them the horse ranch? Or yes, Blanchard's name was on the deed? Believing he had opened a door, Rusty summarized what he saw wrong with the accident scene: Carla being dressed in impractical clothing, the gentle nature of the horse, the time of day and the dark barn. He stopped short of naming the son-in-law a suspect.

"There's talk of a lot of fighting between Carla and Gary and even abuse," he added. "I'm aware of several times when Sheriff Balderson—"

"That's nonsense," Ryder said, stopping him. He braced his palm on the desk blotter and pushed to his feet. "Carla and Gary have their disagreements, but they're no different from any other young couple. And they have the children."

Rusty couldn't easily connect the ideas in those two statements, so he didn't try. He noticed that Ryder spoke of his daughter in the present tense. "Are you acquainted with their hired hand, Luis Ramirez?"

"Of course. He's José's boy."

Rusty couldn't recall if he should know who José Ramirez was, but he definitely didn't know his kid. "Was he the only employee? I thought I saw living quarters in the barn."

"There's a small apartment on the mezzanine, but no one lives in it. Carla uses it as her office. Far as I know, Luis drives to work every day. He lives with his parents. Right now, the whole family's in Mexico and won't be back until after Christmas."

Now Rusty wanted more than ever to look behind the closed door off the mezzanine. Why hadn't Gary simply said Carla had an office in the barn? Was it because an office would have records and personal information? Perhaps a computer? "If their regular employee is away, who helps them with the horses and the chores?"

"Carla and Gary take care of the horses themselves. Sometimes—"

The chime of the doorbell echoed through the house, halting what Ryder might have said. Rusty knew he had lost his opportunity with the father. His whole day had been filled with interruptions, distractions and lost opportunities.

The maid appeared in the doorway and announced the arrival of Hunter Kelso. Rusty might not know José Ramirez, but he did know Hunter Kelso, owner and CEO of Salvation Bank & Trust. The Kelso and Ryder families were friends of long standing.

"You're going to have to leave," Ryder said.

"That's fine, sir. Just one more thing. I want you to know you don't have to worry about the escort to the cemetery. My office will do everything possible to aid you. And if there's anything else—"

"Don't bother. I'll be calling a friend in Austin. He'll arrange it down there through the DPS."

The hackles rose on the back of Rusty's neck. He had seen with his own eyes that calling the Department of Public Safety in Austin, or threatening to, was one of the tactics Ryder had used to keep the former sheriff toeing the line. Rusty had no intention of allowing something similar to happen to him, nor did he intend to be bullied. "It's the county's responsibility, Mr. Ryder. My office's responsibility."

"Don't you dare presume to speak for this county. Your office? You're holding that office only because I haven't had the time or seen fit to do anything about it."

Rusty disliked quarreling with any man in a time of deep grief, but he knew he had to stand his ground. If he blinked, he would be taking the first step into a political trap. "That may be true, but at this moment, I have jurisdiction over what goes on. If the need for the state police's assistance arises, *I'll* make the contact."

Ryder strode to the study's double doors. "Get

out of my house. If I had answered the door myself, you wouldn't have been allowed through it."

He yanked open one of the double doors and Elena stumbled through. Ryder gasped and stared at her. "Daughter! Are you spying on your daddy?"

"No, Daddy. I needed to talk to you. When I heard voices, I didn't want to just burst into your conversation."

Rusty saw that Ryder didn't believe her for a minute. He didn't believe her himself. He tried not to stare at her, but she did look incredible in a soft feminine dress. It was almost the color of her skin. Tan, just as Denise had said.

Ryder's arm looped around her shoulder. "You remember Rusty Joplin, sweetheart. He's come to offer us an escort for our Carla."

Elena looked him in the eye and put out her right hand. "Thank you, Rusty. Neither Daddy nor I have been in a clear state of mind. We haven't planned any . . . details."

Rusty hesitated, looking into her face. She had been crying and he had an urge to take her in his arms, as he had done so many times long ago when she was upset or unhappy. He took her proffered hand. "I'm just leaving. I was telling your dad I'll be in touch with the funeral home and with Gary. You don't have to concern yourself with traffic at the church or the trip to the cemetery."

Elena nodded. "I'll walk you out."

"Benita can do that," Ryder snapped. He stepped out of the room into the hallway and called the maid's name. She appeared almost instantly.

"Walk Mr. Joplin to the front door," he told the maid, "and tell Mr. Kelso to come on back." He turned his back and steered Elena toward the sofa, leaving Rusty to follow the maid.

In the entry, Rusty met the second-richest man

in Sanderson County. Hunter Kelso, well over six feet tall and well over two hundred pounds, was dressed in a suit and tie and hanging on to a big hat.

"Rusty," the banker said quietly, offering his right hand and giving him a chary look. "Sad times. A terrible thing that's happened."

"It sure is, sir," Rusty said, shaking hands with the banker and looking up into his face with his best unflinching gaze. Kelso's breath exuded a strong odor of alcohol.

Rusty didn't trust Hunter Kelso as far as he could throw a grown Hereford bull. The banker, along with Ryder, had put up thousands of dollars in the election to prevent the sitting sheriff's defeat. Rusty wondered if he could build a case for fraud against the group that had fought his election so hard with a barrage of underhanded tactics. But after he won, he had decided to forget it. He didn't have the time and the county's limited resources could be used in a more productive way. He had settled for whipping them fair and square.

Kelso ducked his chin and toyed with his hat brim. "Carla was a special person. . . . A beautiful woman."

The words "beautiful woman" stopped Rusty. "Beautiful woman" seemed an odd thing for a middle-aged banker to say when describing his friend's deceased thirty-five-year-old daughter. "Yes, she was," he replied.

The maid was standing by the door, waiting for him to leave, so he set his hat on his head and said to Kelso, "I've got some questions about Carla and Gary's accounts. I'll be drawing up a subpoena and—"

"Of course, of course. Anything I can do to help. Anything at all. Just call my assistant and make an appointment."

The banker's enthusiasm to be helpful came too quickly. Rusty had the impression that he was squirming. "Yeah, I'll do that," he said. But he thought, *In a pig's eye*. His visit to Hunt Kelso's office would be at his own convenience, without an appointment. "Good night, sir."

Rusty walked out stunned, but not at being kicked out of the Ryder house. What had shocked him was the patriarch's reaction, or lack thereof, to the facts. Facts that, in Rusty's mind, clearly pointed to Carla's husband playing some kind of role in her death.

Chapter 8

The sinking sun had streaked the sky with pinks and purples as Rusty slid into the Crown Vic and cranked the engine. A tragic death had no effect on a spectacular sunset. Still, the day's events had shredded the sense of order in his universe. Exhaustion settled on his shoulders like an anvil. He hadn't felt so drained since taking over the sheriff's office, nor had he faced so much inner conflict.

Even when he had learned his former wife was sleeping with another member of the law firm where she worked, his center hadn't been shaken like it had been today. The cadaverous face of someone with whom he'd had more than a passing acquaintance for more than half his youth wouldn't leave his mind. Nor would the bizarre episode with Elena in Ryder's study. The pair of too vivid images warred with each other in his head and gave the whole day a surreal quality. He wished he could go back to seven o'clock this morning when his greatest concern had been his sunburned skin. He couldn't wait to get home.

The cell phone on his belt vibrated and he keyed in to get the call. Cheryl, giving him a litany of messages, then telling him she had to get home. The dispatcher had sent out a car to Blanchard's place after he had called and complained about two TV vans parked near the entrance to his home.

None of the other messages was manageable until tomorrow.

Home for Rusty was a redbrick, low-slung ranch-style house that, according to the stamp on the toilet tank in the one bathroom, had been built in the sixties. When he had first moved back here from Fort Worth three years ago, he bought it cheap. An old two-story barn bigger than the house, an outbuilding he used for a garage for his five-year-old truck, came with it, along with corrals and 167 cross-fenced acres. He had even gotten the mineral rights, which, in West Texas, was a rare occurrence. Rusty figured he would never find a better deal.

He changed into old boots and jeans and a T-shirt, the soft knit fabric feeling like a gentle caress against his baked neck and back. He fed his two mutts, Shep and Blue, then called his office and told the dispatcher he would be out of touch for a while. He clapped on a bill cap, grabbed a couple of longnecks from the fridge and went to the barn. The dogs followed. His barn cat, Ferocious, came from somewhere and trotted along with the dogs. Banjo, his best horse, greeted him with a nuzzle at his neck. Affection from his horses and pets was all that had been available to him for a hell of a long time.

Until today, that is.

He saddled Banjo, threw the saddlebags across the horse's back and slipped the two beers inside. He could leisurely drink them while riding the perimeter of his quarter section and get back to the house by dark. In another month or so, he would no longer be able to ride in the evenings. Daylight saving time would expire and by the time he got home from his office in town, it would be too dark for a horseback ride.

He swung into the saddle and nudged Banjo

through the corral gate, trying to force the Ryder family and their eccentricities from his mind. Riding alone and having a conversation with his horse and dogs usually cleared his head and helped him regain his perspective. But this evening, though he tried to restrict his attention to the plants he passed and the condition of his pasture, Carla Ryder remained at the forefront of his thoughts.

Because Salvation was a law-abiding, churchgoing small town, the only dead bodies he had witnessed in the past three years, with one exception, had been the results of accidents. The last local murder investigation had been over two years ago when, as a deputy, he had helped the sheriff's investigator go through the motions on a death caused by a fight. That one had been a no-brainer. The identity of the suspect had never been in much doubt and in less than a day he had surrendered without a peep.

Rusty wondered if he had lost his edge, or if he had ever had one. He wondered if he was qualified to build a case strong enough to convict Gary Blanchard. True, he had worked as a homicide cop in the city and had been commended as a thorough and intuitive detective. He had worked with the Tarrant County DA's office and testified in court. Even so, he had been green and in a learning mode. He had never led an investigation. Somebody with years more experience than he had always been in charge.

The same applied to the job he now held. Somebody with years more experience had always held the office of Sanderson County sheriff. Rusty Joplin was the youngest man ever to be elected and he was one of the youngest sheriffs in Texas.

Until he went to work as a deputy, he hadn't known from firsthand experience the broad scope of a sheriff's office. He had studied it in school, but the purity of the classroom setting was a far cry from real life. As an official elected by the people, in many counties the sheriff was the most powerful political figure. That fact was especially true in Sanderson County because the City of Salvation contracted with the sheriff's office to police the city as well as the county.

But he was more than the chief law enforcement officer. He was an officer of the court and responsible for the safety of the sitting judge. The sheriff's deputies were bailiffs, bodyguards and jailers. He, personally, was the administrator of the third-largest budget in the county, behind the school district and the hospital. No doubt holding so much sway for so many years had gone to Jack Balderson's head.

After his election, Rusty had done more than take the oath of office. He had made a personal vow never to take the awesome responsibility of the office lightly nor to take his supporters for granted. And it went without saying that he would cut off his hand before he would accept a bribe.

His mind drifted to Elena again. This evening, it was even more impossible to erase her from his thoughts than it had been fifteen years ago. Her departure from his life and what he had seen as rejection had affected everything in his personal life up to now. Because of Elena, he had married the wrong woman and lived for five long years in the nightmare of his wife's lies and infidelities. Because of Elena, he had exiled himself for years from Salvation and his own family, all of whom he cared about. Because of Elena and their relationship as kids, one of the most powerful men in West Texas despised him.

He didn't need a repeat of all of that.

What had happened in Randall Ryder's study wasn't lovemaking, anyway. It was plain old fucking. He winced mentally at the thought of applying that assessment to sex with Elena. Survivor sex sounded better and was perhaps more accurate. Her desperation had matched his own, he sensed, as if the need to escape a horrible reality, the drive to incinerate an unbearable pain in the heat of lust, had been bigger than they were.

Since coming back to Salvation, he hadn't heard anybody say why she was still single at thirty-three years old. Nor had he let himself dwell on the fact. Now he gave it thought. Why hadn't her father found a man, or men, who would meet his criteria, men who would jump at the chance to marry a woman as beautiful and unselfish—and rich—as Elena? Men who wouldn't mind exchanging their own plans and goals and pride for being Randall Ryder's son-in-law. A man like Bailey Hardin.

What had Elena been doing all these years besides working as an RN at the hospital? He wasn't surprised, really, that she held that job. She had always felt guilty for being rich, had always felt compelled to give back. He suspected she still did.

At home again, Rusty unsaddled with great effort. He hadn't eaten since morning and the beer had left him feeling lethargic. As he swung his saddle onto its tree in his tiny tack room, Ferocious strolled in. The brindle cat leaped up on the saddle seat and watched him.

"You're a sassy cat," Rusty said to him and scruffed his ears. Ferocious purred and swished around his hand.

Rusty hung his saddle blanket over a sawhorse, then took his currycomb to Banjo's stall and began to brush his coat. Only then, in the silence of his barn, surrounded by his pets and horses, did he face his demon. It wasn't inexperience as a cop.

Nor was it Elena that haunted him. She might be tempting as the devil, but she wasn't his demon. The dark thing that gnawed at him came all the way from his very core and he acknowledged it for what it was. Fear and self-doubt. What if he was wrong? What if he had jumped to an erroneous conclusion about Carla Ryder's death?

The consequences of that possibility stopped him. The news of his bad judgment would travel all the way to the state offices in Austin. He stomped back to the tack room and threw the currycomb on a shelf. No, goddamn it. He wasn't wrong. He had worked for the Fort Worth PD almost ten years. He had built a reputation as a no-nonsense, tough but fair cop. He had proven himself. He knew murder when he saw it.

Murder. At some point today, he had come to that conclusion without even consciously knowing it.

The gravity of the realization struck him like a lightning bolt and he thought about his staff. His department had one investigator. Alan Muncy was an honest, hardworking man, but Rusty was positive he had never probed a capital murder committed by an unknown suspect.

Rusty had only two choices: Conduct the investigation of Carla's death himself or turn it over to the Texas Rangers. The very idea of doing the latter was an admission of defeat and a blow to his pride. He had as many years' experience in law enforcement as the younger Rangers had.

Still, he had to ask himself, in the coming challenge of his strength and character, was he man enough to stand the test? Did he have the stuff to follow up on his suspicions, then endure and survive the firestorm they were bound to ignite once they became public? If what he suspected was true, if one of the well-heeled, high-profile citizens of Salvation had murdered his wife, the accusation would create more acrimony than the bitter election campaign had aroused.

Stewing on his worries, he fed all three of his

horses an extra morsel of hay and refilled the cat bowl for Ferocious before going into the house.

Once there, he opened several windows. The temperature had dropped to the low sixties. With the humidity level low, the evening bordered on chilly. Soon the fresh air would cool his house, which had been heated by the sun all day. The desert evenings were something else he loved about West Texas. He hated air-conditioning, but in Fort Worth, where the humidity in the summer months was often as high as the temperature, he had been unable to be comfortable without it.

He called in and told the dispatcher he was home. Then he pried off his boots in the living room, padded to the kitchen and peered into the refrigerator. The contents offered little appeal. His stomach had been unsettled all day.

He grabbed a jar of hot sauce and another bottle of Coors, then pulled some Doritos from the pantry, not unmindful that the combination might give him a worse stomachache. He plopped into his cushy recliner in front of the TV with the supper, but the warble of the phone interrupted. He got to his feet and went to the phone in the kitchen. Caller ID identified his parents' number. Only the family and occasionally his office called him on his landline. "Hey. What's doing?"

"Are you all right?"

"Sure, Mom. Why wouldn't I be?"

"I just wondered, after . . . after everything. Poor Carla."

"Yeah, I know. Look, Mom, you know I can't talk about it."

A pause. "Well, I didn't call to pry . . ."

Rusty knew his mother. She didn't have a malicious bone in her body, but she was a product of years of living in Salvation. Prying was exactly why she had called, though she would never admit it.

With one of the Ryder daughters passing in a tragic event, tonight in Sanderson County the phone wires would be close to melting from the friction of flying gossip. He braced his elbow on the upper kitchen cabinet and propped his head against his hand, waiting for the real reason she had called.

"I just hate to see you getting mixed up with those Ryders and their friends again, David. It could cost you. Don't forget how nasty the election got."

His mother was one of the few people who called him by his given name, David. "I'm not mixed up with them. I'm the sheriff. If something happens to one of them, I have to look into it."

"Denise said you suspected foul play or something."

Rusty searched his mind for what he had said to lead his sister to that conclusion. "Why did she tell you that? I said no such thing."

"Well, I wouldn't be surprised at anything that happened with Carla and that husband. I suppose you know that a few weeks ago he gave her a black eye."

Rusty made a mental note of the remark. He tried to discount hearsay that was inadmissible in court, but every tidbit of information was important in building a picture of a crime. Still, he didn't want to fuel his mother's curiosity or inspire her to chat with her friends about something he might say. On a sigh, he straightened and planted a fist against one hip. "Mom, come on, now. I'm not gonna discuss it. Listen, did you have any problems with that horse Lowell brought out there?"

"No. He's sure a nice horse. Your dad would kill to own a horse like that." She caught a breath. "Oh, my goodness. I shouldn't have said that."

"Tell Dad I'll reimburse him for the feed."

"Oh, he's not worried about that."

"Listen, Mom, I'm beat. I need to doctor my sunburn and hit the sack."

"Rub some aloe vera on it, son. You know that plant I put on your windowsill in the kitchen? If you break off one of the leaves, you'll see a clear juice. Just rub it on your skin. You'll be surprised how much it'll help."

"Okay. Look, I'm gonna go try that now, okay?"

"Well, okay, son. I guess I'll talk to you later."

He heard reluctance in his mother's voice and knew she wanted to ask questions. He also heard concern. She had always worried about him. "Look, Mom, don't be worrying, okay? Everything's gonna be all right."

"Oh, I know."

"I'm gonna hang up now, okay?" He started to put down the receiver.

"David?"

"What?"

"Salvation can be a mean little place. Whatever happens, don't forget we love you and we're behind you."

"I know, Mom. You've always been there."

He placed the receiver back in its cradle. This was one of the reasons he had left a promising career with the Fort Worth PD and moved back to Salvation, wasn't it? Nothing was stronger and more healing than family support and love.

With that thought in mind, he peeled off his T-shirt, snapped a thick leaf off the aloe vera plant and rubbed the juice on his shoulders and arms. It would be nice if he had someone to rub it on his back.

He returned his supper to the refrigerator and went to bed.

Elena strode to her suite, at the opposite end of the hallway from Daddy's. After seeing Hunt Kelso finally out the door, she'd had to help her father to his bedroom and put him to bed. She had warned him several times he would be better off taking the sedative she picked up for him in town than going without supper and belting whiskey with Hunt, but as always, he had paid her no mind.

A dull ache throbbed behind her eyes and between her shoulder blades. She went straight to her own suite, where she ran a bath and dropped in some lavender-scented bubble bath. She wasn't convinced that lavender really had a soothing effect, but she was desperate to try anything that would release the knot of tension that had resided within her all day.

While the tub filled, she exchanged her dress and high heels for a robe and bare feet, pinned up her hair and washed her face, continuing to think about the day and the evening. She had thought Hunt would never leave. The whole time he was here, she sat in the study and listened to him and Daddy and their drunken talk about how to protect for the grandchildren the estate Daddy had given to Carla and Gary. She couldn't keep from wondering why Daddy hadn't already done that. It was unlike him to be so careless with an asset as valuable as Carla's horse ranch.

At the same time she had been pondering that concern, she had been turning over in her mind the things she had heard Rusty say to her father about Carla's death. She wasn't shocked by them. She had been there, had seen the circumstances herself. Rusty hadn't said it in so many words, but he had hinted that Gary had something to do with what happened.

She stepped into the tub, sank up to her neck into the warm fragrant water and turned on the whirlpool. As her tight muscles began to respond to the roiling water, she propped her bath pillow behind her neck and closed her eyes. New thoughts drifted into her mind, gossip she had heard at the hospital about Gary being a philanderer.

She had heard things about her sister, too, but not at the hospital. She had heard them in the English classes she taught at the Catholic church. Her Mexican students, not realizing she and Carla were sisters, talked of Carla being involved with one of their own. Whoever he was, his peers feared for him. They believed Carla to be a threat to him and untrustworthy, and they talked about her influencing him to drink too much whiskey. If Carla's death had not been an accident, could a member of Sanderson County's Hispanic community have had a hand in it?

Elena could find out the name of her sister's Mexican lover easily enough. All she had to do was listen. Or ask. She hadn't done that before because she hadn't wanted to know. But now, did she *need* to?

She should talk to Rusty, should draw him out on the things he had tried to discuss with Daddy. Then she could make a decision if she should tell him about the Mexican man. But she hated doing it, hated to do something that would reflect badly on her family and on her departed sister. A barrier may have existed between her and Carla, but that didn't mean she wouldn't protect her.

At the same time, by learning the Mexican man's name and passing it on to Rusty, she could be putting him in a bad light. People always jumped to conclusions about criminality among the Mexican immigrants. She hated to expose an innocent person to the possibility of something so heinous as an accusation of, dear God . . . *murder*. She could scarcely bear to think the word.

She thought again about the meeting between her father and Rusty in the study and how Rusty had continued to be a gentleman even in the face of Daddy's rudeness. Years back Daddy had hated Rusty. He had suppressed his antipathy for a time, but he had resumed it openly last year when Rusty announced his candidacy against the sitting sheriff, Jack Balderson, a man Daddy and some of his friends had more or less put in office. She knew one thing for sure. Her father never forgot or forgave when someone patently opposed him and/or criticized him, as Rusty had done during the bitter election campaign.

The majority of Sanderson County's citizens had assumed they were stuck with Jack until he dropped dead or chose to retire, but when Rusty announced his candidacy, voter enthusiasm escalated. People turned out in record numbers and voted for Rusty. Her father and their family friend Hunt Kelso put their money and influence behind Sheriff Balderson but to no avail. She secretly supported Rusty. Anonymously, she donated heavily to his campaign from her own account. She voted for him. She could think of no better, more honest individual to be Sanderson County's sheriff. She could think of no one else who would have had the courage to take on her father's toady in an election in Sanderson County. Most people feared Daddy and tried to please him.

Feeling more relaxed, she left the tub, slipped into a thick robe and sat down at her dressing table. The memory of this morning in the study with Rusty came back, as it had done all day. She had tried to will it away, but it had sneaked into her mind constantly. Now, as she rubbed cream onto her face, considering the outstanding man Rusty had become brought up the pesky memories from even further back, all the way back to when they were kids.

They had known each other since she was in

third grade and he was in fifth. They had been good friends years before they became lovers. At times Rusty had been her only friend. He had always been there, ready to help her and steady her. Even as a boy, he was so responsible his mother used to say he was born already grown-up. From the perspective of a lonely girl who never knew quite what to think or do about what went on around her, that seemed like the truth.

When he finished high school and went four hundred miles away to college, she couldn't have been more miserable. She pined for him more than she could ever say and counted the days until he would return on Christmas break. When he returned for the summer, they fell back into the pattern of steady dating again. Many nights that year they had smooched and teased each other in the front seat of Rusty's old truck. She was seventeen, still in high school, and he knew she was a virgin. Though sex was as tempting as the apple in Eden and she had been willing, Rusty always stopped them. They spent the whole lusty summer driving each other crazy.

During the ensuing months, they exchanged letters and phone calls. She had scarcely gone out of the house the whole school year for fear of missing his call. Gossip came back to her that he was dating someone at Tarleton, but she refused to believe it.

She turned eighteen and graduated from high school in the spring, still a virgin. She could hardly wait for his return because she had plans. She was ready for sex and it had to be with him and only him. He had been reluctant, but she convinced him how right they were together. They even discussed the future. In her teenage naïveté, she had believed she and Rusty would be lovers forever.

As the end of summer neared, Daddy told her he knew what was going on between her and Rusty.

He had already arranged for her to stay with her aunt Virginia in Lubbock and go to college at Texas Tech. She protested. Most eighteen-year-old girls were allowed to choose which college they would attend. She had even entertained a notion that she would move to Stephenville and go to college at Tarleton with Rusty, but Daddy wouldn't hear of it.

She had always gotten along with her father better than her sisters had, but that summer, burdened with frustration and resentment, she quarreled with him persistently. She never told Rusty, but it had been extremely difficult to spend time with him and still maintain civility in the Ryder household.

She would never forget the day Carla told her about making out with Rusty, not just once but several times, and even told her details. Nothing had ever been the same after that crushing revelation. Now she wondered if the lie had been planned by Carla and Daddy together.

Of course, she would never know. All she knew was she had given in to Daddy's demands and agreed to go to Lubbock. She hadn't seen Rusty again until he returned to Salvation and went to work for the sheriff's office as a deputy three years back. In all that time they hadn't renewed acquaintance, had rarely even spoken to each other. Even if they found themselves at the same function, they maintained plenty of distance.

She paced her bedroom like a caged cat, debating if she dared call Rusty at home. She knew his personal number was unlisted, but it was on the emergency first responders list she kept in her nightstand drawer.

Chapter 9

In his dreams, Rusty was in the middle of a dangerous arrest with a vicious pack of dogs barking in the background. His eyes popped open. The barking was real. It came from Shep and Blue raising hell in the backyard. His window shade glowed with light from outside. *Headlights*.

He glanced at his bedside digital clock. Eleven thirty. Visitors rarely came to his home unexpectedly and no one came uninvited in the middle of the night. His heartbeat kicked up. He swung his feet to the floor and sat up.

Without switching on the lamp, he yanked on the jeans and T-shirt he had been wearing earlier and shoved his feet into his boots. Then he went to the dresser, took his .45 from the top drawer and stuffed it into the waistband of his jeans, all the while listening to the crunch of tires creeping along his gravel driveway. The barking became even more frenzied.

He stepped to the window and pulled back the edge of the shade just in time to see headlights go out and hear engine noise cease. Now he could see a light-colored SUV bathed in moonlight and parked by his front gate. *Elena*.

"Shit," he whispered, both relieved and perplexed at the same time. He could think of no good reason she should be here. Mentally chastising himself for his cop paranoia, he returned the gun to the dresser drawer and made his way to the living room. He switched on the porch light and pulled open the front door just as she knocked.

"Hi," she said in a tiny voice, her hands clasped in front of her. Her face bleached out by the porch light's glare, she looked small in a too big sweater.

"Hey, Elena."

"Can I talk to you?"

He stepped back from the doorway and allowed her to enter. "Come in. Is something wrong?"

"No, I just—"

"Excuse me a minute," he said. The loud canine chorus in the backyard hadn't let up. He walked to the back door and gave a sharp whistle at the dogs. "Shep! Blue! Cool it. Go to sleep."

The barking dissipated to spasmodic *ruffs* and he returned to the living room and Elena. Discovering that she was his visitor had done nothing to slow his heartbeat.

Puffiness showed around her eyes. She had a disheveled weariness about her, but she still looked fine. He knew how badly his day had gone; he couldn't imagine hers.

She gave him a half smile and brushed a sheaf of hair off her face. "You have good watchdogs. I was almost afraid to get out of the car."

"They aren't used to seeing people around here so late."

"Oh. Of course they aren't. I'm sorry to come this late, but I—"

"Hey, it's okay." He walked over to the old blue sofa he had bought at a garage sale and cleared away the pages of the newspaper. "Here, sit down."

"I had to see you tonight, Rusty. I might not be able to get away tomorrow. Daddy's going to be providing shuttle service from the airport. Gary's parents are coming in from Fresno on an early flight. Daddy's taking him and the kids to the airport in Midland to pick them up. Then Blanca and Bailey are coming in later."

He could see she was uptight. He gestured toward the cleared spot on the sofa. "Here ya go. Have a seat."

She edged between the coffee table and the sofa and sank to the edge of the middle cushion, resting her purse on her lap. "I started to call, but . . ." Her shoulders lifted and she let out a deep breath. "I didn't want to say this on the phone."

"What is it, Elena?"

"I—I came to apologize, Rusty. It's been on my mind all day."

He wasn't surprised. He had known she would feel guilty about the morning's incident in the study. He felt uncomfortable discussing it. "No need. It was just one of those things. I'm sorry, too, about saying Carla's name when . . . well, you know . . . I was rattled. I didn't expect . . . Well, I should have put a halt on things before—"

"You mean Daddy's study? You don't have to be sorry about that, Rusty. It was my fault. I know I embarrassed you. It was dumb, okay? I don't know what got into me. But it won't happen again."

The few minutes of unexpected hot sex had punctuated his entire day and made him a distracted mess. He hadn't even been able to have a conversation with his sister without thinking about Elena's naked body. But now, he felt oddly disappointed at the matter-of-fact way she spoke of it.

He snorted, looking at the floor. Now he really was embarrassed, too much so to look her in the eye. "Well, it wasn't exactly embarrassment."

Several seconds of awkward silence passed.

She exhaled a great breath. "But that isn't what I came to say. What's been bothering me all day is all those years ago, when my sister told me she had been with you, I believed her. Because I took her at her word, I didn't give you a chance to explain or deny what she told me. All this time, all these years, I've blamed her and I've blamed you, when I'm the one who lost faith and ruined everything."

Only Elena would feel a need to apologize for something that had been out of her control and something that had happened more than a decade back when they weren't much more than kids. He sat down on the edge of the seat in his recliner and propped his forearms on his knees. "Why wouldn't you believe something your sister told you? I probably would have done the same thing. I promise, it's okay."

"But it isn't okay with me. I can't keep from thinking what might have been if—"

"Don't think about it. What we had going on back then was one of those kid things, like a million other people go through. I guess it's part of growing up. Like you said, it was all those years ago and we've put it behind us."

Why he had made a statement he didn't necessarily believe he didn't know. He had been wiped out by losing her and had spent the better part of a year convincing himself that they never really had a future together and that an end to what had gone on between them had been inevitable.

She ducked her chin and wiped a tear with a fingertip. "I've cried so much today I have a headache."

"Would you like something? An aspirin? Coffee, water? I've got some Pepsi."

She returned a weak smile. "A Pepsi would taste good. I haven't had anything to drink since supper."

Rusty went to the kitchen and returned with a glass of ice cubes and a can of Pepsi-Cola. She had two tablets in her hand. "Tylenol," she said and sat forward. As she poured the drink over the ice cubes, then washed down the tablets, he again took a seat in the recliner.

"I have to tell you what happened, Rusty. Just so you'll know and so I'll feel better."

He was uncertain if he wanted to hear this. Especially at midnight. He had a helluva day facing him tomorrow. Item number one on his list was to get to Gary Blanchard's early to have the conversation he had wanted to have with him this morning and didn't. Besides that, after the episode in the study, just being near Elena messed with his head and destroyed his concentration.

But what choice did he have? He couldn't kick her out of his house and he didn't want her to see him as an ass. "Okay."

"I never told you," she said, "but that last summer we were together, Daddy badgered me all summer about seeing you. He knew we were, uh . . . I don't know how he found out, but he knew we were having sex. That was why he decided I should move to Lubbock and live with my aunt, then go to school at Tech in the fall. He didn't really care where I went to college. He just wanted me out of Salvation, but still under his control.

"All summer I told him, 'No, no way.' Then, from out of the blue, Carla made this big confession that she had, uh . . . been with you. She said that y'all had done it in your pickup under the railroad bridge."

Rusty was surprised to hear that. The railroad bridge had been his and Elena's secret place, the only place they had found privacy. "You're kidding," Rusty said, his eyes narrowing. He huffed a laugh. "I didn't think anybody knew about the railroad bridge."

"That was just it," Elena said. "I believed her because I had never told anybody where we went.

I don't know how she found out. Someone must have seen us." Her shoulders lifted and fell with a great sigh. "Anyway, I was so hurt and confused. I stopped resisting Daddy and just let myself be swept off to Lubbock."

Rusty gave a bitter chuckle, remembering his own father's words: *Randall's sending her to Lubbock. He wants her to stay with his sister and go to school up there. He's asked me to ask you to stay away from her.* "I remember," he said.

She looked at him and smiled again. "Even though I was mad at you, I still had this fantasy that you'd find out where I was and come and say it was all a big lie. You'd drive up in your old pickup and just spirit me away. And we'd live happily ever after without anyone telling us what to do or how to live our lives."

More of the fateful talk with his dad came back to Rusty. *Then promise me you'll let it be, Rusty. Randall's bigger than all of us. Don't get in a fight with him unless it's worth it. I think you oughtta go on back to Stephenville, finish school and get on with your life. Leave the Ryders to their own doings.*

Rusty smiled, hoping to keep this visit on a lighter note. "We wouldn't have gotten far in that old Chevy. It didn't make it through my junior year."

She didn't reply and more silence loomed.

Hell, why lie? he thought. Believing she had just up and left without so much as a good-bye, then being unable to contact her had fucked him up for months. He had wandered aimlessly through two semesters because he couldn't put her out of his mind. "I couldn't try to find you, Elena," he said at last. "Even if I'd had a decent truck and a job. I promised my dad."

"What do you mean? Promised him what?"

"Randall came to see my dad. I don't know all

that they said, but he wanted my dad to tell me to leave you alone. Dad asked me to promise him I would and I did. I had to. My folks had a lot of faith in me. And they had a lot invested. I'm the only Joplin who ever even went to college, much less graduated. They sacrificed so I could go. No way could I spend a decade getting educated. I had to focus on the two years I had left so I could graduate."

She looked down and began to pull at a thread on her sweater. "I didn't know Daddy did that. But I guess I'm not surprised."

"I did call you several times. I thought we ought to at least talk about it. But the housekeeper, I forget her name—"

"It was Sofia in those days."

"Right, Sofia. She always said you weren't home. When I couldn't get you on the phone, I even drove out to your house, but she told me you had already moved to Lubbock. So I just said, 'screw it' and went back to Stephenville like my folks wanted."

"You never came back here."

"I was back a few times. Christmases. Thanksgiving. That's about it. After I got married, since my wife's family lived in Fort Worth, that was where we spent family time."

"I forgot for a minute that you got married. I suppose *your* dad was happy, too, the way things turned out. Seems like no one wanted us to be together."

"Dad thought we were just kids fooling around. I imagine what he wanted most was not to piss off Randall."

She nodded, still not looking up. "The story of my life. And my two sisters'."

She stood up and walked over to his small fireplace. It was flanked by wood bookcases he had

sanded and refinished himself. It was where he kept
his collection of books—old textbooks, a few books
on American history and paperback westerns. She
pulled a battered western from its home on the
shelf and thumbed through it. "Terry Johnston.
You still read these."

"You know me. I'm kind of a throwback to sim-
pler times."

"I never heard how you ended up working for
the police department in Fort Worth." She returned the book to its slot. "I was surprised when
I heard that was what you were doing. You used
to say you wanted to work for a federal agency."

He felt strange discussing his past life with Elena,
like he was talking about someone other than himself. "My wife wanted to go to law school at TCU
in Fort Worth. One of us had to pay the bills, so
I went to the police academy and got a job as a
street cop. I just sort of wound up staying there for
a while."

"I heard she was a lawyer."

"Defense attorney. One of the bad guys. At
least, from a cop's perspective."

"I was just thinking, you must have gotten married about the same time Carla did." She walked
over to the dining area and looked into the kitchen.
"I like your house."

It was the kind of hollow comment somebody
made to fill silence. Rusty shrugged a shoulder.
"It's small. And old. The barn's better than the
house."

His last statement was a fact not uncommon with
West Texas farmers and ranchers. He had bought
the house from a family estate, a family that had
struggled at cattle ranching all their lives.

"You bought it from the Weaver family, right?"

"Yep. Got it cheap. The heirs were glad to get
rid of it. It was vacant and falling apart."

"I came here with the home health nurse sometimes to take care of Mrs. Weaver after her husband passed away. I can see you've made some improvements."

For a fleeting moment Rusty thought of the disaster the house had been when he first moved in. After spending most of his savings to buy it, he had gutted it right down to ripping up the rugs that stank of pet urine. Everything in the horseshoe-shaped kitchen was new, from the white tile floor to the oak cabinets to the snow white appliances. He couldn't prevent the little bubble of pride that swelled within him at being complimented on the job he had done on the place.

She walked on into the kitchen and he followed her, stopping in the doorway.

"That was tacky the way Daddy treated you tonight. I was in the kitchen eating supper when Benita came and found me and told me *el sheriff* was talking to *Señor Ryder*." She emphasized the Spanish words by crimping the air with her fingers. "So I knew it was you in the study with him. You probably figured out that I really *was* eavesdropping."

Leaning a shoulder on the doorjamb and watching her, Rusty smiled, relieved to change the subject from their past. Apparently his blunder of saying Carla's name had been dismissed. "Look, what your dad says or does isn't your fault. I know he isn't fond of me. I felt like it was my duty to go see him personally. Just like I would anybody else who lost a daughter. I had hoped he might answer some questions for me."

She had reached the sink. She turned, leaned her backside against the counter and crossed her arms under her breasts. The light over the kitchen sink spotlighted her face and he remembered how he had always been awed by how well put together she was. She didn't need to slather on makeup. Her skin was flawless. She had her dad's clear green eyes and her eyelashes were thick and dark naturally. When they were kids, he recalled now, the other girls in high school had envied her.

"But he's wrong, Rusty. He has no reason to dislike you. You haven't done anything to him. Ever." She chuckled and looked down. "Of course, everybody knows that when you beat Jack Balderson in the election, it was a defeat for Daddy as much as it was for Jack. He'd been telling Jack how to run the sheriff's office for so many years."

And probably lining the former sheriff's pockets with an extra stipend here and there, Rusty thought, but didn't say so. He wasn't ready to make the accusation aloud against Randall Ryder and his cronies. Paying the county sheriff under the table was a felony for everybody involved and Rusty had no real proof.

He pushed off the doorjamb and moved on into the kitchen. He, too, leaned against the counter, hooking a thumb in his jeans pockets. "Looks like Randall hasn't changed from when we were kids. Not being one of his lapdogs is still a hanging offense."

She smiled again. "Daddy means well. He thinks he knows what's best for everyone and he's so stubborn. He wouldn't admit that what he did tonight was rude."

"Elena, I don't expect you to come along behind your dad and smooth things over." He lifted a palm, wanting to reassure her. "It doesn't matter. Honest."

She continued to look up at him. "Rusty, I know you didn't accuse Gary of anything, but I can tell what you're thinking."

The remark reminded him just how well they had once known each other. He searched for words carefully, wanting neither to mislead her nor to upset her any more. "He has to be considered. There were some things in that arena that looked . . . well, atypical for an accident. You must have seen that yourself."

She ducked her chin and nodded.

"When an unexpected death is not from illness and not clearly an accident, it always has to be looked into. And a spouse is always suspect until he or she can be checked out."

"Is that all you're doing, just checking things out?"

"More or less."

She turned her head and looked away. He knew she found discussing anything negative about her family difficult. Ryder had instilled a siege mentality in his daughters. In many ways, it was not unjustified. For as far back as Rusty could recall, some member of the Ryder family had been under attack for something most of the time. Rusty blamed money and envy.

"I agree with what you said to Daddy," she said. "Carla might have been as stubborn as he is, but she had more sense than to go into the arena wearing flip-flops. Good grief, she could pick up a parasite, even if she didn't get stepped on by a horse."

"Your dad knows that as well as anybody. Why would he shut me out when I was trying to tell him?"

"I don't know. I think he's still in shock. And he probably can't stand to admit that you could be doing a good job. Besides that, he's getting old. I don't mean that he's a doddering old man, but he just isn't sharp like he used to be."

A frown creased her brow. "Rusty, I don't know if it means anything, but Carla came to the house the night before, uh, before—" She stopped and dabbed at the corner of her eye.

"Benita called me at work and said my sister had

been there and was crying. I called Carla at home, but she sort of brushed me off. Said she didn't have time to talk because she had to get the kids to bed. Said she just wanted to talk to Daddy about something. She thought he was back from Houston." She lowered her head. "That was the last conversation I had with her," she said softly.

Rusty's interest piqued. His mind switched gears. "Do you remember what time you called her?"

"It must have been around eight or nine o'clock. Isn't that what time kids go to bed?"

"She didn't tell you what was on her mind?"

"She never confided in me. She usually went to Blanca, but with her and Bailey gone, I guess Daddy was the alternative."

Rusty thought about the cell phone Gary had told him he couldn't find. "Did you call her on her cell phone or on a landline?"

"Their house phone. Half the time she couldn't keep up with her cell phone."

"Do you know where it is now?"

"Heavens, no. Do you need it?"

"Just asking." He was curious about Carla's cell phone. It could be as important as the barn's locked room. "You're sure she didn't drop a clue about what she wanted?"

Elena shook her head. "I just thought maybe she and Gary had had another big fight. They didn't get along that well. But then, I don't think that's a secret. Gary had girlfriends."

"What about Carla? Didn't she have boyfriends, too?"

Elena paused and began toying with a short fingernail. "Well . . . I think there were men in her life besides Gary."

"Men she slept with?" Rusty sought her eyes, but she continued to avoid looking at him.

"I don't know who they were."

"Then how do you know about it?"

"Because I knew my sister. Men were like a blood sport with her. It was true even when we were in high school. You surely remember. I do know the name of one, but it's old news. Several years ago, before you came back, she got involved with one of the high school coaches. It got out around town. His wife got real nasty. Then he was asked to resign by the school. He couldn't stay in Salvation after that. Carla just blew the whole thing off, like it was nothing. Daddy pretended he didn't know about it, but I've wondered if he had something to do with Coach Callahan being asked to leave."

Rusty searched his memory from his high school years, but couldn't recall a coach named Callahan. A new word entered his analytical process. *Revenge.* "What's the guy's full name?"

"Barry Callahan."

"Never heard of him. Where'd he go?"

"I think he got a job in Brownfield, or some other little town north of here."

"What about this Barry's wife? Did she leave town, too?"

Elena nodded.

"And neither one of them has ever been back here?"

She shook her head.

Rusty made a mental note of the name Barry Callahan. He would try to find out where he was and what he was up to these days. "What about somebody more recent?"

"I suspect there could be someone. Carla always seemed to be out of town or busy or something. It was Gary who always was taking care of the kids. I used to wonder why Carla even had the kids. She wasn't around them much."

"I have to admit," Rusty said, "I can't see your sister as a doting mother."

"Her kids are darling children," she said softly. "Someone's done a very good job with them. Renata, that's the six-year-old, is the sweetest child I've ever known."

Mommy's horse killed her. Are you gonna 'rest him?

Rusty could still hear the little girl's tiny voice and he still had a clear visual of her standing in the Blanchard family room this morning, wearing her little pink pajamas, with her hair all messy from sleeping. He thought he saw an opening to pierce the legendary Ryder family armor. "Elena, what kind of financial arrangement did Gary and Carla have?"

"What do you mean?"

"I know what it costs to take care of a bunch of ordinary horses. I can only imagine what your sister and Gary must have been spending on those high-bred suckers. The cutting horse business is expensive. It costs a lot to travel and compete. Is Gary loaded?"

Elena huffed. "Hardly. I don't think I've seen Gary work since he married Carla. The story we were told at first was that he owned some percentages in well-bred horses. He claimed to be this hot-shot trainer, but other than a little riding, he doesn't even do much with the horses. They hire someone to do most of the work. Daddy's helped them here and there. He's never told me how much. And Carla has . . . had a trust fund."

"Carla met Gary where, at a horse show?"

"At a cutting show in Fresno. She went out there for two weeks. After she met him, she ended up staying four months."

"Was there a prenuptial agreement?"

"No. Carla was in California and pregnant. There was this big rush to get married. If she and Gary had been back here, her being pregnant or not, Daddy would've had Gary surrounded by a gaggle of lawyers before any wedding ceremony took place. That's one of the reasons he doesn't like Gary or Gary's family. He thinks that with Carla being out there alone, without her own family to lend support, Gary and his parents maneuvered her."

And did they? Rusty wondered. He thought of motives as they stood there looking at each other a few seconds. He suspected they were thinking the same thing. Texas was a community property state. It appeared that the horse ranch that had been built by Randall Ryder had been given to Carla and Gary as a couple. Without some kind of legal agreement otherwise, most likely the entire property now belonged to Gary. No more than Rusty had seen of it, he knew the place was worth millions. "How much land goes with their place?"

"Not so much. Around a section maybe."

Six hundred forty acres. Rusty did some quick arithmetic in his head. Even with the depressed real estate values in West Texas, he came up with a number close to a half million for just the land. The house and barns added more than a million more. "Mineral rights?"

"I don't know. You remember Toby Fleming in your class, don't you? His grandparents owned it. They've been in Salvation forever, so it's possible the mineral rights went with it when it sold. Knowing Daddy, he probably wouldn't have bought it unless the deal included mineral rights. I mean, after all, oil is the Ryder business. And a few people are still drilling."

Yep, that sounded about right for a Randall Ryder deal.

Rusty's mental assessment of the value of the Blanchard place multiplied. Tomorrow, he would ask Cheryl to prowl through the county clerk's records for any documents that had been recorded on the place, like leases by drilling companies. "Did Gary and Carla have wills?"

Elena shrugged. "I would think Daddy would have badgered them into it."

"Yeah," Rusty mumbled, "if for no other reason, to provide for those kids."

Elena looked up at him with a troubled expression again. "I know it makes me sound like a traitor, but I can't believe Gary would harm Carla. I know he has a bad reputation and none of us have had much good to say about him, but he doesn't seem like this evil guy who could hurt someone. Physically, I mean. Most of the time when I've been around him, which hasn't been often, I know, but he's always seemed like a good-natured person."

Rusty had come to believe that almost anyone was capable of killing deliberately given the right motivation. And *everyone* was capable of killing in a moment of anger. "What about their fights? Everybody in town talks about their fights."

"I don't know how much of that talk is true. You know how Carla always was. She could be . . . well, provocative. In truth, I've never blamed Gary a hundred percent for the way things were between them. Daddy says it's Gary's fault Carla behaves the way she does. Or did. But he isn't being realistic. My sister's always done exactly what she wanted to."

"People say Gary's a heavy drinker. Is that true of Carla, too?"

She bit down on her lower lip, not replying right away. "I suppose," she said finally. "I don't think she drank as much as Blanca because of the kids."

"Drugs?"

"I don't think they were into the hard drugs."

In Rusty's view, there wasn't much difference. "But they did drugs?"

She shrugged and looked away.

This conversation was getting to be like pulling hen's teeth, but Rusty knew why. Elena had always had difficulty speaking ill of any of her family, or for that matter, anybody, in a negative way, even when somebody had earned it. She searched for and found an excuse or a reason for even a stranger's bad behavior. Now, he guessed her blanket of protection included her brother-in-law.

In their youth, Rusty had teased her and called her Pollyanna, but he had admired how she not only looked for the good in everybody but sincerely believed it was there. It was an ability he had never had himself, even before he lived a number of years dealing daily with the dregs of humanity. Rusty couldn't keep from smiling as that memory of her came back to him. "Well, we got that far."

"Although . . . I hate to say it about my sister," she blurted, "but, Rusty, Gary's no worse than her."

Rusty continued a patient smile, knowing how hard this was for her. "But there's a big difference, darlin'."

"What is it?"

"He's not dead."

Her eyes teared. "I guess I'd better go," she said suddenly and pulled her sweater tighter. "There's a lot to do. These next few days are going to be so hard."

Rusty wished he hadn't been so blunt. Carla was, for all her flaws, her sister. She passed in front of him on her way back to the living room and the front door, leaving a faint fragrance in her wake. He remembered it from the study this morning. "How long will Gary's parents be here?"

She shook her head. "I don't know. Gary hasn't discussed anything with Daddy. He's always been like that. Like he didn't want to be a part of our family."

Rusty could relate. He and Gary Blanchard might have something in common after all. "Did Gary quarrel with your dad?"

"No. They gave each other plenty of room. But the chance was always there. Sort of like a cork holding back a dam leak."

She walked out of the house and Rusty walked with her to the Lexus, a vehicle that looked dramatically out of place parked in his driveway. He opened her door and she slid inside. She looked up at him as she started the engine, her face softly lit by the dash lights. "I've missed you, you know. I've wished a thousand times we could go back in time."

After this morning, a part of Rusty wished the same thing, but it wasn't his head. His head knew better. "Don't, Elena. Let's don't go there. We can't. We're not kids anymore."

She looked straight ahead. "If it means anything, I've wanted to talk to you before now, but . . . well, you know how it is." She put the Lexus in gear. "When this mess gets straightened out, when we all get past it, when *Daddy* gets past it, I wonder if I should think about leaving here."

Now that I'm back? he wanted to ask, but didn't.

He wanted to say, *Don't go,* but he didn't say that, either. What she did with her life was none of his business.

What he did say was, "That's not a decision you have to make tonight."

Chapter 10

As Elena drove the short distance between Rusty's home and the Ryder mansion, all she could think of was how she wished he were a part of her life again. Tonight's visit had only reinforced how much she missed him. She admired him now more than she ever had. He was so smart and strong. He always knew the right thing to do, while most of the time she didn't know where to begin.

She almost couldn't bear being in the same room with him and not feeling free to touch him. Once she had touched him everywhere, kissed him everywhere and she had loved it. And, she remembered all too well, the emotion and the desire had been mutual.

Since his return to Salvation, she hadn't had the chance to stand near him and look into his blue eyes and enjoy the way a smile slowly came to his mouth. A luscious mouth with well-defined, kissable lips and straight white teeth. She hadn't had the opportunity to be near enough to bask in his size and strength. He had been tall and long-boned at twenty, but now his body had filled out. The sight of him in tight Wranglers and a T-shirt was enough to turn any woman's head.

Her thoughts settled, at last, on what distressed her more than she would ever say aloud. No physical relationship with any man had been quite the same as it had been with Rusty. He had been an intense lover—passionate but patient when she felt insecure, raw and primitive when she felt wild and carefree, but ever sensitive to her needs and desires.

And she had, in turn, been an enthusiastic partner in anything he wanted from her. In her mind, she could still see his blue eyes turn to deep violet in a fiery moment. She could recall the heat and the incredible pleasure he gave her, but to her regret, she couldn't remember how it *felt* when he made love to her.

A wave of guilt overtook her for thinking such crazy, selfish thoughts when her sister lay a corpse, possibly even murdered.

At the entrance to the Rocking R, she made a right turn and crossed the cattle guard onto the ranch's long driveway. On either side of her, black pumpjacks seesawed, bringing the Ryder wealth up from beneath the ground and adding more dollars to her and her sisters' trust funds. As she came to a stop in front of the garage doors, she wondered if she could win Rusty back. Once, they had said they would love each other forever. Did that sentiment just go away? Surely some shred of it remained. It wasn't he who had wavered. It was she. She, her sister and Daddy who had ruined everything.

Then she felt guilty again for having such selfish thoughts and casting blame at a time of crisis for her family.

Rusty returned to his bed well past midnight, but he suspected he had already gotten all the sleep he would get tonight. In the silent darkness, the morning's encounter in Ryder's study loomed lifelike in his mind and wouldn't leave.

Suck me. Hurry. . . . That'sit, that'sit. Makeme-come. . . . Makemecome. PleaseRusty.

Even with a murder investigation on his hands, how could he, or any normal man, not think of something personal that had been so intense? How could he not recall how good being with her again had felt? How could he not want making love to her to be just that, making love?

Tonight, seeing her standing there in front of his fireplace, her thick, shiny hair cascading down her back, a part of him had wanted to bury his hands in it and now another part of him wanted more than that.

A distant memory slithered through his mind. A summer afternoon when they had ended a horseback ride over the Rocking R's expansive pastures and her whole family was out of the house. She sneaked him into her bedroom and they made love in a real bed for the first time.

They had already all but done it in the barn when she decided they should go into the house to her room. He was so nervous about being in her bedroom in the Ryder house, he feared he wouldn't perform well enough. Thinking he could end it before somebody came in and caught them, he went down on her. She didn't stop him and he tonguefucked her 'til she came. On fire himself, he shoved into her and they fucked hard and fast and she'd had an orgasm so powerful that afterward she was crying and shaking all over. He had held her in the circle of his arms, while she whimpered against his chest for a long time.

As unsophisticated as he and Elena both had been as lovers, from that afternoon forward, their relationship just got hotter. Elena was more than smart and sweet and beautiful. Beneath her calm demeanor and gentle nature lurked a sexy, adventurous woman who hadn't balked at new thresholds.

Now, pressing his forearm across his eyes, he made

a soft sarcastic snort at his own weakness. He couldn't remember how it had felt making love with his ex-wife, but he remembered details about love-making with Elena.

Shit. He was hard and desire was coiled in his belly like a tight spring. He groaned. He didn't need this. What he needed was a good night's sleep.

From out of nowhere, another memory came to him: That same day, the first time he had been in her bedroom, he'd had to sneak out of the house before her dad and her sisters came home. Though he had followed her to her bedroom often after that, the trysts ended the same way every time—him leaving by the back door so as not to be discovered. Remembering that experience squelched the lust that was threatening to keep him awake the rest of the night.

At some point he drifted into a hard, deep sleep.

He awoke a few hours later logy and tired and still thinking about sex with Elena. "What you need is to get laid, hoss," he mumbled as he assembled the coffeepot. A night or a weekend of raunchy, satisfying sex.

The idea was confusing because over the past weekend in Fort Worth, he had passed up an opportunity for exactly that. He could have spent four nights in Amber Elmore's bed, but he'd had no interest in the talk about "forever" that would have come after the sex. He had already walked away from that with Amber years back. Thus he had declined her less-than-subtle invitation, choosing instead to sleep alone at Mark and Kristy's house.

He halted that bullshit thinking. He had reality to deal with. He had to get to Gary Blanchard before his family arrived from California, before the man became embroiled in the bereavement and burial process.

Up and moving around, Rusty noticed his sunburn was better in the areas where he had been able to apply the aloe vera sap. While coffee brewed, he showered, then broke off another aloe vera branch and rubbed on more of the clear plant juice. He downed two cups of coffee while he dressed. He would survive on that 'til lunch. It was too early for Cheryl to be in the office, so he placed a call to the dispatcher and told her he would be out of touch for a while.

A short time later, in the pink glow of the cool early morning, Rusty was on Gary Blanchard's front porch ringing his doorbell. Blanchard himself came to the door. Shaved and wearing a fresh shirt and clean Wranglers, he looked and behaved like a different person from the uptight individual Rusty had seen early yesterday morning.

Today was the second time Rusty had been within a few feet of Gary Blanchard. He took a close look at him. The two of them were roughly the same age. They both had brown sun-bleached hair in need of a cut. They both had blue eyes and suntanned skin. Yet they really looked nothing alike.

"Let's talk, Gary."

"Sorry, but I don't have time. We're going to Midland to pick up my parents."

"Don't make me do this the hard way, Gary. That won't do any of us any good, least of all your kids. There's time. Let's talk a minute."

Blanchard's head cocked, his eyes narrowed. "Are you making this official? Do I need to get my lawyer?"

Wishing he had brought his portable recorder, Rusty lifted a shoulder in a shrug. "That's up to you. Far as I'm concerned, we're just talking. I'm trying to get a handle on what happened to your wife."

Blanchard held Rusty's gaze a few seconds and

Rusty wished with all his might that he could know what was going on behind the man's eyes. Finally, Blanchard moved back and gestured Rusty through the door.

Rusty lifted off his hat as he stepped inside. Closing the door behind him, he looked around. The entry ceiling was at least two stories high. He hadn't noticed that yesterday. He followed Blanchard into a huge living room, its high ceiling supported by rough exposed logs stained to a honey color. Massive Western-style furniture hunkered on a phony plank floor. A dozen cowhides were scattered over the floor as rugs. If someone had asked him to describe the decor, he would have called it contrived bunkhouse. Some expensive decorator out of Midland or Dallas had tried for the rustic look and gone overboard, Rusty guessed.

Over a white cut-limestone fireplace that climbed all the way to the ceiling hung a life-size oil painting of Carla wearing a long, fancy dress. Rusty stopped and looked at it for a few seconds. Carla's Hispanic side showed in the dark brown eyes that seemed to stare down on them, but all Rusty could see in his mind was the whites turned red with hemorrhage caused by strangulation.

"You hung that yellow crime scene shit all over my barn," Gary said sharply.

"I want to take a look in the upstairs room in the barn. I asked you for permission, but if—"

"Are you saying I'm a suspect of some kind?"

"I don't believe an accident took your wife's life."

"So you *are* saying I'm a suspect."

"I'm not saying anything. I came out here to talk about it. I'm doing you a favor. I could have insisted that you come into town to my office."

"This is bullshit, Rusty." Blanchard threw a palm in the air. "Grandstanding. What're you trying to do? Prove to the damn fools who voted for you that they're getting their votes' worth?"

Confrontation wouldn't accomplish what Rusty had come for. He bit back an aggressive reply.

Blanchard dropped into a leather chair to Rusty's left. "Tell you what, cowboy. I watch TV. I know how this shit goes. You people always think the husband's done something. Go ahead, ask your questions, but get on with it. I'm in a hurry."

You people. Rusty hadn't heard that reference to himself since he left the FWPD. After he became a cop, it hadn't taken long for him to learn that the public perceived the people they expected to protect them as some kind of alien group. He took a seat on a red suede sofa, sitting on the edge of the cushion, hanging his hat between his knees. "I'll get right to the point. Where was Carla night before last?"

"Here. If you don't believe me, you can ask the maid."

"Does she live here with you?"

"Lives in the cottage out back." One corner of Blanchard's mouth tipped up in a smirk. "But you might have a little trouble talking to her. She doesn't speak much English."

"If I need to talk to her, I'll keep that in mind." Indeed Rusty would question the maid. If his own rudimentary Spanish wasn't good enough, he had two Mexican-American deputies to whom English was a second language. "Any idea what time Carla left the house?"

Blanchard sat back in his chair, his arms crossed over his chest, his legs crossed at the knees. "She turned in as soon as the kids went down. I looked in on her when I went to bed. She was asleep."

"What time was that?"

"Before midnight. I watched Leno. Friend of mine was a guest."

Rusty was unimpressed. Name-droppers in the performance horse world were a dime a dozen. The premier cutting horse event, the Fort Worth Futurity, was filled with celebrities who owned competing horses. Most of the real cowboys might know a celebrity's name, but couldn't tell you what made him or her famous. The hangers-on were a different story. Rusty placed Gary Blanchard in the latter category.

"You didn't hear her leave during the night?"

"Nope."

"What kind of rig did she drive?"

"One-ton Ford truck."

"Was it in the garage Tuesday night?"

"Far as I know."

"Was it there Wednesday morning?"

"Yes."

"Okay if I take a look at it?"

"Not today. Like I said, I'm leaving."

Rusty hesitated, regretting that he hadn't asked about or insisted on looking at the truck yesterday. "You said yesterday you and Carla didn't sleep in the same room. Is her bedroom near yours?"

"She slept in the master bedroom. I sleep on the other end of the house, near the kids."

Rusty recalled yesterday morning's observation of the back of the house and the sliding glass door off the patio. The other end of the house was a considerable distance from what he had determined was the master bedroom. "So would her room be on the north end of the house?"

"That's right."

"I'm not trying to be unnecessarily intrusive, but I'm getting a picture here that you and Carla didn't have, um, an intimate relationship."

Blanchard uncrossed his arms and rested them on the chair arm, holding Rusty's gaze. He gave no reply.

"Gary," Rusty said, leaning forward and striving

to gain Blanchard's full attention. "I know it's a personal question, but death is a personal event. Your answer could be important information."

Blanchard looked down, making little circles on the chair arm with his finger. "We, uh, weren't that . . . intimate."

A huge silence grew in the room. Rusty thought of the rumors he had heard about Blanchard's girl-friends and what he had seen with his own eyes. "You must be about my age," he said quietly. "Too young to give up sex. That's why you spend time with Rosa Linda McDowell?"

Blanchard said nothing.

Rusty paused, trying to decide how confronta-tional he wanted to be. What he wanted to ask was with Carla out of the way, did he and Rosa Linda have plans, but it was too soon. What Elena had said about her sister last night scrolled through Rusty's mind. "I'm not passing judgment on that. I understand that people have different ideas of what makes a marriage. Do you know who Carla was seeing?"

"What makes you think my wife was seeing any-one? And just for the record, Rosie and I are friends. That's all."

Rusty hesitated, deciding just how far he could take this without insulting the deceased. "I've known Carla a long time, Gary."

Blanchard braced his elbow on the chair arm again and rubbed his hand down his face. He gave a bitter laugh. "You and how many others?"

"Not me," Rusty said, tilting his head and raising a palm. "Not in the way you mean. I'm just saying I know a little about her activities in the past. And that's what makes me wonder if she had a boy-friend. Or boyfriends."

Blanchard sighed and leaned forward, bracing his elbows on his knees. "I've heard you were some kind of hotshot detective in Fort Worth. Assuming, and all I'm saying is *assuming*. Assuming that what happened *wasn't* an accident, you honestly think she had a boyfriend that had something to do with it?"

"It's too soon to say what I think except I believe the cause of her death is questionable. The first person to consider who could have harmed her is somebody close to her. A boyfriend's a possibility."

Blanchard's blue eyes revealed no reaction to the near accusation in Rusty's last statement. He looked away and sniffed. "If that's what happened, I mean, if someone . . . I mean, if it wasn't the horse . . ." A few seconds passed. Finally he turned back and looked into Rusty's eyes. "It wasn't me," he said softly and Rusty saw a hint of moisture in his eyes. "Honest to God, it wasn't me."

The show of emotion, though only slight, and the firmness of the denial had a ring of truth to it, despite other statements Blanchard had made that Rusty believed to be lies.

"Then it won't hurt to talk to me about it, Gary. I haven't gotten the ME's report yet, but from what I saw yesterday morning, Carla didn't die easy. Strangulation's not instant. It's a brutal, painful way to go out. If you help me, maybe together we can figure out how she got tangled up. Or if somebody did this to her, maybe we can figure that out, too."

Blanchard looked down at the floor and Rusty waited, hoping he had touched the man's conscience.

"I didn't keep up with her activities that much," he said, his tone still quiet. "She traveled with the horses all the time. More than I did. She knew people everywhere, people knew her."

"How about phone calls? Any callers out of the ordinary? Did anyone you didn't know call her here at home?"

"Not that I'm aware of."

"Did she have a cell phone?"

"Everybody's got a cell phone."

"Do you happen to have hers?"

"No. I don't know where it is. Her bedroom maybe."

"Did she have a computer?"

He nodded. "One of those notebook things."

"Did she keep it in an office somewhere?"

"She keeps it with her, wherever she is."

Rusty thought instantly of the locked room in the barn. "I'd like to take a look at the phone and the computer. Think you can find 'em?"

Blanchard hesitated. Rusty almost held his breath waiting for his cooperation. With any luck, there hadn't been the time or presence of mind to erase calls from the phone's caller ID or phone numbers from the contact list. There could be even more information on a computer.

"I don't know where they are."

"Can you look around and see if you can spot 'em?"

"I don't have time to search the house. I've got to get to Midland."

"You could take a quick look, right? I don't mind waiting."

On a scowl, Blanchard rose and left the room, but soon came back empty-handed. He didn't return to his seat in the chair, but stood behind it, his hand resting on the high back. "Can't find the phone, or the computer either."

He had been gone such a short time, Rusty doubted he had made a sincere effort at finding the desired items. He laid his hat on a table beside the chair and pulled his pen and notebook from his shirt pocket. "Okay. What's her phone number?"

Gary stated her phone number and Rusty wrote it down. Even if he never saw the phone itself, he would get the record of calls made. He hated the intrusiveness of cell phones, but loved the records cell phone companies kept. Every call coming in, every one going out. "Is it a Western Wireless phone?"

"We've got Western with all of our phones."

"You have a cell phone, too?"

"Sure."

"Let me have that number, too."

Blanchard didn't answer and Rusty looked up at him, his pen poised to write. Finally, Blanchard said the number. Rusty wrote it beneath Carla's number and added a "G" with a circle around it. He slid the notebook and pen back into his shirt pocket. "Have you found anything like receipts or letters—"

"Nothing." Blanchard rounded the chair. "Are you about finished?"

Rusty got to his feet, leaving no more than a couple of feet between himself and Blanchard. "Can you think of anything else you can tell me about Carla and her comings and goings or her associations?"

"Not anything that matters."

"When someone's passed on, Gary, you never know what matters. Can you think of any individual, man or woman, who might want to see her gone?"

Blanchard slowly shook his head.

"Then there's all the more reason to let me take a look in that office or apartment, or whatever it is, in the barn."

"I'm not sure I should do that. I haven't talked to my lawyer."

"I'll get a search warrant, Gary."

"Maybe. Maybe not. I'm not convinced Judge Potter will let you prowl through my stuff. I can't see that you have a reason to."

Rusty met the challenge in Blanchard's eyes with one of his own. He would get a search warrant sooner or later. That was the best idea in any event. If he found something he felt he should confiscate, he would need the warrant to do so. He dropped the subject for now. "Okay, if that's the way you want it. How about the truck in the garage? It'll just take me a few minutes."

Blanchard looked at the ceiling and mumbled an expletive. "Okay. But make it damn quick."

Rusty picked up his hat and Blanchard led him through the breakfast room into a hallway and finally into a huge garage. Two late-model Ford duallys were parked there. The white one looked used, but the red one sat there as clean and shiny as if it were parked on a dealer's lot.

"The red one's hers. I don't know what you think you're going to find, but knock yourself out."

Rusty opened the driver's door and looked in. The black interior was as pristine as the exterior. He didn't see even dust or dirt on the floorboard. A crime scene investigator might find something microscopic, but that kind of inspection wasn't going to happen.

He saw no laptop computer, no cell phone. He laid his hat on the seat, then ran his hand under the driver's seat. He bent down and looked under the seat, but without a flashlight he could see nothing. Still, he performed the same routine under the passenger seat. He picked up his hat, closed the doors and glanced into the truck bed, then did a 360-degree walk around the vehicle. "She kept her rig in good shape," he said.

Blanchard had been standing by, watching, his arms crossed across his chest. Now he ducked his chin and cleared his throat. "She's . . . she was like that. She wanted everything neat. She had Francisco wash it and clean it every day."

"Francisco?"

"Jacinta's husband. He keeps the yard and does odd jobs around here."

"Did he clean this truck up today or yesterday?"

"He cleaned it yesterday. He hasn't touched it this morning."

Rusty swore mentally, annoyed again that he hadn't insisted on examining the truck yesterday. Still, he doubted he would have found anything helpful. He set his hat back on, then again removed his pen and notebook from his shirt pocket. "What's your housekeeper's husband's full name?"

"Francisco Ayala."

"His wife's name is Jacinta?" Rusty wrote the Mexican couple's names, then stuffed the notebook back into his pocket.

Blanchard pressed a button on the wall and the garage door opened. "You can go out the garage door."

Recognizing that he was again being told to leave, Rusty abandoned the truck and walked out of the garage. Blanchard followed him. Rusty stopped on the driveway and turned back to him. "I'll send my deputy, Jaime Gonzales, out to pick up Francisco and Jacinta and bring them to town to be interviewed. That way, we won't be disturbing you any more than we have to. You might explain to them what's going on."

"Whatever."

"Do Francisco and Jacinta have papers?"

Blanchard didn't answer.

"If they don't have official permission to be working and living in this country, Gary, they're violating federal law. *You're* violating federal law by hiring them. But then, you already know that. I'll have to get in touch with Immigration."

Blanchard's shoulders lifted in a shrug. "Guess there's nothing I can do about that, is there?"

Warning someone like Blanchard about violations of immigration law was a waste of breath. It was a bluff anyway. In all of his years in law enforcement, Rusty had rarely seen the Feds cite an employer of illegal aliens. He and Blanchard stood there, staring at each other. "Nope. Guess not."

So far, Rusty had no solid read on Gary Blanchard and that was unusual. Typically he sized somebody up in a hurry and was dead-on in his assessment. In Blanchard he had seen little that told him anything. Finally, he offered his right hand. "I'd like to think we're allies, Gary. I'd like to think we both want the same thing."

Ignoring Rusty's hand, Blanchard jammed his fists against his belt. "And that would be what? Some boyfriend in handcuffs or my head on a platter?"

Rusty had no reply and perhaps Blanchard didn't really expect one, but the fact that he refused to shake hands rankled. "If there's anything my office or I can do for you or your family, I'm happy to do it. I feel like I've got a little bit of a personal stake in this. All three of the Ryder sisters and I were friends growing up."

"So I've heard."

Still annoyed at both Blanchard and himself, Rusty stopped and leveled a look into the man's eyes. "Just one more thing, Gary." He deliberately paused, letting seconds stretch between them. "It'd be a mistake to try to bullshit me."

Chapter 11

Leaving Blanchard's, Rusty turned his cell phone on and punched in his office number. Cheryl came on the line. "Hey, Rusty, the phone's on fire. Judge Potter's clerk called. The judge is going to be at the courthouse at ten o'clock. The DA called. He needs to talk to you ASAP."

Rusty's thoughts swerved to the injunction Ryder had filed against the autopsy and the unsigned search warrant application stuffed in a file folder on his desk. "Okay. I'm on my way in. Is Jaime working today?"

"Yep."

"Send him out to the Blanchards' to pick up Fernando and Jacinta Ayala and bring them to the office for an interview. And tell Jaime to stick around. Neither one of them speaks much English. As long as we're at it, we should check and make sure they don't have any warrants."

"Will do," Cheryl replied.

"I need something else, too." He came to a stop on the shoulder of the highway and pulled his notebook from his shirt pocket. "Take down these two numbers." He read the numbers of Carla's and Gary's cell phones.

"Got it," Cheryl said.

"Those are Carla and Gary's cell phone numbers. We need their records from Western Wireless for the last, say, two months. We need those today. Tell them we'll follow up with a subpoena as soon as I get one signed." The phone companies were very cooperative with law enforcement when it came to their records. They would send records on a phone call request, but a legal document had to follow.

"Roger," Cheryl said.

"And one more thing. Let's search the county clerk's property records for ownership details of Blanchard's horse ranch, see if any drilling leases have been recorded."

"Will do."

A black Lincoln limousine sped past him, headed in the direction from which he had just come. The only limo that traveled the highways of Sanderson County was the one Randall Ryder owned. No doubt it was on its way to Blanchard's house to pick up Gary and his children for the trip to the Midland airport. He glanced at his watch. The trip to Midland and back took two hours. Given a little time to pick up baggage, he speculated Gary would be back home around noon. If Judge Potter signed the search warrant application, that meant Blanchard, his kids and now his parents would be at home during the search.

He disconnected from Cheryl and keyed in the DA's office number.

"Hi," Kevin O'Neill said when he came on the line. "I heard about Carla Ryder on the radio driving back from Austin."

"Shit. It was on the radio in Austin?"

"On the car radio. I don't know where from. They said it was an accident. Blew me away when I got back to town and found out you think it wasn't. Helen sent me a copy of her order for an autopsy and old man Ryder's injunction. Potter's in today. You and Helen think we got a murder, huh?"

"I know a little about horses and I just don't

think that one did Carla in. Some other things don't add up, either." As Rusty outlined his observations and conclusions, the DA listened without comment. "So you see my point," Rusty said. Kevin's lack of response made him unsure if he had explained the circumstances adequately.

"Yes, I see," the young DA said, but Rusty wondered. Kevin was a Yankee from somewhere in New England. He probably knew nothing about horses and horse care or training.

"Who do you think did this, Rusty? Are you looking at anyone in particular?"

"Gary."

"Holy shit. Is that why old man Ryder's raising hell?"

"Not necessarily. From what I hear, he might enjoy seeing his son-in-law locked up. He's raising hell just because he can. I guess his dislike for me has overridden his good sense."

"It'll turn out," Kevin said. "Even Ryder's money and clout won't do him any good on this one. But I don't understand. My God, it's his daughter. If her death is suspicious, I wonder why he would object to an autopsy."

"I stopped trying to second-guess Randall a long time ago. I hope you're right about Judge Potter."

"He's a judge. He has to follow the law. And he used to be a prosecutor before he became a judge. In my experience, that's a point for our side. Besides, he would have a hard time explaining why he put his friends ahead of an autopsy both the sheriff and one of the JPs thinks is necessary.

"He's got a trial starting, so he's going to rule on the injunction first thing this morning. I've got to get up to the courtroom."

"I'm coming over to the courthouse myself when I get back to town," Rusty said. "I've got a search warrant request to be signed."

"What do you want to search?"

"Blanchard's barn and the locked room inside it. Apparently the room was Carla's office. I asked Gary for permission to take a look at it, but he refused."

"He could have gone in there and destroyed or removed anything of value before you ever got there yesterday morning," Kevin said. "And now twenty-four hours have passed."

Facts Rusty knew only too well. And even if Blanchard hadn't done that, he could have cut the crime scene tape and gone in after Rusty left. "I know, Kevin, but even if he did, he might've overlooked something."

"Do you have a good reason?"

"Reasonable suspicion?"

"That's a stretch. I don't know if Potter will go along with you on that." Kevin laughed. "Even if he liked you. What are you looking for?"

Rusty passed over the joke. "A computer and financial records. Software. A cell phone. Maybe even a murder weapon."

"Be sure and put all that in your application."

"Also, I'm requesting some phone records, so I need a subpoena signed. It's routine. I'll get it ready and get it to you."

Kevin was already arguing against the injunction when Rusty reached Sanderson County's only courtroom, on the second floor of the courthouse. The hearing was short. Ryder's lawyer blew loud and hard, but in the end the judge quashed the injunction. Just as Kevin had more or less said, it would have been highly suspect if he hadn't.

Judge Potter rose and started for his chambers, motioning Rusty to follow, his black robe billowing around him. Rusty took a seat in front of the desk, handed over the warrant application and sat silently while the judge read it. "Porky" Potter was about sixty or so, Rusty surmised. He was of average height, heavyset and puffy, with hanging jowls and skin peppered with brown mottling from years in the sun. Rusty figured his most strenuous physical activity was golf at the Salvation Country Club.

Rusty had requested many search warrants. He was good at preparing them. He wasn't worried that the document would be found lacking by most judges. What worried him with this judge were Blanchard's remarks both times he had talked to him.

If you think ol' Porky Potter's going to let you tear into my barn, you'd better think again. . . . He's a friend of mine. Better yet, he's a friend of Randall's.

I'm not convinced Judge Potter will let you prowl through my stuff.

Finally the judge looked up, his brown eyes boring into Rusty across half-glasses perched on a bulbous nose. "I know Mr. and Mrs. Blanchard."

Rusty began to feel that his nervousness about Judge Potter was right on target. "Yes, sir, I'm aware."

The judge returned to the document. "It's my understanding Mrs. Blanchard was strangled. You expect to find a murder weapon in her office?"

Unfortunately Rusty didn't yet know what the ME would conclude had been used to strangle Carla. But he had seen the bruises on her neck, bruises he believed to be wider than a lead rope would make. He had a theory of his own. "I'm looking for a belt or possibly a thick rope."

"This is a well-written application, Sheriff, but you haven't convinced me those items are likely to be found in Mrs. Blanchard's office."

"But either or both could be in the barn, sir."

The judge cleared his throat and continued to

study the application. "Exactly what kind of financial records are you seeking?"

"I want to know the source of the Blanchards' income. And I want to know how they're spending their money."

The judge stared at him and Rusty could almost feel his contempt. Rusty knew he was asking for broad latitude.

He had to wonder how much Potter really knew about the Blanchards' business. Logically, why would he know anything about it? Being friends with Ryder didn't mean he knew what the Ryder children did with their money. Ryder himself might not even know. Rusty began to sweat.

Finally the judge gave a great sigh. "Randall doesn't believe his daughter was murdered. I'll admit I don't know much about how horses behave, but you haven't convinced me we're dealing with anything more than a tragic accident."

Now Rusty was confused. The judge had just okayed the autopsy minutes earlier. "But, Your Honor, the autopsy—"

The judge stopped him with a lift of his hand. "I went along with the autopsy because the death was unattended and you have Helen's support." He slid the application across the desk, back to Rusty. "I'll allow you to come back to me with this after we know the medical examiner's opinion. Unless, of course, he concurs with Randall."

Rusty knew that most judges would not have denied the search warrant application he had prepared. He left the judge's chambers with a stream of cusswords scrolling through his mind. But as he jogged down the old stairs taking him from the second floor, he began to calm down. He had not a shred of doubt that the medical examiner would come to the same conclusion he had. "Be cool," he mumbled as he crossed the street heading back to his office. "Remember where you are and this ain't over."

In the courthouse annex parking lot, he saw two TV vans, their presence turning his mood darker. He had known that sooner or later all four TV stations out of Odessa and Midland would show up, but he had hoped to avoid them for another day. In the reception area, in addition to the Channel 7 reporter, he found reporters and their crews from the two Midland channels crowded together waiting for him.

"I'll be with you in just a minute," he told them and continued on into his office. As he passed Cheryl's desk, she stuffed a note in his hand. *Jaime and a Mexican couple are in Alan's office,* he read.

In his office, he closed the door and called the Odessa ME. While he waited for the pathologist to pick up, he noticed the cell phone records lying in the middle of his desk blotter. Cheryl had wasted no time. One of the things he appreciated about Cheryl was she got things done and she wasn't afraid to invoke her position as the sheriff's deputy to get cooperation.

The ME came on the line, saying he had already heard about the judge's ruling and was going forward. He would start promptly at seven a.m. if Rusty planned on being there. Rusty assured him he would. The least he could do for a murder victim he had known since they were ten years old was be present at her autopsy.

After he hung up, Rusty walked out and faced the media, overcoming a powerful urge to cover his face with his hands.

"We've heard you aren't treating Ms. Ryder's death as an accident," a heavily made-up reporter said and thrust a microphone in his face.

"We haven't said that. It's an open investigation," Rusty answered. "And the victim's name was no longer Ryder. Her name was Blanchard."

The woman followed up with "We've learned you and the local JP requested an autopsy and the victim's father opposed it. If it was an accident, why are you taking those steps?"

Rusty recalled Judge Potter's reference to unattended death. "There's nothing unusual about looking into an unattended death."

The skinny Channel 7 reporter pushed his wire-rimmed glasses up on his nose and looked up at Rusty with eyes magnified by his glasses' lenses. "Do you have a person or persons of interest? Can you give us a name? Or names?"

"We're still gathering information."

"Was Mrs. Blanchard sexually molested?" another voice asked.

"There's no evidence of that," Rusty was relieved to say.

"Can you tell us what you're doing specifically, Sheriff, to find the person or persons who might have done this?"

"You're jumping to conclusions," Rusty said. "I haven't said *anybody* did it."

"I've been told your investigator isn't even here. Are you considering calling in some outside help?"

He refrained from telling all of the TV viewing audience of West Texas that he had personally investigated more homicides than had the man he had hired to be the sheriff's department investigator. "No. Look, I've got to go. Somebody's waiting on me. When and if we have something to report, we'll let you know. Now, if you'll excuse me."

Cheryl left her desk and tactfully shooed the reporters and the cameramen out of the office. Rusty breathed a sigh of relief. At least the local press weren't the confrontational sharks he had encoun-

tered in the Metroplex. He felt satisfied he had told
them absolutely nothing.

He tapped on Alan's office door with his knuckle
before entering. He found the Ayalas seated in
metal chairs at a brown Formica-covered table in
the corner of the tiny room. Jaime was sitting behind Alan's desk.

Rusty dragged a straight-backed chair up to the
table. He already knew Jacinta spoke little English,
but Jaime told him Fernando spoke some. The four
of them struggled through translation and interpretation. Rusty recorded all of it, but in the end, he
learned nothing new or significant. Jacinta and Fernando reinforced what Blanchard had already said.
Neither of them had heard or seen any kind of
vehicle come or go in the wee hours of Wednesday morning.

He also learned that Jacinta had papers, but Fernando did not. They had been legally married in
church in a village in Mexico. Jacinta had brought
Fernando into America as her temporary guest and
he had stayed well past his permission. Until he
came here Fernando had worked on a watermelon
farm for starvation wages. He had not had a new
pair of shoes for more than four years. He had
lined his old ones with cardboard. They lived on
Blanchard's place in a one-bedroom house behind
the *casa grande*. It was the nicest and largest home
either of them had ever known.

Now Rusty faced a dilemma with which he dealt
every other day. In the state of Texas, it was not
illegal to be an illegal alien. Even if a citizen of
Mexico had sneaked into the state, if he had committed no prosecutable crime, no avenue existed
for holding him and waiting for him to be picked
up by the Immigration or the U.S. Marshals Service. Even if a reason to hold him could be found,

frequently the Border Patrol refused to travel to Sanderson County to take an individual into custody. And even if a Mexican national was unlucky enough to be confined by the Border Patrol, most likely he would merely be escorted back to Mexico and released.

The whole exercise was as ineffective as bailing water from a leaky boat and it was too expensive for a small, financially strapped sheriff's department to handle.

Even if he succeeded in having Fernando sent back to Mexico, it was possible the man would be back in Salvation next week. After chewing it over for a few minutes, Rusty finally told Jaime to order Jacinta and Fernando both to take the English classes at the Catholic church, to lecture them about taking steps toward making Fernando legal, then return them to their home at Blanchard's. The Ayalas were so overjoyed that Jacinta wept and jabbered in a string of Spanish her promise to learn English. Rusty expected the promise wouldn't last any longer than it took them to leave the room.

Randall Ryder barely kept his calm as he left his deceased daughter's home. He had taken Gary and the children to the Midland airport to pick up the Blanchard family—the father, James, the mother, Joelle, and Gary's sister, Starla.

His head pounded. Settling into the leather-upholstered backseat of the limo he had hired to chauffeur them, he tilted his head back against the seat and closed his eyes, trying to will the headache away. Memories battered him mercilessly. He thought about the day of Carla's birth, when he and Magdalena had argued good-naturedly about her name. Magdalena had wanted to name her a distinctly Spanish name. He had wanted something more American. They had compromised on Carla.

She would rest beside her mother. He would make certain of that.

It had sorely pained his heart to be in his daughter's home, surrounded by her belongings and her personality. He stood in front of the life-size painting in the living room for a long while, studying her, and he could hear her voice in his head. Nothing would be the same without her. Seeing her children wandering the house with sad eyes with the anguished adults all around them had almost overwhelmed him.

Her leaving this life was only an extension of a loss that had begun ten years ago when she had married that bastard ne'er-do-well from Fresno. She had changed after that.

Randall's thoughts returned to Gary's family. It had never been clear exactly what they did for a living. They weren't landowners, for sure. James Blanchard held a low-management job as an assembly line supervisor of some kind for some company Randall had never heard of. It wasn't even the same job he'd had when Carla married Gary ten years ago. Randall knew because back then he'd had the Blanchard family researched by the security company he used at Ryder Oil. Joelle did something for a hotel chain and Gary's thirty-year-old sister, Starla, lived in L.A. and had held twenty different jobs while she waited to be discovered by the movies.

Yes, indeedy, Gary Blanchard had hit pay dirt when he conned Carla Ryder into marriage.

And now, because the bastard had been successful in that endeavor, through the three children he and Carla shared he had entry to the Ryder fortune. Well, at least Carla's trust fund was protected from Gary. Randall, his lawyers and his friend Hunt Kelso had made certain it was ironclad and airtight. It would continue to be managed by Hunt and simply transfer to her children when they became older. He may have been uncharacteristically careless on the deed to the horse ranch, but that couldn't be said of the trust fund.

His mind drifted to Rusty Joplin. After that young whelp had seduced his Elena all those years ago, Randall had thought he had succeeded in ridding their lives of him. But then he had come back here and upended the local political system that had worked well for years. Well, at least Elena had gotten past him. Joplin might be a thorn in his side, but Randall believed he was no longer a threat to Elena.

He thought about the suspicions Joplin had voiced last night and he wondered if the kid was really qualified to be making such assertions. Good God, he was talking about, at the very least, manslaughter. And even as much as Randall disliked and distrusted Gary Blanchard, he didn't believe the bastard had the cojones to stand up to Carla. On the other hand, Gary wasn't a brilliant man. Was he stupid enough to destroy the goose that had laid him a golden egg?

The autopsy on Carla was inevitable. Randall had already come to terms with the fact that he couldn't remedy that abomination. He suspected a phone message would be waiting for him letting him know that the injunction his lawyer, Malcolm Freeman, had filed had been thrown out. As soon as the autopsy results were known, he would push the right buttons and get to the bottom of this. He knew people in Austin. Powerful people. If his son-in-law was truly guilty of harming a hair on his precious daughter's head, he, Randall Ryder, would take care of it. He had heard that Joplin had been a good cop in Fort Worth, but this wasn't Fort Worth. He would not allow an upstart to meddle in Ryder business.

Chapter 12

After Jaime left with the Ayalas, Rusty returned to his desk and plopped into his chair, taking a breather for the first time today. He fanned through the pages of the cell phone records and saw that several phone numbers had been highlighted in yellow, so he knew Cheryl had already gone through each record.

She poked her head through his doorway. "Alan called. His brother-in-law got in touch with him up in Lubbock and told him what's going on. He wanted to know if you want him to cut his vacation short and come back to help. He can be here in a couple of hours, you know."

Thank God, Rusty thought. He hadn't opened his mail all week, much less worked on the budget draft that had to be presented to the commissioners' court the coming Tuesday night. If Alan returned, he could give him parts of the investigation and free himself up to spend some time on his administrative chores. "He's willing to do that?"

"Said he was."

"Then tell him to come on back. We can use him. I'm gonna get that search warrant tomorrow."

He had to. Its value diminished with every passing hour. The way the system worked in Salvation, with tomorrow being Friday, he wouldn't see Judge Potter again until Monday.

"I'll tell him," Cheryl said. "I'm going to Taco Delight for some tacos for lunch. Want a couple?"

He glanced at his watch. It was one o'clock and he had been functioning on nothing but the morning's coffee. "You bet."

He and Cheryl often shared working lunches. He reached for his wallet and handed her a twenty.

After she left, working past his lingering anger at the judge, Rusty pulled out a yellow pad. Times floated in his mind, forming no clear pattern. He began constructing a time line. He wrote the words "Love triangle." Beside them he wrote "Gary and/ or boyfriend." On a new line, he wrote "revenge" and "pissed-off wife."

Then beneath that he wrote a column of times, phone calls and activities that he knew about:

Late afternoon Tuesday—Carla goes to see Randall about ??? He circled the question marks.

> *8:00 or 9:00 Tuesday p.m.—Elena calls Carla. Carla puts the kids to bed*
>
> *11:00 Tuesday p.m.—Gary sees Carla asleep in her bed*
>
> *7:00 Wednesday a.m.—Blanchard wakes up, finds Carla in the arena*
>
> *7:13—Blanchard calls hospital*
>
> *7:30—Rusty talks to Cheryl. Ambulance already dispatched*

At the bottom of the column, in large numbers, he wrote *6 to 6:30* and circled it—his own estimate of the time Carla had died.

He had done all he could on the time line with the information he had. All he had to do now was find out what had gone on in Carla's life between eleven o'clock Tuesday night and six o'clock Wednesday morning that had been lethal.

He turned his attention back to the phone records and studied them more closely. Many of the calls were long-distance. On a piece of notepaper,

Cheryl had written a list of the local numbers that appeared most frequently and the names to which some of them belonged. He quickly scanned the list and saw there were frequent calls to the farm-and-ranch supply store. From Carla's phone, there were many calls to Blanca Hardin's number and Randall's, calls to a beauty salon and to Salvation Bank & Trust. On the day before her death, half a dozen calls had been made to the bank. Rusty wondered again what kind of financial activity she had going on.

One other number was on the list Cheryl had made: Diego Esparza. Rusty searched his memory for the name, but other than Esparza being a fairly common Spanish name, it was unfamiliar.

He heard Cheryl come back into the outer office and the anticipation of lunch replaced the task at hand. She came in with the food and he laid the phone records aside.

She sat down in the steel chair in front of his desk and pulled several napkins and tacos from their greasy sack. "I got chicken and beef both." She pushed a cold drink in a Styrofoam cup toward him. "And I brought you some iced tea."

Once Rusty bit into the food, he almost inhaled the first taco. He was even hungrier than he had thought. "Who's this Diego Esparza in the phone records?" he asked as he chewed.

"Beats me. You don't know him?"

Rusty shook his head. "When we're finished eating, run his name through the computer and see what turns up."

"It's moving kind of slow today. Ask your sister. She and Hayden know everybody."

Rusty chuckled. "Too true."

"You haven't said what happened with the search warrant."

"Judge Potter denied it." Rusty bit into a second taco.

Holding a taco poised in midair, Cheryl gave him a pointed look. "I can't believe that."

Rusty shrugged. "He says Randall questions if Carla was murdered. The judge wants to wait and see the ME's opinion. I could tell him what it's gonna say, but he'd rather hear it from Ryder."

Cheryl shook her head, frowning. "I don't know why you even want to be sheriff in this county, Rusty. You're a good guy and a smart guy. You could go somewhere else and be appreciated."

"Somebody has to stand against the Randall Ryders and Hunt Kelsos of the world, Cheryl. Even the Phil Potters. Just because they hold most of the marbles doesn't mean they get to call all the shots. Somebody has to remind them of that. In Sanderson County, I guess that somebody's me."

"Do you know how many people actually challenge those guys?"

Rusty smiled. "It only takes one."

As he helped Cheryl clean up their lunch debris, the name Diego Esparza continued to nag at him and something Elena had told him last night still had to be checked out. As soon as Cheryl left his office he called Denise's drugstore. She answered the phone. Once they moved past the hellos and how-are-yous, he picked her brain about the old scandal involving Callahan and Carla Ryder. Carla had blatantly pursued the coach, Denise told him, and like the mere man that he was, he had succumbed. Still, the community and the schoolkids, loving Callahan as a coach, had sympathized with him and his wife and hated Carla. The upshot was that the coach was forced to leave town, but Carla just went on her merry way like nothing had ever happened. Nothing in the Callahan story filled in any blanks in the case.

"Have you ever heard of Diego Esparza?" he asked her.

"No, but we've got a customer with that last

name. We deliver prescriptions to her. She's old and doesn't drive or have anyone to drive her. She lives in a mobile home on Fourth. Why are you calling and asking me questions?"

Rusty chuckled. "I just love the sound of your voice, sis. Give me that address."

She said the exact address, he thanked her and they disconnected. He wouldn't be content until he knew who Diego Esparza was and what role he had played in Carla Ryder's life. Or death. He could get to Fourth Street in ten minutes.

The mobile home on Fourth was a neat singlewide with siding that looked like white-painted wood. A covered double carport sat a few steps away. The place was well kept, with a rock and cactus bed in the front yard and a long covered wooden porch across the front.

A Hispanic woman answered Rusty's knock. She had piercing black eyes, iron gray hair and red-bronze leathery skin that spoke of her undiluted native ancestry. Rusty could guess her age only as "old." He touched his hat to her. "Señora Esparza?"

Her eyes landed on the badge on his shirt pocket and she began babbling in Spanish. Waving her hands in the air, she rushed away from the door. In seconds she returned and thrust a laminated card through the doorway.

Rusty glanced at the work permit held in a brown hand gnarled by age and hard work, then looked back at her and nodded. "*Habla inglés*?"

"No." Her head shook vigorously.

"*Esposo?*" Rusty often found that even if a Mexican woman couldn't speak English, her husband could.

"No." Her head shook again.

"Uh, *niños*?" Most of the time children could

speak English if they had been attending American schools.

"No here," she said. "He work. No here."

So she must have a son old enough to work. "Uhhum, *su nombre?*"

"Juan Diego."

"Diego Esparza?"

"Sí." She nodded.

Rusty's adrenaline surged. He thanked her, returned to his car and called his office. "I need an interpreter. Find Jaime and send him to 2417 Southeast Fourth."

In a matter of minutes, Jaime Gonzales arrived. The two of them knocked on the mobile home's door again. Mrs. Esparza answered the door weeping and jabbering in Spanish. Jaime spent several minutes calming her and assuring her she was in no trouble and neither was her son. He asked if they could come in for a visit.

She admitted them to a spotless living room. The wooden tables had a low sheen and the place smelled of Pine-Sol. Pictures of Jesus hung on the wall. Several crucifixes made of wood, metal and glass sat in various places around the living room. Decor no different from what Rusty had seen in many Mexican and Mexican-American homes.

From Mrs. Esparza, they learned that Juan Diego was a good son. He was thirty-two years old. He had been born in Mexico, but he was not illegal. He owned the mobile home and took care of his mother. He worked for a drilling company and had been out on a job all week. Mrs. Esparza didn't know his location or the name of the company that employed him. She expected him tomorrow evening.

Mrs. Esparza was typical of most of the older Mexican women Rusty knew. Honest, hardworking, God-fearing. Rusty believed her.

Companies that drilled for oil were no longer plentiful in West Texas, but the five-man crews of the ones that were left covered widespread territory. He removed a business card from his shirt pocket and handed it to Jaime. The deputy in turn gave it to Mrs. Esparza, pointed out Rusty's name and the sheriff's office phone number and instructed her to have her son call.

She broke into tears again and Jaime assured her again that Juan Diego was in no trouble.

Rusty had one last question. "Ask her if her son has a cell phone," he said to Jaime. "And see if she knows his number."

Jaime asked the questions and Mrs. Esparza nodded and said "*Sí. Sí.*" She rose from her chair, went to the kitchen and returned carrying a piece of notepaper. Rusty took the notebook from his shirt pocket and copied the number. Bingo. He recognized it as being the one Cheryl had highlighted on the phone record.

He had to be content with the conversation for now. At least he knew an adult male lived here and that he would be home tomorrow. He debated about calling Esparza on the cell number Mrs. Esparza had given him, then decided against it. A phone call from the sheriff's office might make the guy disappear. Rusty would come back.

He returned to his office to find Alan Muncy back from Lubbock and eager to go to work. Rusty handed over the files he had made and spent the next hour apprising the investigator of what had occurred and the two interviews with Gary Blanchard. They listened to the taped interview with the Ayalas. Statements needed to be taken from EMT Jimmy Don Estes and his partner who rode the ambulance yesterday morning and from Wendy Thayer, the RN at the hospital who took Blanchard's emergency call. A statement needed to be taken from Elena. A subpoena had to be prepared to present to Salvation Bank & Trust requesting Carla and Gary's bank account information.

Last, he told Alan the two of them would be executing a search of Blanchard's barn tomorrow as well as returning to Diego Esparza's home.

With his investigator back to take over some of the work, Rusty tackled the mail and the storm of paperwork that had been accumulating on his desk for days. He opened the BUDGET file again and fiddled with the numbers for two hours but felt he was accomplishing little.

He set the file aside and reached for a thick report the state cops had sent out on the increase of meth manufacturing in rural Texas counties. Beneath it lay another tome on the upsurge of drugs, particularly meth, being smuggled across the Mexican border. He set the two reports in a prominent place on his desk for reading later. Any man in law enforcement could never know enough about the drug business, but he couldn't concentrate on that, either.

An anxiety drummed within him. He recognized it from his days with the FWPD. The hunt had always set his juices to flowing.

Finally, unable to take his mind off the case, he picked up the phone and called Blanca Hardin. A woman with a strong Spanish accent told him she wasn't available.

As the day shift began to leave, Rusty remembered he hadn't gotten much sleep last night and his day tomorrow would start early. He had to be at the medical examiner's office in Odessa before seven. Before going home, he pulled out the sealed sack that had the lead rope inside and placed it in the trunk of his car. He would leave it with the CSI unit in Odessa tomorrow.

Chapter 13

Elena's father's black Lincoln glided along the highway from Midland to Salvation. She, Blanca and Bailey were crowded into the backseat. She had accompanied Daddy to pick up Blanca and Bailey, who had arrived from Atlanta, the last leg of their journey from Italy.

Daddy had been drinking all day and Blanca was well past sober when she disembarked from the plane. Daddy had taken all of them to dinner at the luxurious Cattlemen's Café before starting for Salvation and Blanca had drunk more than she ate. Elena was so uptight she fought not to leap out of the car just so she could breathe again. Sitting by the door, she had a death grip on the latch.

"You're certainly quiet, *hermana*." The Spanish meant "sister." Blanca often used a few words of Spanish when she was drinking. She had learned to speak Spanish before she could speak English.

"There isn't much to be said, Blanca."

"How are the children? Do they know their mother's . . . gone?"

She was gone most of the time when she was alive. "They're with Gary. I'm sure he's told them as best he can."

Elena stared out the window into the black night. Miles across the horizon a tiny row of bright lights glowed. The lights of Salvation.

"Is it Gary who's making the arrangements?" Blanca asked.

Arrangements. As in funeral arrangements. Elena blinked. Indeed, a service hadn't even been discussed. Daddy hadn't been sober and as far as Elena knew, no one had even talked to Gary since early yesterday morning. "No. We don't know when the autopsy will be. We don't know when her body will be released."

"Autopsy?" Bailey asked. "Is that what usually happens when someone gets killed by a horse?"

"Oh, my God." Blanca gave a wailing cry.

Now Elena felt guilty for having them learn about the autopsy without forewarning. When she had called Blanca in Rome, she hadn't mentioned it. She had told Blanca only that Carla had been dragged to death by her horse.

"I filed an injunction to stop it," Daddy said from the front seat, "but Porky ruled against us. I won't forget that."

"Don't they do that within a few days of a death?" Bailey asked.

"We don't know yet," Elena said again.

Blanca raised a tissue to her nose. "I can't believe this."

"Does anyone know exactly what happened?" Bailey asked.

Elena felt her own eyes tear as she remembered Carla's lifeless form covered with dirt and lying in the center of the arena. Only a day and a half had passed, but it felt like a month. "Apparently Carla was in the arena working the stallion she and Gary bought in Fort Worth in July."

"The black one?"

"Yes. The horse must have spooked and somehow the lead rope got tangled around her neck. That's all we know. She had already . . ." Elena paused and swallowed to fight back tears. "She had already passed when I arrived."

"You were there?" Bailey said, a hint of astonishment in his tone.

"A friend at the hospital called me."

"Oh, my God. That's awful," Blanca cried. "Isn't that awful, Bailey? Poor Carla." She stroked a bejeweled hand down Elena's hair. "Poor *hermana*. Something told me before we left on our trip that we should have stayed home."

Elena tilted her head away from Blanca's hand. "I doubt if there was anything you could have done if you'd been here, Blanca."

Bailey sat still as stone, a hard look in his eyes. Finally, he put an arm around his wife's shoulder and pulled her closer. Blanca continued to cry. Daddy didn't turn around.

They arrived in Salvation and their driver slowed his speed. Passing the courthouse, Elena glanced back and saw the lights at the courthouse annex. She wondered where Rusty was and what he was doing. Tonight he seemed like the only person she knew who was sane.

Bailey had already said they wanted to be taken straight home. They were exhausted physically and Bailey had said Blanca had been in extreme distress since she got the news of Carla yesterday morning. Blanca and Bailey lived in the only country club subdivision in Sanderson County. Verandah was also the only gated community. Once they had been dropped off, Elena relaxed for the first time in hours.

When they reached the Rocking R, Elena helped her father from the limo's passenger seat. The driver offered to assist her, but she dismissed him. She accompanied her father to his study. He headed straight for the wide closet that enclosed the bar and brought out the Jack Daniel's and a glass.

"Daddy, I refuse to sit here and watch you drink until you pass out. Please let me help you to bed. You need to rest. Tomorrow's going to be a very long day."

"Go to bed, Elena," he growled.

She watched him as he moved to his desk chair and dropped into it. She could accomplish nothing by staying with him. When Hunt was here last night, she had been trapped while they drank themselves into oblivion. No way did she intend to do the same thing tonight. She turned and went to her suite.

Rusty stamped his boots clean on the pock-marked concrete back porch and entered his house through the back door. He was worn out and starving. Last night he had gotten two hours' sleep and he'd had nothing to eat all day except two tacos.

He pried off his work boots in the utility room. He left them there as he padded into the kitchen in his sock feet, relishing the feel of the cool floor tiles. He grabbed a frozen dinner from the freezer side of the double-door refrigerator. His mother, constantly fretting about him eating a healthy diet, sometimes prepared meals, froze them and brought them over to his freezer in sealed plastic bags, ready to be heated in the microwave. He could cook. He didn't need that service from her, but long ago he had ceased to protest. It was too hard to win an argument with his mother.

Tonight supper appeared to be meat loaf, mashed potatoes and green beans. He slid the meal into the microwave, shut the door with a bang and set the timer. While his meal rotated on the turnta-ble, he crossed the room to take a plate from the cupboard.

A cork bulletin board hung on the wall beside the cupboard. One of the items thumbtacked to it was the Sanderson County emergency call list, phone numbers of first responders in the event of disaster. For no reason Elena's name and phone number jumped out at him. The call list had been hanging there for months and he had never homed in on Elena's name.

The microwave chimed. He abandoned the list, pulled out his meal and took it and the milk carton to his small round table at one end of the kitchen. He mentally scolded himself. He had a hell of a lot more important things to think about than Elena's phone number. The autopsy should be over around noon tomorrow and he intended to be back in Judge Potter's chambers ASAP afterward with his search warrant application.

The fact that he had Elena's phone number continued to peck at him the whole time he was eating. It had to be because cell phones had been so much on his mind today.

He checked in the fridge again and found the pie tin with one last slice of his sister Denise's homemade buttermilk pie. He ate the slice of pie from the tin, then cleaned up the table and the kitchen and put all his dishes into the dishwasher. He still wasn't sure he needed a dishwasher. It took a week to fill it with dishes, so almost every dish in his kitchen was dirty before he ran it.

He moved to the living room and collapsed in his reclining chair. Hoping to find a movie interesting enough to clear his mind, he punched the TV on. His channel surfing stopped when he saw himself on the news. He stopped for a few seconds and watched the report. There were aerial shots of Blanchard's house and layout, aerial shots of the Rocking R and the multistory Ryder Oil Company building in Midland. Shots of Carla. "Shit," he grumbled and surfed on. He found an old western to watch, but Elena's phone number kept calling to him like a beckoning hand.

"Goddamn it," he mumbled. He got up and went to the bulletin board, picked up the receiver and punched in her number. She hadn't answered by the end of three *burrs*. He was glad she hadn't and was ready to hang up when she said, "This is Elena."

He paused, suddenly without words.

"Hello?" she said.

"Hey, whatcha doing?"

"Rusty?"

"Yeah, it's me. I just thought I'd, uh, call and, uh, see how your day went."

She gave a soft laugh. "It wasn't the best day I've ever had. I went to Midland with Daddy to pick up Blanca and Bailey at the airport."

"Oh, yeah. I forgot they had to come from overseas."

"Thank God they were exhausted. All they wanted to do was go home and go to bed. Were you aware how much Blanca drinks?"

"Oh, I might've heard, but I don't pay much attention to talk."

"I think she would be called a two-fisted drinker."

"That's too bad. What drives her to drink?"

"She isn't a happy person." He heard a soft laugh. "But then, what Ryder is?"

"You're happy. I've never seen you when you weren't upbeat. It's one of the things I remember about you."

"Really?" she asked and he heard a brightening in her voice.

"You must be exhausted, too," he said.

"I am, come to think of it. I didn't get much sleep last night. By the time I got home from your place and got in bed, it was nearly time to get up again."

"It's been a long two days." Rusty pulled a chair from the table and dragged it over by the phone, perplexed because he could think of nothing meaningful to say. Hell, he didn't even know why he had called her, much less what to say to her.

"I saw you on the news tonight," she said. "I usually don't watch the news, but I tuned in to see what they were reporting about the Ryders."

"I saw it, too."

"That was a horrible picture they had of Carla. She's . . . she was so much prettier than that."

"No telling where they got it."

"Daddy said Judge Potter ruled against the injunction he filed."

"He sure did."

"So when will they do the autopsy?"

Rusty hesitated. He might not know what he had called to discuss, but he knew this wasn't it. "Uh, it's tomorrow morning."

"Oh," she said softly. "I don't know if Daddy knows that." A pause on her end. "Will you be there?"

"Yes. I will."

"Then what?"

"Then we'll know what caused Carla's death."

"But we know that already."

"But we don't know everything. This is important, Elena."

"I know. You said that. . . . It's just that . . . I've seen autopsies."

Sure she had. Observing autopsies must have been part of her education as a nurse. Now it dawned on Rusty why she had been so upset over it yesterday morning. He chastised himself for being thoughtless. "Don't think about it, Elena."

"I don't suppose you could get me a copy of the report."

He almost said he would, but he stopped himself. "I can't right away. Only the law and the next of kin get a copy. That would be Gary."

"Oh, well. I don't need to see it. I know what it'll say. I'm sure you do, too."

He didn't like the tone of her reply. "I'll be glad to tell you what I can. It'll become public information sooner or later."

"Have you ever investigated a homicide where someone was strangled?"

"A few times."

"Then you must have a theory about what happened to Carla."

Rusty frowned, trying to decide what to tell her. In truth, other than his experience and instinct telling him someone had killed Carla, he knew nothing. Elena sounded as if she was stronger than she had seemed yesterday. His concern was probably unnecessary. Hell, she probably knew more about death by strangulation than he did. "I don't think that lead rope made the marks I saw on her neck. And she had some broken fingernails. I mean, they could have gotten broken, I guess, when she was, uh, dragged across the arena. But I don't think so. Like you said, it's just a theory. The autopsy will tell us facts."

"Daddy always fussed at Carla about those horses." He heard her sniff. "I was so upset I didn't even see the marks."

"I didn't mean to upset you—"

"What happened to the horse?"

"I had him taken out to my folks' place. For his own protection. Sometimes upset people do crazy things. Gary was threatening to shoot him."

"I had heard about him, what a great horse he is. But I hadn't seen him until yesterday morning."

"He's a pretty horse, all right."

"And you think he's being accused of something he didn't do."

"We'll know tomorrow, Elena."

"Why did you call, Rusty?"

"I don't know. I felt like we didn't finish talking last night."

"How'd you get my number? Not everyone has it."

Now he gave a low chuckle. "Believe it or not, I've had it for a long time. It's on my emergency call list."

"Oh," she said.

"Is there anything I can do to make it easier for you, Elena?"

She huffed. "I don't know what it would be. We just have to wait for events to take their course. And I just have to bear up. A good night's sleep will do me a world of good. Did you tell me the time of the autopsy?"

"It's at seven."

"Then I guess I'll be waiting to hear the results."

Rusty didn't want to hang up. He didn't want to break the contact. "I could use some shut-eye myself. I'll be on the road by six."

"I appreciate you calling, Rusty. It means a lot."

"I was thinking about you and I wanted to hear your voice. I wanted to hear you tell me you're okay."

"I'm okay," she said softly. "I'm a lot tougher than you think I am."

"Write down my cell number. So you can call me if you need to."

"I already have it. Your numbers are on the call list, too."

He chuckled again. "I guess I hadn't thought of that. Listen, something came up today. Can you think of a big rich man Carla might have been seeing?"

"No. I know almost nothing about that part of her life. The only big rich man I know is Hunt Kelso. Why? Is he important?"

"He might have been one of Carla's lovers."

"Well, that wouldn't be Hunt. I can't imagine him as anyone's lover, especially my sister's."

Rusty grinned. That was the closest thing to criticism of somebody he had ever heard her say. "Yeah, I see what you mean. Guess I'll say good night."

"Thanks for calling, Rusty."

Chapter 14

The sun was well up in a cloudless sky and Elena had spent a fitful night. Now, still wearing her pajamas and a robe, she sat at the eating bar between the kitchen and the sunlit breakfast room with a bowl of cold cereal. Bailey sat at the table drinking coffee. Blanca was outside on the patio smoking. Blanca and Bailey had come to the Rocking R early and Blanca had made half a dozen trips outside to smoke. Of course Daddy knew Blanca smoked, but he didn't allow smoking in the house.

Blanca came back inside and sat down at the table across from her husband, bringing a cloud of Tresor with her. It had been her signature fragrance forever. She had wept so much her eyes were swollen and her face was as red as the silk scarf tied at her nape and holding her long blond hair. After the alcohol she had consumed last night, she had to have a monstrous hangover.

"I nearly died when I saw those TV vans out by the gate," she said. "Daddy must be having a fit."

Oddly enough, Daddy hadn't said much about the TV people. "He rides past them and ignores them," Elena said. "I just hope none of them approach him."

Blanca pawed through her huge purse. She finally yanked out an ornate silver flask, set it on the glass tabletop with a clunk and scowled at her perfect French manicure. "Oh, damn. I broke a nail."

She picked up the flask and poured a dollop of brown liquid into her coffee.

Bailey glared at her through silver-rimmed glasses that matched his hair color.

"Did you see the aerials of the ranch on TV news last night? And of Carla's house? Channel Seven?" Blanca sipped at her coffee. "They had Rusty on, too. I'll swear, he is the best-looking man. I don't know why some sweet young thing hasn't latched on to him."

Elena's jaw clenched. Blanca had a habit of making remarks about men. If Bailey was bothered by this, he never showed it. In fact, Bailey seemed to be without emotion altogether. Indeed, Rusty had looked handsome in his snow white shirt and his gray Stetson. He had appeared stern and determined, his no-nonsense manner exuding masculinity. Elena had always thought him the total alpha male. And the total hero.

"I hardly ever watch the news," she said.

"If Rusty thinks Carla was killed by someone, why won't Daddy let him get involved?" Blanca said, setting her mug on the table. Her heavy silver and turquoise bracelets clicked on the tabletop. Primitive-looking jewelry was Blanca's usual attire. She dressed in Santa Fe style, traveling to the New Mexico city often to shop for clothing and jewelry in the trendy boutiques. "He thinks someone from Austin would do a better job or what?"

"Daddy has no influence over what Rusty does," Elena said past the food in her mouth. "And I don't know what he thinks about someone from Austin."

"Well, I personally feel that getting the local sheriff involved is a better idea than calling in someone from out of town," Bailey put in. He left the table, carrying his coffee cup, and began to pace in the kitchen. No one could look more out of character than he did this morning, wearing a navy nylon jogging suit. Conservative suits and ties matched his appearance and personality.

"Even if Randall doesn't like Rusty for personal reasons," he added, "some of my friends in Fort Worth knew him when he lived there. They all say he was a damn good cop. The Fort Worth PD hated to see him leave."

"I will not have my daughter buried in California!" Their father's voice boomed all the way from the study and all three of them looked in that direction.

"Is he talking to Gary?" Blanca asked, frowning and exchanging glances with her husband.

"Gary wants Carla buried in California?" Bailey said to Elena, wide-eyed. "Is he crazy? Does he not know Randall?"

"Why, Daddy would hire a hit man before he would allow Carla, or any of us, to be buried anywhere but on the Rocking R," Blanca added indignantly. "Carla should be buried beside our mother."

Elena continued to eat, wondering what Gary was saying to their father. The patriarch suddenly appeared in the room, his lips drawn razor thin. Besides looking angry, he looked tired. After all the whiskey he had consumed in the past two days, he must feel terrible.

A sharp look shot from his green eyes. "Finish your breakfast, Elena, and get dressed," he snapped. "We're going to Carla's house. That sonofabitch thinks he's taking our girl to California, but I'll take care of that."

"But, Daddy, I'm—"

"Don't argue. Just get yourself together."

An hour later, Blanca and Bailey had gone home, Elena had showered and dried her hair, then thrown on jeans and a sweater, and she and her

father were in her SUV, on their way to Carla's
house. As she drove, she sent furtive glances
toward him. He had a sour odor of stale alcohol
about him and it filled the air inside the SUV. His
hands shook and she could see perspiration on his
brow. In general, he didn't look well.

The nearer they came to Carla's driveway, the
more pressure Elena felt to tell him what she had
learned from Rusty last night about the autopsy.
"The autopsy is being done this morning," she said,
looking straight ahead and tuning inflection out of
her voice.

She heard a gasping sob come from him, but she
continued to concentrate on driving. "It had to be
done," she said, quoting Rusty.

At last they reached the long driveway to Carla's
home. Elena turned in and eased up the caliche
road. Horses grazed on either side of them, their
slick coats shining in the morning sun.

"Goddamned horses," Daddy mumbled. "I
never did understand why your sister always had
to have some wild sonofabitch around. I don't
know why she couldn't be . . . couldn't have been
content with an ordinary saddle horse."

His voice faltered and Elena slanted a glance
toward him. He pulled his handkerchief from his
back pocket and coughed into it.

Seeing him in so much anguish caused a pain in
her own rib cage. As a nurse recognizing the signs
of extreme stress and anxiety, she worried about
him. She, better than anyone, knew how he would
hold everything inside, masking just how much he
hurt. The closest he had come to breaking down in
his grief was Wednesday night when Hunt was at
the house and they had been drinking heavily.

She tried not to show her own emotions. "Her
horses are beautiful, Daddy. She thought they were
a good investment."

"Nothing that weighs a thousand pounds and has to be fed every day is a good investment," he growled. "Don't ever forget that. You might as well have a damn pet elephant."

Neither Elena nor her sisters had ever understood Daddy's dislike for horses. The house was full of pictures of him as a young man sitting astride a horse and Elena had faded memories from her childhood of him, her mother and her sisters riding together.

At Carla's house, Gary's father answered the door and invited them into the living room. Elena hadn't been in her sister's home often. From the day Carla had told of sleeping with Rusty, Elena had never trusted her and thus she had always been uncomfortable around Carla when they were alone.

Mrs. Blanchard came from the other side of the room toward them. She first gave Randall a hug and kissed air beside his cheek, then moved to Elena with a like greeting.

Gary came in. He had on ironed and creased jeans and a starched button-down shirt. Knowing Rusty suspected he was somehow responsible for the death of her sister, Elena couldn't keep from staring at his neat, clean look, couldn't keep from studying him. He was bigger than Rusty. Carla had been smaller than Elena. Gary certainly could have overpowered her. Could he really have done what Rusty suspected?

He walked across the room and stiffly shook hands with Daddy. Elena could smell a faint hint of alcohol commingling with strong cologne. Everyone around her seemed to be floating in liquor and perfume.

"Randall, Elena," Gary said, "I wasn't expecting you. You didn't say you were coming over."

"We didn't discuss the autopsy on the phone," Daddy said, "but I'm sorry to say I was unable to stop it. I just now found out it was scheduled for this morning." He reached into his back pocket, drew out his handkerchief and dabbed at his brow.

"I've already heard," Gary said. "It's okay. I think it needs to be done."

Daddy's head shook and he glared fiercely. "No. Not to my beautiful daughter."

"They say they'll release her midmorning," Gary said, smoothly gliding past Daddy's emotional display.

"We, uh, I didn't know," Elena said, unable to control the tremble in her voice.

"I've arranged for Garland Brothers to pick her up and bring her home. Rusty suspects—"

"Don't pay any attention to Joplin. He doesn't know what the hell he's talking about," Daddy said. "Just like he doesn't know what he's doing, either. Unfortunately Phil Potter was in court most of the day and—"

Daddy's words were stopped by Carla's children entering the room. The presence of his grandchildren turned him to jelly. His eyes teared. Austin trotted to his grandmother, but Maggie and Renata came to Daddy. He knelt to their level and wrapped his arms around them. "Oh, my darlings," he murmured.

"Mommy's in heaven," Renata said, her dark eyes round and serious.

"I know, sweetheart, I know."

Tears sprang to Elena's eyes, too. She knelt with her father and her sister's children and hugged them all.

"Don't cry, Grandpa," Renata said. "We're going to California."

Dumbstruck, Elena swung her gaze up to Gary, but her brother-in-law turned away.

"Grandpa will take you to California one of these days," Daddy said and Elena realized he must not have understood what Renata meant. "We'll get on Grandpa's plane and just fly there. We'll go to Disneyland and Magic Mountain and—"

"No, Grandpa," Maggie said. "We're going home with Grampy James and Grammy Jo."

Daddy looked up, his eyes boring into Gary. He released the children and got to his feet. "What does this mean?"

"I've got a lot to do here, Randall," Gary said calmly. "It'll be easier with the kids at my folks' house. I won't have to worry about them. I'll be going out to Fresno myself in a few days."

Only then did the dawning come to Elena, the real possibility that her family could lose these children that they loved so much. Over the years, Gary's parents had visited in Salvation often and built their own relationship with Carla's children. The past two summers, Maggie had spent several weeks at the Blanchards' Fresno home. She talked often of their backyard swimming pool and their next-door neighbor's daughter who was Maggie's age. Indeed, they would feel comfortable with Gary's parents.

"Uh, I think James and I'll take our coffee out on the patio," Gary's mother said hurriedly and leveled a phony smile at Elena. "Would you like to join us, dear?"

"No." Elena wouldn't dream of leaving her father's side when he needed her support.

Mrs. Blanchard hurriedly ushered the children through the French doors to the patio and Mr. Blanchard followed.

"Those are my daughter's children," Daddy said to Gary, wide-eyed, as if he couldn't believe what he had just heard. His face had become a thundercloud.

"Randall," Gary said, holding out an open palm,

"they're *my* children. I've decided it's best for them to stay with *my* parents in California until I can get out there. My mom's at home all day and can give them the attention I think they need at this time. If they stay here, they'll have no one but Jacinta."

"They'll stay at my house," Randall said firmly, as if the decision was his to make.

"No," Gary said, slicing the air with his hand. "They wouldn't be any better off with you. You're all over the damn country and Elena's gone half the time, day or night."

"But I don't have to be," Elena put in urgently. "I can take off work and be with them. I can quit my job. I can—"

"No." Her brother-in-law's head shook. "I've already made up my mind. The funeral will be on Saturday and Mom and Dad will be going home on Sunday after—"

"Funeral?" The look of anger on Daddy's face changed into one of incredulity.

Hanging on to her father's arm, Elena stared at her brother-in-law in horror. He had already made funeral arrangements? Without even consulting Daddy or either of Carla's sisters? She had always been aware of his subtle detachment when it came to the Ryder family, but now it was obvious just how wide the chasm that separated them was.

"I've made arrangements for the funeral on Saturday at the Methodist church," Gary said.

Daddy drew himself up. "My daughter's Catholic."

"Randall. A funeral mass takes all day long. I don't want to put any of us through that, especially the kids. Carla had no loyalty to any church. Believe me, she won't care where her service is held."

"I care," Daddy said. "And her mother, God rest her soul, cares. She raised her daughters to be Catholic."

"She didn't raise her daughters at all," Gary rebutted crossly, his fists jammed against his hips. "And neither did you. They were raised by maids and housekeepers." Gary paused, holding Daddy's gaze. "Everything's already arranged except the cemetery," he said at last.

Elena could see a vein throbbing in her father's temple and she feared for his well-being, wondered if he had taken his medication to control his hypertension. She couldn't hold back tears. "Gary, please try to understand Daddy's loss. *Our* loss. After what's happened, the children mean so much to him, to me, to all of us. If you take them away—"

"Elena, it's already been decided. I'm willing to concede to your dad's wishes that my wife be buried in your family cemetery on the ranch. Carla would like that. But neither your dad nor you has anything to say about the future of my kids."

A muscle worked in Daddy's jaw. Elena had never seen such a dangerous look in his eye. "Blanchard," he said in a fierce stage whisper, "you'll not take my daughter's children out of Texas. I'll kill you first."

He walked out of the house and slammed the door.

Elena stared at Gary. "Do you know what you're doing? Why, Daddy—"

"Elena, let's get something right out front." Gary leaned forward, his face thrust at her, his eyes hard. "I have no reason to stay in Texas. All of my family lives in California. I'm amazed I've stayed here as long as I have, especially considering that Carla and I had a piss-poor life together. If it hadn't been for the kids—"

"Oh, but you did have plenty of prestige, didn't you?" Elena spat, unable to control her hands knotting into fists at her side. "Plenty of my sister's money to spend while you never did a day's work. That's why you came back and remarried her, isn't it? Everything we thought and heard about you is true. You were only interested in her money and the Ryder name."

Gary's eyes narrowed and he sneered. "Are you kidding? Your sister was stingier than a church mouse with everyone and everything except those damn horses. And as for the Ryder name, that's a crock."

Striding away from her, he threw a hand in the air. "Not one person I can think of knew her as Carla Blanchard, my wife. Even after all this time, she was still Carla Ryder, Randall Ryder's daughter. People even assume the kids' last names are Ryder."

He stamped back to where she stood and thrust his face close to hers again, his eyes cold and angry. "I married her a second time for the kids, Elena. And only for the kids. I couldn't stand to see my two little girls grow up to be like their mother."

Stunned to speechlessness and seeing the futility of further argument, Elena backed away from her brother-in-law. When she reached the entry, she turned, ran from the house and followed her father to the Lexus. As she opened the driver's door, she saw the thin-lipped rage in Daddy's face. The last time she had seen him with such a black look was last year when Rusty announced his candidacy for sheriff.

As soon as she slid behind the wheel, he said, "Let's get home. I want to call Malcolm."

Rusty left the nondescript Odessa medical examiner's office knowing four things with grim certainty: Carla Ryder's neck had been broken postmortem. Her death had been caused by ligature strangulation from behind and most likely the murder weapon was not the lead rope that had been found around her neck.

And she was four months pregnant.

Now the ante had been raised. The definition of fetal homicide might be up in the air in the courts and in the national debate, but as far as Rusty was concerned, Carla's killer had committed double homicide.

The question of murder or not had been settled in Rusty's mind since Wednesday, but now even Judge Potter couldn't deny it.

Did Blanchard know about the pregnancy? Was the fetus his child? As far as Rusty could determine, it was possible it was not. In two separate conversations he hadn't mentioned it. So whose baby was it? And did it have anything to do with her murder? Rusty's memory scrolled back to Elena saying Carla had gone to the Ryder home looking for her father the evening before her death.

He reached the highway and headed north to Salvation still sorting his thoughts. He decided that Elena didn't know about the pregnancy or surely she would have mentioned it. Did Blanca know? Possibly. He remembered Elena saying Blanca had been Carla's confidante. He had to talk to Blanca Hardin.

Before leaving the ME's office, Rusty had asked him to fax a copy of his opinion to Helen Grayson so she could make sure it reached Judge Potter as soon as possible. Now Rusty scrolled down the contact list in his cell phone, called the judge's clerk and told him he would be at the courthouse in forty-five minutes to get Judge Potter's signature on the search warrant application from yesterday.

Next, he called Alan and told him to assemble a search team and ask the DA to go along if he was available. In dealing with suspects with as high a profile as the Ryder family, Rusty wanted to have all the support he could get.

He reached the courthouse annex thirty minutes

later. He lost no time in grabbing the file folder containing the search warrant application off his desk. "It's a big barn," he told Alan. "We need four or five people besides you and me. You might have to call in a couple of reserves."

Rusty reached the courtroom and slid onto one of the old oak bench seats just as Judge Potter was pronouncing a sentence on a DUI. Rusty remembered when the subject had been arrested. Hair combed and wearing a suit and tie, he was almost unrecognizable.

Judge Potter looked out into the courtroom and Rusty caught his eye. Before the next case was called, the judge invited him into his chambers and stepped off the bench.

Rusty followed him, carrying the warrant application. He handed the judge the document and took a seat in front of the desk, where he had sat yesterday. He knew better than to expect Potter to admit that he had been wrong in denying it. No one had a bigger ego than a sitting judge.

"Have you made any changes in this?" Judge Potter asked, tilting back his head and reading through his half-glasses.

"No, sir. It's just like you saw it yesterday."

The judge continued to read and a scintilla of doubt began to creep into Rusty. He believed the judge had looked for a reason not to sign the application yesterday. Was he doing it again? Finally, without a word, he picked up a pen, filled in the blanks indicating the time span allowed and scrawled his name at the bottom of the last page. "Seventy-two hours, Sheriff. That's it." He shoved the application back across the desk.

Chapter 15

By the time Rusty returned to the sheriff's office, Alan had gathered the search team. Besides Lowell Giles, Jerry Clay and Marshall Tucker, he had called in two reserves. Kevin O'Neill was eager to be a part of the search, too. Cheryl had made lists of the items they would be seeking. Rusty briefed the group on procedure and cautioned them to be careful to preserve evidence. Kevin cautioned them to not exceed the limits of the warrant.

"Lowell and Jerry and the two reserves will search the barn's lower floor. Alan, Kevin and I'll take the locked room. The Blanchards are probably going to be at home, so Marshall, you get to babysit the family." Everybody nodded and murmured. "Everybody stay focused. Let's go."

Rusty drove his car, followed by Kevin, then Alan, Marshall and Jerry. Lowell and the reserve deputies followed them. Traveling up the Blanchard driveway, they drove past white-fenced pastures and grazing horses and parked in front of the garage behind Carla's red truck. While Rusty wondered why it was out of the garage, the rest of the team pulled to a stop behind Rusty's Crown Vic.

They all climbed out of the cars at the same time to an eerie silence surrounding the sprawling ranch house. The ever-present afternoon breeze had kicked up and carried with it little wafts of sand as

it skated across the flat prairie. Placing a hand on
his hat to keep it in place, Rusty thought of the
green, lush horse ranches around Fort Worth and
Dallas and wondered why anybody who wanted to
be in the cutting horse business would do it in the
windy West Texas desert.

"Oh, my God," the district attorney said, awed
by the display of wealth in front of him. "Would
you look at this place?"

"It's just a house," Rusty said. "And a helluva
lot unhappier than a lot of places smaller and
uglier."

Rusty carried the warrant, with Kevin accompanying him to the front door, and rang the doorbell.
Jacinta Ayala answered with a welcoming smile.
She struggled with telling them no one was home.
They had gone to town. With simple words and
hand gestures, Rusty did his best to quell her fears
and make her understand he and his companions
were going to the big beige barn.

He returned to his car, gesturing for the deputies
to drive to the barn. As they neared the structure,
Rusty could see the yellow and black crime scene
tape he had strung still crisscrossing the upstairs
room's outside exit. To his surprise, it appeared to
be undisturbed.

Downstairs, the massive two-panel barn doors
were closed and latched and not locked. As Lowell
and Jerry swept the doors open and pushed them
back against the barn walls, penned horses whin-
nied and stamped. "You'll have to work around
these horses," Rusty told Lowell, "but be careful.
This is some valuable horseflesh."

"No problem," the deputy replied.

The district attorney, wearing a suit, stood by
with his hands in his pockets. "Are these racehorses?"

"These are quarter horses, Kevin. These particular ones are trained for cutting cattle in competition. It's a popular sport in this part of the country."

Rusty returned to the car and lifted his rarely used crime scene kit out of the trunk, along with his Polaroid camera. With the nearest CSI unit thirty miles away in another town and county, he often had to gather and label his own evidence and take his own pictures.

The trio made its way upstairs single file to the locked room that had been the bane of Rusty's existence since Wednesday morning. He sliced through the crime scene tape across the door with his pocketknife. "Before we force this door," Rusty said, "feel along the top of the frame and see if there's a key."

They found no key, so Rusty applied a hard kick and the door popped open.

They entered a large, dim room. The only windows, one that looked to the outside and one that looked out on the mezzanine and the barn's interior, were covered by closed venetian blinds. Narrow slices of sunlight barely sneaked through the slats of the blind that covered the outside window. Even in the low light, Rusty could see that the room was expensively furnished with massive pieces, similar to those in the house.

"Let's get some light in here," Alan said and walked over and pulled the blind open.

"Oh, wow," Kevin said. "You can see for miles."

Rusty guessed Kevin didn't often get a bird's-eye view of the vast nothingness of the West Texas plain.

Beside the outside window, bridles hung on ornamental iron hooks. With heavy silver buckles and conchos on the headstalls and engraved silver trim on the bits, the bridles obviously had never been used. *More show trophies,* Rusty thought. He noticed one empty iron hook and for a fleeting moment wondered if another bridle had hung there. And if so, where was it now?

The near end of the big room was taken up by a tiny all-white kitchen. The place was neatly kept on the one hand, but on the other, items seemed out of place from where they should be. An empty ashtray was turned upside down on the floor. Documents were strewn in disarray across the end of the kitchen counter.

The entire wall at the far end of the room was covered by a honey-colored bookcase. Rusty quickly scanned the shelves. The few books that were there were related to horses. Framed pictures, outnumbering the books by far, sat on the shelves. The pictures were of Carla and/or Blanchard and various horses. Otherwise, horse show trophies were the decoration.

On the right side of the bookcase a door stood ajar. "I'll take that end," Alan said, and lifted a pair of latex gloves from the crime scene box. He walked toward the open door. "We're looking for a laptop and what else?"

"A cell phone. And a possible murder weapon. Some kind of rope or something you could wrap around somebody's neck."

Rusty pulled on the latex gloves and headed for the kitchen first. He crossed a floor made of the same phony planks he remembered from the living room in the house. A white coffeemaker, plugged into the wall, its ON light still beaming green, sat at the back of the white kitchen counter. The coffeepot was almost empty, but from the brown ring showing near the top of it, Rusty guessed it had been full two days ago. It appeared that the contents had cooked down. Rusty went to it, switched it off and unplugged it.

He picked through the papers on the counter, saw nothing he deemed significant. He determined it was mostly mail. Kevin took the kitchen cabinets and found assorted dishes in the cupboards, clean dishes in the dishwasher.

In the drawer near a wall-mounted phone, Rusty found an address book. When he thumbed through it and saw phone numbers, he decided to take it and compare its contents to the cell phone records he already had. He had just bagged it and labeled it when Alan called from the bedroom doorway, "Hey, boss."

Rusty turned and saw him holding a heavy bit in one hand and a pair of reins and a headstall between the thumb and forefinger of the other. "I found these in the bathroom," he said, "shoved under the sink."

Even from across the room Rusty could see the bridle parts were the fancy kind used in horse shows or as prizes. He couldn't imagine why they would be under the bathroom sink. He glanced at the empty iron hook on the wall and a chill zigzagged up his spine. Alan could be holding the murder weapon. He grabbed the camera and a large paper bag from the crime scene kit and joined the deputy in the bedroom. He held the sack open while Alan dropped the three bridle parts inside.

The bedroom was small and stuffy, less than half the size of the living room, with only one outside window, covered by a closed venetian blind. As the three of them stood in the small space looking around, a pervasive silence surrounded them. "This is where it happened," Alan said quietly. "I'll bet you a hundred. I feel it."

"What are you, psychic?" Kevin said.

"Naw. But I know how things happen. I can see it in my head."

Rusty gave his deputy a look. By city cop stan-

dards, Alan was by no means a highly qualified
investigator, but the man's uncanny instincts had
caught Rusty's attention more than once.

On the floor in front of the dresser lay a framed
picture, facedown. Rusty picked it up and shards
of broken glass fell to the floor. He turned it over
and saw a photograph of the three Blanchard kids.
He laid it on the dresser. "You find a trash can in
the bathroom?" he asked Alan.

"Empty."

Rusty began to snap pictures from several angles.

The only furniture in the room was a queen-size
bed, a bedside table and lamp, a long dresser on
the opposite wall and a wooden chair. Many boot-
wearers kept such a chair to sit on while putting
on their boots. It was easier than sitting on a chair
with a cushion. Rusty himself kept a wooden chair
in his bedroom. The chair sat beside the dresser at
a cockeyed angle from the wall, as if it had been
shoved or bumped out of place. On the wall, he
saw two gouges, almost deep enough to break
through the wallboard.

The bed was made, but the comforter that covered it was rumpled and crooked and half off the
bed. Seeing the comforter, the skewed chair and
the deeply scarred wall, Rusty found nothing wrong
with his deputy's conclusion.

"So what are you thinking?" the district attorney
asked. "They had a fight or something and someone choked her with one of those leather straps?"

"Those are reins," Alan said in a patronizing
tone.

"Carla had a violent temper," Rusty added,
changing the subject. No way did he want one of
his deputies angering the DA. "She didn't worry
about pissing people off. And she wasn't afraid to
go toe-to-toe with the best of them."

Kevin opened the bedside table's drawer and

held up a half-empty box of condoms. "We know what she used this room for."

"It'd be my guess those don't belong to Gary," Rusty said.

"They aren't even hidden," Alan added. "He must not come in here much."

Rusty didn't see the point in explaining that he had come to the conclusion that Gary just didn't give a damn who or what his wife did. "We might as well take the sheets off the bed, have them checked for DNA."

They removed the sheets and stuffed them into another paper bag. A quick search of the dresser drawers followed. All were empty except for some T-shirts and some women's lingerie.

"Let's look for that laptop," Rusty said and they moved back into the living room.

They searched beneath the cushions on the sofa, the chairs, then moved to the drawers in the cabinets under the bookshelves. Bingo. The computer and a battery charger. Rusty carried it to the kitchen counter, plugged it in and booted it up. He didn't know what he expected to find, but a tiny shred of communication could open a large hole.

He didn't know enough of Carla in recent years to guess if she would keep her appointments and business records organized on a computer. And it appeared he wasn't likely to find out in the immediate future because the whole damn thing was password protected. He knew enough about computers to muddle through simple tasks, but he didn't know how to get past a password. "Shit," he muttered and his suspicion about information that might exist in the computer mushroomed.

Alan came up behind him. "Cheryl might be able to get in there," he said. "She's a sharp gal on computers."

"I suggest you turn it over to the crime lab in

Odessa," Kevin said. "This is a homicide. You want all the I's dotted and the T's crossed."

Rusty didn't disagree.

They looked through the apartment one more time, while Rusty wrote the list of items they were taking out of the apartment on the search warrant receipt. Alan spotted a mug with the remains of what looked to be coffee sitting in the sink. He picked it up by the rim, using his thumb and forefinger. "I think I'll take this, too," he said. "You never know. There might be a fingerprint. Or DNA."

They put the evidence they had collected in the trunk of Alan's car and he set out for the crime lab in Odessa. Rusty returned to the house and rang the doorbell again. When Jacinta Ayala came to the door, he used his rough Spanish and managed to make her understand that she was to give the receipt to Mr. Blanchard.

Chapter 16

Back in his car, Rusty turned his cell phone on again on his way back to his office and saw a missed message from Elena. Carla's pregnancy rushed into his head. He drove out of sight of Blanchard's house and parked on the side of the highway that led back to town. After schooling himself into an objective state of mind, he returned Elena's call. She answered on the first *burr*.

"What's up, darlin'?"

"Daddy and I were at Carla's house earlier today. Rusty, Gary's sending Carla's kids to California with his parents."

Rusty's eyes narrowed as his brain tried to assess the significance of that development. "I guess he can do that." He tried to keep his voice even, hoping not to add to her distress. "They're his kids, too, Elena."

He heard her sniffle again. "I know. But Daddy is so angry. You should hear him. He threatened to kill Gary. I know he didn't mean it, but . . . Anyway, now he's on the phone in the study ranting at Malcolm about grandparents' rights. If Malcolm can't stop Gary, we might never see those kids again."

Rusty felt no more than a modicum of concern for Blanchard's safety. Of course Ryder had gone straight to his lawyer. "If your dad tries to bulldoze his way into that situation, he can only cause a helluva lot of hard feelings. I haven't heard a word about Gary being a bad father. In fact, I've heard he's pretty good with those kids."

"Oh, Rusty, Daddy still remembers when Carla and Gary got a divorce and were squabbling over custody of the girls. Gary would come to Texas and take them to his parents' place in California, then Carla would go get them and bring them back. Then Gary would come back here and leave with them again. Daddy worried so much about them being pulled back and forth."

"Maybe your dad should call off his dogs and try a little diplomacy."

"I think it's too late for that. They haven't even brought my sister home yet and Gary's already made funeral arrangements. He didn't say a word to Daddy or to me. He just did it. He's planned her service to be at the Methodist church tomorrow. Our mother was Catholic. And there isn't enough time for everyone to come. Daddy's so upset. I don't know what to do."

Rusty thought about the dichotomy in Elena's makeup. She could calmly and competently deal with a dozen car accident victims suffering from severe trauma and even death and never falter, but she had never known how to deal with her own family. His mind spun back to their youth, when he had played this scene with her many times. She had always wanted her family members to get along with each other and live in harmony with their neighbors. She had never been able to accept that the Ryders weren't a harmonious bunch. With the exception of Elena, every damn one of them was self-centered, with his own axe to grind.

As to the location of Carla's funeral, he couldn't see what difference it made where somebody's funeral was held. But knowing such an issue was important to other people, he suppressed his attitude. "Elena, darlin', it sounds like there's not much you can do. It sounds like it's out of your hands unless you've got some influence over your dad."

"Everyone thinks I can talk Daddy into things and I used to be able to sometimes, but not so much lately. He's getting old, Rusty. It's terrible for all of us losing Carla, but it's devastating for him. If he loses his grandchildren, too, I don't know how he'll stand it. You know how he is. He wants to grab on to everything and hang on to it. He's like a man possessed. I hardly recognize him anymore. He's got high blood pressure now and I know it must be soaring. You're the sheriff. Can't *you* do something?"

If Rusty knew anything about Randall Ryder, it was that he preferred the tsunami approach to opposition over any other. Rusty had had a personal dose of the tactic. With all that had gone on the past three days, he didn't doubt that the man's blood pressure was up. His own blood pressure was probably elevated. "When are they leaving?"

"Sunday. Out of curiosity, I checked flight schedules. I think they'll be flying out around two o'clock."

Why the hurry? Rusty wondered, but he said, "None of this is a law enforcement matter, Elena. And I don't think Randall's interested in my personal opinion or my recommendation. Look, just because Gary sends the kids to California for a while doesn't mean they're gone forever. I'm sure they'll be back."

"I don't think so. Gary's talking about going back to Fresno himself."

That statement brought Rusty's posture straight. He hadn't told Blanchard not to leave town, but obviously it was time he did. "When did he say he'd be leaving?"

"A few days. He's never liked Texas much and all of his family is in California. That's why I think he won't be coming back."

The day's events all rushed through Rusty's head. Nothing had followed a logical path to a reasonable conclusion. Why the hell was Blanchard in such a rush to get himself and his kids out of town? It made no sense.

"Were you at the autopsy this morning?" she was saying.

"What? Oh, yeah. Yeah, I was."

He didn't want to get into a conversation with her about the autopsy sitting in his car on the side of the road. In fact, as much as he would like to continue talking to her, what he wanted more at the moment was to have Gary Blanchard's ass hauled in for further questioning. "Look, I'll have a talk with Gary and see if I can find out what's going on. I'll call you later."

They no sooner had disconnected than the phone vibrated. Cheryl, telling him the funeral home had called with details about Carla Blanchard's service. It would take place at the Methodist church at eleven tomorrow morning, followed by burial at the Ryder family cemetery on the Rocking R ranch and the traditional family dinner in the church community room. She ended by saying she was going home.

So Blanchard would get through the funeral tomorrow, put his parents and his kids on an airplane Sunday afternoon, then spend a day or two, perhaps three at the most, doing something with or about the horses and that horse ranch. Then he would be on his way to California, possibly forever. There was no time to waste.

He radioed the dispatcher and told her to have Gary Blanchard picked up and brought to the sheriff's office for an interview ASAP.

He had just hooked the phone back to his belt

when his chief deputy called. "A protective order showed up in here," he said. "Gary Blanchard's lawyer filed it against Randall Ryder. The lawyer said Ryder threatened to kill his client. What do you want to do about it?"

Rusty huffed and shook his head. The sheriff's department was by no means overstaffed, but it did have a civil deputy who mostly just served warrants. "Get Jerry to deliver it. There's no choice."

While he had Matt on the phone, he put him in charge of the funeral escort to the cemetery. "Ryder wanted to call in DPS," he said, "but I told him we'd handle it. I'm not gonna let him override and go around this office, even for a funeral escort. So keep that in mind."

He pulled back onto the highway and headed for the courthouse annex, thinking about how he would conduct the coming interview.

The sheriff's department didn't have an interview room with video and sound. As cramped and crowded as the facility had become, the employees were lucky to have a bathroom. If Rusty got involved in a suspect's interrogation, he did it in his office and for a good reason. Intimidation. He might not have much wall space or any fancy decor, but he had an impressive stack of diplomas, certificates and awards from twelve years in law enforcement. They hung on the wall above the line of gray filing cabinets behind his desk. If a suspect was sitting in the chair facing him, he also had a plain view of Rusty's accomplishments. It wasn't an ego wall; it was a bluff, intended to make a dirtbag think he might not be so smart after all.

He kept a small recorder in his desk drawer. While he waited for Blanchard, he checked the batteries and found them live. He set it on his desk, hidden from view.

He heard a commotion in the reception room and walked out of his office. Blanchard had come in, escorted by Marshall Tucker. His anger and edginess filled the room.

"I read him his rights," Marshall said, "before we left his house."

Rusty invited Blanchard into his office. He offered him a chair and asked him if he would like something to drink, but Blanchard refused. He sank to the chair and braced his palms on his thighs. "You trashed my barn today," he said sharply and slapped the receipt Rusty had left with Jacinta on the desktop.

"We executed a search warrant, Gary. We never intend to trash anything. But we did look in your barn."

Blanchard's brow furrowed into a deep frown. "I can't believe you sent some damn goon out to my house to haul me in here like a common criminal. And in front of my parents and my kids. What *are* you looking for? Maybe if you had asked—"

"I did ask. Twice. And I told you I'd get a search warrant. Now, I don't know what kind of game you thought you were playing, but you lost."

Blanchard's elbow came to rest on one chair arm. "Why am I here?"

"Are you waiving your right to have an attorney present?"

"I don't need an attorney. I haven't done anything."

Rusty yanked open his bottom drawer and lifted out a waiver of attorney form and shoved it across the desk at Blanchard. "Then sign that."

Blanchard scanned the document, then signed with a flourish and shoved it back across the desk. "Now. Why the fuck am I here?"

Rusty was only too happy to go immediately to the interview he had roughly mapped out in his mind. "I was present at your wife's autopsy this morning, Gary. We now know she was strangled by a ligature of some kind from behind. Murdered. It's no longer speculation on my part. It was confirmed by the Ector County medical examiner."

Blanchard's eyes told nothing, but Rusty saw his throat muscles work. "That really isn't news, is it? I mean, you already told me—"

"There's more."

Blanchard continued to glare, unblinking and waiting.

"She was struck a hard blow in the face at least once," Rusty said. "She was four months pregnant."

For long seconds, the only movement in Blanchard's body was his neck muscle. Finally he dropped his chin and shoved his fingers through his hair. Suddenly he was a deflated balloon. "Jesus fucking Christ," he whispered.

"Did you know she was pregnant?"

He rubbed his hand along his jaw and stared at the floor. "No."

Rusty tilted his head to make eye contact. "Was the baby yours, Gary?"

Blanchard lifted his chin, but hesitated. Finally he said, "I don't know."

The answer caught Rusty off guard. He had anticipated hearing him say no, which would have generated another set of questions.

"We didn't . . . uh . . . often," Blanchard said, "but sometimes . . ." His words trailed off. "I'd have to think back," he added.

Exasperated at being thrown off track, Rusty resisted the urge to let out a huge sigh. He had expected this visit to be a slam dunk, but he could see the news of the pregnancy had left Blanchard shaken. "It was possibly somebody else's?"

Blanchard ducked his chin again and looked at the floor. "I guess so."

As simple as the answer was, Rusty was still surprised to hear a husband calmly say he knew his wife slept with another man. He still remembered what a hammer blow similar news had been to him personally. "Any ideas?"

Blanchard shook his head.

Rusty leaned forward, his face closer to Blanchard's. "Gary. We've got to get to the bottom of this. My God, man, depending on some legal eagle's interpretation, this could be double homicide. You've already figured out that unless you can point me in another plausible direction, you're the logical suspect here. If you really haven't done anything, you have to help yourself. You have to help me. Tell me what you know about Carla's activities, particularly in the past week."

Blanchard looked up and shook his head. "I don't know a damn thing. I just know I didn't hurt her in any way." His voice broke and he blurted, "She's the mother of my kids, forgodsake."

The statement came out with such force and such a ring of sincerity, Rusty almost believed him for the second time. He paused and sat back, seeking a different tack. "Does the name Diego Esparza mean anything?"

"No. Should it?"

"You didn't have a groomer or an exerciser with that name? A barn cleaner or any kind of employee with that name?"

"I said we didn't."

Rusty believed him. No calls to Esparza appeared on Gary's phone record. "Can you think of any reason that name would appear on your wife's cell phone record?"

Blanchard slowly shook his head and Rusty could see in his eyes that he was as puzzled about the name as he, Rusty, was. This time Rusty made no effort to suppress his sigh. "Okay. Just for the record, let's go through this one more time."

Gary made another statement about the events of Wednesday morning and his activities. Rusty prompted him here and there with questions, covering every question he had already asked him, plus some new ones. The man's story didn't change. At least, this time, Rusty had all of it on tape. When he could think of nothing else, he stood. "I think we've covered everything for now. I appreciate your cooperation."

Blanchard looked up. "What choice did I have?"

"A man's always got choices, Gary. They may not be good ones, but they're there."

Now Gary rose, too. "Diego Esparza. Is that her boyfriend?"

"I don't know who he is." *Yet.*

Blanchard started for the door. "I'm outta here."

Before he slipped through the doorway, Rusty said, "I'm told you're planning on leaving town."

"My kids are going home to Fresno with my parents. I'm going out there myself in a few days."

"Don't," Rusty said, looking him in the eye. "If you do, I'll have no choice but to get a warrant for your arrest."

Chapter 17

After Blanchard left, Rusty did the clerical work related to the search warrant. He made copies for his files, but the original warrant, along with a copy of the receipt, had to be sent back to Judge Potter.

The office had cleared out. Except for the dispatcher a few doors away, he was alone. He sat at his desk staring out the window, watching the sinking sun and sorting all that he had learned today.

Who the hell is Diego Esparza? Considering the number of calls to and from on Carla's cell phone record, if he wasn't an employee, was he her lover?

While he contemplated, Alan came back in. "Boy, I just barely made it. Traffic was a sonofabitch. I thought we'd be looking at a month to get into that computer, but their geek says he'll have the password figured out Monday."

"Great. Do you know Diego Esparza?"

"Nope. Who is he?"

"You've never arrested him or run across him anywhere?"

"Doesn't ring a bell. Listen, I need to get home. My little brother's playing tonight."

Friday night. What would West Texas be without Friday night football? It overrode and precluded all else. "Go ahead. I'm quitting pretty soon myself."

After Alan left, Rusty decided to stop dithering and get an answer to his question. He picked up his hat and walked down to the cubicle where the dispatcher sat. "Is Art working tonight?"

"Yes, sir," she answered.

He handed her a note with the Fourth Street address on it. "Call him and tell him to meet me at this address."

He arrived at the Esparza mobile home before his deputy Art Rodriguez did. A new-model dark blue truck sat under the carport. It hadn't been there earlier when Rusty had talked to Mrs. Esparza. As he came to a stop behind it, Art drove up.

Not knowing what kind of individual they would be meeting, Rusty gestured for Art to hang back in case a problem erupted. Then he climbed the wooden steps and crossed the deck to the front door.

A big Hispanic man filled the doorway before Rusty even knocked. He was taller than most Mexicans Rusty knew and as dark-skinned as his mother. His hair was short, clean and a glossy blue-black color. Biceps bulged against the short sleeves of a red T-shirt. He was in good physical shape, like most roughnecks who did the heavy work required of drilling crews. Rusty knew instinctively that this was at least one of Carla Ryder's boyfriends. He had the clean good looks and the overall macho appearance that had attracted Carla for as long as Rusty had known her.

"Habla Inglés?" Rusty said, standing just inside the screen door.

"Sí."

"Can we come in?"

The man glanced to his right, then back at Rusty. "I come out."

Rusty suspected Esparza didn't want to upset his mother any further by having the law enter their home again. The two of them walked across the porch and down the wooden steps into the yard.

Esparza stood with his hands on his belt, obviously nervous. Rusty introduced himself, then Art. "Can I ask where you were Tuesday evening, Mr. Esparza?"

"I work," Esparza said to Art. "Ward County. Able Brothers Drilling."

Rusty knew of the company. He removed his notebook from his shirt pocket and wrote the name. "Where down there are you working?"

"By Pecos."

Pecos was no short trip from Salvation. Definitely not a commute. "Do you stay somewhere down there?"

The Mexican man's eyes squinted and he looked puzzled.

Art stepped in and spoke to him in Spanish.

Esparza tilted his head back. "Ah, *sí.* Motel Six."

"Were you at the motel Tuesday night?"

"Sí. Sí."

"Is there someone who can say you were there? Someone who saw you?"

The Mexican man looked into Rusty's eyes and opened his palms. Rusty couldn't tell if he meant he didn't know or if he didn't understand the question. Rusty turned to Art and the deputy asked the same question in Spanish.

Esparza gave Art a long explanation, out of which Rusty picked up "boss," "friend" and "manager."

Art turned back to Rusty. "He says he drank beer with his boss and two other friends Tuesday night and the motel manager wakes him up every morning."

Rusty listened and nodded, but he didn't take his eyes off Esparza. "But you live here?" He pointed to the mobile home.

"I stay a week. Then come home." Esparza held up five fingers.

Rusty accepted his answer. With the wide area that oil well drilling crews covered, they often stayed near a well site rather than make a long drive to and from home every day. Roughnecks made enough money to afford an inexpensive home away from home.

"Are you acquainted with Carla Blanchard?"

Wariness came into the man's dark brown eyes. He glanced at Art again, then his head nodded once.

"How long?"

"I don' know. Five, six month."

It dawned on Rusty that within that time frame, this man could be the father of Carla's child. "Did you work for her?"

Esparza shook his head. "No."

"How is it that you know her?"

Esparza glanced at Art. "She stop on the road." He followed with another long explanation in Spanish.

Art turned to Rusty. "He says she was parked on the side of I-20 down by Monahan's, with a flat tire on her trailer. The trailer had several horses in it. He stopped and helped her fix the flat. When he found out she could speak Spanish, they became friends."

"Have you ever been to her home?" Rusty asked.

Esparza stepped back and Rusty had the impression he might bolt. He closed the distance between them. "I'm asking you, Mr. Esparza, if you've ever been to Mrs. Blanchard's house?"

Art repeated the question in Spanish.

"Sometime," Esparza said. This time he directed his answer to Rusty. "Short visit." Then he turned back to Art with a long Spanish diatribe that included hand gestures.

"What'd he say?" Rusty asked Art.

"He says he's gone there a few times, but he

never stayed long and he never went into the house. Just the barn."

Rusty's thoughts shot to the locked room in the barn. "Ask him where he went in the barn."

Art complied and again Esparza gave a long answer in Spanish. Art turned to Rusty. "He says he always went upstairs."

Shit, Rusty thought. Not getting into the barn's locked room was impeding progress. "When was the last time you were there?"

Esparza shook his head again. "Month maybe."

"What was the reason for your visit a month ago?"

If Rusty had ever seen a look he could define as "sinking," he saw it now on Diego Esparza's face. But he heard no words from his mouth.

"Was Mrs. Blanchard your girlfriend, Mr. Esparza?"

"Why you ask me question?"

"Just give me an answer."

His dark eyes darted to Art, then swung back to Rusty. *"Sí,"* he said softly.

"Did you have an intimate relationship?"

Esparza cocked his head and looked at Art and Rusty realized he hadn't understood the words. Art asked the question again in Spanish.

Esparza hesitated before answering. Then he gave another long answer in Spanish with even more hand gestures. When he finished, he stuffed his hands into his jeans pockets. Art spoke to him again in Spanish. Whatever he said had a calming effect, because Esparza seemed to relax. "Okay, *amigo?*" Art said to him.

"Sí."

Art turned to Rusty. "He says they had sex in the barn."

"But I no see her no more," Esparza volunteered. "She mad."

"She's mad at *you?*" Rusty asked.

"*Sí.* She tell me no come back."

"Have you talked to her on the phone?"

"She call me." He made a telephone gesture at his ear. "She tell me come back. She *loca* in the head." He tapped his temple with his finger. "She say no come back. Then she say come back."

Crazy. Most men thought women were crazy at some point or other. "And did you go back?"

"I say no. She too rich. She have the rich man."

Puzzled anew, Rusty asked, "What rich man would that be?"

"Don' know. He big." Esparza made a gesture with both arms to indicate a tall, wide person. Esparza himself was a big man, as big as Rusty. The only Salvation rich man Rusty could think of who was bigger than himself or Esparza was the banker, Hunt Kelso.

"Did Mrs. Blanchard tell you she was pregnant?"

Esparza's eyes widened. He gave another head shake.

"Would you be the father of the baby?"

The Mexican man glanced at Art. "No. I don' know. I mean, we . . ." He shrugged.

"Are you aware that she's passed away?"

Now the expression on Esparza's face was one of pure fear. "No," he whispered. "Oooh, nooo."

"Would you know anything about that?"

The man might not fully understand English, but he knew he was possibly being accused of something. His head shook vigorously.

"We believe someone killed her. Can you tell us anything that would help us figure out who did that?"

Art repeated the question. Esparza's head shook fiercely again.

Rusty was losing patience. Sometimes the cumbersome attempt to communicate in a foreign language was overwhelming. He suspected Esparza's alibi would check out. He also believed the man might not have anything else of importance to offer in *any* language.

"Can you give me the exact location where you're working?"

A puzzled look came onto Esparza's expression and Rusty could tell he truly didn't understand. Frustrated, Rusty removed a card from his shirt pocket and handed it over. He could find out the drilling site's location from the company. "If you think of something you'd like to tell me, call this number." He pointed out the sheriff's office phone number on the card.

Esparza took the card and stared down at it while Art repeated the information in Spanish.

Rusty wondered if the minute he left Esparza might hightail it to Mexico. Then again, the man did own the mobile home and his mother seemed well set in it. "I appreciate your cooperation, Mr. Esparza. I hope you'll call me if you think of something you'd like to tell me."

He offered his hand and Esparza shook it. Art said a good-bye in Spanish. Rusty and he walked away together. "He respects the law," Art said. "I think he's telling the truth."

"I think he is, too," Rusty replied. "And that doesn't help us one damn bit."

Chapter 18

As Rusty turned the key in the Ford's ignition, he wondered if Esparza was the man Elena had meant when she said her sister might be seeing someone. Or had she been talking about the big rich guy? If Elena wasn't able to tell him, maybe Blanca knew the answer.

He arrived back at the sheriff's office to find the TV crews in the parking lot. In seconds they were out of the vans and taking pictures and peppering him with questions. They had obtained the cause of death from the autopsy. He still knew nothing to tell them. He gave them the same answers he had given them before.

Before leaving for home, he shuffled through the notes Cheryl had written to him. A cursory search of the deed records on the Blanchards' ranch revealed that the mineral rights were owned by Randall Ryder. That didn't strike Rusty as unusual since Ryder had been the owner of the property before Carla and Gary.

The last note said that Denise had called and said she left a chocolate pie for him to pick up at Mansell's Café. Nobody made chocolate pie like his sister and his stomach reminded him he hadn't eaten since this morning.

His chief deputy, Matt Mercer, was at his desk and Rusty's thoughts switched to the funeral tomorrow. "You got everything organized for tomorrow?" he asked Matt.

"Yeah. I've got almost everybody coming in."

"It's a simple thing, but we don't want to fuck this up. Don't forget, Ryder doesn't want anybody unauthorized past his front gate."

"We don't have to worry about it. DPS is gonna watch his gate. All our boys are doing is minding the traffic on the way out there."

State cops. So Randall Ryder had called his bigshot buddies in Austin after all. Rusty wondered what else he had requested of them. "Was that your idea?"

"I didn't call 'em, if that's what you mean. The word came up from Austin."

"What a surprise," Rusty muttered. "Just don't forget, Matt, the Sanderson County Sheriff's Department is in charge."

"I got it."

With that, Rusty started home. He was hungry, but doing anything in the kitchen was more than he wanted to deal with. He stopped off at Mansell's to pick up the pie and ate supper while he was there—chicken-fried steak, mashed potatoes and gravy and Maybelle Mansell's outstanding homemade yeast rolls.

As he paid his bill, the waitress came from the kitchen carrying a big paper bag. "Denise said to tell you she would have taken this to the office, but she wanted it to be kept in the refrigerator. And she was afraid those chowhounds that work in your office would eat it all."

Rusty laughed and tapped his temple with his finger. "Smart woman, my sister."

He was still smiling when he left the café with his whole chocolate pie. At home, he poured a big glass of milk and cut a slice. Then he sat down to watch the news.

Before the broadcast ended, the phone in the kitchen warbled. Rusty recognized the number as Josh Logan's, his friend from high school he sometimes partnered with in team roping.

"Hey, Rust, you roping out at your folks' on Sunday?"

Rusty thought about the investigation and the budget draft in his desk drawer. "I don't think so, Josh. I've—"

"Aw, no, man. This is the first weekend I've had a chance to be there all summer. You sure you can't make it? I want you to see my new mount. He's a beauty."

"Where'd you get a new horse?"

"Bought him in Fort Worth. Highfalutin bloodlines out the ass. Too bad the sumbitch is a gelding. But that's the way my luck runs. C'mon. Bring Banjo and let's rope."

Though they lived in the same town, Rusty didn't see much of Josh. As a range grass specialist for a major chemical and fertilizer company, he traveled four states. Josh was a cowboy through and through and had even spent some time working as a ranch hand before he finally finished college. Rusty really would like to see the new horse. He remembered Denise saying his sister Sam and her family would be at the Sunday roping, too and wouldn't return to Salvation 'til Christmas. What could he accomplish on a Sunday anyway? He sighed. "Well . . . I guess I could make it. Okay. Guess I'll see you there."

He had no sooner hung up before his sister called. "Did you pick up the pie?"

"Got it. Thanks. I already ate two pieces."

"Listen, about Sunday—"

"Okay, okay," he told her before she could go further. "I'm neglecting my job, but I'm planning to be there. Did you put Josh up to calling me?"

She giggled. "He came in the drugstore, said he hadn't talked to you in four months. The family hasn't heard much from you, either. You should be flattered, hotshot, that everyone wants to see you."

"I'll bet," Rusty said. What they really wanted was to pick his brain. "Listen, you call up Marilee and tell her not to be dragging any extra women along. It's embarrassing."

"I'll tell her, but she doesn't do what I say. By the way, Rusty, I thought you'd like to know. A customer in the drugstore this afternoon told me they passed Blanchard's place and saw a big United Farms real estate sign on it."

"Whoa!"

"Can Gary do that?"

That, plus a dozen other questions raced through Rusty's mind. "I guess he can."

"It doesn't seem right. I mean, that place was a gift from Carla's dad. It's not like it was a set of silverware or something. It's got to be worth a fortune. Do you think Randall knows?"

Rusty wondered the same thing. "Oh, I'm sure if somebody hasn't told him by now, they soon will."

After he hung up, though it was late to call Cheryl, he knew she wouldn't be offended. "Did you know Gary Blanchard has put the horse ranch up for sale?" he asked her.

"Really?"

"I just got the report from the gazette."

"Denise?"

"Who else? Listen, as long as I've got you on the phone, did you learn anything from the computer about Diego Esparza?"

"Nah. Nothing negative. Juan Diego Esparza. I ran that name through everything I could think of. I asked around about him, too. He's a pretty solid citizen, Rusty. He's from Mexico, but he and his mother have been around here for years. His mother worked in the elementary school cafeteria. They aren't citizens, but they're both legal. He even pays income taxes. Is this about the cell phone record?"

"Did you call his employer? I need to make sure if he was working or playing or what Tuesday night."

"That's the one thing I didn't get to. I didn't find out where he works yet."

"He's a roughneck. Able Drilling. I think they're out of Midland."

"I'll be damned. That's Ryder Oil's subcontractor. My cousin works for them."

Rusty huffed a breath. Living in West Texas was like living in a big spiderweb.

He hung up thinking about the "big rich man." He called Elena's cell phone, but she didn't answer. He left a message for her to return his call, but he didn't really expect to hear from her.

Chapter 19

On Saturday morning, Rusty left the sheriff's office in Matt's charge and the murder investigation in Alan Muncy's hands. He dressed in a pair of black dress slacks and a gray suede blazer. He put on a tie and attended Carla Ryder Blanchard's funeral as a family friend.

With his own family being dyed-in-the-wool Southern Baptists, he had never been in the First Methodist Church, the second-largest church congregation in Salvation. The building was an elegant tan brick with a tall steeple and cathedral-style stained-glass windows.

Most of the Joplin family would attend the funeral, Rusty knew, but he went alone and sat alone, taking a seat in the middle pew a few rows behind the section designated for family. As soft organ music played, he looked over the blond maple furnishings, the soft blue carpeting and a stained-glass depiction of the Crucifixion behind the pulpit brightened by the morning sun. The auditorium had the dated but comfortable feeling of being well used. The church had been built before Rusty was born, at the peak of the West Texas oil boom. In those days, the town of Salvation, and no doubt the Methodist congregation, had been larger and much more prosperous.

A multitude of floral tributes filled the air with fragrance and Carla's coffin was covered by a virtual blanket of deep red roses. Rusty heard snippets of whispered conversations speculating about how much they had cost. Some things in Salvation never changed.

Every one of the roughly five hundred seats was taken. Rusty saw that many of the attendees were people he didn't know. People in Western garb, obviously from the performance horse community; people in subdued business suits and ties, obviously out-of-town business associates of Randall Ryder's. Then there were the locals.

In the pew on the left, he saw none other than Josh Logan and he remembered that Josh and Carla had dated for a time in high school. Back then, they had a common interest in rodeo.

The service began with a solo sung by a friend of Rusty's mother's, followed by the eulogy. As the preacher's words droned on, Rusty watched each of the Ryder family members. Randall Ryder sat stoic as granite. Hunt Kelso sat directly behind him and a couple of times he reached forward and squeezed Ryder's shoulder. Elena sat close beside her father, her arm against his, her long hair curling down her back. She wept quietly, her head tilting occasionally and touching her dad's shoulder.

Her emotion touched Rusty's heart and for the first time since seeing Carla's corpse lying on the gurney outside her arena Wednesday morning, he, too, felt grief. In reality, this morning was the first time he had given much thought to the deceased as a person with whom he was acquainted rather than as a victim. In youth, they had been friends. Better than many in Salvation, he knew Carla and her sisters. He knew how losing their mother and being raised by their father with his controlling personality had influenced the adults they had become. For all the Ryder wealth, the lives of the Ryder daughters had lacked much.

Gary Blanchard and people Rusty took to be his family from California sat a few feet apart from the Ryder family, a sight that only confirmed that he wasn't really part of Ryder's inner circle. Rusty studied him, searching for a nuance in expression or behavior that would show him to be a cold-blooded killer, but all that was evident was a mournful man, standing on the edge of an uncertain future.

The three kids clung to him. Every time Rusty had seen the Blanchard children, they had shown great dependence and affection for their father. Though Rusty knew Blanchard to be an unfaithful husband, he had come to believe those who said he was a good dad.

When the music began again, Blanca broke into wails of sorrow and Bailey held her as she staggered from the church. A whispery hum rippled through the crowd. Ryder remained eyes ahead and didn't so much as glance in his oldest daughter's direction as she sobbed all the way up the aisle between the pews and out the front door.

The service ended with a song and a call for prayer. Unlike many funerals that occurred in Salvation, here the coffin remained closed at the end of the service, eliminating the opportunity for the ghoulish to pass by and gawk.

All in all, Rusty thought, as he walked out of the church and into the sunshine and blue skies of a warm fall day, the funeral had been as good a farewell as could be had in Salvation. He was left with a heavy heart and a deep-seated anger. Carla Ryder might not have been a perfect human being, but she didn't deserve to die violently and be left in the center of an arena, covered with dirt and filth.

He paused on the church steps and looked out over the sea of cars and trucks parked around the building. Across the street and down the block, he spotted the TV station vans and revulsion stuck in his throat. He dug his sunglasses out of his shirt pocket and shoved them on. He had driven his own old truck to the service, so he ducked behind a knot of people and managed to get to it without the vultures seeing him.

Given that the state police were managing the gate to the Rocking R at Ryder's request, he didn't make the trip to the family cemetery. The way Ryder felt about him, there was a chance he would have been one of the ones turned away.

At home, he changed his clothing and ate lunch. The silence in his house only added to the depression that had crept in during the funeral service. He switched off his cell phone and made his way to the barn, his mind unable to shut out the murder investigation. His original hunch that Gary Blanchard was a murderer, while not dismissed completely, now held less credibility in his mind.

Then there was Esparza. Had he been nothing more than a toy for Carla? That scenario would be in keeping with the Carla Rusty knew. And if that were true, had Esparza been angry about his role? Had Carla meant something to him? Rusty couldn't tell from the short conversation he'd had with the man. Though logic said the Mexican was a suspect, Rusty still believed he probably had a provable alibi.

He wished again that the crime scene had not been destroyed before he arrived. There was virtually no forensic evidence to use, even if he succeeded in making an arrest. All he had been able to salvage was the lead rope that had been found around Carla's neck and the pathologist doubted it was the murder weapon. He didn't know what to expect from what they had confiscated in the barn apartment.

He saddled the dun he called Lucky and swung

into the saddle, wondering if he should throw in the towel and turn the whole thing over to the state cops. Let the Texas Rangers have a shot at it like Randall Ryder wanted, like most small-town sheriffs were compelled to do. Few towns the size of Salvation had the benefit of a cop with Rusty's experience on their payroll.

Was it arrogance that wouldn't allow him to let go of the case? He didn't want to think that about himself. The keepers of law and order had to make the right choices in standing up for the dead. He wanted to think he was a better man than to let ego interfere with a victim's right to justice.

As he called to his dogs, clucked to his horse and started toward the far corner of his acreage, he had a haunting feeling that possibly his whole future in law enforcement rode on this one investigation. He would be affected forever if he gave in or gave up.

"Forget the Rangers," he mumbled to the air. He had to handle this one himself. Carla Ryder's killer had to be found by his office. Not only did he need that validation for himself, the community needed to know its sheriff was that competent. All he had to do was fall back, regroup and figure it out.

He took his time and made a long ride. He thought about the days of his youth when he and Elena rode horseback together. He thought about her gentleness and her basic goodness. She was a better person than anyone he knew. Since Wednesday morning, she had never been far from his thoughts no matter what he had been doing.

After his ride, he unsaddled, fed his animals, then worked at cleaning his barn until he was physically spent. The dogs had abandoned him and returned to their favorite napping spot in the backyard, but the cat, Ferocious, stayed right with him.

When he could find nothing else to do in the barn, he went into the house and cleaned up. He was hungry, so he drove into town to Sonic and ordered the biggest burger meal on the menu.

He headed east out of town, munching on his burger as he drove. The highway was fairly free of traffic. It wasn't a controlled-access highway, so caliche side roads veered off in north and south directions. Before the oil market collapse, most of the roads went to oil well sites. Now, most of them went nowhere.

He came to one with which he was very familiar, but hadn't been down since his return to Salvation. A thousand memories suddenly assailed him, things he hadn't thought of in years until Elena mentioned it Wednesday night.

Something compelled him to make a right turn. He eased along the rugged surface that wasn't much more than a path grown over with weeds and wild grass. Eventually, he saw it—the old railroad bridge trestle. He drove off the road and came to a stop in the dry creek bed beneath the bridge and looked up at its belly a hundred feet above where he stood. From bank to bank, it was longer than a football field.

Made of wood and supported by massive struts and timbers, the trestle was a nineteenth-century relic. Rusty didn't know what year the train had ceased to travel over it, but in his youth the bridge had been in service and it had been a source of entertainment. He and his buddies, never knowing the train schedule, dared to walk or run across the bridge's open ties, stepping gingerly. Thinking about it now gave him a shiver. The open space was just the right width to trap a boot or a shoe that might not be extractable. If a train had come, their only choice would have been to leap off one side or the other. If they had somehow trapped a foot, the locomotive would have blindly mowed them down.

He and Elena had come here many times. They had parked behind the big boulder on the canyon floor and made love in the bed of his old Chevy truck. Now that he thought about it, he wondered how Carla would have known about that. Elena had said she had never told anyone. He had never told anyone, either, not even Josh Logan.

He drove back up to the canyon bank, his truck's engine and transmission growling and grinding up the steep grade. He parked beside the abutment at the bridge's entrance, got out and walked all the way out to the center of the span. There he sat down, letting his feet dangle over the edge. The sound of silence crackled in his ears. Overhead a hawk soared, floating on a thermal as he hunted his supper.

From here, a man could see for miles. The broad West Texas landscape had a harshness to it that Rusty loved. He came here to live at age ten, when his dad took the job as ranch manager for Goodland Investment Group's many thousand acres. But he had been born on a cattle ranch well north of Amarillo. What he remembered of life there was that winters had been hard and cold, summers hard and hot and live human beings few and far between. As a child, he had spent more time with animals than with people. The solitary life had seated itself in his soul and made him a man of few words.

A deep longing for the arid emptiness of the high plain and its endless vistas was part of what had drawn him back here. Though he had lived in north central Texas more than ten years, he never grew to like the hot, humid climate. He found contentment in wide-open spaces and sparse population. One of the unsettled conflicts within him was the logic that to have the kind of law enforcement career he had once thought he wanted and had educated himself to have, he needed to live in a metropolitan area where major crime occurred. But he hated city life.

As he savored the peace that surrounded him, he sensed a presence. He turned and saw a silhouette at the end of the bridge. He could tell it was a woman. She moved out onto the bridge a few feet before he realized it was Elena.

A surreal feeling came over him, like he had somehow known she would be here. Or vice versa. He got to his feet and moved to meet her. "What are you doing here?"

She looked up at him, her eyes soft. "I come here a lot, when I need to get away. I walk all the way across the bridge and back. Or sometimes, I stop in the middle and look out and things sort of settle in my mind. The sky's so big and the canyon's so deep. Seeing it changes the way you look at things."

"Yeah," he said, squinting against the setting sun. "It's the wide-open spaces all right."

"After today, I just needed to zone out for a few minutes. Imagine my surprise when I saw your pickup. Do you remember when we used to come here?"

He grasped her arm and gently moved them back toward the end of the bridge, stepping carefully. Her smaller shoes were more apt to slip between the ties. "Sure, I do. I took a drive and when I saw the road, I thought I'd just come take a look."

"We had fun here. I used to get so scared when you and Josh would go out to the middle. I had a vision of the train running you down."

He chuckled. "Josh and I didn't have good sense. We thought we were invincible."

"Remember when we used to find those little pools of water in the canyon floor down below and they'd be full of tadpoles? We used to come every day to watch them grow into frogs. I was just thinking about that the other day."

Her eyes lit up and her face became animated and he couldn't stop looking at her. She was beautiful, but she was dangerous. "Yep, I remember that, too. You always wanted to take them home and take care of them. Once you brought them some bread crumbs to eat."

She laughed and ducked her chin and rubbed her forehead. "I did do that, didn't I? But I can't recall if they ate them. Those were carefree days. . . . Since we've been having the drought, there haven't been any little pools of water. I wonder what happens to the tadpoles."

They had reached the end of the bridge and his truck. She looked up at him. "I can't get over running into you here," she said, "but I'm glad. I really needed a change of company."

He leaned his backside against the abutment and crossed his arms over his chest, a defensive move.

"Did you go to Carla's funeral?" she asked.

"Yeah. I sat behind you."

"It was nice. Even if it was in the Methodist church. You know, it didn't really matter. None of us are practicing Catholics."

"People get too strung out over stuff like that," Rusty said. He opened his arms to take in the whole world. "This right here is as good a church as any. Right here, you're a hell of a lot closer to the Being that made it all than you are in that brick building downtown."

Her mouth tipped into a smile. "That's what I always loved about you, Rusty. You're always able to put things in perspective and make them simple."

He smiled back. "What can I say? I'm a bottom-line kind of guy. I don't like unnecessary complications."

"Me, either. I just don't know what to do about them."

"Things getting settled down at your house now?"

She nodded. "It was a bizarre day. Blanca got drunk, so Bailey took her home. Daddy and Gary made up after the big fight they had yesterday. Gary's put the house up for sale and Daddy was upset. Hunt told him he should just shut up and buy it. So, Daddy's thinking about it, but he doesn't really want or need a horse ranch." She smiled. "But yeah, everything's okay."

He didn't want to even think about what *he* had done yesterday, much less talk about it. Being here with her in this place made his job and Salvation seem like a hundred miles away. And something odd was happening to him inside. "Wonder who owns this land now?"

"I've sort of kept up with it. I think some people from Dallas bought it. Some kind of investment group."

"Probably got a good deal. Land's cheap around here now."

Only a sliver of the sun was left showing in the west and twilight was rapidly descending. The soft gold-mauve light turned her skin to copper and she looked like an exotic island princess.

"I have to go," she said. "I need to get back to make sure Daddy doesn't drink his supper. He's been sober all day, but tomorrow's going to be another bad day. We're going to the airport to say good-bye to Carla's kids."

He straightened and she looked up at him. Her

lips were only inches away and he wanted to taste
their sweetness. He wanted to wrap his arms
around her and sink into a repeat performance of
Wednesday's scene in her daddy's study. But his
horse sense stepped in and reminded him who she
was and who he was. And that if he ever got that
close to her again, he might as well go home, take
out his .45 and put himself out of his misery. His
soul would be that lost.

"I'm glad I saw you," she said.

"Yeah. Me, too."

She backed away until she bumped into his truck.
Her SUV was parked on the other side of it, so
she turned and made her way around the truck's
bumper. He stayed where he was, watching as she
climbed in and drove away.

He looked out over the darkening horizon.
"Don't even think about it," he muttered to no
one.

Chapter 20

The next morning, early, Rusty saddled Banjo and Lucky, loaded them into his two-horse trailer, loaded up his dogs and headed for his parents' house on the other side of the county. He needed the R&R, he told himself. A stroll through the fantasy that everything was okay and that the world was not a gritty place every day all the time.

When he arrived at his mom and dad's place, he saw a group gathered around the corral where the black stallion was penned. Two of his cousins were there, along with a couple of his dad's friends. His pal Josh was there, too, looking on as the superhorse stood calmly and allowed himself to be admired.

"This horse makes the one I just spent three months' pay on look like a plug," Josh said as Rusty walked up to the corral.

"This horse makes *all* ordinary horses look like plugs," Rusty replied.

"What're you gonna do with him?"

The question was a good one. The horse's location was probably no longer a secret and Rusty was surprised Blanchard hadn't said one word about him. Indeed, what was to be done with such a valuable, magnificent animal if its owner left town? "Don't know yet."

Rusty's dad had steers penned for roping and a roping team was already at practice in the arena.

A Hispanic neighbor who raised sheep drove up with a trailer full of ewes for the small children to ride and everyone cheered. The sheep rides usually provided a lot of laughs and the kids had a ball. A kid was required to ride a sheep for four seconds. Rusty's mom usually had a prize for the winner, like a book of gift certificates to McDonald's or the Dairy Queen.

Rusty drew away from the corral fence and ambled to his horse trailer. As he began to unload his horses, Josh came over to help him. "I was watching your dad roping earlier. Age hasn't slowed him down a bit. He's hell on wheels."

Rusty grinned. "Yep. Taught me everything I know." He handed Lucky's reins to Josh and began to back Banjo out of the trailer.

"I've missed coming out here," Josh said. "This summer has been a bitch." He patted Lucky's neck. "This that horse you got from Orrin Dolby?"

"That's him."

"Pretty color. I like a dun horse."

"He's seven years old now. Just now getting to be a good horse. You been traveling a lot, huh?"

Blue eyes twinkling, Josh looked at Rusty and gave his devil-may-care laugh. "Sometimes I wake up and forget where I am. I think I was in Oklahoma all of last week."

"Where's that fancy new horse you bought in Fort Worth?"

"He's tied up over at the arena. He's green-broke, but I'm working with him when I can. He'll get better."

They walked side by side, leading Rusty's two horses toward the arena fence. "I was surprised to see you at Carla's funeral yesterday," Rusty said.

"Well, you know . . ." Josh looked at the ground and shook his head. "I tell ya, Rust, I can't believe some fucker choked her. Choking. That's bad, man. Real bad."

"Shit happens," Rusty said, not wanting to encourage a conversation about the investigation, even with a good friend.

"It hurt my heart," Josh said, placing a palm against his chest. "She used to mean a lot to me."

Rusty tucked back his chin. He and Josh had been good friends as teenagers, had played sports together, had even rodeoed together, but the guy had never said a word about a meaningful relationship with Carla. Rusty knew Josh had slept with her, but that wasn't the same as a relationship. "She did? I didn't know it was that way with you and her. I thought you just—"

"You thought I just screwed her 'cause I could? That's what everybody thought. But it wasn't like that. I meant a little to her, too, you know." They reached the arena and tied Banjo and Lucky to a hitching post. "But . . ." Josh lifted off his hat and reset it. "Her old man hated my guts and wouldn't even let me go to their house to see her."

He shook his head and Rusty could see strong—and unexpected—emotion in his pal.

"I tell ya, Rust, back then, the whole thing was just a taller mountain than I was ready to climb. I mean, I was a kid in high school. I didn't know what the hell to do. Then after that, I was a kid trying to go to college. If I had it to do over, I'd just tell her daddy to fuck off and I'd just kidnap her or something." Josh's sly look angled across at Rusty. "I thought it served him right when he shipped her off to California to get her away from me and then she married that dude he'd never even met."

"What do you mean? I didn't even know you were going out with her."

"Well, how could you? You quit coming back here. You had your own thing going in Fort Worth."

"Carla was no kid when she got married, Josh. She must have been twenty-five or so. Old enough to make up her own mind."

"I know. But that doesn't mean her daddy wasn't telling her what to do. I think you know where I'm coming from, buddy. Nearly the same damn thing happened to you."

Rusty snorted. Just as Josh hadn't discussed Carla with him back when they were younger, he hadn't discussed Elena with Josh.

"You know what?" Josh said. "All three of the Ryder girls were good-looking, smart women. If you gathered up all the men who've chased 'em and been run off by their daddy, you'd probably have a roomful of horny dudes. Looks like ol' Bailey Hardin was the only one that came out a winner."

Rusty snorted again.

"When Carla and that Blanchard prick were divorced, I ran into her in Ruidoso. We got us one of those mountain sha-lays and stayed in it a whole week. Didn't even come up for air. I thought that was it. We were gonna be together for good."

"What happened?"

"Aw, hell. I had a couple of customers in the Panhandle whose pastures were in real bad shape. The company wanted me over there, so I had to leave her in Ruidoso. But I told her I'd see her back here.

"It was nearly a month before I could get back. I talked to her a couple o' times on the phone, but by the time I was able to show up in Salvation, she had remarried that prick. I was so pissed off 'cause she did me thataway, I didn't even try to talk to her. Then she was pregnant, so I just forgot about it and moved on." He reset his hat again. "Well, that's not quite true. I moved on, but I didn't forget about it."

"She had a troubled history, Josh."

"But it wasn't all her fault. Ol' Randall never did let those girls think for themselves. I guess he still doesn't. I mean, look at Elena. She looks like a movie star, she's got more money than God, but she still lives at home with her daddy."

"She doesn't have the money. It's all in trust funds."

"Not anymore. Those girls got all their money when they turned thirty. Carla told me."

Rusty cocked his head. He hadn't heard that. "What difference does it make?"

"None, I guess. But you'd think they'd have a little independence. Even when I ran into Carla at the horse show up at Amarillo a few months ago, she was still depending on Hunt Kelso to take care of things for her."

Remembering his sister saying Carla took her liaisons out of town, Rusty suddenly gave Josh his undivided attention. "Exactly when was that, Josh?"

"Oh, I don't know. Let me think about it. Must've been around the end of April or the first of May. Since Ruidoso, I hadn't seen her anywhere where I had a chance to talk to her. She was by herself in Amarillo. We got together for a couple o' drinks."

Rusty stared at him. Was it possible Carla and Josh got together for more than drinks and Carla ended up pregnant? *Nah,* Rusty told himself. The situation was getting to him; he was starting to imagine things.

"Hey, Logan," one of the men at the cow pen yelled. "You're up."

Josh straightened. "Tell ya what, Rust. You catch that cocksucker that choked her and lock me in a room with him. I'll take care o' the problem. Save the county some money." He clapped Rusty's shoulder. "See ya in the arena, pardner."

Rusty spent a couple of hours working with his thirteen-year-old nephew, Hayden Junior, on his roping technique, following that with a long talk about drugs and alcohol use and smoking. The fact that the boy thought Rusty had hung the moon, coupled with knowing Rusty had never used drugs nor smoked cigarettes and drank alcohol only occasionally, went a long way in influencing his nephew. He was glad to aid his sister and her husband with raising their only son to be a good kid. Young boys were under attack from every quarter these days. They needed all the help they could get.

Late in the afternoon, the three neighbors who usually played music, two guitarists and a fiddler, broke into "Rose of San Antone" and a couple began to dance on the portable plywood dance floor that always came out of the barn for these monthly events. Rusty's dad fell out of the roping and started the grill. T-bones were on the menu. One of the perks of Marvin Joplin's being employed by the Goodland Investment Group was all the free prime beef he could use.

To Rusty's dismay, and despite Rusty's earlier instructions, his youngest sister, Marilee, had brought an unmarried female relative of her husband's. Rusty had met the woman before and she was nice enough, even attractive, but he was in no frame of mind to try to be charming or to even pursue an acquaintance.

He had avoided contact with her all afternoon by being a participant in the roping, working with his nephew and helping with the handling of the cattle, but when they sat down to eat lunch, Marilee positioned her family and her friend at the same table with him, Hayden Junior and Josh. Fortunately, there were six other people at the table. Marilee had four small kids. Besides that, Josh was Mr. Personality. Rusty left it up to him to entertain the extra woman.

Seeing his nieces and nephews reminded him the Blanchard children were leaving for California today. He glanced at his watch and saw it was one fifteen. Elena had said their flight would leave at two o'clock. Rusty wondered if she was in Midland at the airport. Then he berated himself for thinking about something he wanted no part of.

The sun had turned into a great orange ball sinking into the unobstructed horizon when Rusty left his parents' place. He drove home slowly with his windows down, letting the cool evening air and the desert scents into his truck cab. The day had been good. What could be better than good food and a few beers with his family and friends and a play day with his horses?

He had been able to politely avoid his sister's friend and except for Josh, no one mentioned the murder investigation. He was sure his mother had lectured everyone before his arrival. She was like that. Being the only male among her four children, he had always been able to count on her to fend for him against the female majority.

He still wanted to casually ask a few questions of his pal Josh about him running into Carla up in Amarillo, but he hadn't wanted to do it at the roping. The remark Josh had made sounded like his and Carla's meeting could have occurred about the time Carla had gotten pregnant.

From the moment he had learned of the pregnancy, Rusty's gut instinct had told him it could be a factor in Carla's death. He had seen a case in the past where an unexpected and unwanted pregnancy had motivated a surprised father to commit murder. He intended to call Josh later from home.

Thinking again about Carla and the pregnancy reminded him he hadn't discussed the DNA of the fetus with the ME. A tissue sample had been obtained at the autopsy, though the Ector County forensics department didn't have the capability of doing DNA testing. The sample was sent away to the state lab in Austin.

As he drove, he organized other activities for tomorrow. He intended to conduct an interview with Blanca Hardin. If Carla's troubles had been disturbing enough for her to go to the Ryder mansion to seek out her father, the thing bothering her could be the very motive for her murder. If Blanca was Carla's confidante like Elena had said, she could have information that would shed light into some dark corners.

The county commissioners' meeting was still scheduled for Tuesday night, but the sheriff's office budget to be discussed and approved at the meeting was still in rough draft stage and untouched by the man in charge of the department, namely Sheriff Rusty Joplin. On his first official presentation since taking office, he didn't want to appear to be a slouch.

At home, he parked the horse trailer beside the corral and unloaded Banjo and Lucky. As soon as the horses were freed of their saddles, they took a good roll in the dirt. They, too, had had a good time today. Banjo liked competition.

After hosing the manure out of the trailer, Rusty backed it into its shed near the barn. With everything cleaned up and buttoned up, he made his way to the back door with a sackful of leftovers his mother had sent home with him. He had enough food to last him a week.

Entering the dark utility room through the back door, he heard the TV in his living room and stopped in his tracks. Adrenaline surged. His heart began to pound as a fight-or-flight instinct gripped him.

He set the sack of food on top of the washing machine. From the darkness of the windowless utility room, he looked through the doorway and scanned the kitchen, letting his sight adjust to the dimness. His eyes landed on a Pepsi can on the counter beside the sink. *Fuck!* No Pepsi can had been on his counter when he left home this morning.

He stood still as his mind ran down a list of possibilities. It wasn't uncommon for illegals fresh from crossing the Mexican border to break into homes looking for food and water or clothing. He thought of Diego Esparza. Rusty hadn't judged him to be a dangerous man, but anything was possible.

Rusty was unarmed. The .45 he carried while on duty was in his top dresser drawer. Other weapons he kept locked in a gun safe in the bedroom closet. A determined thief could get into it. Two shotguns, four high-caliber rifles and half a dozen pistols and ammo would be a treasure trove to a criminal. He eased through the kitchen toward the living room, where a low blue light from the TV screen cast a glow. On the shade that covered the room's only window, he saw an indistinct shadow. He dropped into a combat crouch just behind the doorjamb and saw . . .

Chapter 21

Elena.

Where the hell was her car?

She was sitting in his recliner, her legs tucked under her, absorbed by something playing on the TV screen.

Incredulous, Rusty stood up. "Hey!"

"Oh!" As her head jerked in his direction, her hand flew to her chest and she got to her feet. "Rusty, you scared me."

"What in the hell are you doing in my house?"

She came toward him. "I want to talk to you, Rusty."

He made no attempt to disguise his irritation. "How'd you get in here?"

"Th-there's a trick to opening the back door," she said quickly, her tone defensive. "The home health nurse and I used to have to break in sometimes when Mrs. Weaver couldn't make it to the door. It's really easy." Her shoulders lifted in a shrug and she added, "I parked behind the barn so no one would see my car. I didn't want to sit there in the dark. I—I didn't think you'd mind if I came in."

Her diffident response made him feel like a heel. He hadn't meant to go at her like an attack dog. Discovering that his house was so easily broken into was disturbing and the adrenaline coursing through him had him edgy. His anger waned, but only slightly.

He stepped around her, putting space between them as if they were strangers, and switched on the lamp that sat on the table beside his chair. He wanted a light on for self-defense as much as for any other reason. She might be one of the most harmless people he knew, but after her dad's study, it was himself he didn't trust.

With the room lit, he took one look at her and believed he would have been safer if he had left the light off. She had on a dress and high heels. The dress was soft and green, almost the color of her eyes. It showed her shape distinctly and she had a body built to bring out the basest urges in any man. A rush of heat moved through him. "You're all dressed up."

"I went with Daddy to the airport to say good-bye to Carla's children. It was awful." She ducked her chin and shook her head.

Rusty heard a catch in her voice. He planted his hands at his belt. "That's too bad. But maybe it'll work out."

"I don't know how." She looked up, her eyes shimmery with tears.

Her dark brown hair curled at her shoulders and down her back. He well remembered the times when he had buried his hands in that thick, silky mane and held her head for his kiss. An edge of lace showed in the V-neck of her dress. The latter took his attention to the pillowy slope of her breasts. God help him, his cock sprang to life. "Where does your dad think you are now?"

She shook her head and dabbed the corner of her eye with her fingertip. "A friend's. Or, I don't know. By now, he may not even know where *he* is, much less me."

"What does *that* mean?"

"He started drinking on the way back from the airport and he hadn't stopped by the time I left the house. I told him I had to get away for a while. I told him I was going to visit Manisha and Jiten."

"Who?"

"Manisha and Jiten Shankur. They work at the hospital. They're new here and they don't have any friends yet. I don't have many, either, so"—her palms opened and her mouth quirked—"there you go. We sort of gravitated to each other."

She leveled a look into his eyes. "Except you, Rusty. You've always been my friend. That's why I came to talk to you."

"You said that," he said, having trouble keeping his concentration when her voice was so soft and seductive. "We talked about Carla Wednesday. If you have something else to tell me, you should come to the office like every other citizen."

"No, not in your office. I . . . I didn't come to talk about my sister. I know that makes me sound callous . . . like I don't care about what happened to her, which isn't true, but . . ."

She brushed a sheaf of hair back from her face and hooked it behind her ear. Large gold hoops looped through her earlobes and glinted against her olive skin. "Carla's all I've thought about for days, day and night. My mind is weary from thinking and remembering. I want to talk about us, Rusty. I didn't want to wait until . . . I just didn't want to wait."

He could think of nothing he wanted to discuss less than *us* and she was too damn close again. "Us?" he said, his voice almost a croak.

A tear escaped the corner of one eye and trailed down her cheek. "We take so much for granted, Rusty. When Carla came to the house Tuesday evening, she had no idea she wouldn't see another sunset. None of us did. Even after seeing her in . . . in the arena . . ." On a deep sniff, she lowered her eyes. "Then in her coffin at the viewing Friday night . . . I still can't believe she's gone." More tears came and another deep sniff. "Then, watching her children fly away with people we really don't even know . . ." She shook her head and looked up at him. "It's all been like a nightmare that won't end. It's horrible."

To keep from reaching out and touching her, Rusty kept his hands against his belt. "God, Elena, I don't—"

"Let me finish, Rusty. I have to say this. I've been thinking about it for days." She turned and walked a few steps away as she spoke, as if she were talking to herself. "I've worked in emergency rooms for almost ten years. No one knows better than I how thin the thread of life is or how any one of us can leave this world when we least expect to. Seeing Carla go made me think of wasted time and how a single event can change our lives forever.

"My sister was thirty-five years old and I'm just two years younger. I don't want to waste my life living with my father and having empty relationships only with men he approves of. I want to share my life with someone I care about. I want someone who cares more about me than about Daddy's money. You're the only one who ever has, Rusty. That's why I want to talk about us. I don't—"

"Elena, there is no *us*." He closed his eyes and rubbed his brow with his fingers. As much as it hurt to say it, he had to be honest. "There can't be an *us*."

She turned back to face him. "At the very least, can't we be friends again, like we were a long time ago?" She ducked her chin and wiped her eyes with her fingertips again.

A hollow ache had begun to grow inside his chest. He didn't know what to do. Frustrated, he lifted his arms and let them drop. "I've never said I wasn't your friend. We just never see each other. I'm not exactly in your social circle."

She smiled weakly, but on her even a weak smile was stunning. "I don't have a social circle. You probably don't remember, but I never did."

He did remember. She'd had a girlfriend or two through the school years, but mostly, he truly had been her only real friend. It wasn't that the other kids in school hadn't liked her, he realized now. It was more complicated than that. Her beauty and wealth had made the girls standoffish toward her. The boys had been intimidated. Those attitudes made Elena feel insecure and reticent toward them.

Why she had gravitated to him, Rusty hadn't known, but even as a kid, he had been smart enough to figure out that her need for his company was all mixed up with the fact that he was male and her father had always been the strong figure in her life. Without a mother's influence, maybe that was what happened to young girls who had titans for fathers.

"I don't think we ought to even be discussing this now," he said. "I've got a lot to think about. Maybe later, after things settle—"

"I can't believe you've forgotten." More tears came.

God, he was a sucker for any woman in tears, but he was a total sap for this one. He had been accused many times of having no emotions, but it wasn't true. He was just good at keeping them hidden. Feeling himself weaken, he gave her a narrow-lidded look. "What does being friends again include? We can't go around together. What the hell would the citizens of Sanderson County think if they thought you and me were playing games?"

"You aren't allowed to have friends? It's really no one's business."

"Well, that's just not quite true, Elena. Fifty-five percent of the voters in this county elected me, and not because they think I'm some kind of genius at administration or at law enforcement. They voted for me because they believed I had no ties to your dad and Hunt Kelso. It's a trust they placed in me. No way can I ever betray that."

She had to know that, he thought in exasperation. She wasn't a stupid woman.

"Maybe they elected you because they thought you were an honest, qualified person, Rusty."

He had already stated the argument he believed to be the cold, hard truth. Even if he wanted to recapture old times with the lost romance of his youth, he couldn't. He shook his head. "It just won't work."

"Don't you see?" she said on a sob and came near him again. "Don't you see we were cheated?"

He reached into his back pocket for his handkerchief and handed it to her. "Don't cry, Elena. Please don't cry."

"Why not? We both should cry! When I think about what Daddy did, and your dad, too, I could just—" Her voice hitched, but she regained control. "We may have been young," she said more calmly, "but we loved each other. The adults in our lives treated us like our feelings didn't matter."

That much was true. He had felt it himself once. Indeed, he *had* cried over losing her and had come close to flunking a semester in college. He had excused the emotion by blaming it on youth and insecurity. Even so, he had never let any woman take him to that dark place within himself again and he didn't want to go there now. He had put her behind him and labeled their ill-fated youthful affair as another one of life's bumps in the road.

Hadn't he?

"I know it can't be like it used to be," she said, "but we can surely—"

"We can't go back." He shook his head again. "We just can't do it."

She came even closer and a familiar fragrance filled the air around him. Her mouth was only inches away, her lips parted in unconscious invitation. Sweet. Delicious. He wanted her. The desire came upon him like a craving that penetrated to the very marrow of his bones.

The moment hung between them in suspended silence. He heard his heartbeat in his ears. Accompanying that, warnings screamed inside his head, just as they had last Wednesday in her father's study. He was a damn fool, but he couldn't make himself back off. He bent toward her, cupped her jaw in his palm and placed his lips on hers.

She opened her mouth for his tongue and any semblance of will and resistance vanished. Heat charged through him. He hauled her against him and, like a man dying of thirst, drank of her willingness. She melted into his arms, all heat and softness. Finally he raised his head, his mouth hovering above hers. "Lord, Elena. It'd be better for both of us if you just get in your car and go home."

Her eyes locked on his. She slowly shook her head.

He hesitated, watching reality slink away like a scolded dog. "Dammit," he said under his breath.

Gripping her shoulders, he set her back and stared into her eyes. He would have had to be blind not to read the passion that smoldered there and seeing it fueled his own ardor. "Shit," he mumbled through clenched teeth. Then he grabbed her wrist. "C'mon."

Let's get this over with, he thought, as he pulled her up the hallway toward his bedroom. But in his gut he knew the idea of getting it over with was bogus. This was just the beginning. He was starting something that could only lead to a bad end. But the blood had drained from his brain and no good reason to stop himself came to him.

By the time they reached the bedroom and the edge of the bed, he was devouring her mouth like a starved animal and his fingers were searching the back of her dress for a zipper. She was kissing him back with the same hot impatience and her fingers were fumbling with his shirt buttons.

I didn't come here for this, Elena told herself. She had come to talk. But now, that idea seemed as distant as if it had never existed. Now, a desperation surged through her, a need she hadn't felt in years until Wednesday in her daddy's study. It had been so long since she had touched a man, had been touched by a man. And it had been fifteen years since she had felt the passionate embrace of this man.

"How do you get this off?" he said, tugging at the shoulder of her dress.

"It's two pieces." She stepped back, crossed her arms in front of herself and peeled the top over her head.

As she reached for her skirt's waistband, he leaned away from her and switched on the lamp beside the bed. "I want to see you," he said.

And she wanted him to see her, just as she wanted to see him. She stepped out of her shoes and slid her skirt past her hips. Then it was gone and she was standing there in a puddle of silk clothing with nothing on but green lace underwear and not much of it.

His gaze roved over her. "Lord God, Elena. You'll be the death of me."

She nearly swooned in the aura of his admiration. The fog of fifteen lonely years evaporated. She had never stopped loving him. She hadn't been celibate; she'd had lovers. But she had never stopped loving *him*. And after Wednesday, she knew she had never stopped wanting him. Tears sprang to her eyes. "No, I won't," she whispered. "I want to make you happy." She gave him her back and lifted her hair. "Undo me."

His trembling fingers unhooked her bra. As his arms came around her waist, she let the lacy garment slide down and drop to the floor.

His hands moved up and cupped her breasts. His warm mouth came to the tender spot where her neck joined her shoulder. "Lord," he whispered, "you feel so good."

His fingers found her nipples and she stood there, eyes closed, her back against his muscled chest, wallowing in the wanton pleasure of his caress, the stroke of his fingers. She could feel the pressure of his erection, hot and hard against her bottom.

His hand moved down, inside her panties, where she had grown wet and swollen. She parted her legs, giving his fingers access to her most private place. They easily penetrated and she moaned softly. He began to rub in long, slow strokes. "Feel good?" he whispered against her ear.

"You know it does."

She was so hot and they were too far along to stop. She hooked her thumbs into the waistband of her panties and pushed them down. They slipped to the floor without a sound and she stepped out of them. Then she turned to face him and pressed her nakedness against him. They kissed again, with her hand between them, caressing him. Finally, he broke away, bent down and turned back the covers.

She crawled between the cool sheets and lay there watching him rid himself of his boots, his watch, his clothing. Then, he, too, was naked and she couldn't take her eyes off his penis, standing like a marble column. He gripped it and stroked himself as he came to the bed. All she could think of was its thickness sliding into her. Heat and giddiness coursed through her. She looked up into his eyes and opened the covers.

Without a word, he stretched alongside her and pulled her body against his. They molded together like well-fitting gloves and kissed fiercely. She savored every part of his mouth, his agile tongue, his sweet saliva, his warm lips. His hands and knowing fingers, his open mouth, moved in a heated trail from one of her sensitive places to another until he had touched all of them. All the while he tormented her, he murmured sexy words of passion and pleasure, creating an upsurge of utter joy within her. Her own hands stroked his firm muscles, her fingers traced the efficient planes of his body. She caressed his smooth, hard bottom, loving how his powerful muscles flexed with his every movement.

She had to have more of him. "Come inside," she whispered, and urged him to move over her. Their knees bumped and their hands collided. He seemed to be as anxious as she, as if they had never done this before.

"I'm sorry," he mumbled. "It's been a while for me."

"Me, too," she murmured. She opened her thighs wider, reached between them and guided him and together they maneuvered into position. When she felt the tip of him just inside her, a sense of coming home overwhelmed her and she couldn't stop the tear that escaped a corner of her eye. "I've missed you so much," she breathed.

Rusty felt like a clumsy clod. He hadn't expected to be in this place with this woman ever again in his life, but here he was, hard as a rail spike and every other thought but planting his dick inside her hot flesh had left his brain. Braced on his elbows, he looked into her eyes, trying to calm himself and rein in the primal urge to ravage her. Hearing her whispery voice, seeing love in her eyes, emotion flooded through him. The feeling he'd had for her so many years ago rushed in and filled his heart and mind. "Are you sure about this, Elena?"

"Yes."

As if to prove it, she lifted her knees and he slid all the way to the hilt. Her deepest place felt like a furnace and he clenched his jaw and held himself still for a few seconds to keep from coming. A shudder passed over him. "Damn," he whispered.

"I know," she breathed and kissed him with slow sweetness.

On their own, his hips began to move, awkwardly at first, out of sync with her. A few seconds later, they found a familiar rhythm. Then they were kissing and fucking hard and fast and her breath was coming in quick pants and his chest was heaving like a bellows and all he wanted was to spend the rest of his time on earth right here in this bed inside this woman. He was so ready to go off, but he could tell she wasn't.

She must have sensed his urgency. "Notyet, notyet."

"Christ, I don't think—" He pulled out quickly, before he embarrassed himself again.

"Oh, no. Don't—"

"I have to," he mumbled against her neck. "I'll make it up to you." He ducked his head and sucked at her taut nipple while he caressed her other breast. She took his hand and slid it down the silky skin of her belly to her sex. Releasing her nipple he watched his finger disappear into her thick bush of black curls.

"Oh, *yes, Rusty.*"

Determined to take her to the heights of ecstasy as he had done long ago, he licked his way down her middle and dipped his tongue into her navel. Hanging over her, he circled the indentation with his tongue and nipped and licked her belly. "You're softer than a kitten," he said.

A low hum came from her throat. Her hands fisted in his hair and she pushed his head down, down until the wet pink petals of her open sex were a mere inch from his mouth. His nostrils flared as her scent filled them. His dick grew so hard his balls drew up into his stomach. He slid his hands under her bottom and lifted her and methodically, greedily, partook of every layer of tasty flesh.

She moaned and squirmed, trying to direct his mouth.

"No," he mumbled. "I want to be inside you when you come."

She squirmed more and made little noises, gripped fistfuls of his hair, but he teased her more, careful to avoid the tiny spot that would finish it. Only when she was begging and clawing and clutching at his ass did he crawl up her body again. He kissed her openmouthed. Her tongue thrust into his mouth almost violently and she bit his tongue and lips, licked her own taste from his mouth.

He plunged into her again. She cried out. Her deep muscles enveloped him with pure fire and she came hard, sobbing little "ohs" and squeezing his cock with strong contractions. He let her take her pleasure as long as he could stand it, but he was at the edge. He pumped once and just that fast, blinding pleasure crashed through him. It was physical and emotional and glorious beyond belief. A strained cry burst from his throat and he followed her into a great abyss where nothing else mattered save this one dazzling moment.

He lay sprawled on top of her for a long while before he found the strength to move. When he felt himself slip out of her, he untangled himself from her limbs and rolled to her side, bringing her to face him and enveloping her within the circle of his arms. They were sticky and wet and slick and the strong scent of sex ballooned from beneath the covers. Still heaving for breath, he buried his face against her neck. "Jesus Christ. That nearly killed me."

Elena was breathless. And awash in happiness. Last week, she wouldn't have believed she would ever make love with Rusty Joplin again. Now, here she was, in his arms, in his bed. No matter what happened, no matter how bad things got, she could stand them as long as she had him with her. "Just hold on to me," she said.

He moved his head back and she could see his face. He was smiling and his hand was pressed against her back. He still loved her. She just knew it. She understood his misgivings. Her father was a powerful man. But she was no longer a teenager. She could work it out. "That was wonderful," she said, still so weak her voice trembled. "You're wonderful."

"It's not me. It's you." His voice sounded shaky, too.

As they lay there sharing the pillow and breathing each other's breath, the furnace clicked on and a distant roar filled the silence. She snuggled closer, wanting her body to touch every inch of his warm skin. "You said we couldn't go back, but we have. Nothing's changed."

He smiled. "Darlin', you are so wrong. Nothing's like it used to be."

"We're just older, that's all."

He chuckled. "Don't I know it. I used to be able to go all night."

"Do you hear me complaining?"

They lay quietly until her strength returned. She turned in his arms onto her stomach and propped herself on her elbows. "Do you remember the first time we did it?"

He rolled to his back, his eyes closed. He had a big grin on his face. She felt his hand come to rest on her bottom. "Uh-huh."

They had been on a sleeping bag in the bed of his truck on a starlit night. She thought back about how he had been so careful of her modesty and concerned about hurting her. She laughed softly. "You were so worried."

"Hmm."

"I was never sorry, Rusty. Even after the way everything worked out."

He opened his eyes and gave her an unsmiling look. "Neither was I, Elena."

"Remember how I used to bring that book on sex when we had a date? How we used to try all that stuff in the book?"

Now, he laughed. "Well, we learned a lot."

She gave him a gentle elbow. "Yes, and some other woman got the benefit of all that sex education." That part still gave her a tiny pain. "Those times we used to sneak into my bedroom and cover up with the blankets, thinking no one could hear us? I've wondered a thousand times if Sofia knew what we were doing."

Sofia had been her Mexican "mother-of-the-moment."

"Me, too," he said. "I was scared shitless. I'm surprised I got it up."

"As I recall, you had no trouble." She leaned into him and kissed him.

"It was you. You turned me into an animal." The humor left his expression. His large palm cupped her jaw and drew her face to his. "You still do." Then he gave her a slow, lingering kiss.

"Hmmmm," she said when they parted. "You taste like sex." They readjusted their positions. She slid her thigh across his genitals and placed her head in the hollow of his shoulder. Again, they lay in silence for a long time, wrapped in each other's arms. She could feel his fingers playing with her hair. "What are you thinking?" she asked at last.

"Nothing much. Just . . . how good you feel. How soft. There hasn't been a lot of softness in my life in recent years. I almost forgot how good it feels." His hand came up and brushed her hair back and his beautiful blue eyes looked into hers. "Your hair's still pretty," he said.

"Can I ask you something?"

"Uh-oh. Is it one of those loaded questions?"

"It's just something I want to know."

"Hm. I reserve the right not to answer."

"Since you left Salvation, have you, uh . . . have you had a lot of women?"

"No."

"You were married."

"That's different."

She hesitated, considering what she was about to reveal. But she had to say it. "I cried for two months when I heard you got married."

He didn't respond for a few seconds. Finally, he said, "You shouldn't have done that."

"Would you tell me what happened with your wife? To your marriage?"

"Nothing much to tell. She was real ambitious. She liked lawyers better than cops."

"I shouldn't admit it, but I was glad when you got a divorce. I hoped you'd come back to Salvation. Then one day, Marilee had one of her kids into the ER. She told me you were dating someone. She said your family thought you might remarry."

"Marilee's been trying to marry me off ever since she got grown. I saw somebody for a while after the divorce. Must have been one of those rebound things they talk about."

"What happened to her?"

"Nothing much happened to her, either. It was a long time ago."

Rusty didn't like rehashing his rocky romantic history for anybody, but especially not for Elena. "What about you? Beautiful and rich? There must have been a herd of men in your life."

"I dated a couple of men. Nice men."

He knew without asking she had slept with them and he didn't like knowing it. "I'm surprised your dad didn't find you somebody suitable, like he did with Blanca and Bailey Hardin."

"He tried. But I must have inherited his hard-headed streak. None of his picks were worth keeping."

"You should have chosen one of them, Elena."

"Don't say that. I couldn't. Don't you see, Rusty? I've always known that somehow we'd be together again."

"Then I'm glad you had more faith than I did." He was hard again. He couldn't resist the pleasure and happiness with which she filled him. He took her hand beneath the covers and placed it and one thing led to another. Soon he was impossibly deep inside her again and this time, under control. He watched her face, her parted lips, her eyelids heavy with pleasure as he slowly moved in and out. To his great satisfaction, everything worked better and he lasted a long time.

Still later, she sat up, covering her breasts with the sheet. "What time is it?"

He reached for his watch from the nightstand. "Almost ten."

"Oh my gosh, I have to go. Daddy will have someone out looking for me."

Rusty frowned, trying to remember if he had ever heard a grown woman say that. "Guess we should get cleaned up, huh?"

She looked at him over her shoulder. "Are you going to shower with me?"

"Absolutely." He threw back the covers and got to his feet. "How long has it been since somebody washed your back?"

Chapter 22

Elena brought her Lexus to a stop in the garage. Her dad's two vehicles, the Lincoln limousine and a Ford pickup, were parked in their respective places, so he was home. She checked her clothing. Her dress was wrinkled from lying on the floor beside Rusty's bed. If asked, she would say it got wrinkled riding in the car. She pulled down the sun visor and checked her face and hair in the small lighted mirror.

Satisfied that her appearance looked as innocent as she could make it, she entered the house stealthily through the back door into the kitchen, telling herself she wasn't sneaking in.

Instantly she was surrounded with the aromas of food and piquant spices.

Benita was at the sink. She turned with a smile. *"Hola,"* she said, wiping her hands on her apron.

"Hi, Benita. Why are you here so late?"

The housekeeper continued to smile. "I clean." She gestured around the kitchen.

"Daddy's here?" Elena went to the refrigerator and opened it.

"Sí. In he office."

"Did he eat supper?"

"Oh, *sí.* I make the tamales." An even wider grin spread across her mouth. "He love."

At the Ryder home, the diet was almost entirely Mexican-style cooking. Most of the time, their

Mexican help didn't cook American food well. Elena, too, loved Benita's tamales. A pang went through her stomach. She hadn't eaten since lunch and at Rusty's house neither of them had thought about food. "Were any left?"

"*Sí. Muchos.*" The housekeeper held up ten fingers. She came to Elena's side and pulled a closed plastic container from the refrigerator shelf. "I warm."

"No, no. You go on home. It's after ten o'clock." Benita and her husband, Aden, lived in a separate small house within a short walk of the larger Ryder home. Aden worked as a janitor at the elementary school in town. Elena took the container from her hands. "I can heat them up."

Benita straightened and looked up. At barely five feet tall, she was half a foot shorter than Elena. "I go?"

"Yes. You go on home."

After the housekeeper departed, Elena prepared a plate of tamales and slid it into the microwave. While they warmed, she rummaged further in the refrigerator and found leftover salad. She took her filled plate to the glass-topped breakfast table and sat down. Except for the tinkle of trickling water coming from the summer porch, the house was quiet. It was always quiet. No music, no TV. She listened to music or watched TV only when she was in her suite and Daddy only occasionally watched TV news in the study.

Tonight the place seemed even more silent than usual. And it was cold. The only way to control the ancient air cooling system's temperature was to shut off the water. She went into the laundry room and found her old blue sweater hanging on a peg. She often wore a sweater around the house, even in the summer.

She returned to her meal and ate in silence, lost

in her memories. In her mind's eye, she could see Rusty crossing his bedroom naked as clearly as if she were still there. His body was perfect. Wide shoulders, narrow hips. Not an ounce of fat, muscles where muscles should be on a man. She felt her cheeks heat up and she grinned.

Rusty was the most attractive man she had ever met. Sun-bleached brown hair, wavy and perfect even when it was mussed. And it was all natural. No gels or sprays or coloring products for Rusty Joplin. He would growl if anyone even suggested it. And eyes the color of a clear sky after a spring rain. Eyes that saw everything and penetrated all the way to her soul.

She continued to smile as she ate, remembering making love with him. She still knew how to thrill him, even after all this time. And he certainly knew how to thrill her.

Where would she and Rusty go? Where *could* they go? Would they secretly sleep together from now on? Or would they come to terms with their feelings and give themselves something neither of their parents had been willing to let them have fifteen years ago—a chance to be happy together?

She finished her meal, realizing she still hadn't heard a sound from the study. She placed her dishes in the dishwasher and made her way to the thick double doors. Rapping lightly on the door, she pushed it open. "Daddy?"

She found him at his desk, turning the pages of the photo album that had been lying on the coffee table since Wednesday morning. He, too, was wearing a sweater. He looked up with a long face and rheumy eyes. "What is it, sweetheart?"

Her heart ached for him. Since she saw so much of him, perhaps only she knew the depth of his grief. She glanced at the squatty glass on the desk and the half inch of amber liquid in the bottom. A

Jack Daniel's bottle sat near it. No doubt he hadn't stopped drinking since he started on the way home from the airport.

"I just came to see how you are," she told him.

"I was just remembering," he said softly. He lifted the glass to his lips, threw back the contents, then poured another two inches of whiskey.

She winced. "Can't I help you to bed? If you get a good night's sleep, you'll feel better tomorrow."

His head slowly shook. "Not yet." In front of him on the desk sat a group portrait of Carla and her three children. It had been taken last year. He picked it up and studied it. "The children have landed in California by now."

She heard the slur in his speech. He had to have been drinking even more than she thought for his speech to be so affected. Daddy was a man who could hold his liquor. "Yes, I imagine they have."

"I want you to know something, Elena. I intend to fight Gary. I won't have my grandchildren growing up with criminal riffraff in Fresno, California. They deserve better than to have nothing when I have so much to give."

She sank to a leather chair in front of the desk. "But they won't have nothing, Daddy. Won't they have Carla's trust fund?"

"No. I've blocked the revenue source. Hunt tells me the fund is seriously depleted anyway. In the years Carla was married to that worthless sonofabitch, they managed to damn near squander a goddamn fortune." He slammed the album shut with a loud slap.

Elena jumped and blinked. She thought of the value of her own trust fund. She knew her sister and brother-in-law enjoyed life, but to have spent such a huge amount of money was incredible. "Really? How?"

"They collateralized large bank loans against the

trust fund's assets and never repaid them." Her father was having trouble pronouncing some of his words. He barely managed "collateralized."

"Thanks to Hunt's wise handling," he continued, "Gary's signature, as well as Carla's, is on the notes. Hunt has agreed to call them. There won't be a dime in cash left. Gary will have to relinquish his interest in the remaining assets to satisfy the debt. If he doesn't, the bank will seize them."

"But—but is that legal?"

"It can be done. It'll be a lot of trouble for Hunt, but it can be done." He took a gulp of the whiskey in the glass and coughed violently.

She half rose from her chair. "Daddy, are you—"

"I'm all right." He cleared his throat and wiped his mouth on the back of his hand. His voice became low and gravelly. "If any assets are left, and I have no idea if there will be, they'll be redish—redistributed to you and Blanca."

"Oh," Elena said, amazed. "But you're taking money away from Carla's children."

"No, daughter. The children will be secure. Here. With us. The sonofabitch won't have a penny left to fight me for my grandchildren. Malcolm is preparing the papers now."

Elena ducked her chin and stared at her hands, now clenched in her lap. "It doesn't seem right."

"Right? Look at me, Elena."

She looked up and saw his face thrust forward, his eyes so cold she almost shivered.

"What wasn't right," he said, leveling a glare at her, "was tricking our girl into marriage. Sandoval Security is thoroughly investigating Mr. Gary Blanchard. When I get their report, I'll know everything about him."

"But, Daddy—" His raised palm stopped her. She had meant to say she thought he had already had Gary investigated when Carla married him, but in the face of her father's determination and the amount of liquor he had consumed, a discussion was impossible. She dropped it.

"I've already talked to Garth Jackson down in Austin about his organization taking up the investigation of Carla's death," he said. "The Texas Rangers *will* build a case against her killer, and if that turns out to be her husband, God help him."

"But, Daddy, what about Rusty? If you give him a chance, he'll—"

"No. I will not have Rusty Joplin meddling in our family business, nor will I allow him near a member of my family ever again."

Elena wanted to scream in frustration. "But, Daddy, why?"

"Why? My God, Elena. Have you no shame? He took you like a common slut in the back of his truck."

Elena stared at her father, wide-eyed. In all the arguments they'd had years back, when he had ordered her to stop seeing Rusty, he had never made such a remark to her. "What do you mean? Rusty has never treated me like a common slut."

"And it wasn't just once, Elena. It was a dozen times. Maybe more."

She no longer remembered how many times she and Rusty, with no other place to go, had made love in the bed of his truck. But regardless, how could her father possibly have known even once where they spent time together?

Unless someone had seen them and told him. But even if that had happened, some individual wouldn't have seen them a dozen times.

Had Daddy hired someone to follow them? Had some sleazy spy been watching when she and Rusty had made love, when they thought they had privacy? Was that how Carla had known about the railroad bridge?

The breath almost left her lungs.

Her father was drunker than she had ever seen him. Otherwise he wouldn't be admitting he had done this. Rattled by the revelation, she searched for words. "I—I don't know what you're talking about."

He leaned forward, his eyes narrowed. "I should have taken care of that little bastard back then, you know that? You were underage. I should have had Jack Balderson haul his ass in and charge him with statutory rape. I had the proof. And I would have used it if Marvin Joplin hadn't agreed to intercede and stop his perverted son. Lucky for Rusty Joplin, his father had enough sense to see that I could destroy him."

"I—I was eighteen," she stammered, staring in stunned amazement.

But if he heard her, he showed no sign. And it wouldn't have made any difference anyway. He braced a hand on the chair arm and attempted to rise. His hand slipped and the chair tipped sideways with a thud. He crumpled to the floor, taking his glass, the bottle of Jack Daniel's and his desk blotter with him. A loud growl came from his throat.

Elena leaped to her feet and rounded the end of the desk. He lay in a heap on the floor, struggling to sit upright. Neither the whiskey bottle nor the glass had broken, but the contents of the glass had spilled on his clothing and on the carpet. "Daddy, are you okay?"

Apparently his head had hit the edge of the desk because a small cut on his forehead was oozing blood. She dropped to her knees and turned his face so she could examine his injury. "Awww, Daddy."

She reached for his wrist. While she took his pulse, he rolled to his side and tried again to sit, but couldn't gain traction.

She got to her feet, then stepped behind him and slid her arms beneath his armpits. He outweighed her by seventy or eighty pounds and was as limber as a rag doll, but she managed to get him upright and finally on his feet. Blood dripped from his head injury onto the carpet. He continued to make growling sounds.

"Daddy, let's go into the kitchen where I can get at some water. So I can take care of your cut."

She supported him as he staggered up the hallway, holding on to the wall and dripping blood onto the floor. In the kitchen, she seated him in a chair at the breakfast table. She found a clean dish towel and soaked it with cold water and cleaned the cut. "I don't think you're going to need stitches," she said, examining it again. "I've got some butterfly bandages in my bathroom. I'll be right back."

She hurried to the bathroom and returned with the bandages and antibiotic salve. Cleaning the wound again, she applied the salve and two of the butterfly strips. "Daddy, you have to go to bed. This is awful."

The energy seemed to have drained from him. He offered no protest as she helped him to his feet and walked him to his bedroom. There, she removed his boots, his sweater and his belt, then tucked him under the covers of his king-size bed. She did no more. She couldn't. Her well of affection and compassion for her only parent was strangely dry. His confession had felt like a stake driven through her heart.

She was in tears when she reached her bedroom, the happiness of earlier gone as surely as a yesterday. Remembering that she had left her cell phone on the breakfast table, she returned to the kitchen. She sank to a chair at the breakfast table, staring out into the dark night. She thought about calling Rusty and telling him what her father had just revealed, then thought better of it. What would his reaction be if he knew all that her father had been up to? She would have to tell him sooner or later. She decided not to risk their fledgling reconciliation tonight.

Instead, she dried her eyes and called Blanca. When Bailey answered and said her sister was in bed, Elena glanced at the clock. It was ten thirty. "Is she ill?"

"No," her brother-in-law answered. "She had a little too much wine with dinner and developed a headache."

In other words, she was passed out. Elena rolled her eyes. She tried not to think of her sister as an alcoholic, but the evidence seemed irrefutable.

Well, Bailey knew more about Ryder business than Blanca did anyway. "Um, Bailey, has Daddy said anything to you about Carla's trust fund?"

"It's good as gone, honey. Randall's already on top of it. And high time, too."

"So you know Daddy and Hunt are wiping it out?"

"It's already in the works. Just as soon as all the paperwork is done."

"Well, uh, was anyone going to tell *me* about it?"

"You mean Randall hasn't mentioned it to you?"

"He told me something about it tonight, but if he hadn't been dead drunk, I don't think he would have. I have to say, I'm a little upset because Blanca didn't see fit to tell me."

"Hm. Well, I guess she just assumed you would know, since you live there in Randall's house and all."

She passed over the little dig. She had heard Blanca's criticism of her continuing to live at the ranch many times. "What about Carla's house and land? It has to be worth several million dollars. I heard Gary's selling everything."

Bailey chuckled. "He only thinks he is. The real estate's unsalable, honey, for the price Gary's asking. When your dad purchased that property, before a two-by-four was ever raised on that house, he deeded one hundred percent of the mineral rights to Ryder Oil. In Sanderson County, in the middle of the Permian Basin, I assure you there'll be no takers at millions of dollars for a house and scrubland with no mineral rights. If Gary can sell it at all, he'll get no more than chump change."

Well, there you go, Elena thought. How could she, or anyone, have been so foolish as to think her father, with a reputation for ruthless dealing, would just give Carla and Gary an expensive house and land without somehow retaining control of what might happen to it?

"And the horses?"

"I don't know details about the horses, but I doubt if Randall's involved with them. I'm sure you know he doesn't like the horse business. I do know ownership of a couple of the mares is syndicated. I have no idea how many investors are involved, but I suspect they'll be surfacing soon."

"Does Blanca know where their papers are?"

"I think she told me they're in a safe-deposit box in a bank in Odessa. Carla and Gary did some banking down there. Why the questions, kiddo?"

"I'm just learning things I didn't know before. All of a sudden, I feel like I need to ask questions."

Bailey chuckled. "Well, honey, Randall's business has always been complicated. And he's made it even more so with a few of his personal little idiosyncrasies. But I'm glad to help you if I can. Blanca never concerns herself with it. She just shops."

"Well, I guess that's okay. She always looks nice. It's late. I guess I'll let you go."

Then a sudden memory came from years ago, of

a day in the kitchen, when Carla told her about the strawberry birthmark on Rusty's bottom. Bailey and Blanca had been married two or three years by then and Bailey was already moving up in Daddy's company. "Bailey, do you remember when Rusty Joplin and I dated?"

"Sure," he replied.

"Do you remember when Daddy made me go to Lubbock?"

A telling silence grew on the other end of the line. "Barely," he said after a few beats.

"Back then, did you ever hear Daddy talk about me and Rusty and private investigators or anything like that?"

Silence.

"I've never asked you for anything, Bailey, but I need to know the answer."

"Exactly what answer are you looking for, Elena?"

"I want to know if Daddy hired someone to spy on Rusty and me."

She heard a sigh. "Your dad wanted him out of your life, Elena. At the time, I was pretty young and I thought it was silly. Everyone I knew liked Rusty. But your dad's always had his own way of doing things."

"Do you know . . . ?" She fought back another spate of tears. "Do you know who it was?"

"Well, no. But my guess would be it was someone from the security company he was using at the time. I don't even know if it was Sandoval. I was still fairly new to Ryder Oil, so I wasn't in the loop, so to speak."

She knew a little of how the security companies Daddy hired functioned. Another horror came to her. Somewhere, in some hidden file, did pictures exist of her and Rusty naked together? For herself, she didn't care, but they could be used to attack

Rusty. She was surprised her father hadn't already done that. "I see. Whoever it was, do you think they, uh . . . took pictures?"

More silence.

She gritted her teeth to keep from breaking down. "Please, Bailey."

"I don't know. But isn't that standard procedure?"

She closed her eyes, finally pushing the waiting tears past her eyelids. "Bailey, did you see pictures of us?"

"God, no. I doubt if I could have made myself look at them even if there had been some, Elena. You're my wife's sister. Give me a little credit for decency."

Bailey was a decent man, Elena had to admit. "You know something, Bailey? I don't know how you stand to be in this family."

But she did know. Bailey Hardin's expensive education had been paid for by Randall Ryder. When Bailey and Blanca got married, Bailey's father had been employed by Leow's grocery store as a clerk and his mother had worked in Sanderson's only department store. These days, they were retired and living well. Bailey had always been and continued to be well paid.

"Randall's not a bad man, Elena," he said. "He just tries to have control of everything. You can't blame a man for wanting the best for his kids."

Hearing Bailey was like an echo of herself. She had made similar excuses for her father her whole life. "I know. Look, thank you for talking to me, Bailey. You've helped me a lot."

She left the breakfast room and returned to her father's office.

Four hours later, she had gone through every drawer in his desk. She had lived her entire life in this house. Much of the time she had been alone or under the supervision of a Mexican house-keeper, who wouldn't have challenged anything she wanted to do. Even so, she had never dared prowl in Daddy's personal things.

She had searched the drawers and the shelves in the credenza behind the desk. She found many interesting documents and mementos, but not what she sought. The credenza housed two locked draw-ers. She found the key in a small tin in the desk's middle drawer. And in the credenza's bottom locked drawer, she found a file labeled DAVID W. JOPLIN. She read some investigator's report naming times, dates and places she had been with Rusty. Some of the dates she didn't even remember.

After that, she had gone through the files in every credenza drawer, looking for pictures, but found none. Sixteen years ago, digital cameras weren't on the market. Most of the time she spent with Rusty had been at night. Perhaps no pictures had been shot. She gave up on searching for them. If they existed, without a doubt they would have miraculously found their way to the public when Rusty ran for sheriff. Her father had been that de-termined to see him defeated.

At three a.m., she stopped. She had told the hos-pital she would return to work today. Exhausted, she put the desk and the credenza back in order, only because she was an orderly person. She no longer cared if Daddy knew she had been snooping in his desk.

No parent should treat his child the way her fa-ther had treated her. When he sobered up, she would confront him. But now, as of this moment, she was taking charge of her life. Her father would have to find someone else to manipulate and control.

Chapter 23

Rusty awoke at five a.m. as usual. Even before full consciousness came, the memory of Elena in his bed filled his mind. The pillow on which he slept smelled like her hair. His bed smelled like sex with her. God help him, all he could think of was reaching for her, pulling her soft body close to his and starting all over again.

Typically he would lie in bed a few minutes and let himself wake up gradually. But this morning was anything but typical. A sea change had occurred in his life. He would clear the mystery of Carla Ryder's death and move on, but he might never be able to move on from Elena. He had barely managed to do it once. Twice could be impossible.

But he had to, he argued with himself. They had nowhere to go. He might want to get married again someday, and maybe have some kids, like his sisters had done. Even in his wildest flights of fancy, he couldn't envision that ever occurring with Randall Ryder as a father-in-law.

He wondered if Elena was any more able or willing to stand up to her dad now than she had been years ago. Were things still really like Josh said? Would she always have to leap out of Rusty Joplin's bed and run home to Daddy? *That* he could not, would not, live with. He knew himself too well.

At the same time, the side of him that believed in fair play couldn't expect her to be with him at the sacrifice of a relationship with her only living parent, a father who adored her.

Beyond that impossible situation, his reputation as an honest man was at stake. No way did he want anybody in Sanderson County to construe that Randall Ryder and his network of well-heeled good ol' boys told Sheriff Rusty Joplin what to do. How could that be avoided if said sheriff carried on with the millionaire's favorite daughter?

He didn't know when he would see Elena again, but he had to make her understand that great sex did not a future make.

But first, he had to convince himself.

After he dressed, he stripped his bed. He stuffed his sheets and pillowcases into the washing machine and threw in some soap. As he turned on the machine, he thought about the fact that just a week ago, he had been water-skiing on Lake Worth. Renewing an affair with Elena had been the farthest thing from his mind.

He hadn't been thinking of the cold-blooded murder of her sister, either.

As he put clean linens on the bed, he thought about the need to talk to Blanca Hardin and dig into her relationship with her deceased sister. Last night, he and Elena had been more interested in each other than in anything else. They had avoided the issue of Carla's death, so he hadn't mentioned his intention to call Blanca this morning.

In the kitchen, he made coffee and brought out the makings of a lumberjack breakfast—eggs, sausage, frozen waffles and maple syrup. He was hungry. Last night, he had gone to sleep without supper.

Before leaving his house, he called his own youngest sister, Marilee, who was a stay-at-home mom. With four kids under six years old, she had to be.

"I gotta be in the office this morning," he said.

"Monday's a bitch even when we don't have a major crime under investigation. If I make arrangements for a carpenter to come out here and put new locks on my doors, have you got time to hang around here while he's working?"

"Sure, but I'll have to bring the kids."

"That's okay. Just don't let 'em tear up anything."

She gasped. "What kind of a tacky remark is that?"

He chuckled. "Just kidding. But I know your kids."

"What happened, did somebody break in?"

"I just discovered how weak the old locks are. I've got guns here."

"Well, if I'm gonna bring my kids, lock 'em up in your bedroom or something."

"They're in the closet in a gun safe. But I'll lock the bedroom door before I leave."

"Rusty, can I ask you something?"

"Sure."

"I didn't know Carla Ryder that well, but do you really think her husband killed her?"

He bit down on his lip. "We don't know, Marilee. We're still working on it. When we know the facts, we'll release them."

To his relief, she didn't press the issue.

She also didn't mention the single woman she had brought to yesterday's roping. Maybe she was finally beginning to understand that if he wanted female company, he could find it on his own. He was no Romeo, but he had lived as a single man long enough to know he wasn't chopped liver, either.

After they disconnected, he called the owner of Salvation's only mom-and-pop hardware store and made arrangements for locks, dead bolts and a carpenter to install them on his front and back doors. He wasn't locking Elena out. He intended to give her a key. The thought of her waiting for him in his home was sexy and irresistible.

He next called Blanca Hardin's number, which he had taken from the cell phone records. She told him she would come in for an interview only if her husband could accompany her. Seeing no harm in that, Rusty agreed and they set up a meeting for six o'clock, after Bailey returned from his office in Midland.

Then he told Cheryl to hold the calls while he buried himself in his own office with next year's budget. As an afterthought, he asked her to see if she could find out what horse show had been going on in Amarillo the end of April or the first of May.

Near noon he took a break from the numbers crashing into each other inside his head and called Elena's cell phone. Though he had been mired in accounting all morning, she had lingered in his thoughts. In spite of the problems she brought into his life, he was happy. He was an idiot, but he was happy.

"Ah, the man of my dreams," she answered.

"Hey," he said softly and grinning like a fool. Just talking to her turned him into somebody he didn't even recognize. "Where are you?"

"I'm back to work today. It was time. My being gone for so many days was causing a great strain on the other people here. They're glad I came back."

Rusty didn't doubt the hardship on the hospital. He figured that there were no more than a dozen RNs on the payroll.

A few beats of silence passed. "I thought about you all night," she said, almost in a whisper, "and I've been thinking about you all morning."

He leaned forward, propping his elbow on his desk blotter and bracing his jaw on his hand. "Oh, yeah? What're you thinking?"

She gave a little giggle. "I can't repeat it. Ears, you know. But it's naughty."

He chuckled, too. "I've been thinking about you, too. I'd say last night was worth an encore. We've lost a lot of time. We need to get back into practice."

She giggled again. "You are so bad."

He could hear fun and happiness in her voice and that made him happy. "No, I'm not. You're good."

"Shh. Someone could be listening to you, too. Want to know what else I was thinking?"

"I sure do."

"Wouldn't it be nice if we could just run away? Some place where no one knows who we are?"

"You can never really run away, darlin'. Things have a way of catching up with you. And most of the time, it's when you least expect it."

He heard her sigh. "You're probably right. So, anything new? On Carla's . . . uh, case, I mean?"

He guessed she couldn't bear to say the word "murder." "Don't worry, Elena. We'll get to the bottom of it. I'm gonna talk to your sister later today. She has to know something about what's been going on in Carla's personal life."

"Oh. Well, at least she's in town. I suppose if anyone would know what Carla's been doing, it would be Blanca."

A few beats of silence passed again and a little worry began to niggle at him. Did she object to him talking to Blanca? "Hey, you still there?"

"I'm moving out of Daddy's house, Rusty."

"What? Where?"

"I rented a house this morning not too far from the hospital. It's old, but it's fine. I'll see how it goes. Maybe eventually I'll buy something."

"Elena, you've never lived in a house. I mean, you've lived in a mansion. With maids and gardeners and—"

She stopped him with a laugh. "I'm not dumb,

Rusty. I'm a very capable person. I'm a nurse, for crying out loud. Surely I can manage a house."

"I didn't mean you're dumb. I just meant that's a huge change. What brought this on?"

"I should have done it a long time ago. For years, it hasn't been that pleasant living with Daddy. But you get comfortable, you know? And you don't do the things you should because they're hard and they're a lot of trouble and you don't want to hurt people's feelings. Anyway, what thirty-three-year-old woman still lives at home with her dad?"

Rusty couldn't keep from smiling. He admired her, knowing the difficulty of the decision she had made, then followed up on by actually doing something about it. Elena wasn't like his sisters, he had always told himself, who could rope a steer, slaughter it, butcher it and serve it up for supper.

Then again, he would be the first to admit he still had the image of a vulnerable eighteen-year-old fixed in his memory, when common sense told him no delicate flower worked as a trauma nurse in the ER. For that matter, he had seen her at work and been amazed at her calm competence. Her quiet nature was deceiving. "Okay, so where is this fine house?"

"It's old Mrs. England's house. The one where she lived before she moved to the nursing home in Midland. I got the key this morning from her daughter. I'm going to be moving as soon as possible. I'm going over there on my lunch break at one. Can you meet me and take a look?"

"You bet." And while he was at it, he would go out to his own house, get a key to his new locks and give one to her. "I'll see you there."

He no sooner hung up than Alan Muncy stuck his head through the doorway. "The ME's got a tissue sample. It's on its way to Austin, but I don't know when we'll get the results. Could be weeks."

In reality, it could be months. "Good," Rusty said. "Now we just need to get samples from Esparza and Blanchard."

"I'll work on it." Alan started to leave the office, but turned and came back. "He found stuff under her fingernails, Rusty. So she must have scratched her killer."

Rusty's mind flew back to the day he had seen Carla's corpse in the arena and her broken fingernails. He couldn't recall seeing any kind of scratches or lacerations on Blanchard's hands. And he hadn't even looked at Diego Esparza's.

Elena scrolled down her cell phone menu to Blanca's number, intending to call her and discuss her move and tell her of Rusty's intention to get in touch with her. But before she keyed in the number, something made her stop. Blanca didn't give her the time of day. Elena rarely saw her except for holiday meals at the house. She owed her oldest sister no more allegiance than she owed Carla. And alerting Blanca to Rusty's intentions might even put him at a disadvantage.

Thinking of her sister reminded her of another secret she had kept from Rusty. She hadn't told him about Carla's Mexican lover.

If Elena could have known days ago that she would end up in Rusty's bed last night, she would have already told him about Diego Esparza. But now it was too late. If she mentioned him now, she was sure Rusty would think she was keeping secrets from him. She didn't want him having even one negative thought about her or about renewing their relationship.

Rusty left his desk and ambled out to the reception room at a quarter to one. "Going to lunch," he told Cheryl.

"Turn your phone on," she called behind him, "so I can find you if I need to."

As he walked out the door on his way to a meeting with Elena that could only be tagged "secret," he wondered just how he was going to control this boulder that was suddenly careening downhill.

The house Elena had rented was redbrick with white trim, probably built in the sixties, but it had been well maintained. It was twice the size of his home. She was waiting for him at the front door. They walked together into the living room, which was as large as his living room and kitchen combined. The fall sun sluiced through bare windows against white walls and made the whole house seem bright and fresh.

They couldn't keep their hands off each other, so they strolled through the hallways and empty rooms, his arm around her shoulder, her arm around his waist. His boot heels thudded, her athletic shoes squeaked on the hardwood floors.

"I'm going furniture shopping this week," she told him, her voice echoing in the hollow emptiness. "And I'll have to get some rugs. I don't want to spend a lot on furnishings. This may not work out."

Rusty couldn't keep from thinking of the silliness of the conversation as he recalled Josh's comment at the roping yesterday about the Ryder daughters' trust funds. Elena could probably buy a whole furniture store if that was what she wanted.

And therein lay the obstacle that could not be surmounted by David Wayne Joplin. As much as he might desire Elena or a life with her, his stubborn pride would not let him consent to be a Bailey Hardin.

But it wasn't an issue he had to deal with at this moment. Today, he just wanted to savor being with the woman who had always made him feel like her hero.

She was wearing blue scrubs that looked to be a size too big for her and her long, pretty hair was tied back at her nape with a shiny blue ribbon. Feeling that he was getting acquainted with her all over again, he tugged on her ponytail like he used to do when they were kids. "How come you've never cut your hair?"

"I have it trimmed from time to time. A real haircut would scare me to death."

They had made a circle back to the living room. She turned into him, slid her other arm around his waist and pressed her head against his shoulder. He encircled her in his embrace, placing his cheek against her hair and drawing in the fragrance that had found his nose every time he saw her, the scent of spring rain in the desert.

"You want to know what means a lot?" she asked.

He ran his hands down to her bottom and held her against him. "What?"

"It means a lot that you remember, from so long ago."

"How could I forget? I just hope we aren't sorry we jumped back into this lake."

She scrunched up her shoulders and looked up at him with a smile that challenged the sunlight brightening the room. "We won't be."

His heart swelled until he thought it might burst from his rib cage. He placed his fingertips under her chin and brushed her face with tender kisses, her cheeks, her eyelids, her nose. His mouth finally settled on hers in a languorous kiss that he wished would last forever. He willed himself away with a final kiss to her eyelid. "I guess what I should have said is I hope *you* aren't sorry."

"I want us to have a chance this time, Rusty.

And it could never be if I continued to live at the ranch."

He had neither the heart, nor the will, to discourage her by telling her he couldn't see how they could have a future together. The way he saw it, he would have to compromise most of what made him what he was and he wasn't willing to, even for her. But the temptation of the moment was too hard to resist. Again, he enveloped her in his arms and rested his cheek on her hair. "Your dad must be upset about your moving."

"He's consumed with Carla's death and his grandchildren. He might not even notice I'm gone."

Rusty didn't believe that. "I'll bet."

"He's hired a private detective," she said. "I just found out about it last night after I got home."

Rusty had instinctively known Ryder wasn't standing still. In whatever the dynamic tycoon undertook, there always had been a "rest of the story." There always would be. "What's that going to accomplish?"

"He wants to build a case against Gary."

Rusty set her back and looked into her face. "He honestly thinks a private investigator can discover something I can't?"

She lifted her arms and opened her palms. "You know Daddy. He's a hands-on kind of person." A frown creased her brow. "Well, the truth is, there's more to it than that. He intends to fight Gary for custody of Carla's children. He doesn't want his grandchildren growing up with a criminal."

It wasn't lost on Rusty that Elena always referred to the Blanchard kids as "Carla's children," as if they had been hatched without a father. "There's nothing yet that says Gary's a criminal."

He wasn't ready to tell her, or anybody, that in his mind he was on the verge of shelving Gary as a suspect. Not for any concrete factual reason, but because he believed his story. "And he's pretty good with those kids. I was impressed."

She shrugged. "Daddy's determined."

"This is crazy. All a PI can do is fuck things up."

"I can't do anything about it, Rusty."

"I know." He placed a fist under her chin, lifted it and kissed her. "Who is it?"

"Someone from the security company that does work for Ryder Oil. So he must be from Houston. I don't know his name."

"Well, I guess it doesn't matter. We'll just have to see what the guy does."

"I guess I should tell you Daddy's also been in touch with a man in Austin named Garth Jackson. He has something to do with the Texas Rangers."

Rusty was acquainted with several DPS troopers and Texas Rangers both. He knew the names of many of the DPS administrators and officials in Austin. He didn't know exactly who Garth Jackson was, but no doubt he was high up in the Department of Public Safety's food chain, maybe all the way up to the governor. As open-minded as Rusty tried to be, he couldn't stop the anger that spiked within him. "A county sheriff is elected by the people, Elena. No Texas Ranger is going to take an investigation away from him unless there's a good reason or the sheriff can't handle it. Even your dad can't make that happen. I'm surprised he'd try."

"It's very scary what Daddy's willing to try. There's something else I want to tell—"

The chirp of his cell phone stopped her. "Hold that thought," he said and answered the call.

"You've got company," Cheryl said.

"Who?"

"Turley Holt."

Holt was the Texas Ranger charged with handling major crime in several West Texas counties. "Ten minutes," he told her.

He disconnected and looked at Elena. "Looks like your dad wasn't making idle threats. Turley Holt's in my office."

A troubled look darkened her eyes. "Is that someone I should know?"

"He's the Ranger from Midland."

"Oh, Rusty, I—"

"Shh. Don't worry about it. Everything's okay. I know Turley. We speak the same language."

He dug into his pocket, produced a new brass key that opened both his back and his front doors and handed it to her. "I had the locks changed at my house."

"Oh? You really were that upset because I went in?"

"Darlin', if you can get in, so can somebody else." He closed her fingers around the key and kissed her. "You can go in my house anytime you want to. From now on, just use the key."

She gave him a huge smile. "Okay. I'll be there this evening when you get home."

He smiled back. "I'll try to get there early."

"Are you sure everything's okay?"

"Yep."

That boulder careening out of control downhill picked up speed. But he closed his mind to it and kissed her again.

Chapter 24

Back in the reception room of the courthouse annex, Rusty saw a man talking to Cheryl at her desk in the cluttered room. He wore a starched white dress shirt. A cowboy hat with a tall crown hung on his fingers. Even without seeing his face, Rusty recognized Turley Holt.

Caution surged within Rusty. He knew better than to take Turley's visit for granted. The Ranger stood up and stuck out his right hand. "Rusty. How are you?"

Holt looked so much like the Texas Ranger legend, just seeing him was like stepping back in time. Rusty had a good relationship with him. Both of them were cowboys, both horse owners, both hunters. They always had something to talk about. They shook hands. "Good, Turley. What can I do for you?"

"Someone asked me to come up here and pay you a visit." He smoothed his thick red mustache with his thumb and forefinger.

And I know who that was, Rusty thought. "Come on into my office."

Closed into his crowded sanctum, Rusty laid his hat on top of the file cabinet. They both seated themselves, Rusty in his desk chair and the Ranger in one of the steel armchairs in front of Rusty's battered desk. The gentle breeze from the fan on top of the file cabinet touched their faces and riffled papers on the desk. Rusty had lived with the moving air and the fan's low hum for so long he had learned to ignore it, but the Ranger gave it a hard glare.

"Worn-out air-conditioning system," Rusty said. Rural law enforcement departments never had enough money, equipment or personnel. Most functioned with less-than-perfect office conditions, too. The Ranger chuckled knowingly.

"Who told you to come see me?"

"Someone said you had a little murder up here."

"We do. But in my book there's no such thing as a *little* murder."

"Oh, you're right, you're right." Turley raised a palm. "If it's murder, it's always big."

Rusty propped his forearms on his desk and looked the Ranger in the eye. "Tell you what. Let's clear a question up front. Are you here at Randall Ryder's request?"

"No, no. You know our department doesn't operate that way. Someone just told me you might need a little help."

"I might. But I guess if I figure I can't handle things, I've got enough sense to call on somebody who can."

The Ranger chuckled and nodded. "Oh, I understand, Rusty. I understand. And that's the way it should be. But you've got to understand, too."

"Sometimes I get a headache from understanding."

"So you've about got the bad guy cornered, eh?"

No way did Rusty intend to admit to a Texas Ranger that on Day Six of a murder investigation, his two prime suspects were on the brink of fizzling like a campfire in the rain. "Just waiting for some DNA test results."

"Sent that down to Austin, did you?"

"Yep."

"They'll do you a good job. Might take forever, but they know their stuff."

"Look, Turley, nobody's more aware of this victim's identity or her father's clout in Austin than I am. Hell, I've known this family practically all my life. I know Randall Ryder sent you on this fishing trip. It's personal with him."

"When a man's daughter's the victim, Rusty, it tends to get personal."

"That's not what I meant. I meant it's personal between him and me in a way that has nothing to do with the deceased. The point is, we'll be making an arrest soon. So I guess that's what you can report."

"That's good, Rusty. That's all I need to hear." He stood up. "Buy you a cup of coffee on my way outta town?"

"No, thanks. I just ate lunch."

As Ranger Holt strode out the door, Rusty stared after him, realizing he had been put on notice. Ryder was pulling strings in Austin. The old fucker hadn't been able to engineer Rusty's defeat in the election, so he was employing new tactics. First a private investigator, now a Texas Ranger. Somebody, everybody, anybody was watching Sheriff Rusty Joplin. If he blew this investigation, he would be leaving town with his tail between his legs. And he would be toast in the Texas law enforcement community. He shoved the budget aside again and opened the file he had created on Carla Ryder. He wanted to reapprise himself of the few facts that he knew before his interview with Blanca Hardin.

Everybody but the dispatcher had cleared out for the day when the Hardins appeared in the reception area, right on time. Of course they would be. Bailey was a businessman. Promptness would just naturally be part of his makeup.

Rusty didn't know Bailey Hardin at all except by sight. His thinning gray hair and silver-rimmed glasses fit the image of the vice president of an oil company, which was what he was.

He had to be a few years past forty because he had already graduated from Salvation High School by the time Rusty reached it. Thanks to his engagement to Blanca and the influence and support of her father, Bailey had gone to SMU and earned an MBA from the prestigious business school.

He was known to have a keen mind, but he was the object of countless jokes around Salvation about his marriage to Blanca and the suck-up role he played as Ryder's son-in-law. On the outside, it appeared that sucking up hadn't done him any harm. Many men in Salvation might trade places with him.

But not Rusty Joplin.

As Rusty shook hands with each of the Hardins, he sensed a tightness in their demeanors. An odor of alcohol reached him and he could tell by the glint in Blanca's eyes that she was the one who had been drinking. "Thanks for coming in," he said.

He invited the couple into his office and asked them to take seats. They looked out of place in the crowded, spartan surroundings in which the San-derson County sheriff did business every day. Blanca used to be dark-haired, but now she had that sleek blond and tanned look that seemed to show only on the wealthy, a look that Elena, for some reason, didn't have.

Wearing a pair of starched and creased 20X Wranglers and a starched pink shirt showing a 20X logo, Bailey looked ironed from head to toe. The cowboy hat he carried and the pair of custom-made boots he wore could have cost more than a thou-sand dollars each.

Pink. Rusty couldn't imagine himself in a pink

shirt. His sisters had given him one and told him it was a "hot" color for guys right now. In terms of the clothes he wore, "hot" didn't interest him. He liked blue. If he wasn't wearing a white shirt, he was wearing a blue one.

Rusty took his seat behind his desk and at the same time punched on the small recorder he had placed near his desk calendar. Blanca and Bailey looked at the two gray steel armchairs in front of the desk as if they might soil their clothing. Finally, they sank onto the seats. As Rusty looked across his desk at Blanca, he couldn't keep from thinking that in spite of her flawless hair and makeup, in spite of her being an attractive woman, she looked older than her thirty-seven or thirty-eight years.

"Well, Rusty," she said, "it's strange to be having this meeting. There's been a lot of water over the dam since high school, hasn't there?"

He didn't know her as well as he knew Elena or as well as he had known Carla—she had been a senior when he was a sophomore—but he heard hints of melancholy and nervousness in her voice. And why not? How often in her protected life had Blanca Ryder Hardin been summoned for an interview with a sheriff? He smiled, meaning to put her at ease and reduce the "us versus them" vibe. "There sure has, Blanca."

. "I've been thinking back on all the time you spent at our house when you and my sister were rodeoing," she said. "Seems like only yesterday."

She had to be referring to the years Rusty had roped in high school rodeo and Carla had barrel-raced. Carla had had her own arena to practice in and some of her teenage peers had been invited to join her.

Blanca opened a big purse made of something shiny and fluttery and plucked out a tissue with perfectly manicured fingers. A diamond the size of a dime perched on her left ring finger. She dabbed at her nose with the tissue. "I can't believe all of this. I feel like I'm in some alien world."

"I told my wife it was a good idea to talk to you," Bailey said before Rusty could reply.

"I appreciate that," Rusty said to Blanca. He wondered if she and Bailey knew Randall had hired a PI or that a Texas Ranger was sniffing around the sheriff's office. "This won't take long. I'm hoping you can give me some missing pieces to this puzzle. I'd like to hear about your relationship with Carla."

"Well, we—"

"They were sisters," Bailey said authoritatively, as if Rusty didn't know that.

Rusty raised a palm, stopping him from saying more and keeping his focus on Blanca. "You had a close relationship? Shared secrets?"

She looked down and smoothed the tissue on her knee. "We were close. But I don't know how many secrets we shared. I don't have any secrets and my sister was very good at keeping hers to herself."

"You and Bailey, and Carla and Gary, socialized together?"

She huffed. "Oh, good grief, no. Bailey can't stand Gary. I don't like him, either. He's an arrogant jerk."

"How do you mean?"

"Just arrogant. He always puts Texas down, like he's somehow smarter and cooler than us because he came from California, like we're bumpkins or something. He's made it very clear that he doesn't much like Daddy or the rest of the family, either."

"How about the quarrels and fights he and your sister had? The violence. Tell me about that."

"Well . . . they did quarrel. It's no secret. He did hit her a few times through the years, but—"

"Well, now, just a minute," Bailey put in. "I

don't like to defend him. Personally, I think he's a first-class prick. But when it came to my wife's sister, I wouldn't be surprised if Gary came out on the short end most of the time. I've seen Carla have a fit and swing at him with a shovel. I know she beaned him with a bit once and he had to have a couple of stitches."

Blanca nodded, now folding the tissue on her lap into neat squares. "Carla was like Daddy. If she didn't get her way, she reacted."

Mild statements about the truth from both of them. Rusty had seen Carla have tantrums that bordered on violence when they were kids. Apparently that behavior had carried into her adulthood.

"Were you ever with her when she saw men other than Gary?"

"Uh, no." Blanca glanced at her husband, big-eyed. "Well . . . a few times maybe."

Now, Bailey leveled a stare at his wife. "You went somewhere with her while she was cheating on her husband?"

Did Bailey not know about his sister-in-law's peccadilloes when it came to her marriage? Had Carla used Blanca to cover her activities? Rusty wondered, a little surprised.

A sob burst from Blanca; she stifled it by covering her mouth with the tissue.

"Blanca," Rusty said gently, "it's common knowledge that your sister saw men other than her husband. Nobody's judging her. Can you tell me who they are?"

"Why do you need to know?" She made a deep sniff, pawed in the oversized purse and came up with another tissue.

"Because she was pregnant. And I think knowing who she was seeing could be important."

"Pregnant?" Bailey said to his wife, shock in his

tone. This was evidently the first time he had heard this.

"She wasn't sure yet," Blanca answered, too quickly.

That was a lie. Rusty had three sisters and ten nieces and nephews. No one would convince him a woman wouldn't know she was four months pregnant. But so far, Rusty had run across no one who seemed to know about Carla except the Odessa medical examiner. And now, Blanca.

On the one hand, Rusty felt disappointed that Blanca would lie to him. On the other, police work had taught him that everybody lied. Especially to cops. He steered the conversation back on track, still searching for the truth. "How did she feel about it?"

Blanca glanced at her husband again. "She, uh, well . . . she was, uh . . . well, she was going to have the baby," she said stiffly. Her eyes teared more and she ducked her chin. "She didn't really want to, but I told her I'd take it if she didn't want it."

Bailey came to the edge of his seat, glaring at his wife and propping an elbow on Rusty's desk. "You what?"

Blanca cried out, "I'd rather take my sister's baby than get one from a Third World country! Like *you* want!"

"Hey, hey," Rusty said. "You two can settle that at home. Let's calm down here. This meeting's about a homicide victim."

Bailey sat back in his chair, chastised. He crossed his arms over his chest and cocked a boot across his knee.

"So I take it from what you said that you knew about it and the two of you must have discussed the baby's future. Why would you volunteer to take it off her hands?"

Bailey stared at his wife, but he kept quiet.

Blanca shook her head and turned her attention to her lap again. "Carla let herself get too far along before she started to worry about it. She'd already had two abortions. Besides that, Daddy would just die if he knew she aborted his grandchild. He never knew about the . . . the other times."

Now Bailey was looking at the ceiling and shaking his head.

"I have information that your sister went to see your dad the night before she died," Rusty said. "I'm told she was upset and crying. Would you know what that was about?"

Blanca shrugged. "Even before Bailey and I went to Italy, she was threatening to just go and tell Daddy everything. But I don't know what 'everything' amounted to. Like I said, she kept her secrets to herself."

No doubt Randall Ryder was as hard a man to talk to as he was to deal with. It had to have taken some courage or some desperation for Carla to go to him. But what had she intended to discuss with him? Rusty believed it could be key to the case. "If I guessed that she didn't tell Gary about the pregnancy, would I be right?"

"She was afraid to. I don't think he figured it out."

Well, at least Blanchard hadn't been lying about that. "If Gary had known, would he have been upset?"

"Probably. When she was pregnant with Austin, Gary didn't want him, but he went along. And . . . uh . . . well, Carla wasn't sure the baby was Gary's."

"She wasn't sure the baby she was carrying was Gary's? Or are you talking about Austin?"

Blanca stared at him without answering and Rusty struggled to read what was in her eyes. "The baby she was carrying," she said finally and looked away. She reached up and began to toy with a thick gold earring.

Bailey leaned to the side and pulled a handkerchief from his pocket. He removed his glasses and began to wipe the lenses.

"Let me get this straight, then," Rusty said, bringing Blanca's attention back to him. "This time, you knew she was expecting, but no one, I mean *no one,* else did?"

"I don't think so. She went to the doctor in Odessa."

"If Gary wasn't the baby's father, who do you believe was?"

Blanca sat back in her chair and didn't answer. Bailey looked at Rusty. "So *you* think it *wasn't* Gary?"

"I don't think anything," Rusty answered sharply. "I'm trying to find out." Rusty turned his attention back to Blanca. "And Blanca, it's not helping me or your sister if you stonewall me. Does the name Diego Esparza ring a bell?"

"I know Diego, but he—"

"Who's Diego Esparza?" Bailey asked, gesturing with raised open palms. Bailey, too, wore a large diamond ring.

"He was . . . well, he . . ."

"Diego Esparza was one of Carla's recent boyfriends, Bailey," Rusty told him.

Bailey shook his head. "Blanca, I've been telling you for years your sister's a damn tramp."

"Stop it, Bailey. She wasn't a tramp. She had needs. She was lonely. She knew Gary didn't care about her. She knew he married her to get at Daddy's money."

"If she knew that," Bailey said, "and she wanted to fuck around, then why didn't she just stay divorced? Why did she remarry him?"

"The kids love Gary," Blanca cried. "She didn't want him gone from their lives." She turned back to Rusty. "She was pregnant before she met Diego."

"She was already pregnant while she was having a sexual relationship with Esparza?" Rusty repeated, just to be sure he had the fact solid in his mind.

Blanca nodded.

"Then tell me what her meetings with Diego were like. Did he know she was pregnant?"

"I don't think so. Carla probably didn't tell him. I think he really loved her, but she was always doing things that made him angry."

"When he got angry, did they fight in the way she and Gary fought?"

"No, never. Diego's a nice man. Mostly, he did anything she wanted. You could see how much he thought of her. But I don't know if Carla was capable of loving anyone. What Diego did for her mostly was sex. She used to tell me how hot he was and—"

"Jee-sus Christ!" Bailey was on the edge of his seat again. "Did Randall know anything about all of this?"

Bailey's high-handedness and interruptions had become so distracting, Rusty wished he had asked him to wait in the reception room. "Blanca, what can you tell me about the upstairs room in the barn?"

"Carla used it as her office. But it's also an apartment. It's one of those things where everything's in one big room and there's a tiny little bedroom. She . . . uh . . . sometimes she would meet Diego up there."

Now Bailey got to his feet and loomed over his wife. "Are you saying she met a goddamn lover right under her husband's friggin' nose? While she was pregnant and couldn't even name the friggin' father of her baby?"

"Bailey, sit down!" Rusty ordered.

Bailey glared at him a few seconds, then dropped back to his seat.

Rusty fixed his gaze on Blanca's eyes. "Other than Diego, who else did she meet up there?"

Tell me, tell me, tell me, he willed, *about a "big rich man."*

Rusty couldn't read the emotion in her eyes, but something was definitely there. Was it fear? A few seconds went by.

"I don't know," Blanca said finally.

Rusty continued to hold her gaze. He believed she did know. But what would it take to persuade her to tell?

Rusty dismissed Blanca and Bailey, seeing no point in replowing a field. He was exhausted. When he reached home, he found that Elena had indeed used the new door key. Both delight and chagrin conflicted within him. Last night might have been the most mind-blowing sex he'd had in years, if ever, but he wasn't comfortable with secretly meeting her.

She was in the kitchen at the stove, stirring something in a pot and it appeared she was wearing shorts and one of his shirts. It struck her about midthigh. *Oh, man.*

She put a lid on the pot, lowered the heat and turned to face him. Her hair was disheveled and draped over her shoulder.

"Whatcha' doing?"

She smiled. "I'm heating your supper." She laid the wooden spoon on the stovetop and came toward him. "I hope you don't mind that I borrowed one of your shirts. I came from work. I wanted to get out of those scrubs."

"It looks a heck of a lot better on you than it does on me," he told her. He laid his hat on the table and walked over to where she was. He pulled her against him and kissed her. She kissed him back, but her enthusiasm didn't seem to equal his.

"What's wrong, sugar?"

"Nothing, really. I think it's all catching up with me." She rose on her tiptoes and her mouth teased his with tiny bites and tongue flicks. "I need you," she whispered.

He needed her, too, more than he had let himself acknowledge in the past fifteen years. He pushed his tongue into her mouth and stroked and played. At the same time, he slid his hands beneath the shirt and discovered she had on nothing but panties. Her body felt warm and supple against his hands. He caressed her everywhere he could reach. A surge of pure lust zinged through him and he felt his cock push against his zipper.

"Make love to me," she whispered. "Hold me close and make love to me."

He scooped her into his arms and carried her to his bed.

Later, they lay in each other's arms, well sated. He could think of only one thing. How and why had he lived without this intimacy all these years? Was it possible that every time would be better than the last? And if it was, would he survive it?

His stomach growled and reminded him that he hadn't eaten all day. "What's in the pot on the stove?"

"We had chicken and dumplings in the lunchroom today. I brought some leftovers."

They showered, then sat at the table in his kitchen and ate. The hospital's kitchen was manned by local country cooks. It had a reputation for serving food atypical of hospital fare. Elena seemed preoccupied by something, but he didn't press her. It felt too good just to be close to her in his home. He didn't want the tensions of the outside world to intrude. The more logical, rational side of him told him he was only prolonging the inevitable.

At nine, she went home to Daddy. It didn't matter, Rusty told himself as he pulled on his jeans and a sweatshirt. He was still happy. Who knew? Maybe everything would work out.

Later, while he ate a dish of ice cream, he watched the news and the weather forecast from Midland. At eleven, he turned off the TV. As he started for bed, the kitchen phone rang. He checked caller ID and recognized the sheriff's office number.

"Rusty," the night dispatcher said, "they've got a Code Eight and a Code Three out at Precinct 4, the Owl Club."

Usually, his deputies were casual about using the police radio codes. He thought perhaps the dispatcher had used the "Officer in Trouble" and "Lights and Sirens" codes in error or he had heard wrong. "You sure?"

"I'm sure."

"Who's the deputy?"

"Mike."

Mike Chisholm was more experienced than most of the deputies. If he called for help, he needed it. "Okay, thanks. I'm on it."

Rusty pulled on his boots, strapped on his .45, grabbed his badge and a bill cap and strode from his house. Siren screaming, red and blues flashing, he raced toward Precinct 4.

At a lawful speed, Precinct 4 was a good twenty-minute drive from Rusty's home. Balls-to-the-wall wasn't much faster. The radio calls crackled as different deputies in different parts of the county called in and reported they were en route. Among them was the deputy Rusty knew was Mike's best friend, Ken Carter.

He slid into the Owl Club's caliche parking lot to a kaleidoscope of lights flashing red, white and blue. Four other patrol cars were there, parked at odd angles. He spotted two deputies moving among several clusters of people standing in the parking lot. The ambulance was backed up to the porch in front of the front door. Yellow and black crime scene tape crisscrossed the door.

He bailed out of the Crown Vic and mounted the two steps up to the porch in one stride. Bypassing the crime scene tape, he burst through the doorway. Overhead lights had turned the usually dark room to amber. To the accompaniment of George Jones on the jukebox, Deputies Mike Chisholm and Ken Carter, EMT Jimmy Don Estes and the same female EMT he had seen in Carla Ryder's arena were kneeling over and working feverishly on a supine figure clad in cowboy boots and jeans.

A weeping Rosa Linda McDowell hovered over the back of the female EMT. A creepy feeling slithered up Rusty's spine.

"I'm Jimmy Don," the EMT was saying in a firm voice to the form on the floor. "This is Judy with me. You're gonna be okay. Stay with me, buddy. Fight for it."

A gurgling sound and a few words Rusty didn't understand came from the victim. Deputy Mike Chisholm got to his feet, shaking his head, his shirt and pants stained with bright red blood. "Jesus, Rusty."

"Mike! What the fuck happened?"

The deputy shook his head again. "He had a gun, man. He had a gun. I didn't see it."

Rusty scanned the room. Diego Esparza stood between two deputies. Rusty caught a quick breath.

That Esparza might carry a gun hadn't even occurred to him. "The Mexican had a gun?"

The deputy wiped his brow with his forearm.
"Naw, man. The dude on the floor. Gary Blanchard."

Rusty's heart dropped to his boots. "Who shot
him?"

"Me," the deputy answered.

Rusty's gaze jerked back to the victim. Just then,
the female EMT turned to grab something from
her emergency case and Rusty saw the man's upper
body for the first time. Gary Blanchard lay
sprawled on his back in a wide pool of blood, his
arms at a ninety-degree angle from his body, an IV
plugged into his arm. A huge vivid red blossom
stained the front of his white shirt.

Chapter 25

The EMTs prepared to lift Blanchard onto the gurney. Mike returned to help them. Rusty stood back, to avoid getting in the way of the activity. As Mike and the female EMT rolled the gurney toward the front door, Rusty squatted beside Jimmy Don and the wide pool of blood on the floor. He placed a hand on the EMT's shoulder. "How bad?"

Jimmy Don was hurriedly repacking his equipment case. As he slammed the lid shut and locked it, he answered with one head shake.

"He gonna make it?"

"Don't know."

Rusty took that answer to be a probably not. A heavy lump settled in his gut as he got to his feet. The more he had seen of Gary Blanchard, the more he had begun to form the opinion that the guy wasn't as bad as the local gossip had him. Now, all he could think of was that if he didn't survive, it might never be known if he did or didn't strangle his wife.

As a nonmedical person, Rusty could do nothing for the victim. He moved down his priority list to his next most demanding challenge. A trusted deputy had shot a citizen. When Rusty had worked in the city, there had been a swarm of investigative teams and special service personnel to assist and support in an officer-involved shooting. In Salvation, there was no one but the sheriff. It was an absolute necessity that the investigation of the shooting be beyond criticism. He would be forced to place a call to Turley Holt. An investigation by the Texas Rangers would be as unbiased and transparent as humanly possible.

As Jimmy Don hefted the emergency kit and followed his colleagues out, Matt Mercer came up. "This is a real goat-fuck, Rusty."

"Shut up, Matt, and do what I tell you without arguing." Rusty pointed to the pistol lying on the floor. "Confiscate that weapon and anything else that may be important to investigating this incident." He headed for the door. "Follow me."

Outside, people still milled about the parking lot in hushed murmurs, having been forbidden to leave by two deputies. "Get Marshall and Lowell to take statements from these witnesses." Rusty ran a finger through the air in a semicircle around the parking lot area. "Don't let anybody leave 'til you or Marshall or Lowell has talked to every single one of them. And don't forget to take notes. Let's get Art Rodriguez out here so we can have an intelligent conversation with Diego Esparza."

As the ambulance screamed out of the parking lot, for a fleeting moment Rusty wondered if Elena was on duty in the ER tonight. He didn't know how the ER schedule worked. As a specialist in trauma, she was probably the most capable nurse Salvation's small hospital had on its staff. Even if she wasn't on duty, he suspected they would call her in.

Mike Chisholm and Ken Carter were standing together talking. Rusty approached them. "See you a minute, Mike?"

The deputy quickly gave Rusty his full attention. "Sure, Rusty."

"Let's go over here where it's quiet and talk a minute."

"God, I'm sorry, Rusty," the deputy said, shaking his head as they walked toward Rusty's car. "The guy picked up that pistol off the bar top and that's all I could see."

The deputy had a deer-in-the-headlights look in his eyes and though the night was cool, his forehead shone with sweat. "Take it easy, Mike. Just tell me what happened."

"I get this call from the dispatcher," he said rapidly. He was clearly pumped on adrenaline. "A fight. I figure it's just like a dozen others I've been to out here. But just in case it's worse than usual, I come out here running hot. When I walk in, I see something's fucked, but I can't tell for sure what."

The deputy began to use his hands to describe the action. "This big Mex is at the far end of the bar. His shirt's torn and messed up and he's got blood on his face. I start walking to where he's at and this dude sitting at the bar stands up and turns around. I'm sure he's drunk. Hell, I know he's drunk. He practically fell down. I didn't see the gun 'til he grabbed it off the bar top."

"Why'd he go for the gun? Did you say or do something that threatened him?"

"Naw, man. Like I said, I just walked in. It all happened in seconds, but when he picked up that gun, I didn't see or hear nothin' else. I drew and yelled for him to drop it. He just stood there, Rusty, pointing that fuckin' pistol right at me. Everything just seemed to slow down, like I had all the time in the world. I fired twice. Bang-bang. And he went down."

"Before you got here, Blanchard and the Mexican man were in a fight? Was that what the call was about?"

The deputy rubbed his brow and shook his head. "I guess so, but I don't *know*. I never got a chance to ask any questions. I was pretty sure I got the guy center mass." He patted the middle of his chest with his palm. "When he fell, I rushed to check him out. I saw he was in a bad way. I was trying to help him 'til the ambulance got here."

Rusty sighed. "You're gonna need a lawyer, Mike. I'm forced to call Turley to investigate. You know he'll be fair. But be sure you fill out all the paperwork. It's back in the office. I'll get Ken to take you back and help you. As of now, you're on leave. Leave your weapon with me."

The deputy unstrapped his holster and handed it over.

"That the only one you got?"

The deputy sighed and pulled a smaller firearm from his boot. Rusty locked the two weapons in his squad car's trunk.

"God, I'm sorry, Rusty," the deputy said again.

Rusty liked Mike Chisholm. He was an honest man with two little boys. He placed a hand on the deputy's shoulder. "I know, Mike. We all are."

He called across the parking lot to Ken Carter and the deputy came over. "Ken, take Mike back to the office and don't leave him alone." He turned back to Chisholm. "If there's anything you need, any calls you want to make, just tell Ken. He's your partner for the next twenty-four hours."

"Rusty, am I gonna be okay?"

"If what you told me is true, I don't see why not. But you know the drill, buddy. I'll call Turley first thing tomorrow."

As Ken Carter and Mike Chisholm walked toward Ken's car, Rusty started back into the bar. Just then, a black Ford Explorer careened into the parking lot and skidded to a stop. Buster Arnold, the tavern's owner, climbed out and quickstepped to where Rusty stood, his barrellike belly jiggling under a loud-colored shirt. Arnold, being short and fat, had always reminded Rusty of a banty rooster.

"What the fuck's going on here, Sheriff? I got a call somebody's shot."

"We're working on it," Rusty told him and continued toward the bar's front door. Arnold tagged along behind him.

Inside, the blood pool, marred by the EMTs' footprints, on the vinyl-covered floor had already started to dry and turn dark at the edges. The bar owner stopped and stared at it. "Jesus Christ!"

The jukebox continued to play, a steel guitar twanging in the ominous silence. "Cut that fuckin' thing off," Arnold shouted and the music abruptly stopped.

Rusty spotted Rosa Linda on a barstool, composed but weeping. She looked up when he walked over. Half-moons of smeared mascara showed under her eyes. The red lipstick she typically wore was gone. Her eyes and face looked swollen. Rusty touched the bill of his cap to her. "You okay?"

She looked at him with dead eyes and nodded.

"Wanna tell me what happened here?"

With shaking hands, she lit a cigarette. Rusty had never seen her smoke. When she didn't answer right away, her employer spoke up. "Goddamn it, Rosie, tell him what the fuck happened."

Rusty scowled at Arnold. "Knock it off, Buster. And cut out the gutter talk to a woman." He put his hand on Arnold's shoulder and turned him around. "Why don't you just move on down to the end of the bar, Buster? And in case you need something to do, gather up your licenses and permits."

Arnold opened his mouth to speak, but before a word could fall from his mouth, Rusty raised a finger in front of the man's wide, flat nose and looked him in the eye. "Licenses and permits. I want to take a look at 'em before I leave here."

The bar owner wilted and slunk away.

Rosa Linda blew out a stream of smoke and wiped her nose with the knuckle of her thumb. Rusty pulled his handkerchief from his back pocket and handed it to her. "Now, tell me," he said.

"Gary. He drink too much. I tell him he should drink water. He say Diego screw his wife." She blew into the handkerchief with a loud snort.

Rusty had a sinking feeling as a visual of what had happened began to form in his mind. Blanchard might never have known Diego's name if Rusty hadn't told him.

"Diego no wanna fight. He—he—" She shook her hands frantically, a gesture Rusty recognized as frustration because she couldn't find a word. She blurted a stream of Spanish. From it, Rusty picked up that Diego was a good person. "But Gary . . ." She began to cry and shake her head.

Rusty gave her a squint as a new suspicion came to him. "Are you friends with Diego Esparza?"

"My cousin."

Rusty forced himself not to roll his eyes. The labyrinth of Mexican families and their many children and cousins was a complicated maze.

From Rosa Linda, Rusty learned that Gary had been in the bar drinking for several hours before Esparza came in. Because Diego was her cousin, she had introduced him and Gary. It was Gary who had accused Esparza and started the fight. Rusty also learned that Gary always carried a pistol. Rosa Linda didn't know why it was lying on the bar.

Rusty doubted that she didn't know, but that was her story.

From Esparza, through the Spanish-speaking deputy, Art Rodriguez, Rusty learned the man had no work this week. He came in to drink beer and visit his cousin. Blanchard began to chide him about his sleeping with Carla. Esparza and Gary fought. Other bar patrons broke up the fight. When

Blanchard sat down at the bar, Esparza felt like he was the winner. Then Blanchard took the gun from inside his coat and laid it on the bar top to scare Esparza. That was when someone called the sheriff's office.

Rusty left the scene at the Owl Club in the care of Matt Mercer. On his way back to town, he punched in Elena's cell phone number, but she didn't answer. She had to be either asleep or at the hospital ER trying to save Gary Blanchard's life.

He diverted his thoughts to Mike Chisholm and the mountain of paperwork that had to be completed in an officer-involved shooting. Not the least of his concerns was the state of mind of the deputy. A shooting, even a justified shooting, was hard on an officer and could have dire consequences for his career if not properly handled. Still, while he worried, in terms of the investigation of the incident, the more distance he put between himself and Mike, the better off the deputy would be. He had confidence in Ken Carter. Ken would guide Mike in the right direction.

As he drove he mused that he had broken up many a fight over a woman who was living, but he couldn't remember putting a stop to any fights over one who was dead.

By the time he reached the city limits, he had decided he had to stop at the hospital.

There he saw Elena's Lexus in the employee parking lot. Inside he found the organized chaos that seemed to accompany all medical emergencies. Before returning to Salvation, he had been present at more than he wanted to remember. In Fort Worth, gang activity kept the county hospital busy. Violence and drugs. Two of society's worst ailments.

The hurried activity around him fueled his assumption that Blanchard was still alive. He peeked through the porthole window in the exam room door and saw Elena, her hands busy, her concentration total.

On a sigh he took a seat in a plastic chair outside the exam room door.

While he waited, he called his dispatcher and left a message for Ken Carter saying where he was and that he didn't know when he would return to the office. As much as he hated knowing Mike and Ken Carter were at the office and he wasn't, as the sheriff he felt obligated to be where he was.

Less than an hour later, a hush fell over the hallway and the emergency room. The flurry of activity ceased. He didn't have to be told Gary Blanchard had expired. He got to his feet and stood by, waiting for official word. Two nurses whose names he didn't know emerged and walked up the hall in silence.

Elena came out next, her hair held in a white cap, her clothing bloodstained. Her breath caught when she saw him and their eyes connected. She came to him. He wanted to take her in his arms, but he couldn't.

She peeled the white cap off her head and her hair fell loose. "He didn't make it," she said, her voice weak and shaky.

"I figured," Rusty said solemnly.

She pulled a tissue from a pocket and wiped her nose as she shook her head. "Those kids. I don't know what will happen to those kids."

"How long before you're ready to leave?"

"I'm ready now. I'm really tired."

"Then let's go." He looped an arm around her shoulders and guided her toward the hospital's entrance.

"But people will see us and you—"

"Let 'em."

Chapter 26

In the inky darkness of the early-morning hours, Rusty held Elena in his arms, in his bed. He knew she had been deeply disturbed by attending the death of her brother-in-law. It had to have taken every ounce of her strength. She may not have liked him much, but he had been her sister's husband, the father of nieces and a nephew she loved. In a larger hospital, Rusty suspected, she wouldn't have been required to help in an emergency involving a family member, but in Salvation, perhaps there was no one else.

"Gary didn't have much of a chance," she said, as if she were talking to no one in particular. "Mike Chisholm's a very good shot."

Thank God for that, Rusty thought. Who knew what might have happened if he had been one of those cops who couldn't pull the trigger? His thoughts swung to Turley Holt and the need to notify him.

"One bullet nicked the aorta," she said. "The other pierced the liver. He had almost bled out by the time he reached the hospital. There wasn't even time to call for Life Flight and get him to Odessa. Even if we'd had a good surgeon here, we wouldn't have had enough blood to transfuse."

That explained the inordinate amount of blood on the Owl Club's floor. In Salvation, with its limited resources and services, a serious injury quickly became life-threatening.

He could feel her trembling against his body. "You're strong," he said to her. "You'll be okay. Lean on me."

She clung to him tighter. "I will, Rusty. I always have."

He lay there suspended between wakefulness and sleep, pleased that he could offer her solace and support, much as he had done before. The days of their youth scrolled through his mind. It was no wonder, really, that Elena had latched on to him when they were kids. Her father had traveled extensively in those days and after her mother's death had left her and her sisters in the care of a series of Mexican housekeepers who not only had no real authority over the household, but were probably hiding from the INS. For all practical purposes, the three girls might as well have been alone. Ryder's assistant, who lived in Midland, had occasionally dropped by to check on them, pay the bills and dispense money to them as needed. Elena had often been the target of Carla's temper as well as the target of Carla and Blanca's petty collusion.

Then Ryder would return from wherever he had been and bring expensive gifts and tell them all how much he loved them. Even when Rusty had been a dumb kid, he had spotted the hypocrisy between the patriarch's behavior and his professed devotion to his daughters. That all three of them had grown up to be other than lawbreakers was, in Rusty's view, something of a miracle.

At some point, Rusty finally drifted into sleep. When they awoke a few hours later, they made love in a slow and timeless rhythm. They found an even more profound connection than he had known before, as if the tragedy in which they both played a role created a bond and they could draw on each other's strength.

"I love you," Elena whispered. "I've always loved you."

"I love you, too," he said and the words came easily. He had said them few times in his life, even to the woman he had married.

Loving Elena had always been easy, he remembered. It was dealing with her family that was hard.

Soon, he checked the clock on the bedside table and saw it was nearly noon. "Where are you supposed to be?" he asked her. Since they had resumed spending time together, he had grown more uncomfortable by the day with falling back into the furtiveness with which they had functioned in their youth.

"The hospital usually doesn't expect me to come in after I've worked all night."

"Where's your dad?"

"We aren't getting along that well. For all I know he went back to Houston."

Rusty frowned, unable to remember if he had ever heard her speak of her father in such a rancorous tone.

"To be fair," she added, "he's having a really hard time. And I haven't helped him much."

Rusty had no point of reference from which to relate to the emotions she must be feeling. He couldn't think of a crisis his own family had experienced of the magnitude of what had happened to the Ryders. And if a comparable situation had arisen, his family would have pulled together and supported each other.

For Elena, the family ideal, which had never really existed in the Ryder clan but to which she had desperately clung, was falling apart before her eyes. Other than being supportive, Rusty didn't know what to do to help her.

"I don't guess Randall will get too bent out of shape about Gary."

"He only cares about Carla's children," she said in a soft voice. "What will happen to them now, Rusty?"

"I assume the court will appoint a guardian until somebody can figure out who's gonna raise them."

"They should come home," she said fiercely. "To Texas. They should come and live at the ranch with Daddy and me."

He didn't remind her that she had made arrangements to soon be moving away from the Rocking R. Of course, now it wasn't out of the question that those plans might go by the wayside.

She sat up. Pushing the mop of hair off her face, she walked across the room to her purse and dug out her cell phone. She looked rumpled and sexy and he loved the intimacy of her uninhibited nakedness. He watched the supple movement of her slender body, the smoothness of her olive-colored skin, the dark mane that hung to her waist. He was getting hard again and he thought about coaxing her back to bed.

She looked at the cell phone screen with a frown, then keyed in a number. "Hi, Daddy. . . . No, I'm at Manisha's. We worked so late . . ." She listened, looking up at the ceiling.

As Rusty lay there listening to her lie to her father, he locked his hands behind his neck and watched, savoring the round firmness of her breasts, her large dark nipples, the delta of black where her thighs joined her torso. She was so beautiful she almost didn't seem real. At the same time those thoughts were floating in his head, he also thought of how a shrink could make a career out of studying the relationships between Randall Ryder and his three daughters.

"No, Daddy. It wasn't like that," she said into

the phone. "I don't know any details. He passed away around one or so. I was there. It was very . . . difficult."

As Rusty's thoughts flashed back to the visual of Gary Blanchard lying on the barroom floor in a pool of blood, fighting for life, Rusty was pulled back to reality.

"I'll be home soon. We can discuss it then." She disconnected and wiped one eye with her fingertips.

He threw back the covers and went to her. They held each other for long minutes. She was shaking, so he pulled a blanket from the bed and wrapped it around them both.

"I'm so scared," she whispered against his chest.

"Of what, darlin'? You're not in danger."

She began to cry. "Everything feels so out of control. Every day it's something else. I don't mean to be crying all the time. I'm sorry."

"Shh-shh. Sometimes life's hard, Elena. And you've been through hell this week. You don't have to apologize for being afraid."

Finally she sniffed away her tears and drew back. "I need to shower and go home. So I can see what's going to happen next. I know Daddy needs me."

They showered and dressed, then sat at the kitchen table with cups of coffee. Neither of them was hungry for breakfast. Rusty called his office and got Turley Holt's home phone number from Cheryl, then called the Ranger from his cell phone and explained the previous night's incident. The Texas Ranger gave his assurance he would be in Salvation as soon as possible.

After learning Elena didn't have the Fresno phone number of Gary Blanchard's parents, he placed a call to Information. James Blanchard, his voice weak and shaking, said he would be at the morgue in Odessa tomorrow to pick up his son and take him home. He would not be bringing the

children with him. And he would be consulting
an attorney.

Rusty offered his condolences and hung up on a
sigh. Given the facts, he didn't think a lawsuit would
get very far, but there was always a mad-dog lawyer
out there ready to accuse the cops of the worst.

Since an autopsy would automatically be performed on Blanchard, Rusty's next call was to the
Odessa ME. It was a precautionary call to ensure
that a DNA sample would be obtained and com-
pared to that from Carla Ryder's unborn child and
the material found under her fingernails. And to
ensure that the results would be returned to the
Sanderson County sheriff's department.

Elena sat without comment while he made the
phone calls. After he finished, he dropped her off
at her SUV in the hospital parking lot, without
regard for who might see them. Today he didn't
give a damn.

His office was less than fifteen minutes from the
hospital. By the time he reached it, his mood had
sunk from dark brown to midnight black.

Cheryl was waiting for him. "I've left you messages all morning."

"I know. I've been tied up."

"Everything okay?"

"Hell, no." He moved on into his office to face
the day.

Cheryl came in behind him and closed the door.
"I know what you mean. God, Rusty, I'm just
blown away. Poor Mike." She wiped away a tear.
"Has a deputy *ever* killed anyone in Sanderson
County?"

"If it's happened, it was a hell of a long time
ago. Has anybody heard from him this morning?"

"Ken's wife called. Ken spent the night at Mike's
house. She said he's doing okay. He's not blaming
himself or anything. The preacher from their church

is going over this morning. I already got him an appointment with a psychologist in Midland. The preacher's going to drive him."

"What about his wife and his kids?"

"They went to her mother's."

Rusty nodded, his heart feeling like a lead weight in his chest. Mike Chisholm was a deputy he had personally recruited and imported from Abilene.

"Who's gonna investigate it, Rusty? You aren't—"

"Turley. I'm not touching it. I can't. That's the best break I can give Mike. Call him and tell him to make himself available. Turley should be here soon."

"Those Blanchard kids. What's gonna happen to those poor little kids?"

Indeed. By now he had heard the same question from Elena many times. The image of the younger girl in Blanchard's living room stuck in his mind and he could hear her tiny voice. *Mommy's horse killed her.* "Carla and Gary must have made provision for their kids. Isn't that what most people do nowadays?"

Cheryl nodded. "Hank and I put it in a will. My sister and her husband will be the kids' guardians if something should happen to both of us."

Rusty thought about that. He had asked Elena days back if Carla had a will, but she had said she didn't know.

"I knew you'd want to know," Cheryl said, "so I already checked with DPS. Gary had a concealed handgun license."

Rusty nodded. "He's the kind of guy who would. But it doesn't make any difference. It's still illegal to take a gun into a bar, and you see what can happen when a damn fool does it."

Rusty knew one thing for sure. He was tired of the nonsense. He had to get to the bottom of this crime—and quick. "Where's Alan?" he asked Cheryl.

"Odessa. He got a DNA swab from Diego Esparza. He took it down to the lab himself. He didn't want to take a chance on it getting screwed up."

"Did he say when he'd be back?"

Cheryl checked her wristwatch. "He's been gone over an hour. Should be pretty soon."

Rusty jabbed Kevin O'Neill's number into his phone. The DA didn't even say hello. "Jeez, Rusty, I heard what happened. Is your deputy good on this?"

"I don't think Mike's got any problems. I turned it over to Turley Holt."

"Right. That's the thing to do. Get the Rangers involved. No one can accuse them of bias."

Rusty repeated the story of the shooting to Kevin and the threat from James Blanchard to sue.

"Keep me aware of everything that happens," Kevin said and they hung up.

A feeling that he needed to just start over had been gnawing at Rusty even before Gary got shot. Much of criminal investigative work was experience, gut instinct and judgment based on circumstantial evidence. Only rarely was an abundance of direct evidence available. Yet, in most investigations, things somehow fell into place because a smart cop interpreted events accurately.

In this case, things weren't falling into place. There were too many loose ends. He had missed something. In most crimes, he had always found the devil to be in the details. He closed his door and sat down with the cell phone records again. Holt would show up any minute and Rusty might not get back to the record the rest of the day. He had to make the most of the time he had.

He had eliminated Gary's phone record as being unhelpful, but he still believed he might find an important clue in Carla's. He spread the pages of the record over the top of his desk, comparing dates and phone calls in and out, looking for that person who had last heard Carla's voice while she was living and/or who had last seen her in person.

Last Tuesday had been a busy day on Carla's cell phone. He went over each of the numbers Cheryl had highlighted in yellow again, comparing the times phone calls occurred to the time line he had created and added to the file.

Just then Cheryl stuck her head through his doorway.

"There's a guy out here. Says he's a private investigator."

Randall's man. Fuck. Rusty's bullshit-tolerance level dropped another notch. He had seen too many instances when PIs were only one rung above the criminals they claimed to investigate. "That's just great," he mumbled.

The man came in carrying a bulging black leather satchel hung over his shoulder and a file folder. He was middle-aged with a big smile and teeth bleached white. He introduced himself as Leon Martin. "I've got some information you might find useful," he said.

Rusty couldn't imagine that Randall Ryder's private investigator would be willing to help him in any way. "Have a seat. I'm listening."

Leon Martin set his satchel on the floor and sat down in front of Rusty's desk. "I'm with Sandoval Security." He plucked a leather business card holder from inside his jacket and handed Rusty a card. Rusty accepted it and studied it as the man continued to talk. "My company does background checks on Ryder Oil Company new-hires. However, my particular division goes for a little deeper investigation than your standard criminal record—drug bust type of thing. At Mr. Ryder's request, I've done some work on Garret James Blanchard."

Rusty braced an elbow on the arm of his chair and looked Martin in the eye. "And?"

"Mr. Ryder had us do a little work on Mr. Blanchard some years ago, too." He bent to the side, opened his satchel and pulled out a manila file folder. "We found a few things in his background that didn't make Mr. Ryder happy."

"I can imagine," Rusty said.

"We found that before marrying Mr. Ryder's daughter, Mr. Blanchard was married to the daughter of a wealthy Fresno farmer. They divorced and he received a substantial monetary settlement, which he later invested in racehorses. He also received alimony until he married Carla Ryder."

The first thought that struck Rusty was that if Ryder knew this about Blanchard all those years ago, why had he handed over the horse ranch to Carla and Gary together? By doing so in a community property state like Texas, he in essence put his own daughter at risk for murder by a greedy husband.

"After what happened last night," the PI said, "my job's over. I just thought you might like to know we found little to report on Blanchard in recent years. He's had women friends here and there, but nothing too serious it doesn't appear." The detective shrugged. "He had a DUI in California some years ago. Paid a fine and went to school. So he drank a little too much. But then, a lot of people do that."

Rusty took in the PI's reddened nose, with its spidery purple veins, and didn't disagree. He nodded at the file folder the man had been fingering the whole time he had been talking. "Is that for me?"

"I've made copies of my report. In light of both Mr. and Mrs. Blanchard's tragic deaths, my company has given me permission to share information with you." He handed over the file folder. "Hope it helps you out."

"The information belongs to Randall Ryder. Has *he* given you permission?"

The detective shrugged again. "The information's public, Sheriff. You could find most of it yourself on the Internet if you're inclined to look. We're talking about the murder of Mr. Ryder's daughter. I can't imagine that he'd object to cooperating with your office."

You don't know Randall Ryder, Rusty thought.

After the PI left, Rusty sat at his desk and read the security company's report on Gary Blanchard. For being a summary of the activities of a murder suspect, it was the most benign compilation of information he had ever seen.

The DUI occurred before Blanchard married Carla. Rusty calculated that he would have been twenty-one years old. Rusty read the report again, trying to look between the lines for meanings that weren't there. If anything, the lack of information only made determination of Blanchard's guilt or innocence more difficult. Yet Rusty's gut instinct reconfirmed the conclusion that had already planted itself in his mind—Gary Blanchard had not been his wife's killer.

Finally, Rusty leaned back in his chair and rubbed his closed eyes with his thumb and fingers. He had a dull headache. He had slept only a few hours. He ran back through his memory, searching for what he had overlooked while he was on a wild-goose chase trying to nail Blanchard. Glaring all around him like a brilliant neon sign was the knowledge that two of Salvation's citizens were dead, their three children were orphans and a murderer was still on the loose in Sanderson County.

And the county sheriff didn't have a clue who it was.

And last, but not least, it was Day Seven and a Texas Ranger whose help Rusty had declined would be showing up in Salvation any minute.

Chapter 27

Cheryl came into his office. "The lab in Odessa called while you were talking to that PI. They've already gotten into Carla's computer. You can pick it up anytime."

"Alan's down there, right?"

"No. He's already back here."

Rusty swore under his breath. He needed to be here when the Ranger came, but given what he hoped to find on the laptop, he wanted it now. "Take my unit and go get it," he told Cheryl. "I won't need it. I'll have to be here as long as Turley's here. He'll want to interview everybody involved in Blanchard's shooting."

Two hours later Cheryl was back and Holt had gone out to the Owl Club. He wouldn't return until tomorrow.

"The tech didn't even have to break into the e-mail," Cheryl said. "He just fiddled with words until he came up with the password."

"What is it?" Rusty asked.

" 'Horses,' " she answered. She plugged the laptop in and he stood over her shoulder as they waited for the opening routine to finish. A blue sky and a dozen icons popped up on the screen.

"Let me know the minute you find something interesting," Rusty said. "I'm going back to the phone records." He still believed Carla's killer had to be one of the people to whom she had talked within the week before her death.

The office grew quieter as the daytime crew began to go home. Cheryl stuck her head through his doorway. "You want me to do overtime working on this computer?"

"Are you making progress?"

"Maybe."

"It's important, Cheryl. If you can stay, that would be great. Tell Hank I'll treat you two to dinner."

Her mouth tipped into a grin. "No problem. Except I'm not gonna let you forget that. We don't get dinner out very often."

She closed his office door and he returned to the numbers Cheryl had highlighted in yellow. By now, he knew to whom every number belonged. He had even had conversations with a couple of the people on the list. He began to go down the list line by line whether the number was highlighted or not, listing the numbers on a new page and putting hash marks behind them to show how many calls were attributed to that number. It was tedious work.

When he finished, one number with one hash mark jumped out at him. He must have overlooked it before because he had been focused on the number just beneath it highlighted in yellow. He scrutinized the printout closer, but the number did not appear again. It was an outgoing call. When he was satisfied that only the one call had been made to that number, he picked up the receiver on his desk set and jabbed in the cell phone number. Four rings later, a deep voice said, "Leave me a message at the beep."

The voice had a familiar tone, but Rusty couldn't place it. No reverse directory existed for cell phones. He called the Western Wireless operator, but was told the customer's name was unlisted by request.

Rusty left his desk and carried the phone number to Cheryl. "Is it too late to find out whose cell phone number this is?"

She gave him an evil grin. "Not if I'm rude and aggressive."

"Go for it."

"Good as done." She picked up the receiver. After a series of operators and several invocations of her credentials as a sheriff's deputy, she finally wrote a name on a piece of notepaper. "Hunter Kelso."

Rusty frowned. That wasn't what he had expected. "Thanks."

He walked back into his office, still frowning, and plopped into his chair, wondering if it was unusual for somebody like Carla to have Hunt Kelso's private unlisted cell phone number.

He leaned back in his chair, closed his eyes and rubbed his neck, thinking back and plucking from his memory the conversations he'd had during the past week. *Hunt Kelso*. The only time he had talked to Kelso was in the entry hall at Ryder's house the night after Carla's body had been found.

Carla was a special person. . . . A beautiful woman.

Rusty's heart made a small leap. He had thought Kelso's comment odd at the time he heard it. Was the banker one of Carla's lovers?

Big rich man. Kelso was big and rich, for sure. He had to be six-three, six-four, had to weigh over two hundred. And he had to be a multimillionaire.

Nah. That idea didn't even make sense. Kelso was Randall Ryder's good friend. And he was in his fifties. Rusty tamped down the shock that had kicked up his heartbeat.

But the banker had a relationship with Carla, he reasoned, and with *all* of the Ryder daughters. He had managed their legendary trust funds.

He keyed in Elena's cell phone number. "Hey," he said when she answered. From the background noise, he could tell she was driving. "I need to ask you something personal."

She laughed. "I guess you can get personal with me."

Hearing her voice gave him a lift. He leaned forward, propped his elbow on his blotter and his chin on his palm. Just talking to her turned him into a simpering fool. "Who takes care of your money?"

"What do you mean?"

"Your trust fund. Who's the trustee?"

"I am. Now."

"What do you mean, 'now'? You haven't always been?"

"Hunt Kelso was the trustee until we turned thirty. I'm not fond of Hunt. After my thirtieth birthday, I moved my account to a broker in Midland."

"Why don't you like Hunt?"

"He takes too much for granted. He always acted like our money was his."

"So who takes care of Carla's and Blanca's funds?"

"Well, Blanca has Bailey. I don't know what Carla did. She never told me."

"I don't mean to get nosy, but it's important. On each of the trust funds, how much money are we talking here?"

"You mean just money? Or other assets?"

"Just the money that's easily gotten at."

"I don't know about the others. Last quarter, my trust fund was worth over ten million. That doesn't count stock in Ryder Oil and some other long-term investments."

Rusty's chin almost fell off his palm. He closed his eyes and blew out a breath. The possibility of a future with the woman who possessed ten million dollars in cash just got exponentially harder. "Jesus," he muttered.

He put dollars and cents out of his head. He would have to deal with it soon enough, but he didn't have to do it now. He chose a more cheerful direction to take the conversation. "Did you tell your dad you're moving?"

"Not yet. He's so sad. He thinks he's lost everything. He's been talking to Malcolm. If the Blanchards don't bring the children back right away, he's going to sue them."

Rusty could have told her he saw that coming. "Has anybody looked for a will? Carla and Gary might have specified what was to be done with those kids in the event of their deaths. Most people with little kids do that. Custody could be settled real quick."

"Well, I'm here," she said brightly and Rusty heard the engine noise in the background stop.

"Where?"

"Mrs. Esparza's. I pick her up every week and take her to the English class I teach at the church."

Rusty's hand clenched the receiver. "Esparza? . . . Are you talking about an older woman who lives with her son in a mobile home over on Fourth?"

"Why, yes. Do you know her?"

"Do you know her son?"

Silence met him. "Elena. Do you know her son? Diego?"

Again, she didn't answer right away. "Yes," she said finally.

An icy chill spread over Rusty. Her hesitancy in answering, and the tone of her voice, told him she knew of Diego Esparza's relationship with Carla. And she had known it all along. And she hadn't mentioned it. What else did she know that she had failed to tell him?

A memory from fifteen years back rushed in. He had believed then that she had lied to him. And because of it, his head had been screwed up for a year. Tension grew in his gut. "I'm assuming you know that Diego was one of your sister's lovers."

"But he's a good man, Rusty," she said, the words tumbling out. "He's not a killer. He works hard and—"

"That's not the point, Elena."

"Rusty, I can't talk about this now. Please—"

"Don't you realize you held back critical information about a suspect in a murder investigation?"

And don't you realize the disloyalty you showed to me?

"He isn't a criminal, Rusty. I didn't want to cause trouble for him."

"Well, that's just great." Nonplussed, Rusty plowed a hand through his hair.

"I have to go. Mrs. Esparza's coming out."

"Right. See you." Rusty disconnected.

He sat there, staring at the phone, sorting through what had just happened.

Goddamn it!

He stood up and paced to the end of his small office and back. He had thought she was his ally. She had told him she loved him, but concern for a man she scarcely knew was more important than allegiance to him or even to her sister?

Beyond that muddled thinking, how could he have a future with any woman who had ten million dollars?

As a hollow feeling began to grow inside his chest, conversation came from the outer office. Rusty recognized Lowell's voice. "We played this game figuring out what the most Googled word on the Internet is," the deputy was saying.

"What?" Cheryl asked.

"Guess. You'll be surprised."

" 'Sex.' "

"Nope."

" 'Sports.' "

"Nope."

"Damn it, I'm busy here. Tell me."

"It's 'money.' "

" 'Money'?"

"Yep. That's the most Googled word on the Internet. The thing everybody wants the most."

Money. Rusty's mind swerved to trust funds and millions of dollars. He walked out to Cheryl's desk. "What's the status of the subpoena Kevin signed for us to get at Carla and Gary's bank accounts?"

"Alan's got it with him. I don't think he's had time to get there yet."

He glanced at his watch. The time was six forty-five. *Fuck!* "I've got to get to the commissioners' meeting."

"You want me to stay and keep fooling with this?"

He straightened with a sigh, barely containing his frustration. "No. It'll keep 'til tomorrow. Go on home. I've gotta find a tie and get outta here."

"Your tie's in that flat box in your right bottom drawer. I put it there to keep it from getting wrecked."

"Okay. Thanks."

The commissioners were cranky. They were unhappy about not being able to debate the sheriff's office's new budget, but they understood that Rusty had been shorthanded and buried.

A new agreement had been made with the city whereby the sheriff's office would continue to police the city as well as the county, as it had now done for several years. Rusty had added provisions in the budget for two more deputies and two more vehicles. Unfortunately, that wouldn't be decided tonight.

He sat there choking on his tie and listening to Walt Farber, one of the more vocal commissioners. Someone had called him and reported seeing a deputy's car parked in Wal-Mart's parking lot while the deputy was inside shopping. Rusty had grown accustomed to these ambushes. He explained that just because the deputy may have been inside a store didn't mean he wasn't on call or available to handle a problem. He rarely failed to defend his deputies.

Another member both commended him and complained about a sharp cut Rusty had made in automobile maintenance costs. Rusty had put the work out for bid and taken the best and lowest bid. The auto mechanic who had always done work for the sheriff's department when Jack Balderson was in office had called the commissioner, upset.

And so it went. Not one of the four commissioners seemed to be very concerned that a murderer was running loose in Sanderson County.

It was after midnight when the meeting ended. On the way home, Rusty thought of Elena and wondered if she would be at his house. He hoped not. At this moment, he was in no frame of mind to see her. He still had to think about how he wanted to deal with her lying to him.

Chapter 28

Rusty slept the dreamless sleep of a man exhausted, but he awoke at five a.m and met Cheryl in his office at seven.

"How'd the commissioners' meeting go?" she asked him, taking her coffee to her desk and booting up Carla's laptop again.

"Like it always does." He picked up his mug, too, and stood behind her, watching the computer screen. "Sometimes I wonder just how much a couple of those good ol' boys contributed to Balderson's slick dealing."

She looked up, her brow arched. "You gotta watch your back with them. Jack didn't get to be a crook without a little help from his friends." A move of the mouse and the e-mail mailbox opened. "Okay, what're we looking for?"

"Just like the phone records. Let's see who she was e-mailing and what it was about. See if there's back and forth with Hunt Kelso." He sipped from his mug.

"You don't really think he had something to do with this, do you? Why would he be involved in something this trashy?"

"I just know things aren't always what they seem and neither are people. Even in Salvation."

She maneuvered the mouse and scrolled down the list of e-mails. "Hmm. Lots of horse stuff. Wow, look at that. She talks to some famous people. . . . There's dozens of e-mails here to and from Mr. Kelso. Probably has something to do with her money."

"Let's open the ones from last week."

Cheryl complied and began to hurriedly read through. "Um, mostly money stuff. Put this money here, put some more there. Must be nice to have so much. . . . Wait a minute. Here's one from Thursday week before last. . . . 'Hunt,' " Cheryl read aloud, " 'I told you I'm not doing that anymore. I won't sign it.' "

"Huh. Did he reply?"

She clicked on another screen and scrolled down. "Doesn't look like it."

"Look at last Monday and Tuesday."

"Um, let's see. Last Monday morning, he wrote her he had the papers ready for her signature." Cheryl clicked on another screen. "Less than an hour later, she wrote him back and said, 'Forget it. And I'm warning you, if you forge my name again, I'll tell Daddy.' "

"What?" Rusty said, stunned. He bent over Cheryl's shoulder, squinting at the computer screen.

She repeated the contents of the e-mails. Rusty straightened and went back to the cell phone record on his desk. He checked the date and time of Carla's one call to Hunt Kelso's cell phone. It was Tuesday evening, the day after Monday's e-mail exchange. He looked at the time line he had created. The call was made after she put the kids to bed. He returned to Cheryl's desk. "Look at Tuesday. See if you can find any more e-mails like that."

"Nope," she said after a few minutes of maneuvering the mouse and clicking on messages. "No more good stuff. But she's got an Excel spreadsheet that says 'Investments.' I'm going to snoop around it for a while."

Rusty's cell phone vibrated at his belt. He opened the cover and saw the caller was Elena. He hesitated a few seconds, bringing his thoughts back to their last conversation. "Okay," he said to Cheryl. "Let me know if you spot something."

He walked into his office and closed the door. "Sheriff Joplin," he said into the phone.

"Hi," Elena said in a soft voice. "Did you miss me last night?"

"I was at the commissioners' court meeting. I didn't get home 'til after midnight."

She chuckled. "That must mean you didn't miss me."

He didn't know what to say. He was reluctant to bring up the lie by omission that now loomed as large in his mind as if she had actually spoken a blatant untruth. When he didn't reply, she said, "Rusty, do we need to talk?"

Besides the lie, his mind settled on the two commissioners at last night's meeting who were part of Randall Ryder's network and he thought of the ten million dollars that belonged to her and not him. He paced behind his desk. "I don't know if there's any point, Elena. I've got my doubts that we should have started things up again. When you get down to basics, there's way too many hurdles. It's too hard for you and me both."

A few seconds passed before she spoke. "Rusty, what are you doing? You can't just have this conversation on the phone."

"Elena, I said from the first, that very first night you came into my house, we'd both be better off if you went home. Unfortunately, you didn't and I didn't insist. That was wrong of me. Both our lives were a lot less complicated when we stayed on opposite sides of the fence."

"Rusty, I'm sorry I didn't tell you about Carla and Diego. I didn't know what to do."

"It's not just that. There's more to it. I think we oughtta just take a rest, okay?"

Again, she didn't reply right away. Finally, she

said, "Okay. If that's what you want." Her tone had a ring of finality.

"I think it's best."

She disconnected in his ear. He sank to his desk chair. *Fuck.* Life was so much easier when women weren't in it. Until hooking up with her again, he had been getting along just fine without sex. He had also been getting along just fine not having someone care about him and not thinking about the future beyond his daily existence. "Fuck," he mumbled.

"Hey, Rusty," Cheryl called. He got to his feet and went out to her desk. "Look at this," she said. "Over time, Carla gave Hunt a pile of money and it looks like it's to him personally, not to some investment account."

"What does that mean?" Rusty asked.

"I don't know. I'm not an accountant."

Rusty studied the numbers on the spreadsheet. Six digits here, five digits there, all designated as "Hunt Personal." "Humph. A few zeroes and you get into some real money."

Carla had made notes following many of the transactions. A paper trail. "My God," Rusty mumbled, continuing to study the figures. Beside some figures, there was a note, "Signed by Hunt." "I'm thinking Hunt was taking money from her by forging her name. And she knew about it."

"If that's true, why wouldn't she do something about it? I mean, if some jerk forged my name against my checking account, I'd cut off his balls."

"She didn't do anything about it because they were sleeping together. And he had her bluffed."

"Aww, naw," Cheryl said, wrinkling her nose. "That's sick. He may be rich, but he's a creep. Hell, he owns a bank. Why would he need to take her money?"

"I don't know that yet, but keep digging. If you

find anything else, call me. I need to make a phone call."

Rusty strode back to his office and found Blanca Hardin's number. She answered in a voice heavy with sleep.

"Blanca, something new's come up. I'd appreciate it if you could come to my office for a visit. This morning would be great."

"Bailey's not here," she said.

"It's not Bailey I want to speak to. For your deceased sister's sake, I'm asking you to come and see me this morning."

After a pause, she said, "I just got up. I really can't come without Bailey."

"If you don't do this, Blanca, I think you'll be sorry for the rest of your life."

"What? What's wrong?"

"Blanca, you may be the only one who can help me figure out what happened to your sister. I know you loved her. This has nothing to do with Bailey. Just you and Carla."

The longest silence yet followed.

"If you can't come here, I'll come to your house," he said.

"No," she said quickly. "I'll . . . It'll be a while before I can get there."

"I'll be waiting."

As soon as he hung up, Rusty felt a familiar rush in his blood. He was closing in. At last the pieces were falling into place in his mind, the tiny details that had been there all along, just out of order. Until this moment, the motive for Carla's death had been cloudy. He had tried to tie it to sex and unwanted children and had traveled down the wrong path. And all along, the motive was money.

He called Alan Muncy and reminded him to get to the bank this morning with the subpoena for

Carla and Gary's account records. He expected the bank records would be squeaky-clean. No matter. Even if nothing was obvious in the bank records, he wanted Hunt Kelso to be nervous.

Returning to Cheryl's desk, he watched over her shoulder as she continued to maneuver through Carla's personal records. "It's too bad I didn't get into that apartment and get this computer sooner," he muttered. "Blanchard might still be alive."

"Not your fault," Cheryl said. "You didn't make any of these people what they are."

Cheryl hooked the laptop up to her printer and printed Carla's records for Rusty's file.

Blanca showed up a little before noon, groomed and coiffed as if she were going to an event in downtown Dallas. Again Rusty could smell alcohol on her breath.

"I want you to know," she said crossly, "Bailey will kill me if he knows I came here without him."

Rusty thought it ironic how fundamental some things were. In Blanca's life, a controlling father had been replaced by a controlling husband. He directed her to a chair in front of his desk and offered her a drink of water, which she declined.

"What's this about?" she asked.

"I believe you know something about Carla's affair with Hunter Kelso," he answered, taking a seat behind his desk.

Her eyes rounded and she stared at him. A frown started to mar her perfectly made-up face. "Who said that?"

"Blanca, we've got Carla's laptop and her phone record." He picked up the manila file folder and held it up. "We've got e-mail correspondence between her and Hunt. She kept an extensive record. I can see on paper some of the financial dealings they had. It's gone on for several years. But I want to hear the gory details that aren't on paper from somebody who knows them. I believe that's you."

Her dark eyes darted past his shoulder and he couldn't read what was going on in her head. "I stayed out of Carla's business."

On a deep breath, Rusty pulled the medical examiner's neck-up photograph of Carla Ryder from the file and slid it across the desk. The purple bruise and the knot on the cheekbone showed clearly on Carla's pretty face. The contusions on her neck showed blatantly against her skin.

Blanca recoiled, her eyes suddenly glistening with tears. Rusty saw her throat muscles move.

"This is your sister," he said softly. "You loved her. She was brutally killed by a ruthless bastard. You and I may be the only people in a position to speak up on her behalf."

Blanca broke into sobs. Rusty left his chair and went to the outer office for a bottle of water. On the way back to his own office, he grabbed a box of tissues from Cheryl's desk. When he returned to the office, Blanca had calmed and he handed her the tissues and the water. "I'm sorry this is all I can offer you," he said.

With a shaking hand, she plucked a handful of tissues from the box and began to dab at her eye makeup. She pushed the photograph away and averted her gaze to her lap. "She, uh, has a bruise. Was she hit with something? Do you think she was . . . unconscious when . . ." She looked up at him, her eyes pleading for him to soften what her common sense was telling her.

"She may have been stunned by the blow to the face, but I doubt if she was unconscious," Rusty said.

"You mean she knew what was happening?"

"For a time. The pathologist says she probably

lost consciousness in eight or ten seconds, but she didn't die for several minutes. She fought for her life, Blanca. Some of her fingernails were broken. Material was found under them."

"Oh, God," Blanca wailed, her cry sounding like a hurt animal. "Oh, God. I tried to tell her."

Rusty waited. He could see the torment going on inside her.

After a few minutes, she calmed and blew her nose. "Bailey's always said Hunt's a bastard. He, uh, was the manager of our trust funds for years."

Rusty picked up the photograph of Carla's face and returned it to the file. "I'm not talking about him acting in his role as trustee. I'm talking about your sister making him loans. Or giving him gifts."

"I guess Carla did sometimes give him some money over and above the fees he charged us."

"Gifts?"

"Well, it certainly wasn't loans. There was no way she was ever going to get the money back from him. I told her dozens of times she was being foolish."

"What was Hunt using the money for? He's a wealthy man."

She looked up, her eyes red. "Why, he gambles. On everything. With bookies in Las Vegas. In Shreveport. Carla said he even had a bookie in Houston. Horses, ball games, boxing matches. You name it. I think he's even bet on chicken fights before."

Rusty had never heard this about the banker. Surprised that stodgy banker Hunter Kelso gambled? Yes. Shocked? No. Having become increasingly cynical, Rusty had ceased to be shocked by what he learned about the secret lives of his fellow man. "Do you know how much money she gave him?"

"No. It went on for a long time. I'm sure it was a lot."

"Carla and Hunt were lovers?"

She looked down at her lap and nodded.

"And that went on for a long time, too?"

"Several years."

At least the fatherhood of the unborn child was settled in Rusty's mind, though he now realized it had nothing to do with the murder. "Did he know she was pregnant?"

"I don't know."

"Can you think of anything you can tell me about how your sister felt about Hunt that might help me out?"

She shrugged and looked up. "I thought Carla was out of her mind. But she said she liked Hunt because he was so smart. She got a kick out of being his secret lover. They didn't go places or anything like that. I mean, he's married. I think they mostly got together in the apartment in the barn."

A corner of her mouth quirked and she looked away. "The whole thing was just sick. Carla drank a lot and sometimes she and Gary did drugs. She had gotten to where she didn't care about much of anything but those damn horses. Daddy has always hated those horses. He used to say she cared more about them than she did the kids."

"Blanca, listen to me," Rusty said, bringing her eyes back to his. "This is important. Did Carla see Hunt on the Tuesday before her death?"

"I don't know. I didn't see her myself that day. I mean, I was in Italy." Tears welled in her eyes again. "It's one of the things I regret. If I had seen her . . ." She wiped the corner of her eye with her finger.

Rusty held her gaze. "You were good friends. Even when you didn't see her, you talked on the phone, right?"

She nodded and made a deep sniff.

"Did you happen to talk to her that day?"

She continued to look at her lap. "I spoke to her Tuesday morning. I called her from Rome."

"Is it possible that the thing she went to your dad about Tuesday evening was Hunt mishandling her money?"

"I don't know. I thought she should have told Daddy about it a long time ago. It's funny. Of course, Hunt got fees for managing the accounts. After we got grown, all three of us used to complain at different times about the way he handled the money and his exorbitant fees. But he was Daddy's friend. Daddy always brushed aside our worries." She tucked back her chin and gave a huff. "After Bailey took over *my* money, he said Hunt was robbing us blind. But Bailey would never bring it up to Daddy."

"I've got another important question, Blanca. If I showed you documentation of some of Carla's and Hunt's transactions, would you be able to identify them and testify to the dates and details?"

"I—I think so. Maybe not all of them, but some."

"Do you know what they might have had going on, say in the last ten days or two weeks, something that might have angered your sister?"

"She was angry over the money a lot the last year. She hadn't paid attention to the trust fund for years. Daddy had it set up so that it grew almost automatically, but hers had started to shrink. She and Gary spent a huge amount of money and didn't bring much in. Then adding what she gave to Hunt on top of that . . . well, she had started to worry."

And she had gone to her father Tuesday night to discuss it, Rusty was convinced.

"Is there a reason you're reluctant to speak up about Hunt?"

She looked up at him with confusion in her eyes, as if she couldn't believe he would ask such a dumb question. "Why, he's our family friend. He's *Daddy's* friend."

After a few more questions, Rusty thanked Blanca and told her she was free to go. She rose from her chair, weeping. Shoving the autopsy photo in front of her had been a dirty trick, but seeing the brutality of Carla's death had jarred her into talking to him. Otherwise, he could have waltzed around for days or weeks and ended up in a repeat of the meeting where Bailey was sitting by her side coaching, criticizing and kibitzing. He left his chair, rounded his desk and looped an arm around her shoulder. "I appreciate your help. You've done the best you could do for your sister."

In the reception room, he asked Cheryl to find someone to drive Blanca home.

"I can drive," Blanca said.

"You've been drinking, Blanca. And you're upset. I can't let you leave here driving."

Lowell Giles had come into the office from somewhere. "I'll take her," he said. "Jaime can follow me and pick me up."

Rusty and his deputy walked her outside to her car. She continued to cry even as Rusty seated her in the passenger seat of the silver Mercedes. Lowell scooted behind the wheel. As he started the engine, Blanca buzzed down the window and looked up at him. "Thank you, Rusty. And thank you for Carla."

"No need to thank me. I'm just doing what I'm supposed to."

He returned to the reception room and Cheryl's desk. "Call Elena Ryder and tell her her sister needs her."

"You don't want to call her?"

"No."

Rusty sat in his chair behind his desk for a long time. He believed he now knew what had happened. The phone calls Carla made to the bank

Tuesday were probably made to Kelso. He and
Carla probably had an ongoing discussion about
the money and Carla became upset. She went to
her father's house Tuesday evening to discuss the
situation with him. After she didn't find Ryder at
home, she called Kelso late and made an arrangement for him to come to the apartment. Possibly
to have it out over a loan or a gift or a forged
document or whatever. Maybe she threatened him
with something.

Hunt drove to the barn in the wee hours, his
lights off, and met her in the apartment. They quarreled. Knowing Carla's temperament, no doubt she
attacked him. He hit her, perhaps a reflexive blow,
perhaps with the bit like Alan speculated. Then he
grabbed the reins and choked her.

After he had killed her, he carried her body
downstairs where the black stallion was penned. He
easily found a halter and a lead rope in the un-
locked tack room, put it around her neck, hooked
it to the stallion's halter and spooked the powerful
horse around the arena. That was why the ME had
said her neck was broken postmortem. The only
question left in Rusty's mind was whether Kelso
had killed her in a moment of rage or had gone to
the meeting in the barn with that intention.

Rusty was amazed at the close timing. It was a
wonder that on Wednesday morning Gary Blanchard hadn't walked out of his house carrying his
coffee mug and spotted the incident as it occurred.
Or that the Ayalas hadn't seen it on their way from
their cottage to the *casa grande*. Or that nobody
had seen or heard a vehicle come and go.

Emotion and determination to see justice done
rushed through Rusty. He had looked into the eyes
of many who had committed man's vilest act. He
almost understood crimes of passion. He even sometimes felt sorry for somebody who had snapped in a

moment of incredibly bad judgment and taken the life of another human being. Killing for money, on the other hand, was ruthless, premeditated murder, and the way Carla had been killed was just plain mean. The man who did it deserved the ultimate punishment society could mete out.

He looked at his watch. Alan should be returning at any moment with the records of Carla and Gary's bank accounts.

He jabbed in the district attorney's number. "You gonna be in your office?"

"Yes. What's up?"

"I need an arrest warrant. I'm filing a felony murder complaint against Hunter Kelso."

"Are you kidding me?"

"No. He's Carla Ryder's killer."

"Jesus, Rusty. Are you sure? I don't know if we can count on Judge Potter. He may have to recuse himself."

"Then we've got to find somebody else to sign it. I'm bringing over my file. It's all in there."

Alan came in with a stack of papers. "I thought Mr. Kelso was gonna climb clear down my collar before I got these copies."

"What do you mean?" Rusty asked.

"He sure didn't want to part with 'em much. While the girl was making copies, he had to go over every page before he'd let me have it."

"It doesn't matter. We're going after him with what's on Carla's computer."

"No shit? Then I'd say we'd better hurry. If I ever saw a rabbit ready to run, he's it."

Rusty jabbed in Kevin's number again. "Kevin, that warrant's gotta be signed ASAP. I'm on my way to your office."

Chapter 29

Rusty had the arrest warrant in hand, signed by a judge in a neighboring county. He couldn't imagine the hoops Kevin had jumped through to get the signature. He had new respect for the DA, Yankee or not.

It was near the bank's closing time. He had Cheryl call to verify that Kelso was present.

Salvation Bank & Trust had been founded and built by Kelso's grandfather. The building was a staid redbrick vintage structure a block off the main street near the edge of town. Adjacent to it at the front was a small parking lot that accommodated a dozen cars. The front entrance faced the parking lot.

Rusty and Alan prepared their strategy. They planned to enter the bank through the front door and confront and arrest Kelso in his office. Rusty radioed deputies Marshall Tucker and Billy Bob Jenkins and placed them a block from the bank. He positioned Art Rodriguez and Ken Carter at the bank's back exit and two reserve deputies near the parking lot entrance to detour motor traffic. He was utilizing almost his entire day shift. He didn't expect anything to go wrong, but you couldn't be too cautious downtown where end-of-day traffic could be heavy and sidewalks busy.

With everybody in place, Rusty headed for the bank's parking lot with Alan behind him. As he made a left turn onto the parking lot's apron, a white SUV charged straight at him at high speed. It clipped the Crown Vic's right front fender in the midst of a squealing left turn and blasted up the street toward the Odessa highway. Rusty leaped out, rounded his car's front end and saw a crushed fender, a blown tire and broken tie-rod.

Alan squeaked to a stop beside the disabled patrol car. Muttering a string of oaths, Rusty climbed into Alan's car.

"That's Hunt's SUV," Alan said, plowing up the street on the path of the SUV. "I knew he was gonna run."

Rusty radioed his dispatcher and reported the pursuit of a white Cadillac SUV belonging to Hunt Kelso. In a matter of seconds, the license plate number and vehicle description went out over the airwaves. By the time Alan and Rusty hit the highway, they could barely see the SUV ahead. Alan pinned the accelerator and they raced down the straight highway at ninety miles per hour, headed south for Odessa.

The radio crackled and a state DPS trooper named Pat Harrington reported he was joining the pursuit. Pat was one of the troopers who routinely patrolled the Odessa highway. At the same time the message came through the radio, Rusty saw a DPS black-and-white, siren whooping, red and blues flashing, pulling onto the highway ahead of them, closer to the SUV.

The SUV made a dangerous lane change and passed a car as if it were stalled, still showing no sign of a brake light. Motorists began to pull off left and right as the three automobiles rocketed down the highway. Sweat trailed down Rusty's back, past his belt, gluing his shirt to his body.

Soon a second DPS black-and-white inched up beside them in the left lane and the two of them flew down the highway side by side at a hundred miles an hour.

The first black-and-white pulled close enough behind the SUV to tap its bumper with his. Substantially outweighing the DPS vehicle, the Cadillac was scarcely affected. The trooper didn't give up. He moved in on the SUV's left rear fender with a more powerful hit. Suddenly the SUV spun in a circle, shot across the highway shoulder and through a barbed-wire fence. It came to a stop in a cloud of dust and dirt and flying parts, its rear wheels buried in sand.

The two DPS black-and-whites skidded to a stop. The troopers leaped out of both cars and closed on the SUV, weapons drawn. By the time Rusty and Alan came to a stop, too, Pat had charged the driver's door and broken the window. He yanked the door open and dragged Hunt Kelso out. Rusty, Alan and the two troopers pinned him to the ground and handcuffed him.

Rusty jerked Hunt to his feet and read him the Miranda warning.

Alan was staring into the Cadillac. "Jesus, would you look at this?"

On the passenger-side floorboard they saw a crumpled green paisley valise. The floor and the seat were covered with twenty-dollar bills, some bundled, some not.

"He robbed the goddamn bank," Alan said, an expression of incredulity on his face.

Reining in his anger, Rusty gripped Kelso by the upper arm, marched him to Alan's car and locked him in the backseat. He then returned to the Cadillac. Alan and the two DPS troopers were standing around it, staring at the money and making jokes, letting some of the adrenaline and testosterone dissipate before they returned to their respective cars. Rusty wiped his brow on his shirtsleeve and joined in. He had made many arrests, but he hadn't often been part of a high-speed chase. His heart was racing faster than the chase that had just ended.

Rusty instructed Alan to photograph the money in the Cadillac. Afterward, he and the deputy gathered the bills and returned them to the valise. Rusty strapped the cash-filled satchel onto Alan's patrol car passenger seat, then climbed into the backseat with Kelso.

"You'll never get away with this, Joplin," Kelso said. "Brad Vincent's a friend of mine. He'll wipe his ass with you. Before this is over, at the very least, you'll be impeached."

Brad Vincent was a well-known criminal defense lawyer from Midland, but Rusty, at some point in his trip through society's outlaws and misfits, had ceased to be intimidated by criminal trial lawyers of all stripes. Having been married to one had helped with that. The only difference between the ones with high profiles, like Brad Vincent, and the ones who officed in the cheap-rent district across the street from the courthouse was the source of their fees.

"You're wasting your breath threatening me, Hunt. You're looking at double homicide. Yes, sir, you've got a lot to be proud of. I can't think of another man I've ever known who's fucked around with his best friend's daughter, then robbed her and murdered her and even murdered his own kid."

"What do you mean, 'my own kid'? That's bullshit."

"No, Hunt, it's not bullshit. It's in the science."

"Why, that's crazy. Impossible."

"Don't try to tell me you didn't know Carla was pregnant."

He huffed. "Not by me. I had a vasectomy twenty years ago."

Confused, Rusty stared at him. Had another

foregone conclusion just flown out the window?
"You *were* her lover."

"That doesn't mean I knocked her up."

Exasperated, Rusty replied, "Know what? It
doesn't make any difference whether the child was
yours. It's still dead."

They rode in silence until the city-limits sign
came into view. Rusty leaned forward and spoke
to Alan. "Go around back of the jail."

"I didn't murder her," Kelso said.

No doubt nearing the lockup had finally nicked
the banker's armor. "We'll go through the back
door," Rusty said to Alan.

"I didn't murder her," Kelso repeated, louder.

Rusty sat back against the seat. "Okay. I'm
listening."

"It was an accident. I didn't mean—" He
stopped, as if he realized what he had just said. "I
was defending myself," he said softly. "Sometimes
she was crazy. She came at me like a wildcat. I had
to defend myself."

In spite of the disgust he felt for the man beside
him, Rusty had a clear mental image of Carla doing
just what Hunt said she did. Still, he struggled to
keep an objective demeanor. "What did she do that
gave you cause to think you were in danger?"

"She clubbed me with a goddamn bit. I took it
away from her and I—I lost my head. I might have
hit her back."

Alan pulled up to the jail's back entrance and
stopped. "I'll stay here and do this, Rusty, if you
want to take the car and take care of this money,"
Alan said.

"I've said all I'm going to," Hunt said. "I want
to call Brad."

"You bet," Rusty said. He opened the car door.
"You know something, Hunt? Everybody who
knew Carla, including me, knew she had a hot tem-

per. You might've gotten some sympathy if you had stopped with just slugging her. But once you wrapped those reins around her neck, you entered another realm."

He climbed out of the car, but then ducked back in and settled a look of contempt on Kelso. "What do you weigh? Two-thirty, two-forty? You outweighed that girl by more than a hundred pounds, asshole. Self-defense won't cut it. And I'm gonna tell you why. It's in the medical examiner's opinion. It took several minutes for Carla to die. You had that long to come to your senses and change your mind. She might have regained consciousness.

"But you didn't want that. You wanted her dead. I believe you went to that barn to kill her. I figure she threatened to tell everything she knew about you. She might even have threatened to put your ass behind bars. I'm saying it again: You wanted her dead, asshole."

Kelso opened his mouth to speak, but shut it again.

The fact that he didn't deny choking her with the reins satisfied Rusty that he had put it together right. "We've got the bridle. I'm sure the crime lab will be able to prove the reins were the murder weapon. They may even find a fingerprint on the bit. Smooth, shiny surface like that? Forensics these days is a wonderful thing."

He hauled the handcuffed Kelso out of the backseat and Alan walked him into the jail.

Rusty drove the valise to the sheriff's office, where there was a small safe. He counted $9,220. He locked it up. Afterward he sat down at his desk and made some entries in the file.

The office had cleared out except for the dispatcher. "It must feel good that it's all over," she said.

"It does," Rusty replied.

But he knew it wasn't all over. The most tragic incident that had occurred in Sanderson County in years had only entered another phase. Who knew where it would end or who else it might take down with it?

As Rusty worked, the shakes began and he could scarcely hold his pen. He recognized the adrenaline letdown for what it was. He left the office on rubbery knees.

At home, saddling up Banjo, he struggled through the weakness he felt in his muscles. He put two cold longnecks in his saddlebags and found the strength to climb into the saddle. He nudged Banjo out the corral gate into the pasture and spent the day's end with his horse and his dogs. Maybe this was what fate intended for him.

After his ride, he still felt wired and restless. His heart was still racing. He didn't call the dispatcher and tell her he had returned to the house, nor did he turn on his cell phone. He'd had enough.

He put together a plate of leftovers from the Sunday picnic, grabbed another beer and ate while he watched an old John Wayne movie on TV. Several times he got to his feet and paced aimlessly through the house.

Finally he went to bed and lay there staring at the ceiling, wondering when he would be able to sleep again. A picture of Carla Ryder with Hunt Kelso kept trying to form in his mind, but didn't quite come together. Carla was a pretty woman— not as pretty as Elena but too pretty for a frog like Hunt Kelso.

His mind went all the way back to the morning he had first seen Carla's corpse, through the ups and downs of the investigation, the highs and lows that had gone nonstop for a week. His mind continued its backward journey to the abnormal psychology course he had taken in college and the paper he had written on sociopathic behavior. Did that label apply to Hunt Kelso?

Rusty suspected that when the Ryder daughters' trust funds were audited, it would be found that Carla wasn't the only one who had been robbed.

He thought of the times his sisters and brothers-in-law, or even his dad, had gone to Salvation Bank & Trust, hat in hand, applying for a loan to buy a vehicle or a piece of equipment they needed to support themselves. He thought of the power Hunt Kelso had wielded over the lives of Salvation's population for years. And he thought of the supreme irony that existed in life on this earth and that as a keeper of order, he had seen most of it.

His thoughts drifted to Elena and how abrupt he had been in their phone conversation. He should apologize. But then, a part of him didn't want to mend those fences. Things would be better if they went back to the place they were before last Sunday night.

. . . your family thought you might remarry . . . What happened to her?

His memory traveled even further, to eight years back and the woman Elena had asked him about. Lauren Richards had worked in a bank in Fort Worth. She was smart and ambitious. She came from a farming family and grew up near Abilene. They had much in common. She wanted to get married and have kids. When he heard that was her goal, Rusty had ended their relationship. She accused him of using her to get past his divorce. Now, looking into the darkness, he wondered if that was what he had done.

Using one woman to purge his memory of another seemed to be a pattern with him. He had married Darla Patrick to erase Elena from his heart and soul. Maybe he had deserved Darla's unfaithfulness. She had accused him of never being emotionally present in their marriage.

Then there was pretty blond Amber, whom he had brought to Salvation and introduced to his parents. She was the manager of a day-care center and if a woman had ever been born to be a mom, she was it. She had scared him to death.

Indeed, he was a sorry lot when it came to women and his personal life.

Not liking the direction of his thoughts, he left his bed and went to the kitchen, stood in front of the refrigerator and stared blankly at the contents. He returned to his bedroom and pulled on his jeans and boots and a T-shirt and walked outside. A three-quarter moon lit the cool night and turned his backyard to silver. His dogs, asleep outside their doghouses, lifted their heads and looked at him, then went back to sleep.

Don't you ever get lonely? a woman had asked him once.

If you mean am I unhappy alone, then I guess I'd say no, he had replied.

The answer angered her so, she had thrown a glass at him.

He wandered toward the barn. Ferocious came out, stretched and picked up a pace beside him. And there in the chilly moonlight, in the company of his cat, he let in the thing that had been chafing him for a week, even more than Carla Ryder's murder.

He didn't want to turn into a cantankerous old man living alone with his animals. But he wanted his heart to feel safe.

The only woman who had ever made his heart feel safe had also broken it. Even so, he knew in his soul she could heal it.

And a petty fib and ten million dollars stood between them.

Chapter 30

With only two hours' sleep, Rusty headed for his office at seven, keeping to his routine schedule. He felt tired and wrung out. An adrenaline hangover and a night of soul-searching did that to him.

He called on the discipline by which he lived. He refused to let today be anything other than just another day. And he refused to let the elation he felt at clearing the Carla Ryder murder override the solemnity of the facts. Under no circumstances would he ever give the deceased less than respect.

A preview of the coming events met him when he saw the Channel 7 van parked in front of the courthouse annex. The skinny reporter bailed out of the van and stood waiting for him, microphone in hand. As Rusty slid from behind the wheel, the reporter thrust the microphone in front of his face. "I'm not ready to comment," he told the reporter.

"You've arrested Hunter Kelso. Will you be charging him with murder?"

Rusty wasn't a lawyer, but he could think of a half dozen separate charges to levy against Kelso besides the double murder charge. He hadn't yet spoken to Kevin O'Neill to learn his thinking. Only too aware that the camera was rolling, Rusty carefully sidestepped the reporter and strode toward the building's front door. His antagonist stayed right beside him. "That's up to the DA," he said. "You should talk to him."

The reporter fell back when Rusty opened the plate-glass door and entered the building, but he knew the media retreat was only temporary.

He walked into the sheriff's office reception area to a hush, an atmosphere no less than he expected. No doubt the whole county was stunned to silence. "Alan in yet?" he asked.

"No," Cheryl answered. "Want a cup of coffee?"

"That'd be great. Thanks."

In his office, he sat down and began to organize his thoughts. He pulled out his files and started through them, making sure everything was in order and in its place. Accurate, reliable details would be important to Kevin.

He heard a commotion in the outer office and looked up.

Randall Ryder strode through his door, his face a red portrait of rage. "I'll have that badge on your shirt for sure this time." He shook his finger in front of Rusty's nose. "I've already called the attorney general."

Rusty got to his feet. "Mr. Ryder, you—"

"How dare you? How dare you accuse a fine man like Hunt Kelso? Why aren't you out looking for my daughter's real killer?"

"Mr. Ryder, if you'll have a seat—"

"Daddy!"

Rusty shot a look to the door and a voice he recognized. Elena stood in the doorway, dressed in green scrubs. "What are you doing, Daddy?" She came to his side and put her hand on his forearm. "Daddy, please. Don't do this." Her voice trembled. She turned to Rusty, the pain in her eyes palpable enough to touch. "Is it true? You've arrested Hunt Kelso for Carla's murder?"

"Yes."

"Oh, my God," she said, her brow deeply furrowed.

"It's crap," Randall Ryder exclaimed. "All crap." He put an arm around Elena's shoulder and turned her toward the doorway. "But don't worry, sweetheart. I'm taking care of it."

She jerked free of his grasp. "No! Stop it, Daddy! You can't take care of it. Maybe if you'd taken care of it years ago when all of us wanted you to, Carla would be alive today."

Ryder drew himself up to his full height. "Why, daughter, who do you think you're talking to?"

"I know Rusty's right. Or he wouldn't have made the arrest. Blanca knows all about it, too." Elena began to cry. "Daddy, can't you understand?" She raised her hands, fingers rigid and splayed. "Don't you see? This—this dirty old corrupt man that you've called your friend all these years killed my sister." She began to sob. "You didn't see what he did to her. It was awful, Daddy." She turned to Rusty again. "He stole Carla's money? He killed her for her money?"

Rusty rounded the end of his desk and put his hands on Elena's shoulders. "Elena, let's everybody just calm down—"

"No!" She shoved his hands from her shoulders and jerked away from him, too. "I don't want to calm down. I'm tired to death of all the insanity that goes on around me." Her heated glare came at him, a look he had never seen. "I'm tired of you, too. Everything's about you and how *you'll* be affected. Your job. Your career. Your feelings. You're not the one with a family member who's been murdered."

She turned back to her father. "Look at yourself, Daddy. Look at what you've sacrificed. And for what?"

Ryder's eyes teared. "Elena, please, sweetheart. I—"

"Oh, Daddy, don't you see? It's all so phony.

We're so phony." She put an arm around his back. "Come on, Daddy. I know you aren't feeling well. I know how upset you've been. Just let me take you home. We can talk. And I can help you straighten things out. Let me help you."

They were both in tears. She urged him forward and walked him out of Rusty's office as if he were a child. She didn't look back. A feeling that if he let her walk through that door he would lose something irreplaceable overwhelmed Rusty. But he resisted following her.

When they were well out of the sheriff's department, Cheryl came in. "Holy cow. That was different."

Rusty shook his head. "Jesus," he mumbled, rubbing his brow with his hand. His heart was beating a tattoo. Little by little the Ryder family was disintegrating before his eyes and seeing it left him shaken in an unexpected way. Randall Ryder had always been the epitome of arrogance and authority. Of strength. Rusty couldn't keep from worrying how hard this must be for Elena.

"You don't really think he called the attorney general?" Cheryl said.

"Why not? He's been after my ass. He called the Texas Rangers. He hired a private investigator. Why wouldn't he call the attorney general? I'm sure he knows him. But you know what, there are some things money can't buy."

"Don't say that," Cheryl said, frowning. "Remember O.J."

Rusty left for home at five o'clock for the first time in many days. To his relief, the Channel 7 van was not in the parking lot.

Though he was almost too tired to function, he drove to his parents' house, seeking the comfort and the company of someone who was normal and without guile. Someone he knew loved him and always thought of his best interest.

He went through the back door. The ranch house where his folks lived was old and comfortable, with hardwood floors that squeaked in places when you stepped on them. He found his mother in the kitchen, which was where he usually found her. The large room smelled of something sweet and spicy. She came to him, put her arms around him and hugged him. "Are you here for supper?"

"I'm not that hungry," he said, setting his hat on the end of the counter. "Where's Dad?"

She stepped back and returned to peeling potatoes. "Up at the north pasture. He'll be in soon."

"What're you cooking?"

"Steak and fried potatoes. Your dad still has to have potatoes with every meal, even though he's putting on weight." She put a handful of potato slices into a big bowl with others and covered them with water. "So has the dust all settled?"

She didn't have to clarify the question. Rusty snorted. "It may never settle."

"I know what you mean. I don't think there's ever been a cold-blooded murder in Salvation."

"I don't think so."

Wiping her hands on her apron, she went to the refrigerator and brought out a gallon jar of tea. She filled two glasses with ice and poured the brown liquid over them. She carried the two glasses to the long pine table in the dining area off the kitchen and took a seat at the end of the table. When he was growing up, with his friends and all of his sisters' friends, sometimes a dozen people dined at this table. "Come sit down with me," she said.

For years Rusty had tried to avoid talks with his mother, but today, something inside him wanted it. He followed her.

"Are the people in town giving you a hard time?"

He shook his head. "I think everybody's still too blown away. They haven't gotten around to criticizing yet."

"Such a shocking thing."

"Murder's always a shock to somebody, Mom."

"It's just that we don't see that kind of thing in Salvation." She plucked a napkin from a holder in the middle of the table and wiped away a ring of moisture under her glass. "And how's Mike Chisholm?"

"I think he's gonna be okay. Turley hasn't found anything out of line with his performance. He was just doing what he's been trained to do. Bottom line, you can't point a gun at a cop without consequences. Only fools and drunks try it."

She nodded. "I'm glad he's going to be all right. I saw his sweet little wife in the grocery store and she was so worried."

From where they sat, Rusty could look out a bank of windows and see the small pasture off the corral where the black stallion was grazing.

"I heard you're seeing Elena again," his mother said.

"The grapevine, huh?" He squinted his eyes and took in the horse's black coat shining in the late-afternoon sun. The animal didn't have a smidgen of white on him anywhere.

"A little bird told me you picked her up at the hospital the night Gary Blanchard got shot. And you dropped her off the next morning."

"What, people are spying on me now?" he said, annoyed.

"There are no secrets in Salvation. Not really. I'm not nosing into your business. I know how much you used to care about her. I've wondered many times if your dad was wrong to interfere all those years ago."

Rusty sat back in his chair and stared out the window. "Mom, if one of Dad's best friends killed one of us kids, Dad wouldn't defend him, would he?"

She frowned and tucked back her chin. "Of course not. Is that what's bothering you?"

"I can't get past it. I don't know if it's denial or what, but Randall Ryder refuses to believe Hunt Kelso killed Carla. He's more pissed off because Hunt's been arrested than he is about what happened to his own daughter."

"David, Randall must be getting close to eighty. He and Hunt have been friends forever. Lord, Randall was friends with Hunt's daddy. I'm sure he's having a hard time. Look at all that's happened. I'm surprised he doesn't have a stroke or something."

"Knowing Randall as I've always known him, I never would have expected him to defend the man who killed his daughter."

"People react in strange ways to high stress. You must know that better than anyone. How's Elena holding up through all of this?"

Rusty lifted a shoulder. "Okay, I guess. She's probably the strong one."

"Who's helping her?"

"What do you mean?"

"I mean she's always been alone. Are you the one she's leaning on?"

"No," he answered and a cloak of guilt settled on his shoulders.

"Wouldn't you like to be?"

He couldn't answer.

"David," she said, reaching out and clasping his forearm, "of all my children, you're the one I worry about the most."

"Why?" he asked. From his perspective, he was better off and more secure than any of his sisters.

"Because you're so hard on yourself. And you expect so much from other people. And you're always disappointed when they don't live up to your expectations. You were that way even as a little boy. I know what's going on in your head, son. You're beating yourself up because Elena's rich. You're worried that if you follow your heart, everyone in Salvation will think you're taking bribes from Randall."

Rusty sipped his tea.

"She can't help it if she was born rich. What do you want her to do, give all of her money away?"

"Well, no, but—"

"You're being foolish. As for people thinking you're on Randall's payroll, no one who knows David Joplin would ever believe that. You have to have that much faith in yourself and in other people."

"Half the time, Mom, I don't have *any* faith in other people."

"Then you have to work on that. If you don't conquer it, you'll be miserable the rest of your life. Unless you want to go off to some mountaintop and be a hermit, you have to live in the world with other people, David. And you can't do that very well without a little trust."

"What if the person you want to trust isn't honest with you?"

"Oh, phooey. What has Elena done that isn't honest? I don't know anyone who doesn't have the utmost respect for her, unlike how they feel about the rest of the Ryders."

Rusty leaned forward, his elbows braced on his thighs. "She didn't tell me something she should have. It was something important."

"Maybe she had reasons that were good ones to her. Did you talk to her about it?"

"No."

"Well, that's your first mistake." His mother leaned forward, too, and they sat there, their faces inches apart. "Stop and look at Elena's life, David. She might be rich and pretty, but as near as I can tell, she doesn't have much to look forward to. She's lived there all these years in that huge house with her daddy and done his bidding. Never married, never had a family. She works long hours at the hospital. I don't know what they'd do without her. The Mexican community adores her. She teaches them and helps them take care of themselves. She's a loving, giving person, David. Talk to her. Don't let her escape again."

Rusty cocked his head and stared at his mother. Part of him wanted to fall into her arms and cry. Fearing he might lose control and do that very thing, he got to his feet and walked over to the window where he could take a closer look at the black stallion. "Wonder what that horse's name is."

His mother came up beside him and slid her arm around his waist. "I've been calling him Blackie. He and I are getting along just fine. I give him mints and he gives me kisses."

"You're the one taking care of him?"

"I've even ridden him."

"Mom! You can't do that."

"Well, I sure can. He's living at my house, isn't he? I just wanted to see if he's as mean as people are saying."

Rusty stared at his mother. She never ceased to surprise him. If he could find a woman like her, he would marry her in a heartbeat.

"He's a sweetheart," she said, still watching the horse. "Very well-mannered. He's been driving the calves crazy, wanting to play with them, but that's the kind of horse he is. That's the 'cow' in him. I love him."

"Hunh," Rusty muttered. "Well, don't get too attached to him. He's probably worth about three hundred thousand dollars."

"Well, he's still just a horse. Kind of like people. No matter the trappings, people are just people."

Rusty gave his mother a flat look. "Okay, Mom. I get it."

"What are you going to do with him?"

"Haul him back over to Blanchard's, I guess. There's about a dozen others over there that somebody's gonna have to do something with."

"I suppose Blackie belongs to the Blanchard children now."

Rusty nodded as the image of the three Blanchard kids formed in his mind. It was a picture that cropped up often, one he couldn't seem to erase. And he remembered that he still didn't know who was the father of Carla's unborn child. Knowing was no longer important, but he couldn't keep from being curious. "I suppose so."

His mother sighed. "I wish we could keep him."

"You know what, Mom? If I had three hundred thousand dollars to burn, I'd buy him and give him to you as a present."

She laughed. "And you know what? I'd take him."

They both laughed and he felt better.

Chapter 31

It was nearly dark when Rusty headed home. He had stayed and eaten supper with his parents, something he hadn't done in more months than he could count. He and his dad had walked through the pasture and the barn lot looking at and discussing the livestock. They hadn't done that since Rusty was a boy.

When he pulled off the highway onto his driveway, he saw a car parked beside his house. As he got nearer, he saw it was Elena's Lexus. He felt a tiny lift in his heart.

He came to a stop behind her SUV. She got out and came toward him. "Hey," he said, sliding out of the Crown Vic. "Why didn't you go in the house? Don't you still have a key?"

"I didn't feel like I should. I didn't know if I'd be welcome."

The answer sent a little stitch of pain through him. "I've never seen your dad like that. Did you get everything calmed down?"

She smiled sadly. "I don't know if Daddy's going to survive this. He's lost so much. His daughter, his grandchildren, his best friend."

Rusty wasn't unsympathetic. He doubted that Randall Ryder had ever faced so much lack of control of people and events all at once. "Everybody's lost something in this."

She looked up at him. The breeze blew strands

of her hair across her face and she brushed them back with her hand. "I may be one of the lucky ones. I've found something. Did you know I have a half brother?"

"In Salvation?"

She shook her head. "He's in the army, deployed in Iraq. He's a lieutenant. His name's John Cruz. He's half Mexican, like me."

Rusty was surprised, but not shocked. He was growing accustomed to a daily dose of new news in the Ryder family. "No kidding. How old is he?"

"He's twenty-eight. His mother lives in Midland. Her name's Pilar. She used to be Daddy's assistant. Do you remember her?"

Rusty searched his memory. He remembered the name, but couldn't produce a face to go with it. "Vaguely."

"It's sad that Daddy didn't remarry and raise his son. If he had, he might not have felt a need to meddle in his daughters' lives so much."

"I guess so," Rusty said. "How'd you find out?"

"Daddy told me this afternoon when we talked. I'm going to write to John and invite him to come to Salvation. As soon as things calm down a little, I'm going to visit his mother."

"Wow. Who knew? People sure make messes of their lives. I mean, we only get one shot at it. You'd think people would work a little harder at getting it right."

"Messy lives. Would that include you and me?"

He shrugged. "I said my piece on that."

"I don't believe you don't love me, Rusty."

"It's not that I don't. I'm just not sure that I can."

"Because of Diego? Or is it the money?"

He shrugged again.

"I didn't lie to you about Diego, Rusty. I've known the Esparzas a long time. I know they're honest, good people. Even though I knew he had something going on with Carla, I blamed her, not him. She was like that. She always wanted to do something she thought was dangerous. . . . Anyway, I took a look at the situation and decided what harm would it do if I just didn't mention it?

"Then later, after . . . well, after you and I got together again, I was afraid to say anything about it. Because I knew what you'd think."

He smiled and brushed some strands of hair from her face. "So it's my fault that you didn't tell me?"

"Of course not. But does anyone have to be at fault?"

"Somebody usually is."

"You live in a black-and-white world, Rusty. You've always been able to say, 'This is the way I see it,' "—she sliced a hand down through the air—" 'this is the way it is and this is the way it's going to be.' "

"You're saying I'm hardheaded."

"I'm saying you've got a confidence that you're always right. It's never been that easy for me."

"The truth is, it isn't that easy for me, either, Elena. But I have to do what I have to do. I have to be able to look myself in the mirror."

"I know, Rusty. You were like that when we were kids. That's why I've always trusted you."

"I have to tell you something. I made a mistake in this investigation. And it may have cost Gary Blanchard his life. That's a heavy load. It'll always haunt me."

"But you did the best you could. That's what most of us do, Rusty. Even Daddy."

She paused, looking at him long and hard. He began to feel nervous. "I don't like that look in your eye," he told her.

"I didn't just drop by to visit. I came for a reason."

Not liking the sound of that, he cocked his head and leveled a look of his own at her. "What is it?"

"I found Carla's and Gary's wills."

"Where? In the bank?"

"Blanca told me they did some banking in Odessa. Bailey got Judge Potter to sign a court order, and Blanca and I got into their safe-deposit box."

"Did the wills mention the kids?"

"They left guardianship of their children to me."

"Huh," Rusty said. "I thought Carla had the best relationship with Blanca."

"I can't explain it. Maybe it's because I'm the youngest. Or maybe it's because I kept the kids quite a bit and they like me. Or maybe it's because Carla and Gary didn't like Bailey much. He was extremely critical of how they lived."

From his one encounter with Bailey Hardin, Rusty believed that. "What about Gary's parents?"

"They're in their sixties. I doubt if they want to raise three small children, even their grandchildren. In any event, I wouldn't keep them from spending time with them."

"So what're you gonna do? Move them to the Rocking R?"

"If I decide to take them, I'll buy a house in town. Maybe I'll buy Mrs. England's house. It has four bedrooms."

"What do you mean, if you decide to take them? If you don't, they'll stay in California and you'll probably not see them again."

"I know." She chewed on her bottom lip.

"Okay," he said. "What's the other shoe?"

"I wouldn't be so scared of taking them if they had a father figure to look up to."

Rusty gave her another look. What was she getting at? "Yeah?"

She held his gaze for a few beats, then she turned

away and elbowed him in the side. "C'mon. What've you got to lose? They're good little kids."

Oh, no. No way. The last thing Rusty had ever expected to do with the rest of his life was take another man's kids to raise. Though he had to admit he'd had a special feeling about the Blanchard kids from the first time he saw them. He shook his head. "Lord, Lord, Elena. This is just too fast. I'm not sure what you're getting at, but I'll tell you right now, I don't know anything about being a father."

"All you do is love and take care. I've seen you do that with adults."

He shook his head. "Won't work. We couldn't just live together. We'd have to get married. There's too much money. No way could I ever be a kept husband."

"It's crazy to let my money be such an obstacle. I can't help it because I've got it. It has nothing to do with who I am."

"I know that."

"Then what's the big deal?"

Now his head was spinning. Did he have an obligation to those Blanchard kids? Because of the role he had played in their father's passing, was it now his duty to take responsibility for them? "I don't know. I'd have to think about it."

She smiled. "While you're thinking, do you think you could take me in the house and ravish me?"

A weird feeling of euphoria filled his head. What the hell was it? Happiness? Love? "Lord, Elena. This is crazy." He laughed, hooked an arm around her neck and planted a hard kiss on her mouth. "I've missed you."

She just kept smiling at him. "But I haven't been gone."

But he had. And he had come within an inch of

losing her again. Finding her SUV parked in his driveway when he came home must surely have been a message from fate. He pulled her close and kissed her long and tenderly. And in the process, that weird dizzy feeling took over and he gave her his soul. It was meant to be. For fifteen years he had been on a journey back to this place and the arms of this woman. No other woman he had ever known could compel him to make the commitment he had made in his heart. When he finally lifted his mouth from hers, he looked into her eyes and saw love. "Have you eaten?"

"Yes. Why?"

"I just want to be sure you've got the strength to be ravished."

Epilogue

Rusty sat at his desk with two DNA profiles before him. Life-changing events had occurred in the six and a half months that had passed since the day Carla Ryder's body had been found in her arena.

The most earth-shaking, from Rusty's perspective, was that he now had a wife and three children. And he was living in town in old Mrs. England's house while his own place underwent expansion. The remodel was being done with Elena's money, which was a burr under his blanket, but there had been little choice. No way could a family of five live in his tiny two-bedroom house.

The black stallion had been sold for a shocking amount of money, which had been deposited in a trust fund in the names of the Blanchard children. The remaining Blanchard horses had been either claimed by their investor groups or sold at auction. The Blanchard horse ranch was still on the market.

He studied the DNA profiles, digesting all that had come to light. He couldn't keep from pondering the vagaries of the human condition. The identity of Carla Ryder Blanchard's killer was now known and Hunt Kelso was awaiting trial. Yet, no one knew who had fathered the child she carried. DNA profiles had eliminated all three of her known recent partners.

But Rusty believed *he* knew her secret. Carla and her high school lover had gotten together in

Amarillo at the Panhandle Futurity. Rusty suspected Josh Logan had no idea his child had lived in Carla's womb.

The decision Rusty had to make now was if and what he would tell Josh.

Shouldn't a man know he had fathered a child?

Or would everyone be happier if he just put Carla's closed file in the back of the file cabinet's bottom drawer and moved on? He hadn't even told Elena of his suspicion, but should he?

As he pondered the question, the phone on his belt chirped. He checked caller ID and saw his own home phone number. Elena. As much patience as she had, she could well be running short. The Blanchard kids had just returned from spending spring break in California.

"Hey, darlin'. What's up?"

"Hi. Are you coming home soon?"

"Yep. What are the kids up to?"

"Blanca took them for the weekend. Being able to take them to Six Flags was her reward for staying sober three months. Bailey's going with them."

"Oh, yeah? We're all by ourselves?" Rusty could feel a grin crawling across his mouth. He and his bride hadn't had a lot of private time together since their hurry-up wedding. "What are you doing?"

"Cooking. I'm making Benita's enchilada recipe. It's in the oven now."

"Are you naked?"

She giggled. "No, but I could be by the time you get here."

"Fifteen minutes," he said and disconnected.

He picked up his hat and strode from his office. Life was good again. Better than a hardhead like him had any right to expect.